SOMEWHERE IN SPACE

And Other Stories

The Best of C.C. MacApp
Volume 1

The DANCING TUATARA PRESS
Books from RAMBLE HOUSE

CLASSICS OF HORROR

1   Beast or Man! — Sean M'Guire
2   The Whistling Ancestors — Richard E. Goddard
3   The Shadow on the House — Mark Hansom
4   Sorcerer's Chessmen — Mark Hansom
5   The Wizard of Berner's Abbey — Mark Hansom
6   The Border Line — Walter S. Masterman
7   The Trail of the Cloven Hoof — Arlton Eadie
8   The Curse of Cantire — Mark Hansom
9   Reunion in Hell and Other Stories — The Selected Stories of John H. Knox Vol. I
10 The Ghost of Gaston Revere — Mark Hansom
11 The Tongueless Horror And Other Stories — The Selected Weird Tales of Wyatt Blassingame Vol. I
12 Master of Souls — Mark Hansom
13 Man Out of Hell and Other Stories — The Selected Stories of John H. Knox Vol. II
14 Lady of the Yellow Death and Other Stories — Selected Weird Tales of Wyatt Blassingame Vol. II
15 Satan's Sin House and Other Stories — The Weird Tales of Wayne Rogers Vol. I
16 Hostesses in Hell and Other Stories — The Weird Tales of Russell Gray Vol. I
17 Hands Out of Hell and Other Stories — The Selected Stories of John H. Knox Vol. III
18 Summer Camp for Corpses and Other Stories — Weird Tales of Arthur L. Zagat Vol. I
19 One Dreadful Night — by Ronald S.L. Harding
20 The Library of Death — by Ronald S.L. Harding
21 The Beautiful Dead and Other Stories — The Weird Tales of Donald Dale
22 Death Rocks the Cradle and Other Stories — Weird Tales of Wayne Rogers Vol. II
23 The Devil's Night Club and Other Stories — Nat Schachner
24 Mark of the Laughing Death and Other Stories — Francis James
25 The Strange Thirteen and Other Stories — Richard B. Gamon
26 The Unholy Goddess and Other Stories — The Selected Weird Tales of Wyatt Blassingame Vol. III
27 House of the Restless Dead and Other Stories — Hugh B. Cave
28 Tales of Terror & Torment Vol. 1 — Edited by John Pelan
29 The Corpse Factory and Other Stories — Arthur Leo Zagat
30 The Great Orme Terror and Other Stories — Garnett Radcliffe
31 Freak Museum — R. R. Ryan
32 The Subjugated Beast — R. R. Ryan
33 Towers & Tortures — Dexter Dayle
34 The Antlered Man — Edwy Searles Brooks
35 When the Batman Thirsts — Frederick C. Davis
36 The Sorcery Club — Elliot O'Donnell
37 Tales of Terror and Torment Vol. 2 — Edited by John Pelan
38 Mistress of Terror and Other Stories — The Selected Weird Tales of Wyatt Blassingame Vol. IV
39 The Place of Hairy Death and Other Stories — An Anthony Rud Reader
40 My Touch Brings Death — The Weird Tales of Russell Gray Vol. II
41 Echo of a Curse — R.R. Ryan
42 The Finger of Destiny — Edmund Snell
43 Laughing Death — Walter C. Brown

CLASSICS OF SCIENCE FICTION AND FANTASY

1   Chariots of San Fernando and Other Stories — Malcolm Jameson
2   The Story Writer and Other Stories — Richard Wilson
3   The House That Time Forgot and Other Stories — Robert F. Young
4   A Niche in Time and Other Stories — William F. Temple
5   Two Suns of Morcali and Other Stories — Evelyn E. Smith
6   Old Faithful and Other Stories — Raymond Z. Gallun
7   The Alien Envoy and Other Stories — Malcolm Jameson
8   The Man without a Planet and Other Stories — Richard Wilson
9   The Man Who was Secrett and Other Stories — John Brunner
10 The Cloudbuilders — Colin Kapp
11 Somewhere In Space — C.C. MacApp

DAY KEENE IN THE DETECTIVE PULPS

1   League of the Grateful Dead and Other Stories — Day Keene in the Detective Pulps Vol. I
2   We Are the Dead and Other Stories — Day Keene in the Detective Pulps Vol. II
3   Death March of the Dancing Dolls and Other Stories — Day Keene in the Detective Pulps Vol. III
4   The Case of the Bearded Bride and Other Stories — Day Keene in the Detective Pulps Vol. IV
5   A Corpse Walks in Brooklyn and Other Stories — Day Keene in the Detective Pulps Vol. V

SOMEWHERE IN SPACE

And Other Stories

The Best of
C.C. MacApp Volume 1

C.C. MacApp

Edited and Introduced by

John Pelan

RAMBLE HOUSE

The Mercurymen, *Galaxy Magazine,* December 1965
Tulan, *Galaxy Magazine,*
For Every Action, *Amazing Stories3,* May 1964
Trees Like Torches, *Worlds of Tomorrow,* May 1966
A Pride of Islands, *If,* May, 1960
The Fortunes of Peace, *If, September* 1967
A Flask of Fine Arcturan, *Galaxy Magazine,* February 1965
The Drug, *Galaxy Magazine,* February 1961
All That Earthly Remains, *If,* July 1962
Somewhere in Space, *Worlds of Tomorrow*, November1964

ISBN 13: 978-1-60543-723-1

Cover Art: Gavin L. O'Keefe
Preparation: Kathy Pelan and Fender Tucker

Dancing Tuatara Press
John Pelan Presents:
Classics of Science Fiction and Fantasy #11

SOMEWHERE IN SPACE
And Other Stories

TABLE OF CONTENTS

INTRODUCTION: ALL THAT REMAINS   9
  – JOHN PELAN

THE MERCURYMEN   17

TULAN   69

FOR EVERY ACTION   91

TREES LIKE TORCHES   99

A PRIDE OF ISLANDS   127

THE FORTUNES OF PEACE   147

A FLASK OF FINE ARCTURAN   171

THE DRUG   181

ALL THAT EARTHLY REMAINS   197

SOMEWHERE IN SPACE   219

MAD SHIP   263

ALL THAT REMAINS . . .

A funny thing happened on the way to preparing the second collection by Evelyn E. Smith, (*Call Me Wizard*, which will be a later book in this series) . . . *this* volume happened . . . During a conversation with my good friend D.H. Olson, (who has helped behind the scenes on more of my projects than it would be possible to list here); I was rattling off the titles of the preceding books in the series and those planned for the future when he suggested I consider a collection by Charles De Vet, with the comment that all of his work was in the 1950s and 1960s, but that that timeframe might be too recent for me. I replied that while we do indeed go back to the 1930s, the "sweet spot" for this series is actually the 1940s through the 1960s, so that an author whose work was primarily in the 1950s and 1960s would actually be right in our sweet spot. I recalled reading some De Vet stories, enjoying them, but I couldn't recall exactly where and asked where I should start looking . . .

Dwayne replied that his work had shown up everywhere from *Imagination* to *Planet Stories* to *Galaxy* and *If*; and that, knowing my collection of pulps and digest magazines, I was bound to have quite a bit of his work on hand. I said, "He sounds like he's exactly the type of author this series is all about . . . Prolific in the magazines and underrepresented in terms of short story collections, much like Robert F. Young and C.C. MacApp, they were everywhere at their peak and pretty much out-of-print now . . ." (I fully realize that Robert F. Young has two excellent collections published during his lifetime and a splendid sampling of his work released as an e-book a few years ago. However, those three publications account for about 10-12% of his short fiction. That's still under-represented as far as I'm concerned.)

C.C. MacApp. Oddly enough, until that moment I hadn't really considered a MacApp collection. Certainly I remembered his novels, most of which were expansions of novellas that ran in *Galaxy*, *Worlds of Tomorrow* and *If;* and even more importantly for us, I recalled the excellent novelettes such as "The Mercurymen", "Prisoners of the Sky" (both the original novelette and the book-length expansion), and the tales that chronicled mankind's battles against the Gree and the Gaddyl. My recollection was that during the mid-1960s he seemed to be in every issue of the Galaxy Publishing trio. And as far as I knew his short fiction had never been collected.

And with that an evening of digging through several boxes of magazines followed. As it turns out, I owned nearly every magazine that Mr. MacApp had appeared in and thus I was in a much better position to work on this book than on the De Vet collection, (which will appear in due course). While I was an admirer of MacApp's fiction, I didn't know a great deal about the man himself. It was no secret that behind the byline was San Francisco chess master, Carroll M. Capps (in fact, one of his novels was released with his real name on the cover and the copyright attributed to the pseudonym!). Several phone calls to Bay Area friends who might have met him revealed that while very active in chess circles, Capps didn't seem to have much of (if any) presence in SF fandom. However, every person I talked to had fond memories of his stories (though, oddly enough, no one mentioned the same stories, perhaps indicative as to why I remembered him as being in nearly every magazine . . .).

As it turns out, I had misremembered the volume of MacApp's output. As opposed to appearing in every issue of the three magazines as I had remembered, his actual body of work totaled less than thirty stories. Why such a strong impression then? Two words, quality and variety. As to variety, readers familiar with these stories who are buying the book simply for the convenience of having all these terrific tales in one place would likely agree that "Somewhere in Space" is as different from "A Flask of Fine Arcturan" as "The Mercurymen" is from "All that Earthly Remains," and none of these bear much resemblance to "Trees Like Torches" or

"The Drug". MacApp's versatility is almost Kuttneresque, and truly remarkable when one considers, that with a couple of exceptions, the content of this volume is all from the early years of his career (1960-1965). That this collection is comprised primarily of early stories was not at all by design. Those of you familiar with my patterns in assembling single-author collections know that I generally eschew chronological collections in favor of presenting as wide a variety of an author's work as possible in each collection, so as to show their full range to best advantage. It just so happens that the three volumes of non-series MacApp stories that took shape did so almost of their own accord and it turned out to be this first book which is comprised mainly of early work, the second volume draws mostly from the last years of his career, and the third volume mainly from 1965-1966 (his peak period, when he also has the popular "Gree" series running in *Worlds of Tomorrow*).

That I speak of MacApp's career in three parts may seem a bit odd, as his entire career spanned just over a decade, beginning with the publication of "A Pride of Islands" in May of 1960 and ending with "Hot World" in November of 1971. However, looking at his bibliography, his career does indeed break up into three parts, just ten science fiction stories and two fantasy novelettes published from 1960-1964, the "Gree years" of 1965-1966, where most of his efforts concerned this series, and then a veritable explosion or "nova" starting in 1967 that saw seven books published and over a dozen excellent stories, most of which were at least novelette length.

Sadly, C.C. MacApp's life and writing career share some unfortunate commonalities with another popular author in this series, Malcolm Jameson. Both began writing (or at least selling) rather late in life (in their forties), and both died far too young. MacApp was in his early fifties when he passed away in 1971 and, in terms of popularity, just beginning to hit his stride. Having expanded several novellas into novel length, his publishers were no doubt hungry for more and we can only speculate that he would have responded with several more novels.

Another similarity with Jameson, is that he started out at a fairly high level and went up from there. His first story, "A Pride of Islands," written in 1960, was picked up for an anthology appearance alongside heavyweights like R.A. Lafferty and Daniel F. Galouye in 1965, the same year that "The Mercurymen" was a contender for the Nebula Award. When we look at the quality and quantity of his production during the last five years of his life there's little doubt that he was well on the way to being a major name in the field. Had he been granted anything like a normal span of years, (say, even to age 72), it's reasonable to speculate that even if had he slowed just a bit in later years, we might well have seen something on the order of another forty or so stories of substantial length and perhaps as many as two-dozen novels!

One of the most interesting features of MacApp's work considering the time when he debuted is that (much to his credit) he seems to have ignored the New Wave entirely. Not that he was a reactionary like Lester Del Rey and some other authors from the so-called "Golden Age" who loudly proclaimed that the New Wave would be the death of science fiction. No, it was more a case of MacApp ignoring both sides of the raging debate as he quietly went about his business turning out one excellent story after another. As an aside, despite Sturgeon's Law being true of the New Wave, the 10% that was good was very good indeed, Some of the best material it produced is still eminently readable today, with works by the likes of Brian Aldiss, J.G. Ballard, John Brunner, Samuel Delaney, Thomas Disch, Harlan Ellison, and Roger Zelazny rightfully being considered classics today. On the other hand, more traditional authors such as Poul Anderson, Gordon Dickson, Daniel F. Galouye, Keith Laumer, Katherine MacLean, Clifford D. Simak, and Richard Wilson were producing some of their best work and, of course, the awesomely talented quartet of Philip K. Dick, Fritz Leiber, Theodore Sturgeon, and Jack Vance stood above the fray like Olympians peering down at Troy by virtue of having always been so brilliant and original that all four men could be said to have been "new waves" unto themselves.

But back to C.C. MacApp. Unlike many authors who debuted in the early sixties, his work was much more in the mode of the traditionalists, which may go a long way to explaining MacApp's general absence from Judith Merrill's "Year's Greatest" anthologies. The Merrill anthologies became progressively more idiosyncratic after the editor's pronouncement that the "S" stood for "speculative" as opposed to *science*. Apparently no one was on hand to gently inform Ms. Merrill that all fiction is, by definition "speculative." Coinciding with MacApp's ascent to the top ranks in the field was a growing loss of credibility in a series that snubbed stories such as "The Mercurymen" and "The Fortunes of Peace" in order to make room for what passes for poetry by Randall Garrett, macabre cartoons and nearly anything from mainstream magazines that could conceivably earn the rubric of "SF".

Were I editing a "Year's Best" back then, I'd have to say that most years from 1960-1969 would feature a MacApp tale. In fairness to Ms. Merrill and also to Messrs. Carr and Wollheim (who only selected a couple of his tales for their annual anthology), it's likely that the author's preferred working length was one thing that worked against him. Many editors are somewhat gun-shy about using novelettes and looking at my list of the MacApp pieces that I'd consider necessary to include in a "Year's Best" collection, only two are truly *short* stories, three come in at just under 10,000 words, and three tip the scales at well over 20,000 words! Most editors would be very likely to turn away from these tales is favor of using three or even four shorter pieces and thus getting more names on the table of contents. Just in case anyone ever gives me a chance to do a series of retro "Year's Best" anthologies, here are the MacApp stories that you can expect to see:

1960 – "A Pride of Islands"

1964 – "Somewhere in Space" (As much as I like "For Every Action", I'd opt for the longer piece.)
1965 – "The Mercurymen"
1966 – "Prisoners of the Sky"
1967 – "The Fortunes of Peace"
1968 – "Where the Subbs Go"
1969 – "Mad Ship"

A pretty impressive listing, and while I don't feel anything from the missing years quite meets "Year's Best" criteria, he certainly had good stories in the missing years, but the competition was exceedingly fierce as well. As to the lack of awards (and only one nomination, that for "The Mercurymen"), there was a odd tendency from the late fifties through the mid-seventies to bestow awards and nominations for same in the short fiction categories primarily to those authors who were also novelists, (the notable exception to this phenomena was Harlan Ellison). Certainly one line of thought would have it that writers who are successful enough to sell novels are probably at least commercially competent and thus their short fiction is also probably of a fairly high level; but I'm not one to discount the tendency of people to vote for familiar names when push comes to shove and I suspect that a lot of excellent magazine writers got the short end of the stick in this regard. The Ellison exception is likely due to two things: the exceptional quality of his work which simply could not be ignored, and his very visible public persona which more than made up for a lack of novels. (After all, I don't think there's a science fiction fan who was alive during the 1960s that didn't own, or at least read, *Dangerous Visions*.)

By the end of the decade MacApp was appearing regularly in paperback, mostly with expansions of novelettes into novels. In all cases, these expansions are quite successful and read as though they were planned at that length in the first place. I suspect that few readers would know that *Worlds of the Wall*, *Prisoners of the Sky*, *Subb*, and *Omaha Abides* all had their genesis as shorter works in *Amazing*, *If*,

Galaxy and *Worlds of Tomorrow* if the data wasn't on the copyright page. Unlike many instances, where the expanded work merely seems a short story with a case of the bloat, MacApp's expansions are all effective as novels.

Of course, with this mining of earlier material, one has to wonder what a hypothetical future career would have looked like. Would MacApp have jumped into the paperback original market with both feet, creating completely new worlds, or would he have continued working at the novella or novelette length and then expanding select works to a longer form? Sadly, we'll never know.

I like to think that we probably would have seen some truly intriguing new worlds and new societies postulated. After all, one of MacApp's real strengths was convincing world-building. His alien societies while having some reference points to Terran analogues still manage to convey that sense of true otherworldliness that is so much a part of the sense of wonder that can be instilled by the best science fiction. This book presents eleven very different worlds from the fertile imagination of Carroll M. Capps, we hope you enjoy visiting them all.

John Pelan
Near Area 51
New Mexico
2013

THE MERCURYMEN

I

TEM WAS MANY KILOSTRIDES rootward from the last settle-
ment, in a part of the stalk that was not planted nor grazed
because nearly half the diameter was filled with icy water
and the air was cold. Nevertheless, it was not too cold for
fish nor for some of the quadrupeds, and he loved to come
here when he had free time.

He lay concealed in the throat-like constriction between
stalk sections. He was watching a wild tomcat fishing. The
luminous moss grew feebly here, and he could barely make
out the cat's dark form inching along the giant fronds at the
water's edge. He wondered why tomcats would come this
far (and even farther, he knew) when, in warmer but still un-
settled parts of the vine, there were lizards and mice and
birds to hunt. Maybe they liked the dim light and the soli-
tude, and the vastness of the sections. Personally, he found
the size of the sections a little frightening. The one before
him was a good two hundred strides in diameter, and over
half a kilostride long.

Now the cat was out of sight entirely, but he kept his eyes
on the spot where he'd seen it last. There were no bird songs
here; no sound at all except for a faint trickling of water
somewhere. He pulled his goatskin hood closer about his
cheeks and waited.

There was a leap and a splashing. Then the cat's dark form
went bounding up the steep wall. He caught just one glint of
silver at its head as it disappeared into some hidden cavity.
Presently he heard eating sounds.

After a while he gathered himself, squirmed free of the
bulbous growths which, legend said, would swell to an air-

tight seal in case the section were seriously punctured, and picked a way back along the near-vertical side of the next section. He plucked a vine-fruit, but it was tart and he only swallowed a few bites; they seldom ripened this far root-ward. He thought he might do a little hand-fishing himself farther along, where it was warmer. But then, he ought to be getting back.

The kilostrides passed. The sections were smaller, with much less water in them so he could walk nearer the bottom of the curve. The luminosity brightened. He reached sections planted to rice; then, finally, one where grass grew almost halfway up the circumference. He smelled goats ahead. At the next section-joint he had to let himself through a netting.

As he skirted the grazing animals, the herder, a young man a few orbits older than he, called out. "You better hustle, idler! The Elders have been looking for you!"

Tem grunted an acknowledgement and continued his cas-ual pace. As First Son of the Chief he didn't feel he should let goat-herders hasten him. Nevertheless, when he was out of sight he walked faster. He couldn't imagine why the Eld-ers would want him.

The first huts came into sight. A little later a band of chil-dren spotted him and came running, babbling and shrieking, each vying to be the bearer of the news. "Tem! The Chief is dying!"

They'd already bled the Chief and given him fermented rice, but even so, his face was set against the agony and eyes were dull. It was the sickness that strikes in the right side of the belly. He raised his hand feebly and took Tem's. His voice was weak, but calm. "I affirm that you are my true First Son. I invoke the Law of the Migration." He let his hand drop and closed his eyes against the pain.

Tem knelt, trying to find words.

How was this possible? The strongest and wisest of the vine . . .hardly into middle age . . . He looked around at The Elders, wanting someone to tell him it wasn't so, that this was cryptic charade, and that his father would throw off the act any instant and bound to his feet with a guffaw. But he recognized the Conclave of Death. Besides the Elders, none of the vine was present except six other first sons who were older than Tem but within the age limits for migration.

One of those, a man named Buld, scowled and said harshly. "Why does he not disown this stripling so we can elect a real Leader?"

The dying man's face only tightened more, but one of the Elders said, "Do not speak blasphemy!" Each of the Elders took one step forward, signifying their intentions of enforcing the Law if necessary. Buld looked sullen, but said no more.

Numbly, Tem got to his feet and stood at his father's head, as the conclave demanded. He wished he could leave to find his mother and comfort her, but of course he could not; nor could she join the Conclave.

From the Book of Truths: And within the menagerie, these things shall ye take, lest the new vine know them not: the fruits and the grains, and the fishes that swim and the fowls that fly, and the things that creep, and the tiny things and the things that suckle their young . . .

II

Since this was a season when the sin was already retreating Brightward (everyone kept looking apprehensively at the corona above the horizon), the migration could start as soon as it was ready.

Tem had been Outside before, of course, as part of his training but he'd only left the lock and walked a few steps on the gravel above the vine, and it hadn't seemed real. Now, ostensibly overseeing preparations (though the Elders' who'd been on their own migration to this vine, were the actual experts), he had to stay out here for twenty or thirty kilopulses at a time, and Outside was all too real.

He was glad the suitmakers had done a good job on his suit. The face part was of the clearest rubber possible, with very few bubbles or white spots of undried vine latex, and the fit was good. It was awkward moving, with the weight of the backpack full of air-freshening fungus pulling him off balance. But they'd assured him he'd get used to that. They'd also promised the pleats at knee and elbow joints would stop sticking together when the latex cured a little more.

He kept tilting his helmet to look up at the Stars, though it made him ill to think of such emptiness above him. He could believe the Stars were fantastically distant, all right, but were they really Gods? And if so, were they watching?

For that matter, he'd never been quite clear in his mind about the relation between sun and Sunn. Was the sun Sunn's weapon? Or his dwelling? or what? Of course Sunn could probably travel around anywhere invisibly, even to Darkside; though the Law didn't say; and asking such questions got you admonitions instead of answers.

He turned and stared the way they'd be going. That was another confusing thing. The Law said you must go in the direction of your right hand as you stood facing Brightward. Clearly there was distance there, and ground to walk on, but was it a direction? One was used to two directions— rootward and leafward. Or, to use other terms, darkward and brightward. Anyway, they had to go in this new 'direction', across an unknown number of vines, until they found an un-inhabited one fit to settle. The guess was that it would be as much as four hundred kilostrides. They could go that far before the sun began to return, if they didn't lag.

He saw an Elder frowning at him, and turned his attention to the work.

They were bleeding air out of the lock now, into big rubber bags; carrying those over and squeezing the air into the menagerie. Big as that was—with a dozen wide carts under it—the animals, and the human couple who'd live in it to care for them, would be cramped. Most of the space was filled with the air freshening fungus. Still, they'd be more comfortable than he and the others, living in suits with only an occasional visit into the resters.

The menagerie was the biggest airbag, by far. There were smaller ones; air fresheners, the resters, and simple bags of spare air. There were waterbags and bags of food, and bags of liquid vine latex for future use. There were two carts loaded with great sheets of rubber, already cured, for constructing the lock when they found their vine. There were loads of rope, and the precious tools. And seeds, of course. There was no assurance *what* would have spread to a new vine.

The lock was sagging now, into the slanting tunnel that let it meet the vine at a good angle. It was time for a shift to go in. He walked over and helped push on the big end-plug until it gave way and the remaining air gushed out. They trooped in, replaced plug and held it hard against seating. Someone opened the valve from the vine, and the lock began to fill again. Soon Tem's suit lost its rigidity and hung upon him, and the end plug would stay in place by itself. They pushed open the inner plug and entered the vine, and filed down the ramp that had been built up to the lock. It was good to be able to look in any direction and see solid walls around him again. He began unlacing his suit.

He met people, all wanting to stop and talk, and excused himself politely. He was headed downvine toward his home, but there was another stop to make first.

He reached the right section and paused in the throat, in sudden despair. It was strange, he thought, how it took things a while to hit. Slowly, he started down and to the right, until he was walking in the grass beside the narrow lake. Near midsection he turned right, through a fruit orchard to where some huts nestled on the curve of the vine.

Neena's father sat there, turning a roast over a small fire. He looked at Tem silently for a few pulses, then said, "I'm sorry, lad, but you both knew what to expect."

Tem didn't answer that. He said, "Could I see her?"

Her father nodded rootward. "Two sections down, in the rice."

She must have been expecting him, for she was working near this end. He walked out and began gathering handfuls

of the tall grain. It was not censorable for them to work together and talk.

They worked silently for a while, then he said, "I could refuse to go. But then I'd be in Bottom Caste, and so would
you if you married me. We never really talked about it, did
we?"

She was calmer than he expected. "No, we didn't. I suppose you'll take up with my sister. I've seen the way you
look at her."

He flushed. "I do not! She's four or five orbits older than I
am!"

She shrugged. "Anyway, I guess you don't really care
much about me, or you'd find some way to take me along."

He frowned at her. "What kind of talk is that? Even if we
dared defy the Law, do you think the Elders are blind?"

She glanced around and said in a low voice, "I'm the same
size as my sister, and we look alike. I don't think any of the
Elders would know the difference if I were in her suit."

He was so shocked he cringed, half expecting Sunn to send
a meteor and destroy the section. Slowly, he straightened.
Really—in all his experience—Sunn had never punished
anyone, preachments notwithstanding. It was always the
Elders who handed out punishment. And there'd be no way
they could pursue the migration. He said unsteadily, "But
your sister . . ."

"I've already talked to her," she said, "and she's willing.
She's afraid to go anyway."

III

The Elders gave the fainthearted no time to rebel. The lock's
inner plug closed behind the migration like the cutting of an
umbilical cord. Thirty-nine men and forty-three women—all
the healthy firstborn of the vine whose ages fell between
seventy and one hundred orbits—turned and gazed across
the bleak country.

The hardest thing to get used to, Tem decided (after the
suits and the awful emptiness above them) was the harsh

lighting. One compressed glare from the sun's corona lit the uneven rock, leaving shadows so sharp-edged and black it was hard not to think they were bottomless holes. The stars, dazzling as they were, helped very little to light those shadows.

Even where it was illuminated, the ground was frightening. Gravel extended for a few strides, where the vine's growth had shattered the rock; but beyond lay the undulating plain, punctuated here and there by hills or ringwalls, dotted with loose rocks from the latter.

Another disturbing thing was the silence. He could see lips move, see people clap their gloved hands together to soften the gloves, and strained his ears for the sounds. But inside his suit he could hear too much—his harsh breath, his blood pumping.

He could see bitterness in some of the others' faces. The Law did seem inequitable, requiring that the first generation born in a new vine supply the migration, on the death of the first Chief. Why couldn't older vines send the migrations, if migrations were necessary? There was some vague principle that a colony too long in a vine might grow soft, but it seemed to him that a generation or two might go by without that, so that a vine could better afford to equip a migration. And why such long migrations? If fewer vanguard vines had to send them out, they wouldn't have to leapfrog so far to find empty vines.

He could sympathize with the bitterness, for he himself was feeling for the first time—really feeling it inside—how cruelly they'd been thrust out; how unreachable the old vine was now. What brought it home to him as the way he'd parted from mother. She'd come to the lock with a last present—a newly braided belt and scabbard with his father's knife—and she'd helped him on with his suit. They hadn't said much. He'd been almost gruff, because he was afraid she'd embrace him with everyone looking and all. She'd surely known how he felt, and she hadn't done it; but he wouldn't soon forget the look in her eyes or the little gesture of her hands as he looked back for the last time. If he'd really realized it was the last time—that he'd never hear of her again, or when she died—he'd have certainly embraced her.

He decided they'd stood here feeling sorry for themselves long enough. He gestured to the team he'd chosen, and bent to pick up a tow-rope of the menagerie. The others added their weight to his and the menagerie began to move.

When the team was pulling together well, he turned his place over to another man and walked back along the column. The other carts were moving. One man on a tow-rope was limping, and gestured that his suit was chafing him badly. Tem transferred him to a scouting squad that was to move a little ahead. At least the man could walk gingerly, with no load to pull.

He looked back to make sure there were no stragglers, then walked forward along the column.

They were able to travel fairly straight, with only short halts to rest, for what he judged was ten kilopulses (though one's heart was a poor chronometer under this exertion). Then, glancing back, he saw there was some disturbance in the column. He started toward it.

The man he'd left in charge of that unit hurried to meet him, and they touched helmets so the small metal contact-plates would carry their voices. The man said, "One of the women insists she has to visit the rester."

Tem walked back with him and discovered that the miscreant was Neena. He halted, dismayed, then slowly advanced and touched helmets with her. "You must have been drinking water! Didn't your sister tell you not to until you really needed it?"

"I was thirsty," she pouted, "and I didn't think . . ."

He looked at her in exasperation. "Can't you wait until we camp?"

"No!"

He spun away from her, growling to himself. A fine start! The vine still in sight, and he had to make camp. Sullenly, he signaled the order, and the column closed up to the tight pattern that would conserve warmth. At least, they did it efficiently—all of them (except Neena) remembered their teaching.

Buld took the opportunity to criticize his leadership.

Before they started on, he delivered a lecture in pantomime; and he kept them moving faster than he might have on the next jaunt. After a while he could see they were very tired and legitimately needed to camp. But by this time a large ringwall was looming ahead. He decided to keep on and camp just to brightward of it.

Presently a long line of other objects poked above the horizon. He knew they were the leafages, at section-joints, of a vine. He hoped the lock, if any, wouldn't be in sight. There was danger that individuals might sneak away and try to enter a strange vine, even at the cost of becoming Bottom Caste among its inhabitants. That was less likely now, of course, than it would be later when people were really discouraged or sick.

However, when the column was already skirting the ringwall, he saw a chasm in their path, stretching from the ringwall brightward. This was trouble.

IV

He turned over responsibility for making camp to a man named Bannow, passed back along the column to see that things were all right and to exchange glances with Neena, then headed out to the ringwall.

He climbed slowly, with frequent rests, because one was warned that if he used air too fast he might grow foolish without realizing it. The fungus should be doing well, though, with the light from the corona falling directly on his backpack.

Long before he got to the top he could see that the chasm went as far as the horizon, but he kept climbing because he wanted to see the country ahead. Again, he had the experience of sudden realization. One moment, the scene was like a painting; then, abruptly, he felt the vastness.

The ringwall was perhaps twenty kilostrides across. Inside, it was hollow just as he'd heard them described. It was dark in there, the light from the corona just hitting the top of the far wall, but as his eyes adjusted could see by Starlight that the floor was deeper than outside, and smoother, though there were a few small craters. Uncomfortable, he turned away.

The column was neatly camped, a cluster of toys to bright-ward. It was queer to see only their shadowed sides and a rim of corona light at the top of each. He looked, hesitantly, at the corona. From up here it seemed definitely bigger and brighter, especially at the base.

The chasm went straight brightward, swerving once to a smaller ringwall. Obvious, it was the bed of an old vine, chopped off by this ringwall—a comparatively recent me-teor hit—and left to die from there up. He couldn't see the darkward of ringwall, but he knew the stalk would have sealed itself, sent out feelers, found its way around the new obstacle, and gone on, paralleling the old, shriveling stalk. He could see that it had drawn close so it could consume the old vine via small local roots. It *had* consumed it, leaving the ditch, something like two hundred strides across and nearly as deep.

The new vine was only halfgrown (not inhabited, surely) but it was his first good view of a vine. Along the length, the thin layer of gravel was clearly distinguishable from solid rock. The leafages were great bursts of spear-like growth, fanning out in semicircles above each section joint. Some, he knew, were fifteen times the height of a man. They were said to shade the path of the vine and, by evaporating water, keep the vine's temperature down when the sun struck here. He'd seen a piece of one once, freshly brought in; eight inches in diameter, moist and woody inside, covered outside with hard, rough very white scales.

He moved on a little way to see farther ahead, and a spot of very bright light came into view on the horizon. It must be a high mountain peak, catching the sun. He considered. Theory said sunlight reflected from a mountain was safe, and wonderful for the fungus, and warm. This mountain might be a hundred kilostrides away; still, they had to go farther than that. It was a little to brightward, but by the time they got there the sun would have retreated farther. It would be a good place to camp and freshen up everyone's air, and catch up on whatever else needed doing.

Besides, he wanted to see a mountain.

The land between, so far as he could see, had no serious barriers. There were ringwalls of various sizes, some simple hills, a few cracks. He fixed those in his mind so he could avoid them.

This present chasm was the thing to worry about now. It would take too long to build a ramp across it, and the alternative of going back around the ringwall—and passing in its cold shadow—wasn't attractive.

Could a way be cleared along the base of the ringwall itself? A thought struck him. There must have been other migrations by here, unless they'd all passed farther darkward. He went a little way down the slope, and grinned with delight. There *was* a path of a sort, where boulders had been moved and holes filled in. He was very lucky this time.

Before continuing down, he looked around for one more thing. It was earlier in the season than the Traders appeared at the vines, but no one knew where they came from, and legend said they sometimes attacked migrations. However, there was no movement in sight, and nothing that looked like a camp, and that was the best he could do. He started toward camp.

Before he'd gone far he noticed that he was breathing hard, even though he was going downhill. He began to have trouble controlling his limbs. Once, when he jumped between boulders, he misjudged and fell hard.

He hauled himself up painfully. Nothing was broken, but he knew he'd overestimated his air, especially since his backpack was now turned away from the corona. He wasn't silly yet, but he might not be far from it. And—he realized with shock—he'd violated an elementary principle. He'd come alone.

He got down safely, but by now his mind was very muggy and his limbs alternated between aching and numbness. He concentrated on getting one leg ahead of the other, stopping now and then to stand with his back to the corona, head down, almost falling asleep.

He hardly knew he'd reached camp until he stumbled into it. He was vaguely aware of Buld confronting him with a scowl, but couldn't seem to keep his mind even on that.

The next thing he knew Bannow and some others had a fun airbag attached to the suit's intake nipple, and an empty one on the exhaust, and were squeezing air through. His head cleared, though he was still very tired.

Bannow told him, "You made a bad mistake sneaking Neena into the migration. She raised a fuss about your being gone so long, and somebody recognized her."

V

There was no way Tem could have blocked a Council even he'd tried. He called it as soon as he'd refreshed himself. There were six of the maturest men, beside himself.

The cumbersome touching of helmets slowed things so he had a chance to think. He listened woodenly to Buld's argument at since he'd broken the Law, he was no longer fit to lead; and at they'd better depose him.

He let them wait for his answer while he thought it out. Buld's argument was hypocritical, but how to demonstrate? He said, "Why is Buld so anxious to get rid of me? Does he want to be Leader himself?"

Buld declared he was thinking of the migration. Tem said, "Buld must have gained respect for the Law quite suddenly. When my father was dying, Buld wanted him to avoid the Law by disowning me."

That produced nods and one or two grins. Buld said, scowling, "That was just a suggestion to the Elders. What I wanted was a grown-up Leader. Besides smuggling in a brat who doesn't belong, this stripling has brought us too close to Brightside, and now he's got us trapped so we have to go back around this ringwall. He'll get us all killed before he's through."

Tem said, "You don't know anything about how far Brightside is, or how far we can go."

Buld glared at him. "My father was on the last migration too!"

"He wasn't Leader," Tem said, "and no one voted for him for Chief. I'm the only one who's really trained. As far as Neena's concerned; which is better—a girl who wanted to come, or one who was afraid to?"

Buld and a couple of the others spoke of the Law again. Tem said, "If Sunn wants to punish me, he can do it right now. I'm ready." He stood up and walked a few paces away.

One of the men presently came over to him, with a glance toward the corona, and said, "What about this chasm you've got us up against?"

Tem went back and sat down. He thought he might get Buld to stick his tongue out a little farther. "What *should* we have done?"

Buld said, "We should have camped farther back while someone scouted."

Tem said, "By the same reasoning, we'll have to scout the other side now. Do you want the job? You can take a partner and some bags of air."

Buld glared. "We've all heard how a big meteor kills a vine, and that's obviously what's happened here. Why do we have to scout the other side?"

"Well," Tem said, "I wonder how you know for sure that this meteor killed this vine. What if the vine was already dead? We'd go all the way around and find we couldn't pass on that side either. Is that your idea of leadership?"

He was glad Buld wasn't quick-witted. Buld flushed and said, "Well, I would have found out before."

Bannow looked at Tem keenly and said, "Can you get us across without going around?"

"Of course," Tem said casually.

The vote was four to two in his favor.

Afterward, he was astonished at how alert and shrewd he'd been. Eloquence had never been his strong point before. He decided that it was because Buld had been trying to take something away from him and he just didn't want to let go.

They took the path he'd seen, finding only a few boulders to move, then crossed over the young vine. By now, everyone understood that he'd outsmarted Buld, and he saw many grins. That was good for morale, he decided. So was the evidence that another migration had passed this way, sometime. Tem wondered how that one had made out.

He didn't dare speak often to Neena, and though the other women, misty-eyed, had adopted her, she was glum. As the march dragged on, so were others.

But glumness wasn't the worst. One woman, taking her turn in the rester, refused to put her suit back on and had to be forced into it, screaming. She quieted later, but her face worried Tem and he could feel the whole column reacting. He made camp sooner than he might have, close to a vine, hoping that would raise spirits a little.

It turned out to be a mistake. While he was climbing a nearby ringwall to scout, the woman broke from camp and ran toward the vine. Others pursued. He had to stand helpless and watch the whole thing from a distance. She threw herself down, clawing at the gravel. Then, before they could reach her, she must have deliberately undone the lacings of her suit.

The suit went limp, and that as all.

Sick, he started down without finishing his scouting. He knew now what he should have done. He should have given her something to carry, walked her until she was exhausted, and let her sleep.

Another thing he'd been neglecting was religion. He'd have to appoint a preacher to talk about Sunn. It looked as if a Leader had to know and understand almost everything.

On the way down, he thought, it might have been Neena. What had happened to Neena?

They crossed a number of vines before he saw a lock, and that was in the distance. He made sure the column didn't see it.

The dazzling mountain was getting nearer, and he made a point of how they'd rest up when they got there, but some of the migration seemed to find it frightening rather than reassuring.

The supplies, including the air, were holding up pretty well, but there was trouble in the menagerie. Some of the goats got sick, and one died, for no apparent reason. Finally Tem discovered that some of the air-freshening fungus was spreading into their compartment, and they were nibbling it. It wasn't supposed to be poison.

Some of the birds, confined so long, were pecking others to death. They had to be separated.

He'd expected conflicts among the people, but there were surprisingly few. Presently, from his own behavior, he understood why. He found himself withdrawing into the world of his suit, paying less and less attention to other people. One thing particularly struck him. The right arm of each suit was deeply pleated under the armpit, with an external grip so the gloved left hand could pull down and outward. That enabled the wearer to get his right arm inside. He noticed many right sleeves hanging empty before he realized he was doing the same thing himself. Thereafter, he kept his arm in the sleeve, unless he had to bring it inside to eat, drink, or scratch himself. It was odd, but the sleeve somehow felt outside the suit.

VI

After they'd crossed a few more vines, they found what was left of an old migration. Tem thought it was probably the one that had built the path back there.

There were no corpses in the sagging menagerie except those of cats, small birds, and fish. The goats and larger fowl were gone. There were several empty suits lying around, and four that weren't empty. There were waterbags, airbags, two resters, some air-freshener carts and some empty carts, all falling apart, the wood shrunk and warped, the rubber brittle and cracked from Sunn knew how many seasons' exposure. Tools, rope, and personal belongings were scattered about. It looked as if the survivors had taken what they could carry, and just walked. There was a vine within ten kilostrides, but no lock in sight.

Maybe the Traders had gotten them, or maybe Sunn had swallowed them up.

The column wasn't visibly much moved by the relics, but during the next camp a couple—a man and wife who'd had to leave two young children with relatives—quietly killed themselves. They didn't take the simple way of just opening their suits. They got knives inside, lay down together, and stabbed themselves.

That shook Tem worse than anything so far. He made up his mind to reach the sunlit mountain in two marches if he possibly could, with one brief stop between.

He pushed the column through the first march, crossing two closely spaced vines without even slowing, camped briefly, and bullied them on. The mountain was awesome now; stretched diagonally ahead in one long blaze of light. He could feel the warmth of it already, and his eyes ached. Nevertheless, his vision was adjusting amazingly, so he could tolerate the light, though he couldn't look directly at it. The ground was mountain-lit by now. The corona was a faint ghost, and so were the stars, though space was black as ever.

He could see some of the people about to rebel at this light, and that Buld was getting ready for another try. Then he found the ideal spot.

There was a large ringwall some kilostrides from the mountain, itself aglow with mountain light. Closer to the mountain, and near this end, was a much smaller one. He could go to brightward of the smaller one, for shade from the mountain, and enjoy the twice-reflected, tamer light from the big ringwall.

They dragged to the spot and made camp. The light was stronger than any in a vine, but comfortable. There was no more hunching of shoulders against the cold as one's warmth leaked away to the sky and to darkward. The fungus fairly puffed out fresh air, and the animals grew frisky.

They had the cleaned and exposed carcass of the goat that had died, and now Tem decided they could build a small fire in the menagerie and have fresh meat for once. People revived visibly.

By his count of vines, they might be close to half way through their journey. Before they left here, he'd have scouted enough to make a closer guess.

The lower slope of the mountain, below where the sunlight hit, could be climbed, he thought, to an elevation higher than any ringwall he'd seen yet. So, as soon as people were fed and resting he took Bannow and started that way.

He got used to looking at the mountain through a murky part of his helmet, so the light was cut down.

The mountain was probably twenty kilostrides long, and half that high at the peak. It was really a long ridge, set at an angle to the sun, and he had a feeling it was not very thick through. It curved down at each end, tapering into darkness.

The upper part of it was sheer cliff, lit part way down now. Below the cliff, and barely visible with one's eyes dazzled so, was a steep but even slope, apparently of rock crumbled from the cliff by the sun's timeless hammering. Already Tem was perspiring. He touched helmets with Bannow to say, "We'd better turn from side to side so we won't melt our suits."

Actually, it didn't turn out to be that bad. They had shade from huge boulders, and could hurry across open stretches; and one could always turn his backpack to the cliff and let the fungus soak up some of the light.

They kept on until they were more than halfway up the rubble slope, then the heat was finally too great. They sat down in a shadow.

Gradually Tem's eyes adjusted, but it was still disappointing how little he could see of the country. Things close by were brightly lit from the mountain, and tended to dazzle his sight. Things farther away weren't lit much. He could see the two close-spaced vines they'd crossed (both squeezing around the obstacle of the mountain) and some ringwalls he remembered. In the other direction, beyond the far end of the mountain, he thought he could make out the leafages of another vine, but he wasn't sure.

He said to Bannow, "I guess that ringwall would be a better vantage point after all. Maybe we can walk part way around it and climb."

Bannow didn't answer. Tem drew aside and looked at him. Bannow's eyes were fixed down the slope, and when Tem followed the look he saw four suited figures, tiny in the distance moving toward the slope. They were spread out widely, carrying something in one hand. A moment later he saw a fifth. He decided the things they carrying were some of the sharpened stakes intended for fastening the lock onto the new vine. In addition, the fifth one dragged two airbags.

Bannow started to rise, and Tem pulled him back. Bannow touched helmets. "It's Buld and his bunch! They intend to kill us!"

"I know," Tem said, trying to keep the trembling anger out of his voice, "but let's stay here for a while and think. They can't see us. Remember how it was looking up?"

Bannow sat down. "But we've got to get around them and get back to camp!"

"How? If we climb down they'll see us, and move to intercept. We'll run out of air before they do. They've probably told the camp they were just climbing that small ringwall or something. We can't expect any help in time."

"Well," Bannow demanded, "what are we going to do?"

"First of all, let's act as if we didn't see them. We can go along this slope to the end of the mountain and get into shadow. They may not see us at all; and even if they do, we'll be out of their reach, so probably they'll just wait."

"Then what?"

"Well ... at the worst, we might go clear around the mountain and get back to camp from the other end. I figure it wouldn't be more than sixty kilostrides. If we're very careful with our air, we might make it."

Bannow looked very doubtful. "It'll be cold on the other side."

"Maybe not. The heat may go clear through. Anyway, it's better than just sitting here, isn't it?"

Bannow hesitated, but finally nodded.

They went carefully, seeking shadows, but presently it became clear that Buld had spotted them. They kept on, rounded a bulge, and were in darkness.

VII

Now even the corona-light was hidden. Gradually the stars grew into brilliance, as if the distant gods were drawing closer to watch.

To Tem's surprise, this side of the mountain was a gentle slope, with a surface much like level ground. Below them was a small ringwall, ghostly in the Starlight. He could feel his warmth leaking away, so he turned a little uphill. If there were warmth coming through the mountain, it would be nearer the top.

They moved on slowly. Tem was paying close attention to the footing so he wouldn't trip, when a vaguely seen motion ahead brought him to a startled halt.

Bannow had seen it too. Tem bent his head to touch helmets, but said nothing. The movement was not toward them, but up the slope from below, crossing their path. It was not a man, nor any single creature, but a vast moving pack. As well as he could make out in the dim light, the individuals stood half as high as a man and moved on many legs, though they didn't seem to have horizontal bodies like cats or goats. Finally he said, in a cautious whisper, "Do you suppose these are the things the Book speaks of? The metal things that crawl?"

Bannow's voice was awed. "I don't know. Shall we turn back?"

"Let's stand still for a while."

The vanguard of the pack was nearing the top. Suddenly a line of light grew along the peak, toward them, so bright and so startling that Tem threw an arm before his eyes. He felt Bannow whirl away from him. He himself took a step backward and stumbled over Bannow, who'd evidently tripped with the first step. He jerked his head around to look back. The line of light was still advancing, and he pushed himself erect to run, but before he did he realized the line was not aimed at him, but was just growing along the peak. It was not a solid line, he saw as it came closer, but consisted of thin upright sticks, like a row of very bright, perfectly matched firebrands. It was not straight, but irregular, with dips and rises and gaps.

Something brushed by him. He flinched, but didn't panic. Now he was surrounded by the things, which felt solid and heavy when they bumped against him, but paid him no attention. They scuttled to the peak and aligned themselves along it, thrusting up fingers or feelers into the sunlight, jostling for places in line, crowding each other where there were too many. Then there were no more around him, but farther along they still swept up.

Bannow got to his feet, pawing at his suit. Tem moved close and touched helmets. The man started, then said, "Sunn! They walked right over me! I though . . . is my suit punctured? I can't—I don't hear any hiss . . ."

"You're all right," Tem told him. The suit felt rigid as ever, but there was a little roughness. "I guess they have very small claws, if any." He looked toward the peak. "They seem to eat the sunlight, or drink it."

A few stragglers were arriving, to push their way into line. Tem moved after one, trying to see it.

There was a central body, the size of a man's head. A number of legs, each as long as Tem's arm but no thicker than a finger, grew from the body on all sides. These were flexible, and while about half of them clung to the rocks, the rest were held up so that two inches of the tips were in sunlight.

Now the things were motionless except for an occasional shifting of stance or a wave of an upthrust leg. They stretched along the mountain as far as Tem could see in either direction.

A very strong urge gripped him to climb and get one quick glimpse of the sun. He took a few steps before he caught himself. He looked at Bannow, then reluctantly turned to go on. There was no time to investigate this wonder now.

Bannow drew alongside, wanting to talk, but Tem put off touching helmets. These creatures were apparently a form of life that didn't need air; could wander at will. Could things be learned from them that would free men from dependence on the vines? Could a man, or a small group, find an empty vine nearby and make trips to study them?

He turned to Bannow, and as he did he saw a line of luminous blobs moving up the slope toward them.

He crouched, suppressing his impulse to run, but Bannow's nerve finally broke. The man whirled and ran back the way they'd come. Tem shouted uselessly, then started after him. The blobs of light suddenly reacted, moving to cut Bannow off.

Bannow might have outrun them, but instead he turned and ran up the slope. Tem, suddenly realizing the danger, ran as fast as he could toward him.

He was too late. He saw Bannow's helmet suddenly turn blinding bright as it popped into sunlight. Bannow's eyes stared for just an instant, then snapped shut. The man clapped both hands to his face, whirled, and plunged down the slope. Tem saw him go headlong and slide. Then the suit suddenly went limp.

He stopped, fighting nausea, forgetting the blobs until a knot of them gathered around Bannow's corpse. By then he could see they were men in suits, with very large backpacks that gave off the glow. Shortly, several surrounded Tem. He thought of looking for a rock to defend himself, but they didn't act threatening, though two of them held tapered, sharp-tipped swords.

One of them made incomprehensible hand-signals, then, as Tem shook his head, pointed at Tem's helmet and his own, and pantomimed bringing them together. Tem nodded and they touched helmets.

VIII

The man's speech was only slightly odd. "You from a vine near here, son? What are the two of you doing up here, anyway?"

Tem tried to get his voice working. "We—I guess my friend isn't doing anything, anymore."

The man shrugged. "Too bad. But it would have been besten if he didn't panic. Why were the two of you up here?"

Tem hesitated. Maybe he oughtn't to tell them about the migration. "Some men were trying to kill us. We came to this side of the mountain to get away."

The man looked thoughtful. "Your vine very far?"

"Well . . . quite a ways."

The man studied his face and finally said, "You're from a migration. Got yourselves in some kind of trouble, and ran. Besten you not be so close-mouthed about it. We won't take you back."

Tem said indignantly, "It isn't that at all!"

The man scowled. "Well, we can't stand here jabbering. You can come with us, or die here." He glanced at the two with swords, then turned and went down the slope. The two armed men waited motionless.

Others had taken Bannow's suit off his body, and were carrying the suit away. Tem started toward the corpse, changed his mind, and walked after the spokesman.

The line spread out again, so it was hard to see anything but the glowing backpacks. There were about thirty, all told. A little way down one of them bent to pick up a thing and carried it in one arm. Tem saw legs dangling, and realized it was one of the metal things, dead. Another man found one, and so it went all the way down the slope, until each man was carrying two or three. Finally the spokesman turned back and handed Tem a pair to carry. They were fairly heavy.

Beyond the end of the slope, other figures moved about, apparently also gathering the dead things. Soon Tem saw that there were carts heaped with them. Imitating others, he went to the nearest cart and deposited the two he had. No one gave him any instructions, so he just stood.

Presently they stopped looking for the things and threw over each cartload a rope net, tying it securely. Someone looked at Tem and pointed to a tow-rope. He picked it up and pulled with the others, wondering if they just wanted to get some work out of him before killing him.

It seemed a very long time that he trudged, his hands on the rope first cramping painfully, then going numb. His feet grew clumsy. He stumbled along, knowing his air was bad. Finally he must have fallen, for the next thing he knew he was draped face-down across a cart-load, and tied on so he wouldn't slide off. The jolting ride went on for a long time.

He realized that they were clear into Darkside now.

Then they halted, and he managed to raise his head and saw another cliff, this one lit only by starlight, and with no rubble at its foot.

There were four tunnels in the cliff, each with a clear-rubber airlock. One of the locks was open, and the carts were being rolled in.

Dull as he was, the lock fascinated him. It was made more intricately than the ones he knew, with hoops along its length and pleats between. The three not in use were folded against the tunnel-mouths. His mind worked at that. Why, they must squeeze the air back into the tunnels, instead of losing it!

He got a chance to observe that, as his cart was in the next batch that went in. The tunnel itself seemed to be a second lock, as it had a plug in its middle, and another at its inward end. When that was opened, light as strong as a vine's spilled in.

Inside, they unloaded him and laid him on the floor, face up. Someone began unlacing his suit. A little pressure seeped out, then his helmet was pulled off and he was breathing pure, rich air.

As soon as he could, he sat up and stared around at things he only gradually understood.

This was evidently a great natural fissure, twisting back into a mountain, but it had been much reworked. Rock was hewed away in places. At others, walls of squared stones, cemented with latex, sealed openings or supported ceilings.

A series of shelves hacked from the walls were planted with some kind of shrubs Tem didn't know. There was a stepped wall down the middle of the fissure, similarly planted. Luminous moss grew on vertical surfaces and on ceiling.

The artificial wall where the tunnels came in drew his awed attention. There were great abutments supporting massive machinery—more metal than he'd supposed existed. Some men were turning a giant's windlass, slowly raising high a huge boulder that dangled on a rope as thick as Tem's thigh. At the other end of the wall, a similar boulder descended slowly, turning a heavy shaft to which were geared a dozen strange devices. Rods moved in and out of smooth round holes, with a hissing that could only be the intermittent escape of air under pressure. Great pulleys creaked as the monstrous ropes snaked around them.

Eventually he understood that all this machinery operated the locks, squeezing air in and out.

The tunnel he'd come through opened again, and the last of the expedition came in. The man who'd talked to Tem unfastened his helmet and removed it, looked around checking men and carts, and finally glanced toward Tem. He came over and said, "I'm Hannult. I'll want to talk to you later, but meanwhile I'll take you to the Young Bachelor's chamber and leave you with Oskir. He's boss there."

Oskir was older than Tem, blond, and large. He looked Tem in the eye without expression, then walked around him studying his suit. Finally he said, "No marvel your air got bad. Is this the besten you Vinies can do?"

Tem flushed. "I've trekked two hundred kilostrides in it!"

Oskir's eyes showed a trace of amusement. "With airbags and big carts of freshener, and such. What's your name, and how old are you?"

Tem started to blurt out angrily that he was a Chief's first son, but saw the futility of that. He'd have a better chance of escaping if they didn't know he wanted to get back to his migration. He said sullenly, "My name's Tem. I'm seventy orbits. And a half."

The amusement flickered in Oskir's eyes again. "Tell you, then. There's roast goat over there, and some milk. This ditch is for bathing, and the way you smell, besten you do that first. Hang your suit here." He indicated a peg, then waved a hand toward a low dark tunnel. "We sleep in there. You'll take the pad nearest the inlet." He turned and walked away.

Tem glared at him, then hung his suit on the peg, removed his underthings and stepped into the water. It was tepid, and smelled of some pungent herb. He scrubbed himself with a wad of coarse vegetable fibre, got out, rubbed himself dry, started to dress, then decided he'd better not. He dumped the clothes in the water to soak, and went over to eat. When he'd done that, he rinsed the clothes, wrung them and spread them on the floor under his suit.

Oskir and some others, deliberately ignoring him now, were squatted in a circle, gambling with odd-shaped stones. Five or six more worked on their suits or tinkered with various things. There were about twenty in the group.

Tem ducked through the tunnel and found there was a spacious chamber beyond. There was no luminous moss, but enough light came in so he could see that the walls were cut into shelves and planted. The pads were spaced far apart, probably for ventilation. He lay down on the first, wincing with lameness, and tried to relax.

Evidently these people didn't intend to kill him, but would he ever get a chance to escape? And if he did, what then?

He wondered what Buld had told the column. Possibly that Tem and Bannow had deserted and surrendered to a vine. He wondered what would happen to Neena.

For all he knew, these people might hunt down the column and plunder it. He listened to the low hum of talk in the outer chamber. These were the Traders, of course. At least they were human, though they had odd ways of living.

Eventually, from exhaustion, he slept.

Oskir woke him by toeing him in the ribs. He rolled aside and got to his feet. He felt rested, so some time must have passed. Oskir nodded toward the tunnel.

In the outer chamber were all the young men he'd seen before, plus two or three others. They stood along the walls, with an air of waiting.

Oskir said, "Turn around." When Tem did so, Oskir hit him on the chin hard enough to knock him down.

Tem came up like a cat, and didn't forget to poke out his left fist before swinging his right, but somehow both punches bounced off Oskir's thick forearms. Oskir hit him again. He staggered, caught his balance and tried to dodge in close. He got his left to Oskir's cheek, but not solidly, and took a hard punch he didn't even see coming.

After that it was one long series of stunning blows. He fought back as well as he could, but he was groggy and Oskir was too strong, and too clever with his fists. Tem went down repeatedly. Each time, he hauled himself up, until finally, after a punch that didn't feel any harder than the rest, he found his legs wouldn't work. He had the will to get up, and his mind was fairly clear, but his limbs would only make uncoordinated pawing motions.

They picked him up, dowsed him in the bath water, and swabbed off his face. He was still too weak to stand alone, but his thoughts were remarkably clear, if inclined to wander. He was bleeding a little from the nose and from a small cut in his upper lip, but he knew he wasn't badly marred.

Most of the punches had been clean ones to the chin. He realized Oskir had deliberately avoided messing him up.

He was almost strong enough now to start swinging again, but something in their attitude stopped him. They were looking at him with casual approval. Finally Oskir said, "I'm going to parley besten I can Hannult let you join."

Tem glared at him. "Oh? And suppose I don't want to?"

Oskir looked mildly surprised. "What else can you do? You spect we'd let you go back to a vine, now that you've seen this much?"

IX

As the newest member of Oskir's dormitory, Tem drew the menial tasks. Every three sleep-cycles (as marked by the growth of moss along a measured path) he had to bail the bath water into bags and carry it around to prescribed places to be used for irrigation, then refill the ditch from the nearest reservoir. He had to sweep the floor, air the pads, ventilate the dormitory by using fans, fetch food, bring in fertilizer for the plants and take garbage to the fertilizer factory. He smouldered, but held his temper. Aside from his occupations, he was treated as an equal.

Oskir, who seemed to know everything, personally took charge of his training. One big job was to build a new suit for himself, and he had to perform every bit of the work to Oskir's satisfaction, even if it had to be done over ten times. The backpack was complicated. Instead of a simple honeycomb of fungus, as in his old suit, this one alternated layers of fungus with layers of luminous moss, which gave enough light to keep the fungus working. There was also a better way of feeding in nutrients, and a better method or circulating the air. It was twice as heavy as the old pack.

Equally fascinating was the jettison lock in the front of the suit, at waist level. It had ingenious valves so it could be worked from either outside or inside. Using little bags for body wastes, this made it possible to live in the suit for a long time.

There were also improvements at the ankles and in the soles, which made for better climbing and less danger from sharp rocks. All in all, he was delighted, and he nearly blurted out that such suits would make travel between vines easy. He caught himself in time.

The cycles flowed past. His despair about the migration dulled a little, so he could live with it. He was able to pretend he was content here. He wasn't quite accepted into the clique, but aside from a certain amount of joking about his Vinie origin, there was no hazing. He was willing to let things rest there.

He supposed the migration would be close to finding its vine now, if it hadn't run into bad trouble. He worried about Neena. They might put her in Bottom Caste, since she didn't belong, which would make her a virtual servant to the whole vine. He supposed Buld would get himself elected Chief. That thought brought up shaking hot anger; and that was one feeling that didn't grow dull.

He thought now, that he should have killed Buld right at the start. It wouldn't have occurred to him then, of course, but that seemed to be the logic of the thing. He could have found some way to make it look like an accident.

He shuddered and put that thought from his mind.

Some younger men were elevated to Oskir's group, and took over the menial chores. Tem was put to work in the shops where the metal creatures were cut apart and things made from the metal.

He was a flunkey, but not the only one, and the place was so fascinating he didn't mind. Sometimes he worked a hand bellows that forced air into big rubber bags, for the smiths to use with their fires.

In the vines, small open fires had been used for cooking, or to cure rubber, but that was all. These fires were even smaller, and confined within stone boxes through which thin jets of air were blown. The flame came out pointed and incredibly hot, and would even melt iron.

The metal creature's legs were partly iron, but their body-cases were of some other metal. They were cut open, the insides were taken out and sorted for various metals, and the cases were hammered flat, then trimmed six sided. The edges were heated soft and joined together. Finally, when a sheet of them was big enough, it was hammered on great anvils until it was very flat and smooth and the joints could hardly be seen.

Also, using the fires and anvils, with some special tools, the smiths made all sorts of tools and weapons. There were the straight tapered swords he'd seen, and a variety of knives that made his own look crude. There were scissors; dainty ones for tailoring, large, long-handled ones for cutting tough vegetation or even metal.

One tool in particular took his eye—a saw for cutting the hard hulls of vines.

Once he helped carry some new gardening tools to a branch of the cave where grains were planted. For the first time, he saw women of the cave close up. They wore ordinary clothes and looked no different from vine women. When he heard one speak, he was sure she *had* come from a vine. He wanted to talk to her, ask her how she'd come here, but he didn't get a chance.

He worked in the smithies and at other jobs until he knew most parts of the cave, and most of their equipment. Then a time came when Oskir told him, "You'll be getting a chance to try out your suit. Hannult says besten we take you on a foray and see how you act."

There were about forty men on the expedition, including Oskir, Tem, and half a dozen others of the dormitory. They took eight medium-sized carts, a few tools, some empty bags, and some extra air and water. They headed deeper into Darkside, and now there was something different about the ground. It was darker and harder to see in the starlight, and slick at times. He had to walk carefully.

This suit held the warmth better; and, after a good twenty kilostrides, he couldn't feel any deterioration of the air.

They kept going almost in a straight line until a ringway lay ahead. He studied it curiously. Not only was it low in relation to its width, but it lacked the rugged outlines he was used to. They reached the skirt and he found he was walking on gravel among half-buried boulders. He saw signs that people had been here before, shoveling away the gravel, and that was apparently what they were going to do now.

They laid out small-meshed nets of strong cord, and he was given a shovel and told to heap gravel on one of them. When it was fairly covered, four men took hold of one side and four of the other, and rolled the load back and forth so that the fine stuff sifted through. They discarded the coarse stuff and started over. As the fine material piled up, they shoveled it into the box-like carts.

Tem's curiosity overcame his pride. During a rest period, he touched helmets with Oskir. "What is this for?"

"Dirt."

Tem flushed. "I mean, why are we getting it here?"

Oskir grinned. "Cause we don't want to take it away from Vinies." In a moment he went on, "If you just take rock that's been burnt in the sun and crush it, there ain't muchen good in it. This is the besten for growing stuff, sept you can get goat manure or rotted rice or such. You got to find a ringwall like this one, in Darkside."

"Oh," Tem said. "What makes this one different?"

Oskir shrugged. "My father told me it was because a meteor was ice, not rock like most. It went in a ways and exploded, and threw out this fine stuff. Times, you'll dig down a ways and it feels wet, a little. This is the only one I been to. I can parley it makes stuff grow, all right."

Tem digested that. Then, as Oskir seemed in a talkative mood, he brought up something he'd been wondering about. "You people never talk about Sunn. The god Sunn, I mean. You always try to explain how things happen by themselves. Don't you believe in Sunn?"

Oskir pulled his helmet away and chewed on some dried meat for a while. Then he joined helmets again. "There's those talk about Sunn. I spect it's how you feel inside. I never could see much proof one way or the other. Looks to me, if there's a Sunn, he put things so they run mostly by themselves. Looks to me, people are supposed to make their own, not sit down and wait for some god to give it to them. He put plenty, sept a man don't try."

Tem drew back, uncomfortable. This might be blasphemy, but it made more sense here Outside than in a vine. It would explain how a man like Buld could just take what he wanted, Law or no Law, if no one stopped him. And keep it, if no one took it back.

They filled seven of the carts, packed the tools and other things in the eighth cart or on top of the dirt, and started Brightward. Judging from Hannult's caution now—sending scouts, camping in cover—there must be some danger. Also, they seemed to be mapping, as Hannult kept making notes and sketches.

Finally, when the gossip was that they were nearly out of Darkside, they made camp on a moist gravel patch that Oskir said lay over the base of a vine. They were going to get water here. While a pit was being dug, Oskir took Tem to the nearest ringwall on sentry duty.

They left relays of man for contact with camp, and moved around to brightward of the ringwall before climbing. From the top, the corona was faintly visible, and Tem could see the dark line of gravel where the vine ran up-country, though there were no leafages here. He wondered if a vine seeped water all along its length. He turned to ask Oskir, and found Oskir's back to him.

It occurred to him it would be very easy to pick up a rock and hit Oskir on the head. The inflated helmet was rigid, but would move easily, and (as Tem knew from more than one tumble) wouldn't protect the skull. He could roll the corpse down inside the ringwall, where they'd be a long time finding it. He owed Oskir some lumps.

However, he found he didn't want to kill Oskir. He'd repay the beating sometime, as a matter of principle, but he didn't really resent it. After all, that had been a matter of principle too; a duty with Oskir. Anyway, he'd better stay with the Traders until he learned more, and at least knew where he was.

Oskir turned. Tem touched helmets and asked, "That dark streak. Is that because it's moist?"

"A little. Those are reservoir sections of the vine."

Tem said, "What do you mean, reservoir sections? There's water in every section, even up near Brightside."

"Sure," Oskir said, "but these here are full; no air space at all. They're deeper under, too, so they're safer from meteors. If a vine gets hit farther up, this water'll stay here until a new vine grows."

"Oh."

Oskir nodded up-country. "You can't see the first leafages from here. I spect it'd be about eighty kilostrides. That's where the vines start to have air in them, and come up near the surface. Hey. You tell me how the Vinies decide where to put their locks."

Tem said, "The Law sets it. You're supposed to have at least forty leafages below the lock, but not more than eighty. That puts it in a comfortable part of the vine." He looked at Oskir, then touched helmets again. "You ever been as far up as the locks?"

Oskir grinned. "I been on trading trips for the last nine orbits. Last orbit I was clear to the leaves."

"What?"

"Sure. Hannult took me along. Ten of us went."

Tem said, "How did you stay alive?"

"We didn't walk out in the sun, stupid. There's ringwalls and mountains, like here, for shade. Besides, the leaves grow three times as high as here, and thick, and make a shade. Only thing is, the ground's hot in places. We found one place you could stand on a mountain and look at the sun through a thick piece of rubber."

Tem snorted.

Oskir said, "Your friend did, didn't he? Only thing, he didn't have enough rubber in front of him. Course, you can only look for a couple of pulses, or the rubber melts."

Tem, the notion spinning in his head, began to believe. "To go all the way to Brightside!" he muttered. "And look at the sun!"

Oskir chuckled. "You spect that's something? Look here." He turned and pointed the way he'd been looking before. "See that bright star, right above the horizon?"

"Yes. That's really bright."

"You should see Venus when it's in the sky. This one's Earth. See the real faint one, kind yellow, right beside it? That's the moon. It goes around Earth. You know about Earth?"

"Well ..." Tem said.

Oskir's voice was soft. "That's where people come from in the first place. Some day, we'll find out how; then we'll go see what happened to them. Maybe they're still there, but just need a little help of some kind." He stood looking for a while. "I spect it won't be in my lifetime. No more of this parley, now. We're supposed to be up here on watch."

X

When they got back to camp, the pit was thirty feet deep. They ate, rested briefly, and joined the digging.

Before long the hull of a vine showed. Now men brought a pipe, ten feet long, made of wooden strips glued together, with an iron tip honed to a slanted cutting edge. Hannult jabbed at the vine, twisted and pulled the pipe free. An iron rod was thrust in from the other end, to punch out the chunk of vine that had stuck in it. Hannult kept deepening the hole until some water, bearing chips and strings of latex, gushed out. Now the pipe was thrust clear in, and water swelled from the tip.

They collected the water in bags, but to Tem's surprise they didn't seal them at first. They dumped the water into the dirt laden carts. The water soaked into the dirt, and the carts still weren't any fuller!

When all the dirt was mud, they did fill the bags and seal them. Iron bars went over the mud, and the bags were tied on top.

The hole in the vine plugged quickly when the pipe was removed, and they filled in the pit before leaving. There were traces of mist here and there, just above ground, and puddles that evaporated quickly.

Now they turned darkward again, but angled away from the vine, to the right. If Tem had his directions correct, they were headed home.

When they'd traveled about sixty kilostrides they met the trouble Hannult had been expecting.

They were nearing a large ringwall when a scout who'd climbed it began signaling; turning his backpack toward them, then away, in a complex sequence. He was relaying something from scouts farther around the crater.

Hannult sent two men running ahead to find a hiding place, and took the column straight to the ringwall. Two other men backtracked to make sure no telltale debris had been dropped along their path. Then Hannult talked briefly with Oskir, who gathered Tem and his other young men.

The column found its hidden cave, and there was a hasty transfer of good on the carts. The cart with no mud in it was fitted out with a few tools, one of the tapping-pipes, a bag of air, and two bags of water; along with some food. Oskir's bunch seized the towropes and ran around toward the dark side of the crater. They were going all out, and Tem's lungs soon burned like fire. Even this suit would never keep up, at this rate.

Before long, though, they slowed to a leisure pace. The main column was getting ready to go around the bright side if that were clear, or hide if it weren't. Obviously, this single cart was a decoy.

When they'd gone a little farther, Tem saw in the distance a whole army of backpack glows. There must be over a hundred. Oskir held the casual pace, moving darkward from the ringwall. Presently it was clear they'd been sighted, for a dozen men broke away from the army and ran to intercept them. Oskir went on a little way, then stopped so suddenly the cart almost overran Tem. Then Oskir threw his weight forward again, and so did the others. The cart began to bounce over the rock, headed away from the strangers now.

Of course they couldn't escape with the cart, but Tem supposed any time gained would be vital to Hannult. Scouts climbing the crater might pause to watch the chase.

The pursuers were getting close now. Oskir dropped the rope and ran. The others went with him, but Tem had no warning. He stumbled and fell. By the time he got to his feet the raiders were nearly upon the cart. They were making derisive gestures, apparently with no intention of chasing anyone so long as they got the cart and supplies.

Tem could still have fled, or he might just have stood there meekly, but something in the face of the nearest stranger reminded him of Buld. Shocking, unexpected fury exploded within him. He leaped to the cart and grabbed the tapping pipe; spun it so the point was toward the stranger, and lunged. The man stared for an instant, then twisted frantically. The point raked along his side, and for a split instant Tem thought he'd punctured the suit, but it only snagged and pulled free, intact. He took a step back, ready for another thrust, but all the strangers had leaped out of reach. Now each put an arm behind him and pulled, from somewhere, a sword. They spread out to surround him. He gave ground, darted to one side and menaced a man, who drew back. Beyond them he saw more men leave the army, carrying long spears that would out-reach him. The local group pressed him back slowly, gaining time. He felt very foolish now. What had he accomplished? Well, at least, he was being a good decoy, and that was the intent. But he'd soon be a dead one. His stomach felt as if it were full of gravel.

Then a rock sailed past him and made one of the strangers duck. More came; obviously Oskir hadn't run far. But throwing-size rocks weren't plentiful. Tem hesitated.

Shouldn't he take this second chance to run? After making such a fool of himself, he was ashamed of himself, he was ashamed to have Oskir and the others put themselves in danger.

But before he could make up his mind, the strangers were suddenly retreating toward their own army. Only one of them—the one Tem had attacked—stayed for a moment. That one, keeping the cart between himself and Tem, ran forward and jabbed his sword into first one, then the other, bag of water. Then he grinned at Tem, made an obscene gesture, and ran after the others.

Bewildered as he was, Tem had wits enough to go to the cart and press a hand over the cuts in the bags. Oskir arrived, furious, and bumped helmets! "Fool! You might have gotten us all killed! Why didn't you follow the plan?"

Tem thought about it. He could hardly explain. He said meekly, "Nobody told me any plan."

Oskir glared, speechless. Then the glare began to fade and finally he was grinning. "Well, besten we not stand here. Another army's coming, or they wouldn't have run like that. Likely they're loaded with plunder and the owners are chasing them. I spect you'd want to fight them, too."

XI

They found Hannult before he reached the cave. He was delighted that they'd saved the cart and supplies, and if he didn't think well of the way it had happened, he didn't say so directly to Tem. However, as soon as they were home Tem was put on crash program of learning the hand signals, also the backpack signaling. He was told in blunt language that, while feuds of varying deadliness existed between tribes of Traders, this cave wanted none. Evidently it was considered a sport, not a hostile act, to capture carts out in the open.

Sport or not, when the cave sent out the first trading expedition of the season, a few hundred kilopulses later, it was large and well-armed. Even some of the women went along to handle chores.

This was more like a migration than a foray. There were carts with air-fresheners, resters, extra air, extra water, and many empty bags. There were tools and metal in sheets, rods, and bars, for trade; and bags of rock salt mined in the cave. They also had a few woven fabrics to offer, and some articles of wood, but these were just camouflage, to mask their dependence on the vines.

Their own more sophisticated tools, including the vine-tapping pipes and the saws, were kept out of sight, with the weapons.

To Tem's disappointment, they headed the opposite way from the migrations, slanting brightward. When they'd gone a ways he found a chance to talk to Oskir. "That mountain where I was picked up must be near here."

Oskir shook his head. "We aren't that far yet. That's just about the end of our territory."

So they wouldn't get to Tem's old vine. He asked, "Do we trade all the way out to the newest vines?"

"No. The last eight or ten belong to that bunch you tangled with. The newest are too poor to trade much, anyway. That's why we never bother with migrations, either. Sept sometimes we steal a girl or two."

They passed the mountain eventually, but now only the very peak was lit, giving little warmth or light. They turned brightward to a large ringwall and made camp in a hidden niche. Oskir took Tem to one of the resters, handed him another suit, and said, "You're picked for the trading party. Go inside and they'll fix you up."

There were two men inside who helped him out of his suit, then proceeded to smear his face with greasy stuff that stained it red. A pair of goggles hid his eyes. Finally they helped him into the second suit, and he was disgusted to find that it was his old one. Later he saw that the whole trading party—twenty men—were similarly made up and were wearing Vinie suits. Then he understood. They didn't want the good suits seen.

With two cartloads of goods, they approached the first vine. Two Elders were in the lock, pretending to be making repairs. Tem grinned. He knew the eagerness and unease they were hiding.

Hannult did the bargaining, standing outside the clearest spot and gesticulating, as items were brought up singly for display. He put on a show of fierceness and weirdness. Tem, carrying an axe head to be shown, grimaced and made hostile gestures, and enjoyed the Elders' expressions. That earned him a scowl from Oskir that was half grin.

When the Elders were convinced there'd be legitimate trading, the inner plug opened. Mosslight spilled out. A procession came out, bearing bags of fruit and grain, cooked fish, cooked fowl, and raw carcasses of goats. There were a few small bags of water, handled as if they were very precious. Larger bags contained liquid vine latex, which could be used as glue or for making rubber.

Hannult accepted the edibles and the latex, and solemnly purchased a small bag of water, as if it were a great luxury. He concluded the trading with mysterious genuflections, and led the party away by a roundabout path.

As soon as they reached camp, the women went to work on the goat carcasses. The meat was cut in strips and mauled with spike headed hammers, then laid out on the surface rock so the warmth would speed drying. When it was dry, it was powdered with a little salt and sealed into small bags. Oskir said it would keep a long time.

They worked back across the vines, re-passing the high mountain, gradually exchanging the metalware for edibles and latex, and some articles of wood. It became obvious to Tem that they wouldn't get within two hundred kilostrides of the newest vine.

Nevertheless, he made preparations. He found a chance to steal a saw and hide it. He got several bags of the powdered meat, too, and some grain. Water would be a problem. If he couldn't steal a bag of the right size, he might have to get it from vines, which would take him farther to darkward than he wanted to go. Tentatively, he took a small bag.

Toward the end of the trading, there was much sentry duty. When sentries were being changed, he slipped away, got the stuff he'd hidden and kept on going.

XII

After crossing several vines, he nearly blundered into the foreign trading expedition, but they didn't see him. He detoured around them, then moved darkward and turned across country, crossing below the lock of each vine.

He walked, rested, and walked, until he lost all count of the stops. He ate enough to keep up his strength, but drank sparingly. Gradually he slid into the familiar half-daze, and had to make an effort to think at all. After a while he realized the corona had made its farthest retreat and was beginning to return.

He crossed yet another vine, noting with vague puzzlement that its lock was below instead of above him. Then something snapped awake in his mind. This was what he'd been looking for! He shook himself awake, sipped a little water, and turned down the vine. Buld had been afraid of the corona, or had pretended to be. If he'd taken the column darkward, his lock would be down here.

When he was close to the lock he stopped, with an odd reluctance. The trek had become such a part of him, it was somehow wrong that it should be over. Yet this was a new lock. The puffs of latex where the stakes were driven into the vine hadn't collapsed yet, nor had the vine begun to grow over its wounds.

He looked around at the scattered debris, and recognized some of it. Where was the menagerie? He stared back across country. Finally he saw one of the carts, tilted, with one wheel missing, its towropes sprawled where they'd fallen. They hadn't done much salvaging; even precious rope lay around. The tunnel wasn't nearly deep enough, so that the lock met the vine very near the top, and at a bad angle.

At least, they were in a vine. They wouldn't starve, though they might get pretty lean if they had to live on vine-fruit. And he hadn't come here to commiserate. First of all, he had to get into the vine, and this was no place to do it. He ate and drank a little more, then squeezed the last of the water into his suit-reservoir. He salvaged some rope and started down the vine.

What he wanted was a section too cold to have been explored yet, but not too far from the lock. He settled for the twentieth one down.

He chose a spot twenty strides below a leafage, and began scraping away the gravel. When he'd cleared a circle of hull, he jabbed the point of the saw in and twisted. It was very hard cutting, but he chipped out a hole and was finally able to thrust the saw through. Bits of vine blew out and thudded on his helmet, and he was spattered with strings of latex. The blast of air was like a solid thing. The hole plugged quickly and he shoved the point in again and began sawing a straight line, holding his arm out to one side to avoid the latex. The stuff set very fast, and stuck hard, out here.

The cut sealed fast behind the saw, but it left a line of weakness. He sawed three sides of a rectangle big enough to drop through, suit and all. Then he paused to consider. If he sawed the fourth side, the plug might blowout and smash him like a bug. If he left part of the fourth side it might act as a hinge, so the plug would just flap back.

When he'd done that, he still had to go around the old cut again. The plug blew out with awesome force, but the hinge held. The saw was knocked from his hand and bent, but he wasn't hurt. Now the blast of air was incredible. Latex, draining from capillaries, formed strings in a virtual tube around it, whipping madly. The blast went on so long he began to fear the whole vine was emptying. At last, though, it slackened. Eventually, he could peer in.

The section was full of mist, but seemed to be clearing. The luminous moss was still glowing, though it might be dead now. He tied a rope around the hinge and let it fall inside. He tugged at the flap, and it moved slowly.

Eventually, to get it shut behind him, he had to tie another rope around the free end and strain at it. When it was closed—with the ropes still dangling—it stayed. Oozing latex should seal it fast, and the vine would soon heal.

He cut off one rope a few feet down to tie on the end of the other. Together, they reached within an easy drop of the bottom. He'd cut a little too far from the leafage, though, and had to drop into water. He felt ice crumble beneath him, but the suit protected him.

Now, if what he'd been told about vines was correct, he was in good shape. He climbed toward the throat, where the bulbous growths had swollen shut like a clenched fist. If they didn't open until capillaries filled the section, he was in for a long wait.

However, there was evidently, as he'd been told, some other mechanism or intelligence in the vine. In not more than three or four kilopulses, the throat began to open and air poured in. When the blast lessened, he squeezed through and started up the vine.

When water filled only a fourth of the diameter, he got out of his suit and hid it, taking part of his food with him. The air was chilly, but it felt wonderful to be out of the suit.

He found that the vine wasn't a completely barren one. There was grass, and wild rice, and insects and lizards, and fish; things that had come through the seeding-shoot from some parent vine. He saw no mammals, and no birds.

He'd reached territory where he had to go cautiously, peering into each section before entering it, so he saw the seven people before they saw him.

XIII

They didn't look well-fed, and they didn't look cheerful.

There were two married couples and three single men. Tem had to think a moment to remember all their names.

Should he show himself? Why not? He had to make contact sometime, and these weren't part of Buld's clique. He walked toward them and called out, "Kliv! Jellen!"

The seven of them whirled and peered toward him. Then Kliv's eyes went wide. "Tem!" One at the women screamed. The whole seven fell back.

Tem grinned at them. "Relax. I'm not a ghost."

Kliv was the first to accept that. "Sunn!" he exclaimed, "I'll never doubt miracles again! How——?"

Tem had already decided on a story, or a hint of one. "Ours isn't the only migration that ever travelled." Let them do some guessing.

The others had come forward now. Jellen said wonderingly, "You found another migration? But we thought . . . Well, I see. Buld *did* lie, even though he didn't kill you and Bannow. He said they saw both of you vanish in bursts of flame near that mountain. Some of us doubted it and wanted to go looking for you. It almost came to a fight right then, but they'd grabbed everything that could be used for a weapon. Anyway, we didn't even know what direction to look, so . . ."

"I'm glad you didn't," Tem said. "How did things go after that?"

"Bad. As soon as we were past the mountain, he led us darkward. It was cold, and we made poor time and used too much air. Then we got into some tough country and had to detour. We lost the menagerie, except for some of the fowl; and eleven more people died on the way, and six more escaped with some supplies. We think they surrendered to a vine."

Tem said, "Neena?"

"She stayed with us." Kliv acted a little embarrassed.

"Well," Tem asked, "What'd happened since? Why are the seven of you here alone?"

Kliv said, "Buld has a grip on everything. We thought he'd probably kill us, because we spoke against him, so we ran.

He hasn't come after us yet. I guess he doesn't really have to."

"Did any of the grain get through? And no goats."

"Yes, but no goats."

"You can live without goats," Tem said. He refrained from saying that, if the colony grew prosperous, there might be ways of getting goats. "How many would resist Buld if they had a chance?"

"I don't know. Most of them resent him, but there's not much fight in them. They just want to forget the Outside."

"How many will fight for Buld?"

"His clique, and two or three more. Maybe nine all told."

"Is there much fight in *them?*"

"Yes. They're getting most of what eggs there are, and most of the meat we salvaged. They'll fight to stay on top."

"Well," Tem said, "*you* haven't much to lose. If you'll follow me, we'll get rid of Buld and make this a decent vine to live in."

The two women showed distress. The men looked at each other. Finally Kliv said, "We'll go with you if you can show us we have a chance."

Tem left the married couples and one of the single men to improvise clubs from vine fronds and to follow a few sections behind. He, Kliv, and Jellen started up the vine, scouting each section before entering it.

Twelve sections up they found two of Buld's friends, fishing with a net. They were evidently there as an outpost, as each had handy a six-feet wooden staff, sharpened at each end, evidently made from a cart. They wore knives at their belts.

There were only a few clumps of fronds along that side. Tem said to Kliv, "Do you think you could creep fairly close to them?"

"Maybe."

"Pretend you're trying to steal their fish. Get them to chase you this way."

He and Jellen found places in the convolutions of the throat, as far into the other section and as high on the sides as possible. He didn't think Buld's men would be reckless enough to pursue blindly through the throat, but if he could get them close . . . He raised his head enough to peer out.

Kliv was going on all fours. He got within nine or ten strides before his cover played out. Then he leaped toward the bucket of fish just a few steps behind the men.

The farther man glanced up and shouted. The nearer dropped the net and hurled himself toward Kliv, reaching for his knife. Kliv got a hand on the bucket, then, as the man was on top of him, swung it into the man's face, knocking him off balance. Fish spilled from the bucket. Kliv wheeled and ran with what were left. The two grabbed their spears and came after him, bellowing. Now if they only didn't look up too soon . . . Tem's limbs felt weak and shakey.

Kliv leaped for one of the bulbous growths, and from there to a higher one. The first pursuer jumped mightily, landed on a growth, and struggled for balance as the stuff gave. His eyes fell upon Jellen, who was tensed to spring, and he jerked his spear around.

Without conscious planning, Tem had already launched himself. He arced down, missing the man, but a murderous instinct made him reach out with the saw. It ripped awfully across the right shoulder and the man went down, screaming. Tem landed, tumbled, trying not to cut himself on the saw, then writhed to his feet and faced the second man. But there was no fight left in that one. He just stood, jaw hanging, spear adroop. Tem said, "Drop it!"

They bandaged the hurt one as well as they could, then got the fishnet and cut cords from it to tie both men securely. They waited for their five friends to come up, left them the prisoners and one knife, and started on.

The next dozen people they met (scattered along the vine, fishing) were friendly or neutral. Tem deliberately used the shock of his reappearance, commandeering instead of asking. He added two reliable men to his advance squad. Since

none were armed, he sawed a few clubs out of fronds and
left his noncombatants hacking out more with a knife, with
instructions to hold the upper end of a certain section. Then
he climbed into the throat to scout the section. He hoisted
himself to a growth, and without warning confronted two of
Buld's cronies starting through.

He made a move as if to retreat, hoping to draw them after
him. However, after a moment of gaping, one seized the
other and whispered urgently. They both turned and ran. The
quick-witted one must have realized Tem would have allies,
and that the thing to do was to get to Buld immediately. Tem
gestured to his handful to follow him, and leaped after the
pair. He drew ahead of his underfed comrades, gaining a little on the quarry. At the end of the section, he bounded far
up the curve to see whether they kept going.

They did.

There were several people in this section, who straightened
and stared. Tem yelled for them intercept the two, but only
one moved, and the fugitives threatened him off with their
spears. At least, though, the man joined Tem.

Two sections later Tem saw he'd lost the chase. He
stopped in the throat, watching the quarry flee up the lefthand side of the fairly wide lake. In their path were about
fifteen new huts, with the bulk of the colonists working
around them or lounging. The two shouted at the people,
threatening them with their spears. The people listlessly allowed themselves to be herded toward the other end of the
section.

There was a smaller group of huts there, partway up the
curve. Coming at a run were Buld and four other men, all
armed with spears.

Tem ran down the slope, shouting. The people looked back
and stopped. Buld's pair prodded them on, and now Buld
was bellowing at them. Most of the people started on, staring
back over their shoulders. One man broke away and ran toward Tem, then several others. Tem heard Neena scream,
"Tem!" and saw her start toward him. One of the armed pair

herded her back, spear poised. She turned and went with the others, face buried in her hands.

Tem counted eight men and three women who'd escaped and were running to him. He scanned each face, and didn't think any of them were enemies.

That left about twenty, mostly women, in Buld's hands. Tem went over things mentally. Not counting his own two captives, there were about thirty either with him here, or behind him in the vine. There were five or six unaccounted for, who might be farther up the vine.

The eleven who'd defied Buld just now gathered around Tem. He cut off their questions. "You, and you. Take these women down to where the others are. You other six—will you fight?"

They all nodded.

Tem looked around. Kliv was just coming through the throat. A moment later Jellen and the other three men appeared, panting for breath. Now Tem had eleven with him who'd fight, against Buld and six allies. But Buld had hostages; and if he could recruit a man or two among them, he had plenty of knives and spears.

Buld had the hostages herded up near his own hut now, and his men were busy tying some of them so they couldn't escape. Tem watched with mounting frustration. He could hardly attack now. Of course Buld couldn't afford to kill the hostages—they were his security—but what if he killed one at a time? Or threatened to torture them?

Could Tem pretend convincingly that he didn't care what happened to the hostages? No; not if Buld put it to the test.

What if he just seized the vine, moved up it and left Buld penned up here? Again, Buld could use the hostages.

What Tem had to do was work on Buld's nerves somehow, quickly, before he had time to think. Or, try to split away some of Buld's men.

There *was* the fact of Tem's sudden reappearance, which must be mystifying and dismaying to Buld. While that lasted, could anything be done to amplify it?

What if Tem acted like a ghost, or something else super-natural?

Whatever he did, he ought to get out of this section, so Buld couldn't threaten him with the hostages. Should he go back down the vine? Buld must be wondering what was down there.

Maybe he could act as if there *were* something frightful down there. Maybe he could even act frightened himself.

That began to feel promising. He said to Kliv, "How many people up the vine? Any of them hostile?"

Kliv said, "I don't think so."

There are just a few, tending the fowl."

"How far up?"

"Well, the lock's in the next section, and there are a few huts in the one beyond, then two sections with fowl in them."

An idea began to stir. "The lock's in the next section? Where are the suits, and the other stuff?"

"Right under the lock. We just left everything there that we didn't have use for."

Tem thought hard. He turned to Jellen. "Go back down-vine and get everyone here in a hurry. Act as if there's something terrible coming up the vine. Look as scared as you can, but don't explain. Can you do that?"

"Yes, but—"

"I'll explain later. Hurry!"

Jellen left. Tem took his other ten to the far end, across the constriction from Buld, and made a show of scouting the throat. Then he waited, acting nervous, paying little attention to Buld but staring downvine. Finally the rest of his people came hurrying into the section. He gestured them on, posted his armed men between them and Buld, got them all through the throat.

Buld called out, "What nonsense are you up to now?"

Tem yelled, "You'd better surrender while you can."

Buld laughed. "I've got these people here. You can't do anything."

Tem looked as worried as he could. "You'd better let them go." He turned toward the throat, turned back irresolutely, and finally hurried into the throat. He put one man where he could watch Buld and signal Tem if Buld moved.

XIV

No ramp up to the lock had been started. Rope ladders dangled the full distance, only a little off the middle of the vine. Equipment, including suits, lay scattered about at the edge of the lake. Tem glanced back at his watchman, then chose two suits. He told the people, "Carry the rest of these upvine. Go at least five sections before you stop, then wait until I come." As they stared at him, he said harshly, "Hurry!"

His own bunch stayed with him, but he told them, "Help Kliv and me into these suits, then you go upvine too. Make sure nobody comes back down. We're going to let the air out of this section." He smiled grimly at their expressions and said, "I know what I'm doing."

They trotted off, and he and Kliv began the climb. When he could just see the lookout he'd left, he gestured to the man, pointed upvine and held up five gloved fingers. The man left his post and started through the section. Tem hoped he'd understand and keep going.

The climb was long and nerve-wracking, with the ladders swaying, and carrying the saw in one hand didn't make it easier. Finally, though, Kliv reached the crude platform hung below the lock, and reached down to give Tem a hand.

The inner plug came unseated easily, since there was still pressure in the lock outside, maintained by leakage. They wedged it where it couldn't swing shut, and stepped out.

Getting the outer plug loose, of course, would be beyond their strength, lacking levers to pry with. He looked for a thin spot in the rubber, found one where it bulged, and poked the saw at it gingerly. He thought it would penetrate easily when the time came.

Now Kliv's face showed understanding, and horror, but he didn't protest. They went to where they could peer obliquely into the section, and waited.

He was gambling that Buld would come scouting without being prudent enough to bring hostages. The man would suspect a trap, of course, but he wouldn't be sure, and as time passed his nerves would get worse. If he did bring hostages, maybe he could be trapped anyway—it should be possible to let enough air out of the section to render everyone in it unconscious, without killing them, then get the inner plug back in place.

Time dragged. Kliv got up and paced in the lock, but Tem stayed where he was, grimly. At last Buld and another man trotted into sight, headed upvine.

By the time Tem could see them, they were a third of the way into the section. He tensed. Should he spring the trap now, or wait? He didn't know how quickly the throat would close when air started to escape. Would they have time to get back? Would Buld glance up, and understand the significance of the open inner plug?

Buld stopped suddenly, eyes fixed on the spot where the suits had been. Tem leaped away from the opening, shoved Kliv to safety, jabbed the saw into the thin spot. The rubber split, and the split ran halfway around the lock. A mighty wind knocked Tem down. His suit puffed suddenly rigid. He crawled toward the vine opening, but the wind shoved him aside. He hauled himself clear of it, got to where he could see in slantingly. Buld and the other men were sprinting downvine. They went out of sight, and Tem strained his neck to see farther, but could not.

He had to wait, not knowing whether they'd got clear or not, for what seemed eternity. Mist formed around him. He went to touch helmets with Kliv, but the wild air battering on his suit drowned out their voices. Finally he forced himself to sit down and wait.

At long last the wind lessened, and he could push his way to the side of the opening and force his head in.

The two men lay at the throat where they'd collapsed, clawing at the great growths. The throat was squeezed tight.

He raised a hand to beckon Kliv, intending to say they should get inside to the platform and be ready to replace the inner plug before all the air was gone. But he hesitated, and Kliv stared at him, obviously seeing his indecision.

Tem tried to sort out the muddle in his own mind. He'd come all this way to kill Buld, hadn't he? He wasn't sure. A man's motives seemed to be such mysterious things. He couldn't feel the slightest concern now whether Buld, and the other man, died or not. Maybe all he'd really wanted was to regain his leadership and prove that he was the better man.

A kilopulse longer, maybe less than that, and the air in the section would be too thin. Right now, he could take Buld alive and let the colony decide what to do with him. On the other hand, Buld would always be a threat to the colony. They'd have to watch him constantly. If they ...

They?

Yes, he said to himself, I'd have known it long ago if I'd stopped to think about it. I'm not of this colony any more. I'm not of the vines.

As long as he didn't care one way or another, why leave Buld to worry the colony? Why even bother them with the decision?

He stayed where he was and watched the bodies begin to puff. When he was sure they were dead, but before they got too ugly, he motioned Kliv and they crawled in to replace the plug.

XV

As soon as the first urgencies were taken care of, he and Neena strolled a few sections below the lock. He had to assure her several times that none of the throats would suddenly squeeze shut without reason, or with diabolical reason, as they were passing through.

She said, "I didn't take up with anyone else, but I want to tell you the truth. I did think about it. There was one man who paid special attention to me, and I didn't avoid him. I thought—" She searched his face. He said nothing, and she went on, "I was sure you were dead, and I thought they'd make me Bottom Caste because I didn't belong; but if I married this man, they wouldn't."

He said casually, "Was it Buld?"

She colored. "No. But it was one of his friends."

He said, "I don't think anyone would have blamed you. I wouldn't."

They walked in silence for awhile, then she said, "It does make things complicated, though. They'll think—" She stopped and faced him. "I want to be sure *you* don't think it!"

"Think what?"

"That I just want to be the Chief's wife."

He nearly smiled at that. "I don't think that. And they won't because I'm not going to be Chief."

She stared at him. "What do you mean?"

"Will you try to imagine it like this? Suppose we went to another vine, the two of us, that was an easier trip from here. I don't mean a deserted vine. There'd be other people, and we wouldn't be Bottom Caste, and we'd be comfortable. We'd just be plain people. Would you come?"

The bewilderment in her eyes made him put an arm around her shoulders. "Well?" he said, for he daren't waste much time.

She drew back. "You mean, put on a suit again and go Outside? And leave everyone we know?"

"Maybe one or two others could go with us."

Suddenly she flushed.

"What's gone wrong with you? Why can't you be Chief and—and live a normal life?"

"I'm not going to be Chief. I'm sorry, Neena. I want you to come with me, but I'm not going to stay."

She wouldn't talk for a while, just sobbed and thrust his hands away. Finally he said, "Do you suppose you might feel differently if you had some time to think about it?"

She pulled herself together. "Would we be married and live here while I think?"

This time he did smile. He couldn't be angry with her; she'd been through more than any girl deserved in a lifetime. "Suppose I came back, in another orbit or two. Would you want to talk about it again?"

"I don't know. You don't seem to—to care about me at all. I feel as if you were some—I feel as if I didn't know you."

He kissed her gently on the forehead and left. He didn't look back and she didn't call after him.

He hurried, for he had to get to his hidden suit before anyone came looking for him. He felt badly about her, but he had to admit that his other feeling was relief. People did change. He wasn't really Tem any more. He didn't even remember, exactly, what Tem had been like.

His mind grew busy with schemes for getting back to the cave. There'd be difficulty leaving the vine by the way he'd entered, without getting blown out through the hole; but with arrangement he could do it. He'd be on short rations for the trip. And he'd have to talk fast, convince Oskir and Hannult he hadn't given any secrets away to the Vinies.

Vaguely, he wondered if it were quite normal for a young man to walk away from a really pretty girl like that . . .

But before he was out of the vine, Neena was out of his mind. There was a whole worldful other things to be pondered. A whole skyful, in fact.

TULAN

WHILE FACING the Council of Four his restraint had not slipped; but afterward, shaking with fury, the Admiral of the Fleets of Sennech slammed halfway down the long flight of stone steps before he realized someone was at his elbow. He slowed. "Forgive me, Jezef. They made me so mad I forgot you were waiting."

Jezef (adjutant through most of Tulan's career, and for some years brother-in-law as well) was shorter and less harshly carved than his superior. "So they wouldn't listen to you. Not even Grefen?"

"Even Grefen." That vote had stabbed deepest of all.

Jezef took it with the detachment that still irritated Tulan. "The end of a hundred years of dreams; and we go back under the yoke. Well, they've always been soft masters."

They reached the ground cars. Before getting into his own Tulan said coldly, "Since you're so philosophical about it, you'll be a good one to bear the sight of men saying good-bye to their families. We're to take full crews to Coar and surrender them with the ships. Requisition what help you need and get everybody aboard by noon tomorrow."

Jezef saluted with a hint of amused irony, and left.

Whipping through the dark icy streets, Tulan smiled sourly, thinking how Sennech's scientists had reversed themselves on the theory of hyperspace now that Coar had demonstrated its existence. Maybe the Council was right in mistrusting their current notions. As for himself, he saw only two things to consider: that with Coar swinging behind the sun, the accuracy of her new weapon had gone to pot; and that before she was clear again he could pound her into surrender.

His swift campaigns had already smashed her flabby fleets and driven the remnants from space, but the Council, faced with the destruction and casualties from just a few days of the weird surprise bombardment, was cowed.

He'd spent the previous night at home, but wasn't going back now, having decided to make his farewell by visiphone. It was the thing he dreaded most, or most immediately, so as soon as he reached the flagship he went to his quarters to get it over with.

Anatu's eyes—the same eyes as Jezef's—looked at him out of the screen, filling him with the familiar awkward worship. "You've heard?" he asked finally.

"Yes. You won't be home before you go?"

"No; I . . ." He abandoned the lie he'd prepared. "I just didn't feel up to it."

She accepted that. "I'll wake the boys."

"No! It's—" Something happened to his throat.

She watched him for a moment. "You won't be back from Coar. You've *got* to speak to them."

He nodded. This wasn't going according to plan; he'd intended it to be brief and controlled. Damn it, he told himself, I'm Admiral of the Fleets; I've no right to feelings like this. He straightened, and knew he looked right when the two sleepy stares occupied the screen.

Their hair was stiff and stubborn like his own, so that they wore it cropped in the same military cut. It could have stood a brush right now. They were quiet, knowing enough of what was wrong to be frightened.

He spoke carefully. "I'm going to Coar to talk to them about stopping the war. I want you to look after things while I'm away. All right?"

"All right, Dad." The older one was putting on a brave front for the benefit of the younger and his mother, but the tears showed.

As Tulan cut the connection he saw that Anatu's eyes were moist too, and realized with surprise that he'd never before, in all the years, seen her cry. He watched the last faint images fade from the screen.

Sometime near dawn he gave up trying to sleep, dressed, and began composing orders. Presently Jezef came in with cups of steaming amber liquid. They sipped in silence for a while, then Jezef asked "You've heard about Grefen?"

Tulan felt something knot inside him. He shook his head, dreading what he knew was coming.

"He killed himself last night," Jezef said.

Tulan remembered the agony in the old Minister of War's eyes when he'd voted for surrender. Grefen had been Admiral in his day; the prototype of integrity and a swift sledgehammer in a fight; and Tulan's first combat had been under him. A symbol of the Fleet, Tulan reflected; and his death, yes, that too was a symbol—what was there but shame in surrender, for a man or a fleet or a world?

His hand clenched, crumpling the paper it was resting on. He smoothed the paper and re-read the order he'd been writing. He visualized the proud ranks of his crewmen, reduced to ragged lines shuffling toward prison or execution.

It seemed impossible, against the laws of nature, that men should strive mightily and win, then be awarded the loser's prize. His anger began to return. "I've a mind to defy the Government and only take skeleton crews," he said. "Leave the married men, at least."

Jezef shrugged. "They'd only be bundled into transports and sent after us."

"Yes. Damn it, I won't be a party to it! All they did was carry out their orders, and superbly, at that!"

Jezef watched him with something like curiosity. "You'd disobey the Council? You?"

Tulan felt himself flush. "I've told you before, discipline's a necessity to me, not a religion!" Nevertheless, Jezef's question wasn't unfair; up to now it really hadn't occurred to him that he might disobey.

His inward struggle was brief. He grabbed the whole pad of orders and ripped them across. "What's the Council, with Grefen gone, but three trembling old men? Get some guns manned, in case they get suspicious and try to interfere."

Blood began to surge faster in his veins; he felt a vast relief. How could he have ever seen it differently? He jabbed at a button. "All ships' Duty Officers; scramble communication circuits. This is the Admiral. Top Secret Orders . . ."

Shortly before noon the four-hundred-odd ships lifted out of Sennech's frosty atmosphere, still ignoring the furious demands from the radio. Fully armed, they couldn't be stopped.

Tulan's viewer gave a vivid picture of the receding fifth planet. The white mantle of ice and snow was a backdrop for blue artificial lakes and the dark green of forest-strips (hardy conifers from Teyr) alternated with the lighter shades of surface farms. The ice had been almost unbroken until men came, bringing more heat than Sennech had ever received from a far-off sun.

That had been before the First Solar War, when Teyr (the race of Aum had originated there) ruled. That awful struggle had bludgeoned the home planet back to savagery, and left Coar and Sennech little better off.

With recovery, Coar had taken over and prospered immensely. Teyr stayed wild except for small colonies planted there by the other two planets, and Sennech lagged for a while.

Within Tulan's lifetime his world had found itself ready to rise against the lax but profit-taking rule of Coar, and that rebellion had grown into the present situation.

Sennech's wounds were plainly visible in the viewscreen; great man-made craters spewing incandescent destruction blindly over farm, city, or virgin ice. The planet was in three-quarters phase from here, and Tulan could see the flecks of fire in the darkness beyond the twilight zone. Near the edge of that darkness he made out the dimmer, diffused glow of Capitol City, where Anatu would be giving two small boys their supper.

He checked altitude, found they were free of the atmosphere, and ordered an acceleration that would take them halfway to the sun in fifty hours. It was uncomfortable now, with Sennech's gravity added, but that would fall off fast.

Jezef hauled himself in and dropped to a pad. "I wish I had your build," he said. "Do you really think we can pull this off?"

Tulan, in a good mood, grinned at him. "Have I ever led you into defeat yet, pessimist?"

"No; and more than once I'd have bet ten to one against us. That's why the Fleet fights so well for you; we have the feeling we're following a half-god. Gods, however, achieve defeats as terrible as their victories."

Tulan laughed and sat down beside Jezef with some charts. "I think I'll appoint you Fleet Poet. Here's the plan. No one knows what I intend; we could be on our way around the sun to overtake Coar and either fight or surrender, or we might be diving into the sun in a mass suicide. That's why I broke off the siege and pulled all units away from Coar; the fact that they're coming back around to meet us will suggest something like that."

"Are they going to join up?"

"No; I want them on this side of the sun but behind us. I have a use for them later that depends on their staying hidden. Incidentally, I'm designating them Group Three.

"In a few hours we're going to turn hard, this side of the sun, and intercept Teyr. I want to evacuate our forces from the moon, then decoy whatever the enemy has there into space where we can get at them. That's their last fleet capable of a sortie, and with that gone we can combine our whole strength and go around to Coar. She'll probably give up immediately, on the spot."

Jezef thought it over. "Will they be foolish enough to leave the moon? As long as they're safely grounded there, they constitute a fleet-in-being and demand attention."

"We'll give them a reason to move, then ambush them. Right now we've a lot of reorganizing to do, and I want you to get it started. We're splitting this Force into Groups One and Two. Here's what I want."

They cut drives and drifted in free fall while supplies were transferred between ships, then Tulan held an inspection and found crews and equipment proudly shipshape. Despite the proliferating rumors, morale was excellent.

A few hours later the realignment began. Space was full of the disc-shapes; thin, delicate-looking Lights with their projecting external gear, and thicker, smoothly armored Mediums and Heavies. He had twenty-three of the latter in Group One, with twice as many Mediums and a swarm of smaller craft.

Group Two, composed of the supply ships and a small escort, was already formed and diverging away. That was a vital part of his plan. From a distance they'd look to telescope or radar like a full combat fleet.

He was almost ready to swerve toward the third planet and its moon, but first he had a speech to make. It was time to squash all the rumors and doubts with a dramatic fighting announcement.

He checked his appearance, stepped before the scanner, and nodded to Communications to turn it on. "All hands," he said, then waited for attention.

The small monitor screens showed a motley sampling of intent faces. He permitted himself a tight smile. "You know I have orders to surrender the Fleet." He paused for effect. "Those are the orders of the Council of Four, and to disobey the Council would be unthinkable.

"Yet it is also unthinkable that a single ship of the Fleet should surrender under any circumstances, at any time; therefore I am faced with a dilemma in which tradition must be broken.

"The Council of Four has lost courage, and so, perhaps, have many of the people of Sennech. We have ways of knowing that the people of Coar, far more than our own, clamor at their government for any sort of peace.

"Coar's fleets are smashed and the remnants have fled from space.

"Clearly, courage has all but vanished from the Solar System; yet there is one place where courage has not wavered. That place is in the Fleet of Sennech.

"At this moment we are the only strength left in the Solar System. We dominate the System!

"Would we have history record that the Fleet won its fight gloriously, then cravenly shrank back from the very brink of victory?

"We left Sennech fully armed, though our orders were directly opposite. I need not tell you that I have made the decision any man of the Fleet would make.

"This is our final campaign. Within a short time we shall orbit Coar herself and force her surrender. That is all."

There was a moment so quiet that the hum of the circuits grew loud, then the monitors shook with a mighty cheer.

Later, alone, Jezef congratulated him amusedly. "They are certainly with you a hundred percent now, if there was any doubt before. Yet there was one argument you didn't even hint at; the strongest argument of all."

"What was that?"

"Why, you're offering them a chance at life and freedom, where they might be going to imprisonment or execution."

That irritated Tulan. "I'm sure you're not so cynical about Fleet loyalty and tradition as you pretend," he said stiffly. "I wouldn't affront the men by using that kind of an argument."

Jezef grinned more widely. "Did it even occur to you to use it?"

Tulan flushed. "No," he admitted.

Teyr and her moon Luhin, both in quarter-phase from here, moved steadily apart in the viewers.

Group One's screen of light craft probed ahead, jamming enemy radar, and discovering occasional roboscouts which were promptly vaporized. Far behind, Group Two showed as a small luminescence. It would never be visible to Luhin as anything else, and then only when Tulan was ready.

They reversed drives, matched speeds neatly, and went into forced orbit around Luhin. On the flagship's first pass over the beleaguered oval of ground held by Sennech's forces—unsupported and unreinforced since the home planet's defection—Tulan sent a message squirting down. "Tulan commanding. Is Admiral Galu commanding there? Report situation."

The next time around a long reply came up to them. "This is Captain Rhu commanding. Galu killed. Twenty percent personnel losses. Six Lights destroyed; moderate damage to several Mediums and one Heavy. Ground lines under heavy pressure. Ships' crews involved in fighting at perimeter. Food critical, other supplies low. Several thousand wounded. Combat data follows." There was a good assessment of the struggle, with some enemy positions that were known.

The Fleet Force that had escorted nearly one hundred thousand ground troops included five Heavies and other craft in proportion, besides the transports and supply ships. Alone, they'd been pinned down by superior enemy ground forces and by a sizable fleet holed up all around the satellite. With Tulan's support they could be taken off.

Tulan composed orders. "Withdraw ships' crews from lines and prepare to lift. Get wounded aboard transports and prepare to evacuate troops. Set up fire control network to direct our ground support."

The tedious job of shrinking the perimeter, a short stretch at a time, began, harassed by the quickly adapting enemy.

During the first twenty hours the hostile fire was all from ground projectors, the enemy ships not risking detection by joining in. By that time one section of the front had pulled back to where several ships, sheltered in a crater, would have to lift.

Lines of men and equipment converged on the ships and jammed aboard. The actual lift was preceded by a diversion a few miles away, which succeeded in pulling considerable enemy fire. The ships got off in unison, slanting back across friendly territory and drawing only light missiles which the defenses handled easily.

Then, suddenly, a salvo of heavy stuff came crashing in, too unexpected and too well planned to stop. One of the lifting ships, a transport, vanished in a great flash.

Tulan yelled into his communicator. "Plot! Where did that come from?"

"I'm sorting, sir. Here! A roboscout got a straight five-second plot before they downed it!"

"Intelligence!" Tulan snapped. "Get the co-ordinates and bring me photos!"

There were already pictures of the area where the salvo must have originated, and one of them showed a cave-like opening in a crater wall. "That's it!" Tulan jabbed a pencil at it. "You could hide a dozen ships in there. Let's get a strike organized!"

The strike group included four Heavies besides the flagship, with twelve Mediums and twenty Lights. They slanted down in a jerky evasive course while pictures flashed on screens to be compared with the actual terrain.

Ground fire, chemically propelled missiles, erupted ahead of them and the small craft went to work intercepting it. They were down to a hundred miles, then fifty, streaking along the jagged surface so close they seemed to scrape it. This was point-blank range; as the computers raced with the chaos of fire and counter-fire, human senses could only register a few impressions—the bruising jerks, the shudder of concussions, white streaks of rocket-trails, gushers of dirt from the surface, winking flashes of mid-air interception.

Then the Heavies were on target. The flagship jumped as the massive salvo leaped away—not chemical missiles, but huge space torpedoes propelled by Pulsor units like the ships' drives, directing their own flocks of smaller defensive missiles by an intricate network of controls. The small stuff, augmented by fire from the lighter ships, formed momentarily a visible tube down which the big stuff streaked untouched.

The whole crater seemed to burst upward, reaching out angry fingers of shattered rock as they ripped by, rocking and bucking with the blasts. Tulan's viewer swivelled aft to hold the scene. Secondary blasts went off like strings of giant firecrackers. Great black-and-orange fungi-like clouds swirled upward, dissipating fast in the thin atmosphere. Then Tulan spotted what he was looking for: three small ships flashing over the area, to get damage-assessment pictures. There was still a lot of ground-fire from farther out, and it caught one of the three, which wobbled crazily then disappeared in a flash which blanked out the viewscreen.

"Intelligence!" Tulan shouted. "Casualties?"

Intelligence was listening to his earphones and punching buttons. "Two Lights lost, sir. Slight damage to seven more and to one Medium."

"All right. Get a telecopy of those pictures as soon as you can; we certainly hit something. Maybe a Heavy or two." He relaxed, aching, and reflected that he was getting a little mature for actual combat.

The pull-back went on, drawing only the local ground-fire now that the enemy had been taught his lesson. Groups of ships lifted almost constantly. The final position was an oval forty by sixty miles, held almost entirely from the sky. The last evacuees straggled in like weary ants, and when the radio reported no more of them the last fifty ships lifted together and ran the gauntlet with slight losses.

Tulan pulled the Force away for rest and repair. Group Two was idling at extreme radar range, making a convincing blip, and he designed some false messages to be beamed toward it with the expectation of interception. The impression he wanted to give was that Group Two was the Force that had been bombarding Coar, coming in now to join him. Actually, the latter fleet was farther away, hidden in the sun and, he hoped, unsuspected.

Things were going according to plan except for one puzzling item: there was no message from Sennech's small garrison on Teyr. All he could get from the planet was a steady radar scan, which might mean that Sennech's colony had been conquered by Coar's.

He'd been hoping to get certain supplies from Teyr, and now he took a strong detachment in close to the planet to find out what was wrong. The threat finally raised an answer. "This is the Chief of Council. What is it that you want?"

"Chief of Council? What are you talking about? I want the Garrison Commander."

"I suppose you're Admiral Tulan. There's been a change here, Tulan; Teyr is now an independent planet. Your garrison, with Coar's, comprise our defense forces."

Tulan stared at the planet's image. "You're at war with Coar!"

"Not any more, we aren't." There was a chuckle. "Don't sound so shocked, Admiral; we understand you're in mutiny yourself."

Tulan slapped the microphone onto its hangar. He sat, angry and bewildered, until he remembered something, then buzzed Communications. "Get me that connection again. Hello? Listen. I have sixty thousand troops in transports, with almost no food. I intend to land them."

"They're welcome as noncombatants, Admiral. They'll have to land disarmed, in areas we designate, and live off the country. We've already got more refugees than we can handle."

"Refugees from where?"

"Haven't you been in contact with Sennech at all?"

"No."

"Oh." There was a thoughtful pause. "Then you don't know. There's bad radiation in the atmosphere and we're hauling as many away as we can. We can use your ships if you're finished playing soldier."

Tulan broke the connection again and turned, fuming, to Jezef. "We'll blast our way in and take over!"

Jezef raised his eyebrows. "What good would that do?" he asked.

"Why; they—for one thing, we've got to think of those troops! We can't land them unarmed and let them be slaughtered by the savages!"

Jezef grinned. "I doubt if they'll refuse to let them have enough small arms to defend themselves. They can't stay where they are."

"But they're military men, and loyal!"

"Are they? The war's over for them, anyway. Why not let them vote on it?"

Tulan jumped up and strode around the command room, while Jezef and the staff watched him silently. Gradually, the logic of it forced itself upon him. "All right," he said wearily, "We'll let them vote."

A few hours later he studied the results gloomily. "Well, after all, they're not Fleet. They don't have the tradition."

Jezef smiled, then lingered, embarrassed.

"Well?" Tulan asked.

"Sir," (that hadn't come out, in private, for years) "I'd like to be relieved."

It was a blow, but Tulan found he wasn't really surprised. He stared at his brother-in-law, feeling as if he faced an amputation. "You think I'm wrong about this whole thing, don't you?"

"I'm not going to judge that, but Sennech's in trouble far worse than any question of politics, including your own family."

"But if we turn back now Coar will recover! It's only going to take us a few more hours!"

"How long does it take people to die?"

Tulan looked at the deck for a while. "All right. I'll detach every ship I can spare, and put you in charge. You'll have the transports too, as soon as they're unloaded." He stared after Jezef, wanting to call out to him to be sure to send word about Anatu and the boys, but somehow feeling he didn't have the right.

He took the fighting ships away from Teyr, to where Group Two could join up without being unmasked, then started sunward as if he were crossing to intercept Coar. A few miles in, where they'd be hidden in the sun, he left a few scouts.

As he saw it, the enemy commander on the satellite, noting the armada's course and finding himself apparently clear, would have no choice but to lift his ships and start around the sun by some other path to help his planet.

That other path to Coar could be intercepted, and as soon as Tulan was lost near the sun he went into heavy drive to change direction. He drifted across the sun, waiting for word from his scouts. At about the time he'd expected, they reported ships leaving the satellite.

He looked across the room toward Plot. "Plot! Feed that data to Communications as it comes in, will you?" And to Communications: "Can we beam Group Three from here?"

"Not quite, sir; but I can relay through the scouts."

"All right; but make sure it's not intercepted. I want Group Three under maximum acceleration for Luhin, and I want them to get running reports on the enemy."

"Right, sir."

Tulan was in the position he wanted, not needing to use his own radar, but able to pick up that of Coar's fleet at extreme range, too far to give them a bounce. He'd know their course, speed, and acceleration fairly well, without even being suspected himself.

He held that position until the enemy was close enough to get a bounce, then went into drive on an intercepting course.

One of the basic tenets of space maneuver was this: if two fleets were drawing together, with radar contact, neither (barring interference from factors such as the sun or planets) could escape the other; for if one applied acceleration in any direction the other could simply match it (human endurance being the limitation) and maintain the original relative closing speed.

When the enemy commander discovered Tulan's armada loafing ahead of him, he'd been accelerating for about ten hours and had a velocity of a million miles per hour, while Tulan was going the same direction but at half the speed. The quarry began decelerating immediately, knowing it could get back to Luhin with time enough to land.

Tulan didn't quite match the deceleration, preferring to waste a few hours and lessen the strain on his crews. He let the gap close slowly.

He could tell almost the precise instant when the other jaw of his trap was discovered, for Plot, Communications, and Intelligence all jerked up their heads and looked at him. He grinned at them. What they'd picked up would be an enemy beam from Luhin, recklessly sweeping space to find the Coar fleet and warn it of the onrushing Group Three.

The enemy commander reacted fast. It was obvious he'd never beat Group Three to Luhin, and he made no futile attempts at dodging, but reversed drives and accelerated toward the nearest enemy, which was Tulan. Tulan was not surprised at that either, for though Coar's fleets had bungled the war miserably, when cornered they'd always fought and died like men.

He matched their acceleration to hold down the relative speeds. The swift passing clash would be brief at best. He formed his forces into an arrangement he'd schemed up long ago but never used: a flat disc of lighter ships out in front, masking a doughnut-shaped mass behind. He maneuvered laterally to keep the doughnut centered on the line of approach.

Roboscouts appeared and blossomed briefly as they died. The fuzzy patch of light on the screens swelled, then began to resolve into individual points. The first missiles arrived. Intricate patterns of incandescence formed and vanished as fire-control systems locked wits.

A sudden, brilliantly planned salvo came streaking in, saturating the defenses along its path. Ships in Tulan's secondary formation swerved frantically, but one darting, corkscrewing missile homed on a Heavy, and for an instant there were two suns.

Tulan, missing Jezef's smooth help, was caught up in the daze and strain of battle now. He punched buttons and shouted orders as he played the fleet to match the enemy's subtle swerving. Another heavy salvo came in, but the computers had its sources pinpointed now, and it was contained. These first few seconds favored the enemy, who was only fighting the light shield in front of Tulan's formation.

Now the swelling mass of blips streaked apart in the viewers and space lit up with the fire and interception. Two ships met head on; at such velocities it was like a nuclear blast.

Then Coar's ships crashed through the shield and into the center of the doughnut. Ringed, outgunned, outpredicted, they hit such a concentration of missiles that it might as well have been a solid wall. Ships disintegrated as if on a common fuse; the ones that didn't take direct hits needed none, in that debris-filled stretch of hell.

Tulan's flagship rocked in the wave of expanding hot gasses. There was a jolt as some piece of junk hit her; if she hadn't already been under crushing acceleration away from the inferno she'd have been holed.

From a safer distance the path of destruction was a bright slash across space, growing into the distance with its momentum. It was annihilation, too awful for triumph; there was only horror in it. Tulan knew that with this overwhelming tactic he'd written a new text-book for action against an inferior fleet. He hoped it would never be printed. Sweating and weak, he slumped in his straps and was ill.

While brief repairs and re-arming were under way, he sent scouts spiraling out to pick up any radio beams from Sennech or Teyr. There were none. The telescopes showed Sennech's albedo down to a fraction of normal; that, he supposed, would indicate smoke in the atmosphere. He wavered, wondering whether he should detach more ships to send out there. Reason and training told him to stick to the key objective, which was Coar's surrender. He waited only for Group Three to achieve a converging course, then started around the sun again.

They didn't encounter even a roboscout. He crossed the sun, curved into Coar's orbit, matched speeds, and coasted along a million miles ahead of the planet, sending light sorties in to feel out any ambushes. Still there was no sign of fight, so he went in closer where the enemy could get a good look at his strength. Finally he took a small group in boldly over the fourth planet's Capitol and sent a challenge.

The answer was odd. "This is Acting President Kliu. What are your intentions?"

Tulan realized he was holding his breath. He let it out and looked around the silent command room, meeting the intent eyes of his staff. He had an unreal feeling; this couldn't be the climax, the consummation—this simple exchange over the radio. He lifted the microphone slowly. "This is Admiral Tulan, commanding the Fleets of Sennech. I demand your immediate and unconditional surrender."

There was something in the reply that might have been dry amusement: "Oh; by all means; but I hope you're not going to insist upon an elaborate ceremony. Right now we don't give a damn about the war; we're worried about the race."

There was more silence, and Tulan turned, uncertainly, looking at the bare spot where Jezef ought to be standing. He buzzed for Communications. "Connect me with Captain Rhu. Rhu; I'm advancing you in rank and leaving you in charge here. I'm going down to accept the surrender and find out what this man's talking about."

Kliu was gaunt and middle-aged, wearing, to Tulan's surprise, the gray of Coar's First Level of Science. He was neither abject nor hostile, agreeing impatiently to turn over the secret of Coar's weapon and to assist with a token occupation of the planet. Again Tulan had the unreal, let-down feeling, and judging by Kliu's amused expression, it showed.

Tulan sent couriers to get things started, then turned back to the scientist. "So you have had a change of government. What did you mean, about the race?"

Kliu watched him for a moment. "How much do you know about the weapon?"

"Very little. That it projects matter through hyperspace and materializes it where you want it."

"Not exactly; the materialization is spontaneous. Mass somehow distorts hyperspace, and when the projected matter has penetrated a certain distance into such distortion, it pops back into normal space. The penetration depends mainly upon a sort of internal energy in the missile; you might think of it more as a voltage than as velocity. You've made it very hard for us to get reports, but I understand we successfully placed stuff in Sennech's crust."

"Yes; causing volcanoes. Our scientists speculated that any kind of matter would do it."

"That's right. Actually, we were projecting weighed chunks of rock. When one bit of matter, even a single atom, finds itself materializing where another already is, unnatural elements may be formed, most of them unstable. That's what blew holes in your crust and let the magma out."

Tulan considered the military implications of the weapon for a few moments, then pulled his mind back. "I see; but what about the radiation? It wasn't more than a trace when I left."

Kliu looked away for a while before answering. "When we learned you'd defied your government, our own military got out of hand. They had a couple of days before the sun cut us off completely, and they began throwing stuff as soon as it could be dug and hauled to the projectors. They used high energies to get it past the sun. As we realize now, a lot of it hit the planet deeper than at first, below the crust. Under such pressure a different set of fissionables was formed. Some of them burst out and poisoned the atmosphere, but most of them are still there." He leaned forward and eyed Tulan hard. "We've got to get an expedition out there to study things. Will you help?"

There was another of the palpable silences, and when he spoke Tulan's voice sounded unnatural. "I—yes; we'll help. Whatever you want. Is . . . Sennech finished?"

Kliu smiled tightly. "Sennech, for sure; and she may take the rest of us with her. Nobody conceived what this might come to. A lot of those deep materializations produced pockets of dense fissionables, and they're converging toward the center under their own weight. When they get to a certain point, we'll have a fine monument to Man's ingenuity. A planet-size nova." He stood up. "I'll start organizing."

Tulan existed someway through the preparations, and when they were in space again the solid familiarity of his ship helped. His staff was carrying on wonderfully; shielding him, he suspected, from considerable hostility. Discipline held up.

A technology that had spanned five orbits and probed beyond was at bay, and the expedition was tremendous. Hardly an art or science was unrepresented. If need be, whole ships could be built in space.

A beam from Teyr as they passed told of refugees by the hundreds of thousands, dumped in the wilderness with a few ships still trickling in. Tulan would have traded everything he could command to hear a word of Jezef or the family, but Teyr wasn't concerned with individuals and he didn't ask.

Sennech was dull gray in the telescopes, showing, as they neared, flecks of fire. They went in fast, using her gravity to help them curve into a forced orbit as they strained to decelerate. Thermocouples gave readings close to the boiling point of water; that, probably, was the temperature of the lower air.

Roboscouts went down first, then, as conditions were ascertained, manned ships. Tulan took the flagship down once. Her coolers labored and her searchlights were swallowed in murk within a few feet. Sounds carried through the hull; the howl of great winds and the thumps of explosions. Once a geyser of glowing lava spattered the ship.

Within hours the picture began to form. The surface was a boiling sea broken only by transient mountain peaks which tumbled down in quakes or were washed away by the incessant hot rain. It would have been hard to find a single trace of the civilization that had flourished scant hours before.

The slower job was learning, by countless readings and painful deduction, what was going on inside the planet. Tulan occupied himself with organizational tasks and clung to what dignity he could. After an eternity Kliu had time for him.

"She'll blow, all right," the scientist said, sinking tiredly into a seat. "Within half a year. Her year."

"Twenty thousand hours," Tulan said automatically. "How about the other planets?"

"Coar has one chance in a hundred, Teyr possibly one in ten."

Tulan had to keep talking. "The outer satellites. We can do a lot in that time."

Kliu shrugged. "A few thousand people, and who knows what will happen to them afterward? It's going to be a long time before the System's inhabitable again, if ever."

"Ships . . . people can live a long time in ships."

"Not that long."

"There must be something! The power we've got, and this hyperspace thing."

Kliu shook his head. "I can guess what you're thinking; we've been all over it. There's no way to get to the stars, and no way to move a planet out of its orbit. Don't think we haven't been pounding our skulls, but the figures are hopeless."

Tulan stared at the ulcerous image on the screen, built up by infra-red probing through the opaque atmosphere. "She looks ready to fall apart right now. How much of her could you blast off?"

Kliu smiled wearily and without humor. "We've worked that idea to the bone, too. If you could build a big enough projector, and mount it on an infinitely solid base, you could push something deep enough and accurately enough to throw off stuff at escape velocity, but it's a matter of energy and we can't handle one percent of what we'd need. Even if you could generate it fast enough, your conduits would melt under the current." He got up and walked a few steps, then sat down again. "Ironic, isn't it? All we can do is destroy ourselves."

Tulan's mind couldn't accept it; he was used to thinking that any amount of energy could be handled some way.

"There must be something," he repeated, feeling foolish as he said it.

He went over the figures he knew so well; the acceleration and the total energy necessary to drive a ship to the nearest stars. Even a ship's Pulsors, pouring energy out steadily, were pitiful compared to that job. Schoolboys knew the figures; mankind had dreamed for generations . . .

He sat up abruptly. "This hyperspace; didn't you tell me there were such things as velocity and momentum in it?"

Kliu's eyes focussed. "Yes; why?"

"And that a projector could be built to put an entire ship into hyperspace?"

Kliu stared at him for a second. "Kinetic energy! Built up gradually!" He jumped to his feet. "Come on! Let's get to the computers!"

Several hundred hours later Tulan lay watching the pinpoint on his viewscreen that represented Sennech. He'd been building up speed for a long time; he ached from the steady double-gravity. The ship, vastly beefed up, was moving at a good fraction of the speed of light. It wouldn't be much longer.

The cargo of carefully chosen matter, shifting into hyperspace at the right instant, would be taken deep into Sennech by the momentum he'd accumulated in normal space. If the calculations were right, the resulting blast would knock a chunk completely out of the planet. Each of the thousands of other ships tied to him by robot controls would take its own bite at the right time and place. Providing the plan worked.

The Solar System would have a few hot moments, and would be full of junk for a long time, but the threatening fissionables inside Sennech would be hurled far apart, to dribble away their potence gradually. Kliu admitted no one could calculate for sure even how much, if any, of Sennech would remain as a planet, but Teyr, at least, with her thick atmosphere, should withstand the rain of debris.

He wondered about his family, and Jezef. Kliu had tried to get word, but the tragically few refugees were scattered.

He smiled, recalling how severely he'd had to order his staff to abandon him. He was proud to remember that much of the fleet would have come along, if he'd let them; but live men were going to be at more of a premium on Teyr than heroic atoms drifting in space. Machines could handle this assault. He himself had not had to touch a single control.

The indicators began to flash, and, sweating with the effort, he hauled himself erect to attention. It was good to be winding up here in his own command room, where he'd lived his moments of triumph. Still, as the red light winked on, he couldn't help thinking how very quiet and lonely it was without Jezef and the staff.

FOR EVERY ACTION . . .

Date: 5 June 1987.
To: Commandant, USSR Hq., Mars. (Personal).
From: Commandant, USSR Pluto expedition.
Code: TS Perishka C.
Subject: Mad American Spaceman.

Wofka: I am taking the precaution of sending this to you personally, because of the obvious possible booby-traps. Perhaps discreet espionage on Mars or Earth will reveal what sort of shell-game the Americans are up to now, before we involve ourselves in some propaganda debacle.

Twelve hours ago radar picked up a small object in space, moving in an orbit that would intercept us fairly closely but at a slightly lower speed. Knowing that an American ship was already near Pluto, and that they surely knew *we* were approaching, I at once placed my ship in a state of maximum defense. However, closer approach revealed the object to be not a mine or torpedo, but a space suit with a number of objects attached to it. Of course the suit or other objects *could* have contained explosives, so I maintained caution.

When we were quite close we picked up a weak radio transmission in English that appeared to be beamed not at us but in the opposite direction. If it was in code we have been unable to break it. Our interpreter, whom possibly we had better investigate, again, could tell us only that the voice, a male one, was reciting some sort of nursery rhyme called Mother Goose. The recitation was monotonous and repetitive.

Shortly thereafter telescopic examination revealed the following:

1—space suit, evidently occupied.

2—tanks of approximately 300 litre capacity, fixed to the suit by short rigid rods.

4—bundles, approximately half a meter cubed, lashed to the legs of the suit.

1—cylindrical container, approximately three metres long by zero point seven metres diameter, fixed between the legs of the suit in such a way that the occupant appeared to be riding as you would ride a horse.

1—large bow, with which the occupant of the suit fired or shot arrows in a direction normal to the orbit of Pluto (that is, away from us) at intervals of eight seconds.

The arrows came from the long cylinder he was riding.

Upon discovering our approach the occupant of the suit stopped shooting arrows and said in English, "If you can still hear me, fellows, I've found Ivan." (His knowing my first name is significant!). He repeated the transmission several times, then waited with apparent calm for us to pick him up.

Upon examination of his equipment, we found no explosives. The small bundles contained batteries to keep the suit operating. One of the 300-litre tanks was about half full of gruel; the other about half full of body wastes. The gruel was made accessible to the spaceman by a plastic tube which had been sealed through his helmet at the front, so he could draw upon it merely by putting his mouth on the tube and sucking. The removal of body waste was accomplished by a similar but more permanent arrangement which was surprisingly effective, though an obvious indignity and by his testimony uncomfortable. The suit's maintenance machinery was in good working order, and the air inside was breathable though not as sweet as one might prefer. The long cylindrical tank was about one-third full of arrows, the rest having been expended. The arrows were cut from steel (evidently the hull plates of a ship) by means of a hack saw or some similar implement. The bow was of springy metal and the string of braided fine wire. Both were alloys that held their flexibility in the cold of space.

Quite obviously the shooting of arrows had provided reaction to slow the spaceman's orbit to a speed where we would overtake him. Nevertheless the calculation and execution of such a maneuver would be difficult to the point of believability. The man's story is that he was reciting 'The House That Jack Built' as a sort of mnemonic to maintain the proper rate of fire, and that the arrows averaged out to a chosen weight and the bow delivered consistent reaction when drawn to a certain point. He sticks to this story through all interrogation, and says he was sent to ask us to rescue his comrades, who are (he says) floating in a small portion of their ship in an orbit dangerously close to Pluto. Of course I do not swallow his story. Nevertheless I do not see any harm in cautiously approaching a little closer to investigate. I am confident we can handle any trickery the Americans may have in mind.

The entirety of his statement is so ridiculous that I will not attempt to abstract it, but will attach it in full. I'm sure you will exercise caution equal to mine in sending this to you personally. Old comrades must stick together.

Signed, Ivan Dzbrown.

commanding.

Statement of mad American spaceman:

Hi. No, I don't speak Russian. I know a few words of Basque, though, from my mother's side, if that'll help any. Oh, you speak English! Jeez, you speak it real good. You say you were born in Massachusetts? Nice place. I was there a while when I took my Ph.D.

Well, here's the scoop. I guess you heard about us making up our minds to get to Pluto first. It only cost us four hundred billion bucks, ha, ha! You should have heard old ex-President Johnson yell. Well, anyway, we made it off Mars in real good shape, and we were latching onto Pluto good too, but then we noticed the jets weren't working right, and after a computer check and all we decided somebody better go outside and take a squint. I got picked because I've got the most experience in suits. That's why I'm here, too.

Well, right away when I got aft I could see that there was something stuck around the jets; it looked like cinders at first. When I got closer I saw that it was more like as if some grapes, the black kind, were clustered around the orifices. While I was bent down looking, something came along and gave me a hell of a whang on the butt. Right away I thought Jeez, a meteor; but it didn't penetrate the suit and I was all right. Then I began to see more of them coming and I hauled on my line and got away from the jets because that was where they were all headed. I talked to the skipper and he told me to stay out there and watch if I wasn't in any danger.

They were coming from all directions and collecting around the jets like a swarm of bees. But they were not coming as thick and pretty soon they stopped coming entirely. Then after a while some of them began to go away. They didn't all go, though, and enough of them were still around the jets to goof up the action. Once in a while a single one or two would break off and go away, and maybe a couple more would drift in and gather on.

I took one of the tools that we have on the suits, I guess probably you people have got the same kind of thing, and hacked away at them but they were on tight. The only ones I could get loose seemed to be the ones that were letting go anyway.

Well I got hold of one and let it go right away because I could feel it sort of squirm, even through the mitten, but it wasn't actually squirming as I found out when I let it go. It was shaped like maybe two-thirds of a marble, one about five-eighth of an inch in diameter. I guess maybe you people work in millimeters', and your kids don't get to play marbles, huh? Let's see ... two hundred and fifty-four times six hundred and twenty-five is ... carry the two ... where the hell would I put the decimal place ... say, like a dull black iron ball-bearing about fifteen point eight seven five millimeters in diameter, with one-third of it sawed off flat. A blue light came off of this flat side and it gave the thing quite a boost of acceleration and that was what I felt. I was worried at first that it was some kind of an ion drive that would burn a hole in my hand or the suit, but it didn't do anything like that. I watched a few more and I saw that they could turn themselves any way they wanted to by giving out a faint glow on one edge of the flat place, then when they wanted to light out and go they just turned it all on. We did some fooling around with them later and found out they could exert about—but there's no sense going into all that now. We've got the figures in the ship, or what's left of it: and hell, the least we can do after you rescue us is let you in on them. Scientific cooperation, ha, ha!

Well I took a chance because I was pretty excited and the next one that drifted in I grabbed it and held it so the blue light was away from my hand. I could feel the push but it wasn't strong enough to get away from me. That may be why they stay out there, where they don't have to deal with fast orbits and stronger gravity close to the sun. They were far enough from Pluto so it wouldn't pull them in.

When I talked to the skipper again he thought sure as hell I'd flipped and got me in right away, but I had the thing to show them. It turned out I was not so damned smart; because I had to go right back out and watch what happened when they gave the jets a little gentle goose. I wished I'd kept my big mouth shut for a little while.

I'll tell you, when those jets went on I thought I was going to get it. Those things came flying from all directions like hornets. You know how an orifice heats up, even with a short burst, and how fast it cools off afterward in space? Yeah, I guess you would. Well, every time we gave it even a little goose, those things came flying. I found out the way to do was to stay a few yards forward of the jets and stand still, and they'd go around me to get at the jets. As soon as the metal got cold, some of them would go away. But some stayed on. Just lazy, I guess.

Well, we were pretty excited and we tried to radio Mars; Earth's behind the sun right now you know; but the transmission didn't seem to get through. I suppose you can figure

out who had to suit up and go outside finally to see what was
wrong with the antenna, after the skipper and the Communications Officer had a hell of a beef. And you know what?
Every time we tried to transmit with any power at all those
damn sawed-off ball-bearings came gathering around the
antenna, just like flies around manure. You people've got
that, I'm sure; I read somewhere how you were pretty big in
ranching and all. It began to look to me like they could soak
up any kind of radiant energy, from radio on down to infra-
red; and that's the way it turned out. And we found out they
could resist heat, too. We couldn't even faze them until we
got them damn near hot, and that killed them. The trouble
was, even though some of them got themselves incinerated
in the jets, by that time they were welded on. The orifices
got so clogged we didn't dare fire them anymore.

Of course we tried a lot of things like sawing the jets clear,
but it wasn't any use. Every time we turned on even a little
squirt we got those damned things back again.

Well then naturally we didn't want to go barging in on
Pluto out of control, so we used the retros and spinners to
slow ourselves down into a stable orbit. I suppose you've
got what's left of the ship on your radar by now. We
couldn't go anywhere and we couldn't transmit, but we
could hear incoming messages all right, and we heard how
you people were headed out this way and we figured if we
could warn you soon enough, you could stay down here and
pick us up if we could get down far enough. There don't
seem to be any of those things this far in. The crew can
make it down here all right if you've got room for us. I see
you've got a good big ship here.

Well there wasn't any way we could contact you by radio so
we talked over how one of us could get down here, and it
figured out that we didn't have enough air tanks and so on to
jet a man in. That wouldn't have attracted any bugs. We call
them bugs, but I suppose some damn scientist will look at
one through a magnifying glass and put some silly name on
it.

There was plenty of time, we knew you wouldn't be here for a while yet, so we had a chance to think things over and make a few haywire experiments, and that rig you saw me in was what came out of it. I practiced guiding myself around for about three weeks. When I want to go in a straight line I just shoot arrows the opposite way. You know, for every action there's a ... And when I went to put on a little spin I just hold one of the arrows out away from me and give it a flip away in the right direction. I'm pretty good at it now. In fact, I figure I can be the world's champion. Maybe in the next Olympic games ...

You saw all the rest of the stuff.

So that's the scoop, and I don't mind saying I'm damned glad to see you, even if you are a bunch of—even if I don't speak your language. From here you can transmit to what's left of our ship, and the boy'll start coming. They had enough suits rigged for everybody, and by now they ought to have the whole rear end of her sawed up into arrows.

(Statement ends.)

Date: 6 June, 1987
To: Security Officer, USSR Hq., Mars. (Personal.)
From: Commandant, USSR Hq., Mars.
Code: STS Babushka Y.
Subject: Commandant, USS Pluto expedition.

Nikolai: Please check subject once again for possible instability or disloyalty. Also find whether he has sent any coded messages to anyone other than me. Also check the security of Code TS Perishka C.

I hope your family is well.
Signed, Vladimir Czmith,
commanding.

Date: 10 August, 1987.
To: Ambassador to USA.
From: Kremlin.

Code: None.
Subject: Capitalist propaganda.

Protest vigorously at once ridiculous and insulting story in American newspapers of Soviet spacemen floating in space singing Volga Boat Song and throwing spears.

Signed, J.

TREES LIKE TORCHES

I

MURNO, ON HIS BELLY under some bushes on the eastern slope of a mountain, accepted the telescope from the man beside him, laid it across his left wrist to steady it, and focused on the small clump of trees far out on the flat. Early afternoon shadows made it hard to see pair of men sitting there, but he finally handed the scope back said, "Two's all I make out. No sign of the children."

Pete nodded. He was a scout for the Sierra Norms with whom Murno and his family had found sanctuary this past year. "Just rear lookouts. The main band'll be several hours ahead. We gave them a lesson the last time they tried this."

Murno, whose ten-year-old daughter was one of the kidnapped youngsters, felt annoyed at Pete's casualness. He said nothing and studied the flat. The country just east of the Sierras was certainly different from the western slopes— much drier; its short grass brown now, brush or scattered oaks only along the few dry washes. There was one creek with a little water in it, a few miles south. In the low spots of the flat without drainage, alkali stopped all growth except a certain sparse grass.

He said to Pete, "You call it two nights' trek across the flat. What's beyond?"

"Hills, high enough to catch a little rain, fairly well wooded. Beyond those, there's supposed to be ten thousand square miles of basin that water draws into from all sides, covered with what's called the Black Grove. The renegades we caught last year said that was where they intended to trade the children."

"To whom?" Murno asked, "And for what?"

Pete shrugged. "The ones we caught didn't know."

Murno suppressed irritation. "Who are these renegades, anyway? Are they Norms? Where do they come from?"

"Norms; what else?" Pete shifted position. "They hole up somewhere south of the Black Grove. There must be quite a colony of them. They raid free farmers and anyone else they can." He scowled. "I'm not keen on taking the field with Bluies, even if they *are* supposed to be our allies now."

Murno didn't answer at once. From habit, his eyes scanned the sky for Gaddyl aircars, or the aliens' mutated hunting-birds, called gee hawks, even though he wore strapped to his left forearm an instrument of the Sierra Norms that would locate radio sources too far away to be seen. Finally he said, "When you get into strange country you may appreciate the Bluies and their talents."

The sun was long lost behind the Sierra summit when the rest of the expedition arrived.

The first inkling Murno had was when he began to imagine that a feline—lighter in color and more compact than a tiger, but bigger and bunchier than a puma—was about to pounce on him from behind. He thrust the thought away; he'd chosen this cover carefully. Then he had the feeling that the bramble thicket behind him was much thinner than he'd thought, and the cat had found a way through it. The feeling was so strong that he turned his head to reassure himself. The bramble was as thick as it was supposed to be.

He grunted in annoyance and wriggled clear—to where he could see the five young-looking blue men, grinning, their hands still poised in the intricate gestures that could make false thoughts in a man's head or put him to sleep. They were nude except for G-strings, moccasins, and leather belts from which hung darts and throwers and a few small bags. Their skins were hairless and quite smooth, matching the deceptive smoothness of their muscles. They were running four cats, which—tails lashing, not happy at being re-strained—sat on their haunches a few feet away.

Pete came out from under the bush, saw the cats, cried out in shock and raised his airgun.

Murno knocked it aside. "These are friends." To the blue men he said, "It's good to see my hunting companions again." They nodded, but said nothing. He noted, with a grin, that their scalps were clean-shaven again. The loss of hair-patches and the vow of silence no doubt meant they'd been caught playing pranks again. He said, with a little malice, "This is Pete. He claims that every one of his ancestors was a Norm, and that none of them were ever conquered by the Gaddyl."

Pete reddened and mumbled, "What's wrong with them? Can't they talk?"

"Not for a while," Murno told him. We went over to make friends with the cats. Two of them already knew him, but he wanted to be sure all four would recognize him by smell if he happened upon them in the dark.

A more mature-looking blue man, with a full though close-cropped head of hair, came down the slope. "Murno! It's been almost a year!" He frowned at the five younger ones. "Have my nephews been pestering you again?"

"No, no," Murno said. "Kal-Let, this is Pete." He waited for the two to exchange nods, then asked, "How is the Old One?"

"He is well," the blue man said. "He sends you greetings and bad news. Many of your former neighbors have been caught. The fief Guddun has killed some and re-enslaved others. Also, he has alerted the other fiefdoms that there are hostile Norms in the mountains, and he appeals to the Planetary Prime for more weapons and aircars."

Munro listened soberly. The only reason Earth had been allowed to return to wilderness and partial freedom was that, for the Gaddyl, it was an out-of-the-way planet, only occupied by fifty or sixty isolated Gaddyl fiefdoms, and not exploited much. Guddun, however, who had just inherited a fiefdom, had a grudge against free humans. Murno asked, "What of your own people?"

Kal-Let told him, "Some of us have been killed. And we have killed Gaddyl."

The other Norms arrived in a few minutes. There were twenty of them, men of the summit, like Pete. All were carrying airguns, all wearing the camouflage coveralls of woven fabric, green splotched with brown and gray, heavy ankle-length shoes, brimmed hats covered with netting into which foliage or straw could be stuck. The young Blues took time from soothing the cats to grin at the clothing. Murno, whose lighter leather garments were more practical, made a mental wager that the Norms would be shedding before they'd gone far.

It was dark enough now to start. Murno of course could not match the Blues as a stalker, but he was the only leader acceptable to both groups. He pointed out a dry wash he'd chosen earlier. "We'll go down that until we get a track."

The cats, playful with the coming of dusk, sported about investigating this and that, but there was usually at least one out ahead. Pete's men traveled single file, their shoes making more noise than Murno liked, so that he moved on ahead with two of the younger Blues. Kal-Let and the others were at the rear, in case something hunted the hunters.

Nothing much happened in the first two hours. Once the cats flushed something bigger than themselves—a lion, maybe, or some Gaddyl-mutated beast—and there was a contest of snarls, but the thing fled. Another time, the instruments picked up an aircar going over. But it was high, and if it had geehawks they weren't flying.

Not long after that the cats began sniffing around the clump of trees where the renegade rear-scouts had been. Kal-Let came up, listened to the cats' scratching about, and said, "They must have left before sundown. Is it your wish to catch them?"

"Not yet," Murno told him. "That would warn the main group. If we can just get past them and gain as much time as possible on the others."

Pete was nervous out here in open country. He put in, "The kids won't be able to travel very fast."

Murno didn't argue that point, though he thought if the youngsters had nothing to carry they could keep up with adult Norms. He asked Pete, "Is there anything they'd have to detour around?"

"Not that we know of."

Kal-Let said, "In that case, they are going just a little south of east. If you wish, Murno, I can scout ahead with the cats and locate the two."

"No, I think not. Let's angle off southward, so tomorrow we can use the telescope with the sun at our backs."

II

With the first light of morning they found the best cover they could—a group of five fair-sized oaks. After scouting it they chose lookout posts in the trees. Murno, Kal and Pete went aloft while the others made themselves as inconspicuous as possible on the ground. The sun began its climb. The Sierra men began shedding garments.

Murno eased his weight around carefully, so as not to shake the foliage, and chewed dry cooked venison highly seasoned with salt and onion. It was going to be a long day.

In such open country they could only travel at night—not only because the renegades might spot them, but because geehawks probably would. There were a few of the big birds aloft already, to the north, soaring high up in wide circles that gradually moved this way. There was a fiefdom somewhere north a hundred miles or so, but these birds wouldn't range that far; they must belong to some hunting party. Murno was in the position of hoping the renegades would be careful.

It was mid-morning before he saw the two renegade rear scouts again. He wouldn't have seen them at all if one hadn't got up to stretch just when Murno was looking. They were under a pair of trees more than a mile away. Silently, he

pointed, and Pete squirmed into position to use the telescope. "Same two."

Kal, in an adjacent tree, said, "There are others north and
east of those, I think."

"Where?" Pete demanded.

"I do not know," the blue man said, "but those two look in
that direction, and once they signaled."

Pete grunted. Murno waited nervously, but Kal didn't take
offense.

After that, Murno spent most of the day watching the two
renegades or scanning the sky for hawks. The blue men appeared to nap much of the time. The cats were off somewhere, probably in a dry wash where they'd gone at sunup.
They'd have sense enough to stay out of sight and not wander beyond call. It was the Sierra men who were miserable.
Stripped to their underwear, they tried sleeping, talking,
gambling, eating, working at their guns, without easing their
boredom. Around midday one of them demanded of Pete,
"Damn it, why can't we go off south somewhere and hunt
fresh meat? No one's going to see us."

"What would you hunt?" Pete asked him. "We haven't
seen anything bigger than a rabbit all day."

One of the young Blues said, "There is a herd of bovines
only a few miles away, beyond that slight rise. Have you not
smelled them?"

Pete scowled. "All I smell is—"

Murno interrupted hastily, "Keep your voice down!
There's also an aircar somewhere south, maybe after those
same bovines." He hadn't seen the car, but he'd watched the
hawks move south, then converge and drop from sight.

An hour later his guess was confirmed. There were rifle
shots—the chemical-explosive kind the Gaddyl used for
sport—from beyond the rise. He told the men, "Get in close
to the treetrunks, and bring your clothes with you." He
peered southward. This side of the rise, he saw one of the
cats creep up out of the dry wash and lie on its belly, head
on the ground, listening. Kal saw it also, and said something
to the young Blues. From the ground they couldn't see the

animal, but one of them sang a soft high note and the cat's ears twitched. A moment later it retreated to the dry wash.

Murno never did see the aircar; maybe it was staying within a few feet of the ground. But late in the day the hawks went north, in a group and not very high, which meant they'd been released from hunting and were going somewhere to be fed. The aircar might or might not have moved off in another direction. Sometimes, if there were a lake or river, the nearly-amphibious Gaddyl sportsmen stayed out overnight.

He turned his attention back to the renegade scouts. Before the sun dropped behind the mountains, they left their post and trotted eastward. No doubt they'd speculated as he had about the Gaddyl party, and were risking an early start rather than staying here. He resisted the urge to follow.

That night he pushed his own party hard, only stopping twice to rest briefly, swig from waterbags and chew dried meat.

It was still dark when they reached the wooded hills.

These were pines, of a sort that had branched trunks and didn't grow very tall; good cover unless something happened to pass directly overhead. One of Pete's men immediately demanded, "What about fresh meat?"

Murno hesitated. After all, these Sierra men had been dodging the Gaddyl for generations. "All right. A couple of you can hunt. But don't go more than a mile from camp."

He himself took two of the younger Blues and headed up a hill to the north. From the top, he could see back over the way they'd come during the night. There was a small dust cloud on the horizon—the bovine herd, possibly, running from Gaddyl huntsmen, or a band of wild horses. Closer, a few solitary animals were grazing. His instrument showed no aircars or radio-carrying geehawks within range. A few miles south there was a stream, as he'd suspected, following west from these hills.

He inclined his head to the blue men and started over the crest of the hill. Suddenly he stopped.

The valley to the east was deeper and greener than he'd expected. He asked quietly. "Is there water?"

Now, under necessity, the young mutants could break silence. One—Murno thought it was the one called Liss—said, "There is water. I hear no ripples, except from the north, I think it is a lake."

Murno considered. There might be game, and the Gaddyl might come here. He could retreat swiftly, or try to have a look first.

He wet a forefinger in his mouth and held it aloft. What breeze there was wouldn't carry their scent down the slope. He unslung his bow and held it, with two arrows, in his left hand, then stepped warily down the slope.

There was a lake; narrow, fed by a stream from the north. The outlet was undoubtedly the stream that turned west onto the flat, so the lake was quite long. He stood still for a minute, listening for sounds that the Blues, never having had much contact with the Gaddyl, might not recognize.

It was lucky he did; for though he heard nothing, he saw something that made his stomach knot.

Slipping among the trees on the opposite slope, silently, was a band of breloons—the Gaddyl's fierce, oversize, keen-scented mutant baboons. That they ran silently indicated a fresh track—not a man's or they'd have been in full clamorous cry. But they were headed upstream and were likely to cross a fresh trail of the renegade rear guard.

What to do? Run back to camp, get the others to the stream and intercept the beasts? Too little time. Anyway, at least some of the breloons would have radio-collars, and Gaddyl monitors would be listening. Divert them? That was just as bad.

The cats! He stared up the valley, where he could still see an occasional flash of brown. There'd been at least a dozen breloons; too many for the cats. But maybe dart-wounds would look like claw or toothmarks, when the Gaddyl got there. There'd still be a hunt, but maybe the cats could evade it. He whirled to Liss. "Can you mind-talk to your brothers from here? And to Kal?"

Liss looked doubtful. "Feelings—danger—maybe. What is your idea, Pale One?"

"Kal will know what to do! Try to send a . . . a conception of the creek, and breloons moving up the far bank. And the cats fighting them!"

Liss and his brother frowned in concentration; began moving their hands, faster and faster. Liss sang, very softly, a tuneless little song to himself. His face twisted, as if he watched some swift drama. Murno's own head filled with shadowy pictures . . . Breloons loping silently . . . A stream, burbling down a valley with the sun rising beyond it . . . *East,* East, beyond the ridge . . . The cats charging! A tangled fight! Murno clamped his lips on a cry; pressed hands to his temples—

Then the pictures were gone. Liss said proudly, "It is done! I did not think that—no one of our generation has handled such a complex thing!"

Murno turned and hustled diagonally up the slope, toward camp. Before he was halfway he heard a sudden bedlam up the valley. The roars and shrieks lasted only seconds, then there was only the terrified chatter of the breloons, fleeing back downstream. He'd never known breloons to act like that. His two companions were grinning, trotting easily beside him while he pounded along, struggling for breath.

They reached camp and found Pete's men crouched with their airguns ready. Pete called to Murno, "What happened? The Bluies suddenly took off with the cats as if all the Gaddyl in the world were after them! Then that racket—"

Liss told Murno, "My brothers and my uncle put thoughts in the minds of the breloons. The beasts saw a whole mountainside full of cats charging at them, each ten feet tall. They will not come this way again."

Pete started to say something and Murno cut him off. "Quick! Over the ridge!" He himself started off at a run. They topped the ridge and met the other Blue returning. He waved them back toward the stream, beyond which could be seen at least two dead breloons. "Upstream, in the water! We can't leave a trail!"

The Sierra men cursed at getting their shoes soaked, but everyone obeyed. Murno didn't dare take them more than a mile. At the first break in the hills on their right, he led them out of the valley and eastward.

There was danger, now, of being spotted by renegade scouts, but the vital thing was to get far from the dead breloons. Things weren't as bad as they might be, of course. Fresh packs of breloons would only pick up the track leading out onto the flat, and the one he and the two young Blues had made, looping to the lake and back. And by the time those were chased down and puzzled over and rejected he'd have some distance.

III

Pete walked in surly silence for a while, then fell in beside Murno. "These damned Bluies. I never believed all the stories that they could read minds and hypnotize people and all that. Tell me straight. *Can* they do things like that? What are they, anyway? Aliens, like the Gaddyl?"

Murno sighed. He'd told the Sierra leaders all he knew about the mutants, but they hadn't seen fit to spread it. "A thousand years or more ago, the Gaddyl were still experimenting with human mutations. They produced a few specimens with blue skins and very keen senses. For what purpose no one knows. But the specimens turned out to have talents the Gaddyl didn't expect, so they were killed. But two males escaped and were never caught. One survived and hid somewhere on the western slopes of the Sierras until the search was abandoned. Apparently the Gaddyl didn't know that, besides the other things, he had a very long life span. Eventually he mated with Norm women—maybe from your own ancestors—and all the Blues are descended from that. So they're all half Norm. The original escapee was killed in a hunting accident when he was six hundred years old, but I've met a surviving son. They call him the Old One, and he's a loose ruler of all the tribes. He and his sons have a lot of the original talents, including the ability to communicate clearly with each other over long distances; but each generation has less talent and a shorter lifespan, and looks more like Norms. The vow of silence is imposed on children to make them use what talents they've got. If they communicated by speech, they'd never develop it."

Pete clumped along, muttering, for a while; then, "That's what they *told* you, maybe. But how come the Gaddyl have left them alone until just recently?"

Murno said, "Remember that generations of Gaddyl have come and died. Most of the fiefs have been easy-going. The Blues took pains not to bother them or interfere with their hunting. And the Gads couldn't flush them out except by destroying game refuges."

Pete spent a while absorbing that. Finally he growled, "Suppose all that's true. I'm still not going to *like* anybody that can do things to my head whenever he wants to."

Murno didn't exactly like that himself. He said, though, "They've vowed allegiance against the Gaddyl, and they'll keep the vow. If these five young ones act up a little, try to remember they aren't really mature yet."

Pete said, "That's another thing. They claim to be brothers, but they all look the same age."

Murno grinned. He thought he'd better not mention that the youngest was one hundred twenty-eight.

Before mid-day they had to take cover because geehawks were circling overhead.

At least the Sierra men weren't bored now. They sat with their backs to treetrunks, or lay in underbrush, eyes fixed on their instruments. Murno couldn't help wondering if they realized how feeble their own painfully acquired technology was compared to the Gaddyl's. They hadn't seen much of the latter.

There'd been no indications of breloons on their trail yet, but it wasn't likely the false leads would occupy the search much longer. Murno had chosen the hardest, driest ground practical, and on a warm day like this the track shouldn't last more than five or six hours. Still, the hawks here proved the Gads were suspicious, and serious. All they knew, probably, was that something very ferocious had routed a band of breloons; but they'd want to know a lot more. What Murno feared most was that the renegades' main group would get too worried and flee, leaving the kidnapped youngsters to occupy the breloons. It was possible their rear guard had heard the fracas. They knew about the lake; they'd taken a route to pass north of it. And they'd surely seen the hawks by now.

Did the Gads know that renegade Norms roved this country? If so, what was their attitude? This was beyond the borders of the west coast fiefdom where Murno had spent his early years—Guddun's fiefdom, now—but unless some other fief claimed this territory, any Gaddyl might come here to hunt.

In mid-afternoon the hawks found something. The ones overhead all soared away northeast and the instrument Murno carried showed aircars headed that way. The men realized now what that could mean. Several, who had sons or daughters among the kidnapped, conferred excitedly then came to Murno. "We've got to help if we can!"

Murno swept a quick look across the sky. "Keep your voices down. That's probably the rear guard they've spotted, which means that's exactly where we don't want to go." He stood pondering. "Liss, can you keep contact with your brothers, all alone?"

Liss got to his feet in one easy motion. "At least partially, Pale One."

"Come with us, then. Kal, will you take the others and the cats and keep north of us for a screen?"

Kal grunted assent and beckoned to his nephews. The cats, relaxed in the shade, leaped to their feet and followed. Murno started southeast at a trot. Pete caught up with him. "Why this way?"

Murno hid his impatience. Pete wasn't very sharp in the field. "Because if that's the rear guard, the main group's farther east; and I want to keep south of them if I can." He set the hardest pace he could. Occasionally, Liss would pull ahead, stop, and seem to be concentrating. After a few miles he said, "Pale One, my relatives are trying to tell me something. There are hawks, circling again, and the sound of breloons tracking men."

Murno demanded, "Where are Kal and your brothers situated? Can you see?"

"They are on a hillside, well hidden, above a creek—the same one we crossed. The valley below them is thickly wooded. The hawks do not have sight of anything, and the breloons are not close to their quarry."

Murno sighed in relief. The main group, with the children, wasn't involved then. The rear guard, knowing the country, had a chance. If they were caught—well, it was a harsh thought, but he hoped the breloons would kill them before they could be interrogated.

He turned and slogged on grimly. The main group would be pushing the children hard.

Within ten more miles, the country changed abruptly. There was open rolling land again. On the horizon was a low dark line that must be the Black Grove; a good four hours' hustle away, he thought. The only cover between here and there was a stream, a couple miles to the north, bordered by large trees that looked like cottonwoods.

That would be where the renegades had gone, of course. He'd been a little cautious and gotten farther south of them than he intended. He peered around, unhappy with the layout. Following that creek down to the Grove would not only risk an ambush by the renegades, but also discovery by the Gaddyl if they picked up the fugitives trail quickly. Yet he couldn't cross in the open, in daylight. And neither could he wait. So it was the creek, and he'd better not delay. At least he had Kal somewhere to the north to warn him of trouble from that direction. He gestured to the men and led north, the edge of the hills.

Half an hours' hard going brought him to where the creek left the hills. He stared out cautiously from cover, wondering if Kal had had to stay holed up farther west. He turned to Liss and found the blue man grinning. "All right, what's the joke now?"

Liss pointed. Murno looked and saw Kal beckoning to him, half a mile down the creek. With a curse, he called to Pete and led the way to the creek.

It was easy going in the screen of cottonwoods. When they reached Kal-Let, the blue man took in Liss's grin and frowned. "Liss could have told you, Murno, that we were ahead of you. When we saw the breloons were all busy, we came this way fast. I thought it best to scout the creek at once. The ones we hunt passed this way about noon, hurrying. The children were with them. They are tired, judging by the tracks."

Murno was already moving. The sun would be down before they reached the Grove; the renegades might already be there by now. If it were as thick a forest as Pete thought, the chase wouldn't be easy.

A few miles along, Kal and Liss stopped suddenly, raised their heads as if listening, beckoned to Murno, and hurried on. Presently Murno saw them gathered with their relatives and the cats. Two renegades, disarmed and scared, were backed up against a big treetrunk.

Murno hated to spend the time, but he knew it was best to interrogate them. He walked to within a few feet and held out his hand to one of the cats, which hurried over and stood beside him hopefully. He told the ruffians. "If you talk fast and truthfully, we may not kill you. Where were you taking the kids?"

One of the men blurted, "To the edge of the Grove, to trade to the Bigears."

Pete arrived in time to demand, "What the devil are the Bigears?"

"Mutants," the man said, eyeing the cat nervously, "That live in the Grove."

Murno asked impatiently, "What do they want with the children?"

"I—I don't know." The man's guilty face implied he'd made some unpleasant guesses.

Murno demanded furiously, "How long will the trading take? Are the Bigears always waiting?"

"I ain't ... sure," the ruffian pleaded. "I've only been there once before. The way I understand it, we were going to tie the kids to trees and leave, and the Bigears would come and get them after dark. They never come out in the daytime. Can't stand the light."

Murno fought for calmness; started to turn. The man said, "We were only hired as scouts. We didn't have anything to do with—"

Murno turned back to him, murder in his veins. "You live somewhere south of here?"

"That's right. Yeah."

Murno told him, "You'd better go that way, fast. I guess you know there'll be Gads here before long. And if *we* see you again we'll kill you. Now scoot." He was moving as soon as they were, with only a couple of backward looks to make sure they were obeying.

He led the way recklessly, relying on the cats to nose out any ambush in time. There was none. The renegades had evidently only left two men behind as a precaution. The sun seemed to plummet into the west. It went down, and the Grove was still only a black line in the east. Another hour, and he could smell the dankness of it; feel the moister air.

Still, it was two hours after sunset before they reached· it. He posted lookouts, then risked torches to learn what he could from the tracks.

The story was plain. The children had been tied to treetrunks with leather thongs, and their captors had gone south along the edge of the Grove, on the run, no doubt desperately worried about Gaddyl. Someone—the footprints were bare, and not much bigger than the children's—had come, cut the thongs and herded the youngsters into the Grove.

Murno, sick with exhaustion and despair, stared at the tunnel-like black hole where the creek, and a path to the left of it, went in. The cats were sniffing about, intrigued but wary. Finally he mustered enough decision to say, "I guess we'd better not take torches."

Pete protested, "Are you crazy? You'd walk right into treetrunks in there!"

Kal put in, "Torches would only make us good targets. We and the cats will go first. The rest of you follow by ear."

Pete glared at the blue man. "To hell with that. Wait for morning!"

One of the other men said harshly to Pete, "You don't have a child in there."

Murno said firmly, "We'll go without torches, at least as far as there's a well-worn path."

IV

It wasn't comfortable. The path was smooth and he could feel his way somewhat, through his moccasins; and the creek rippled enough so he didn't blunder into it. Ahead, he could hear the cats sniffing and mouthing soft complaints. He kept both hands out in front of him so he wouldn't bang into trees. Behind him the Sierra men were having hard going, and swearing about it under their breaths.

An hour, more or less, passed. There should be a moon by now, but the foliage overhead hid it completely. He wasn't surprised. If, as the renegade had said, the Bigears couldn't stand daylight, this must be a pretty dark place even at noon. He pushed himself another hour, then called a halt.

The men grumbled again about the dried meat, and quarreled disheartedly among themselves. Murno thought ten minutes had passed, but he couldn't resist a few more.

Suddenly, a tree beside the path glowed like yellow-hot iron.

There was an uproar. The men were shouting; jumping to their feet and stumbling over each other. One of the cats leaped over Murno's outstretched legs. It landed in a crouch and whirled this way and that, snarling. The blue men were on their feet, knives in their hands. Murno got as far up as all fours, then stayed there, bewildered. It appeared they hadn't been alone.

Five or six small men, not over five feet tall, crouched scant yards off the path, as startled as he was, huge bulging eyes covered by tight squeezed lids. Their ears were bigger than a man's open hand, and stood out from their heads. Their skin was dark gray. They wore practically nothing and carried some kind of dart-throwers. An instant, and they whirled away and vanished among the trees, jabbering in ludicrously deep voices. Murno caught, in the distorted dialect, the words, "Great One" and "Norm-devils." The latter, he presumed, fit him, as well as the Sierra men. Something huge moved at the edge of his vision. He jerked his head around and saw, back along the trail, a great bear-like shape shuffling into darkness. An owl swooped away in startled curves. Mice, squirrels, other small things he didn't know—all with huge eyes and ears—scurried away from the light, protesting in various ways.

Incredibly soon, everything was gone. Now he had time to realize that the tree was not giving off heat, and that it glowed all over, from the base of the trunk to the highest leaf he could see. Those leaves were round, six inches across, and as thickly packed as they'd have to be to cut out all daylight. Eight or nine feet up the straight trunks branched. There short spines or barbs, with thick stems and enlarged, pointed heads, radiated out as if to repel climbers.

This tree was not the kind at the edge of the Grove.

The glow persisted a minute longer, then cut off suddenly. Now the dark was a frightful thing. Murno was glad when one of Pete's men struck a match and lit a torch.

Pete said huskily, "Let's get out of here!" and turned.

A man stepped in his path, jaw set. "No. My boy's in here somewhere. But it looks now as if we're better off with torches."

Kal said calmly. "We do not need torches. Nothing will bother us in the dark. But the light may anger them."

Pete fairly yelled, "Nothing will bother us? Are you stupid? Didn't you see—"

Kal smiled. "They have been around us all along. We knew, but did not want to alarm you. There is no radiation of menace. Even the bear was only curious, and now that he's seen the size of our cats he'll stay away."

Pete muttered an obscenity and raised his airgun a little. Murno's patience shattered. "Damn it! If you're not up to coming along, go on back! Or follow us with torches. I'm going ahead!" He turned and followed the blue men.

It was surprising how far down the path the torch light traveled, and how stubbornly his instincts clung to it. But once he was beyond it—the men were following, slowly—the prickling of his skin eased a little. He was all right.

This wasn't a normal forest. Well, he could accept that. He didn't think it was Gaddyl technology, and he had faith in Kat's ability to sense menace. And now, without the comparatively noisy Sierras close behind him, he could hear more—the soft footfalls of the blue men, who, he was certain, deliberately allowed themselves to make a little noise for his guidance. And as time passed and his eyes struggled for ultimate adjustment, he became aware that the darkness was not absolute.

The trees all glowed, very faintly; not enough so he could see their shapes, but enough so he could half see the path and the blue men trotting ahead of him. He resolutely ignored the other things with which his imagination peopled the Grove.

Yards ahead, someone screamed. Murno crouched, knife drawn, straining his senses. There was no further sound except some faint vague murmurs—not human, he thought. The cats were very silent. Kal said, "It was this tree."

Murno moved close to the blue men. "What are you talking about?"

Kal took Murno's left hand and placed it against a smooth trunk. "I am glad the other Norms have dropped behind. They would have panicked. Here, trees make sounds and give off light. They are sentient, too. We can feel it dimly. Though I do not think they have real minds."

"But to *scream* . . ."

Kal said, "One of the girls screamed as she passed here, and the tree is only imitating the sound."

Liss put in, "You are brave and wise, Pale One, and the best bowmen we have ever seen. But your ears are dull. We have been near the trees ever since we entered."

Kal said, "Yes. And not all of the sounds are reassuring. But if you want to go on, we will not flinch."

Murno said. "I'm going on. At least, until one of these trees decides to knock me down and sit on me."

In the darkness, the young blues chuckled.

It was an hour more, at least, when he heard a distant call from behind, "Murno! Breloons!"

He stopped, almost beaten down with a sense of futility. The Sierra men—he thought it was Pete's voice—had just put themselves in bad trouble to warn him, and he couldn't go back to help, though he wasn't sure Pete had wits enough to evade the breloons.

He turned slowly, and heard the blue men start on. And now, as he followed on legs that shook with exhaustion, the forest murmured and remurmured the strange new sounds, "Murno. Breloooons. Murno."

It was morning, and the only way he knew it was that they passed a break in the forest, where the sky was visible, and around which the path detoured widely. The place looked like an old bomb scar. Years ago, probably, some Gaddyl hunting party had made an entry for themselves.

He only allowed himself a minute or two in the light, then forced himself on.

Sometime later, when there seemed to be more light again, he thought at first that he was getting a little delirious. Soon, though, it was unmistakable. The foliage was much thinner, and the trees grew farther apart. He became aware that the path had dwindled until it hardly existed, though they were still near the stream.

Presently the blue men stopped, looking puzzled. The cats plopped down wearily. Kal said, "The scent is no longer here."

It took Murno a moment to realize he meant the children's scent. "Well, did they turn off?"

Liss back-tracked; found a place where the creek was shallow. "They waded across here. But something is not right."

Silently, Murno waded across and watched them searching for a track. Presently they moved on, away from the creek, southeast by his compass. The cats plodded behind, complaining wearily. Then the blue men halted again. Kal said, "The scent is all around us now."

Murno said impatiently, "Well, then, they rested here a while."

"No; it is not that." Kat stood, frowning, then suddenly blink in surprise. "The trees are reproducing the scent!"

Murno stared at him, then snarled, "Hell! Now what?" He tried to get his tired brain working; finally said, "Well, I've got a compass. We'll just go on in a straight line, scent or no scent!"

A tree whimpered somewhere. Liss, ears cocked, said, "Let us try what we can feel." He sat down, cross-legged, and his brothers did likewise, forming a circle. They closed their eyes in concentration. Liss crooned a few soft tentative notes, and the forest shuddered. He opened his eyes, grinning like a child with a new toy, and sang a clear high note.

Back it came from every direction, loud and pure. Kal burst out, "Enough! Do you want the Gaddyl swarming around?" They got up, sheepishly.

Kal stood frowning for a minute, then said in a tone of wonder, "Why, they *belong* to someone! Someone—

something—*uses* them! But in addition they have dim feelings of their own . . ."

Somewhere overhead there was the 'whoosh' of a fast-moving aircar.

Murno, remembering the Gaddyl had instruments to find fugitives by body-heat, stared upward, fists clenched with hate. "Let's move!" He forced himself into motion.

Here and there as they went the blue men found visible footprints. Liss said, "The Bigears did not come this far. The children went on alone. They walked close together, as if they were afraid. Maybe the trees talked to them, do you think?"

Murno didn't answer, His heart was pounding now, knowing as he did that the trail was only two or three hours old. Then he heard a child's voice, off to the left.

He whirled toward the sound, but Kal said, "It is only a tree. They will try to mislead us now."

While he stood in doubt, Murno heard, somewhere back along the path, faintly, a breloon. He snarled an oath. *"That was no fake!"*

Kal's face was alert. "No. They are coming."

That galvanized Murno's mind into action. "You, Kal. If Liss comes with me, can the rest of you intercept them as you did before?"

"Maybe." Kal was already moving back the way they'd come; and Liss was starting on in the other direction. Murno struggled to catch up with him. Young voices were babbling now, tantalizingly, as if the children were just out of sight to the left. He looked appealingly at Liss, and flushed at the blue man's patient expression.

The voices stopped abruptly, as if their instigator recognized futility. Murno slowed. They ought to get off the direct track, he thought; parallel it to one side to avoid ambush. Then he realized the trees could see them anywhere.

Another aircar whooshed overhead. He halted long enough to swivel his instrument about. At least two Gaddyl craft were close by, and others not far away. He ran on.

He heard a child crying softly, somewhere ahead.

V

Futile or not, he and Liss circled and approached the spot from another direction.

The children were all there, looking scared and tired, but apparently unharmed. Sis, in her boyish leather clothes, sat against a tree trunk, knees drawn up before her, arms and head resting on them. One of the other girls was nibbling on a thumb-sized yellow fruit, and a couple of the boys were chewing what seemed to be dried meat. There were two waterbags near the base of a tree.

Murno listened hard to the Grove noises for a minute, glanced at Liss, got a shrug, and stepped forward. "Sis!" he called quietly.

Her head jerked up and she stared at him an instant before bouncing to her feet. "Oh, Daddy!" She ran to him, threw her arms around his waist and buried her grimy face against him. "I knew you'd try to find us, but then I thought—I thought—that black woods was so awful! And we—we couldn't see the men who were b-bringing us, and—" She broke down in sobs.

The rest of them were gathered around now, jabbering in hushed voices. "Quiet!" Murno told them, gruffly to hide his own emotion, "We're not out of here yet!" He looked at one of the oldest boys. "Have you seen anyone since the Bigears—those little men with the deep voices—left you?"

The boy shook his head vigorously. "No! But there was food here. And every time we tried to leave, something snarled at us. And the trees told us not to be afraid and just wait here."

Murno glanced around. "All right. Listen, all of you. There are breloons on our track, and Gaddyl flying around, so we've got to hide for a while. First of all we'll go"—he looked at his compass—"west. That way. Until we're near the dark part of the forest and not too far from the trail. We'll wait very quietly and listen. If things work out, we'll go back along the trail, but it won't be for a while. You've got to be very brave and quiet. Understand?"

They nodded. He told, them, "Gather up the food, and those waterbags."

They started westward, the youngsters fearful at first. The trees made no sounds beyond faint echoes.

Before long there was an outburst of breloon cries from the direction of the trail. Murno faced that way, hands cupped behind his ears. The uproar turned to a rout, with the breloons fleeing westward. He listened until he was sure, then waved the children on. The breloons wouldn't run forever, which meant they'd be somewhere along the trail for a while. He asked Liss, "Do you feel anything from your brothers?"

"Only a . . . feel of caution. Or—yes! They're coming this way, but not in a straight line. They're separating. They're bothered about something, and—"

A deafening blast interrupted him. The ground shook; leaves rattled and some fell. Murno grabbed arrows, unslung his bow. The Gaddyl bomb couldn't have been more than a hundred yards behind them. He waved violently to Liss. "Get them moving! I'll stay back a minute to—"

"Daddy!" Sis protested in terror.

"Go on!" he told her savagely, "Liss can take care of you better than I can!" He gave her a shove; gestured fiercely at the rest of them. They went, in a ragged run, turning their heads to stare back.

He took cover behind some saplings and waited.

He could no longer hear the children, though the forest was deathly silent now. It occurred to him that whatever controlled the Grove wouldn't want to show its tricks with Gaddyl around. He listened for their voices, but there was no indication they'd landed. A bird flew by, silently. He looked at his instrument. There was an aircar very nearly in the direction he'd sent the children. He turned that way, took a step.

A ripping sound came from that direction.

He recognized it—a heavy laser burning down through the trees. He ran as hard as he could, bow and two arrows gripped in his left hand, right grabbing for another. Girls screamed. There were sudden Gaddyl shouts and the excited barking of breloons. Now the forest was full of sound— shouts as if a large group of Norms was running toward the action. He heard a Gaddyl shout in the Gaddyl tongue, "Ignore that! It's a fake!" Breloons bellowed their sighting-call. Through the trees, he got a first glimpse of a child running this way. Then the others were in sight, and, beyond them, breloons coming fast. Somewhere, judging by the sound, Liss was surrounded and fighting. He yelled at the panicked youngsters, "Climb trees! They can't climb as high as you can!" He paused an instant to see Sis shinnying up a slender trunk, and others at least grasping the idea. He dashed toward the leading breloons, roaring as loud as he could, and they paused.

Now the trees took up his roar and further distracted the beasts. He flung himself toward the nearest one and it darted aside, snarling, uncertain. Then he saw Liss, backed against a tree, knife flying. Several breloons darted about him, warily. Two lay dead.

An aircar rested on the ground not far away, branches still smoldering around it. Two Gaddyl had stepped out with light hunting-rifles, and grinning, were ready to cripple Liss so the beasts could tear him apart. They saw Murno and their faces changed. An instant, and their rifles were moving.

He recognized one of them as Guddun's younger brother.

He was astounded at the mad hatred that rose in him, even as his hands nocked an arrow, drew, and aimed. The young Gaddyl screamed just before the shaft reached him. It plowed into his midriff and his rifle went off wildly. Murno had another arrow nocked, but the second alien's rifle was already pointing at him and he knew he'd be too late.

Shafts suddenly converged on the alien, battering him down in a bewildered, crumpled heap. Other arrows—they had to be called that—struck at the breloons, not only the ones around Liss, but those that ringed Murno. Some collapsed in the first awful barrage. Others raced about mind-lessly, shrieking, as Murno stood stupified at the source of the arrows.

The short thick barbs he'd noted on the trees were swiveling to follow the darting beasts. The individual aim wasn't per-fect—but the cumulative effect was awesome. Each barb, as it came to aim, suddenly elongated itself and shot with terri-ble force away from its trees.

Within seconds there wasn't a breloon on its feet. Each one that lay stirring drew more shafts, until the last moan of agony was still.

Somewhere behind Murno a voice said softly, "This way, Murno. I may not be able to repel other aircars from this spot."

He whirled, eyes darting, then realized some tree had spo-ken. Another, farther away, called softly. He went that way.

Liss, grinning with no sign of nervousness but robbing at a few minor wounds, caught up with him. The children, urged gently by the trees, climbed down to follow. Liss said, "I am not unhappy that this weird forest had turned out to like you, Pale One." Murno grunted doubt, and looked at his instru-ment. Aircars were headed this way.

Then he heard a clear high call, somewhere in the forest to his left.

Liss said casually, "Kal and my brothers will handle the other Gaddyl. The aliens will return home convinced the two dead ones were turned upon by their own breloons, and that they saw nothing else significant."

The children had all caught up by now. The voice came again. "The young ones are to stay here."

There was a chorus of protests, but the voice said firmly, "Stay here! The Norm called Pete and his men will be guided here and will escort you home."

Sis said forlornly, "Do I have to go with Pete, Daddy?"

Murno told her reluctantly, "I think you'd better, honey."

Now he and Liss were led for a long time, doubling back and circling. Murno recognized that a puzzle was being constructed for possible scent trackers. As nearly as he could judge, they were several miles from where they'd left the children, and were somewhere near the creek, when the voice said, "Wait."

A few minutes later a huge blue form came into sight.

VI

Murno could only stare; and for once Liss's composure was missing too.

They both knew the Old One, of course—Liss's half-mutant ancestor—but this man, or creature, was to the Old One as the four friendly cats were to the huge maned lions of the Sak Toe valley. He was a foot or more taller than Murno; gnarled and knotted with muscles; his hands big enough to wrap around a Norm's throat, his biceps the size of Murno's thigh. His skin, like Liss's, was hairless except on the scalps and the long pointed ears, but it was as leathery as a bull's. Yet for all his bulk he walked as lightly as the Old One— only a little less lightly than Kal or his nephews. His face was lined and weathered with age, but he was nowhere near senile. Scars crisscrossed him, some of them fearful. At least two fingers were missing.

He smiled at Murno's wide-eyed inspection. His voice was powerful, with a deep timbre, but not loud nor harsh. "In the first few centuries of my life I was reckless and not very shrewd. Now, I give more thought to my survival and that of the descendants I hope to have." He turned to Liss with an almost eager expression. "You, young one. Are you in some way a relative of mine? I have never heard of beings such as you."

Liss was too awe-struck to do more than mumble. Murno said, feeling half in a trance, "A thousand years. You're one of the two who escaped! It must be! How—?"

The being looked at him, a little impatiently. "I made it look as if I'd died, of course. You're the first Norm to see me in six or seven hundred years. If I let you and your daughter and the others go, you're never to tell about me. Do you understand? I have ways of killing you if you do."

Murno's face grew hot. "If you're the one who controls these trees, you know I'm no pal to the Gaddyl."

The being's mien softened a little. "That I saw. And it's one of two reasons you are still alive. The other is the blue companions you brought. Since this young man appears tongue-tied, can you tell me if I'm right in guessing they are part Norm?"

"Half Norm," Murno told him.

Liss finally found speech. "You have the ability to control trees. Can you not link minds with us as the Old One, our first ancestor, can?"

The huge being shook his head. "Plants I can control, and mutate, and understand. That was the reason we were created—to be gardeners. But we turned out too strong to suit the Gaddyl. This Old One? He is the son of a Norm woman and the mutant who escaped with me. Does he resemble you?"

"To some degree," Liss said, "but we are drifting back toward Norms with each generation."

The big creature was thoughtful for a while. "Then I am saved several hundred years of experimentation. I have mated with women of the Bigears, and with other mutants to the east, but none have born children. That is why I caused those Norm youngsters to be brought. Now—" He looked Liss up and down keenly. "What do you think, young one? Will I have to kidnap women of your people, or will it be arranged peacefully?"

Liss grinned. "You can discuss that with my uncle when he arrives. I, for one, want to know how three-quarters Blues will turn out."

The huge blue man said, "My trees tell me he'll be here before long." He turned to Murno. "I am glad I do not have to kill you, Normal; I like what I've seen of you. Go now, and catch up with your daughter, and begin inventing stories to hide my existence. I'll watch you safely out of the Grove. It may be that we shall meet again."

Murno looked at Liss, who showed no inclination to leave, then turned and plodded away. He did not permit himself to look back.

He was thinking with regret that, with only a normal life-span, he would not live to see much of the Three-Quarters Blues.

A PRIDE OF ISLANDS

ALYARSMIT CLUNG to the top of a tall swaying hair and squinted toward the ponderous caterpillar-shaped beast way off in the very far distance.

"It's coming this way, all right," he called down to Brusmit, who was leaning against the base of the hair. "It's moved half a length since we first saw it."

"Do you think it sees us yet?" Bru asked uneasily. From up here, six man-lengths above the skin, he looked even shorter and pudgier than he was.

Alyar grinned down at him, then looked toward the front of their own beast. "I think so," he said. "Our eyestalks are up and signaling. The pincers aren't active, though. It must be a friend-beast."

"I don't see how they can recognize each other this far apart," said Bru doubtfully. "We'd better go tell Paboss."

"He sees it." Alyar looked aft to where the leader of the smit clan perched on another hair, a good shout from Alyar's.

"You'd better come down," said Bru. "He clobbered Jorsmit for being in sight, the last time we met another beast."

"He doesn't care when we're this far away." Nevertheless, Alyar climbed down; it wasn't all comfort at the top of a hair, especially when the beast felt you and twitched. "Let's go back there. He might know who it is."

He started through the thick growth of shorter hair, and Bru followed. They moved carefully, listening; it would be nip-and-tuck if only the two of them encountered a fley. They heard a few, detoured around them, eventually reached Paboss's outpost.

The leader was down from the hair, sitting with his back against it, munching dried meat. Three spearmen with him jumped up when they heard Alyar and Bru coming, then, recognizing them, relaxed.

Pabosssmit grunted and gestured toward the joint of meat beside him. "Help yourself." He eyed Alyar keenly. "That you on the hair up forward?"

"Yes, boss. But I made sure I came down in time."

"Don't go showing yourself again before we make contact."

"I won't. Could you tell who it was?"

"Looked like the jaksin beast."

"Oh. We don't fight them, do we?" Alyar was a little disappointed; he'd never been in a fight.

Paboss grinned. "No, but we don't trade with them, either. Pabossjaksin doesn't like me."

Alyar remembered something he'd heard. "Was that where you stole Maboss?"

The grizzled leader filled his thick chest and chuckled. "That's right. Stole her right out from under his nose!" He extended his arms, showing some scars. "Here's where he got me, before I knocked him out. Here's where Ma bit me."

"She bit you?"

"Sure. Any girl worth stealing'll put up a fight. I had to haul her along, kicking and screaming, and fight off half the jaksin clan at the same time. It was some party."

Alyar sighed, thinking what it must be like to go raiding. "I'm old enough to have a woman of my own," he mused.

Immediately, Paboss glowered. "Don't you go getting any ideas, hear? I don't want an open war with the jaksins. We've got enough trouble already, with the grans and the kendies." He put a hand tentatively on his club. "You hear?"

"Yes, boss," said Alyar hastily.

During the rest of the day the two beasts halved the distance between them. Near evening, Alyar led Bru, protesting, up to the smit beast's head and down over the edge where they could see forward and remain hidden in the short hair. It was dangerous; the beast might mistake them for fleys and reach up with a pincer-tentacle, which could move fast, considering the size.

When the slow hunching gait stopped and the beast settled down for the night, they went back to the thickly furred spot where the clan lived. Two of the moons were up, and with the excitement of being near another clan, nobody wanted to sleep yet.

Alyar left Bru with an audience of young people who hadn't seen the other beast yet, and went looking for the older men. They were in a clearing, rehashing stories about other clans, especially about the jaksins, which was an old one with a fine repertoire of legends. Maboss had naturally brought the stories with her.

Just now, Paboss was retelling a fascinating, if ridiculous one, about how people had originally come from another world on a beast that could fly.

Alyar sat and listened for a while, then, when the icy evening rain broke up the session, went to his sleeping place in a patch of protecting curly hair. After the first sleep, when it was midnight and dry again, he sneaked to where Bru slept, hissed at him, and drew him away. "Are you game for a little trip?"

"Where? You mean up front again?"

"No. Over to the jaksin beast. Just for fun."

Bru was horrified. "At night? We'd freeze! Anyway, you heard Paboss!"

"We can find something to put on over our own clothes, and wrap our feet in leather. All Paboss said was I mustn't try to steal a girl. Nobody'll miss us for one day, and the beasts will be together by tomorrow noon. We could bring back some kind of souvenirs."

"You must be crazy! What if the jaksins caught us?"

"They'd only haze us a little, if we hadn't done anything. Think of it—besides Paboss and Maboss, only seven smits have ever been to another beast!"

Bundled in extra garments, they sneaked to the curve of the beast's side. Bru acted as if he were going to his own funeral. When they got down to where the hair grew out horizontally, they moved out beyond the short stuff and dropped from one coarse emergent to another; then, finally, to the ground. Apparently no one had heard them. They ran toward the front of the beast, staying as close to the furry belly as possible, for warmth and concealment.

The jaksin beast was due north, half-hidden by the horizon and hard to make out against the background of the tremendous Forest where it had been feeding. Beyond the trees and a little to the right was a volcano, exhaling fiery clouds but not muttering audibly at the moment. East of them was a river; to the west, on the far side of the beasts, another Forest. It was not surprising that the two beasts had met, since they were on a narrow strip of hardened lava between river and Forest.

They traveled in long jumps, gradually closing the distance to the jaksin beast. Near it, they saw that it was awake, with all four front eyestalks and one pair of pincers extended toward them.

They halted out of reach.

"Do you think he'll know we're not jaksins?" Bru whispered.

"I don't think they care *who* lives on them, just so we keep the fleys down. Let him get a good look at us and he'll see we're people."

He was right, but by the time the huge appendages began to retract, the cold was getting through the clothing. They hurried for the shelter of the hair. Warm again, they chewed some of the meat they'd brought along and considered what to do next.

"We'd better go along the ground to the rear," Alyar said. "The men will be mostly near the front, on guard. Back there, there'll only be women and children."

"But we'll be a long way from home. What if the beasts don't come together?"

"Oh, they usually stop and talk, or whatever they do, for three or four days. We'll have a chance to sneak back."

"Why don't we just cut off some hairs right here for souvenirs and go home?"

"Don't you even want to spy on the clan?"

Bru sighed unhappily. "You're not actually going to try to steal a girl, are you?"

"Well—no. But it would be fun, wouldn't it?" His imagination began to percolate. "We're not far from the Warm Ground. That's what the first smit did. He stole a girl and couldn't get home with her, so they lived for a whole season on the Warm Ground until they found a young beast and started their own clan."

"If you've got any crazy ideas like that, you can count me out. People who get lost from their beasts get caught by Demons, or outlaws, or eaten by terrible animals. Next you'll be talking about going to Iron Mountain and fighting the Iron Fley!"

"Huh. The explorers who came back with all those stories probably exaggerated to make themselves look braver. Anyway, all I'm asking you to do is climb on the back end of this beast and spy on the jaksins."

It took the rest of the night to reach the blunt rear end, which had only one pair of eyestalks and one of pincers. They went through the process of letting the beast see them again, so it wouldn't think they were fleys when they began to climb, then picked a low rigid hair to start on.

It was a good four man-lengths up, too much of a jump even in this light gravity for Bru, who missed and floated back to the ground, contorting, while Alyar tried to control his laughter. He uncoiled a rope. "You need a good lively girl to work some of that fat off you," he chuckled as he hauled Bru up.

Panting, Bru pulled himself onto the hair. "You'll get me killed before I ever have a chance to get married. Do you think they heard us?"

"No. We haven't heard *them* yet, and they're bound to be jabbering like women always are." He coiled the rope and they began to climb.

When they were halfway up, there were squeaks and rumbles below them. They stopped, holding their breaths, while the tentacle curled toward a spot only thirty or forty man-lengths away and the great claw began digging at the fur. Evidently something itched there; and in a few moments, they did hear the screech of a hurt fley. They resumed climbing.

When the skin was level enough to walk on, they began hearing voices—the giggling of girls and the drier chatter of older women, but no men's voices. They crept forward, parted the hair very carefully, and peered out.

They must have found the quarters of a very important family, for the clearing was freshly cut and expensive woven rugs covered the skin. The walls were evenly trimmed, with several hung paintings. Sleeping places had been cut into one side and lined with soft leather from the underparts of fleys.

Alyar had only a glance for all this luxury, though, for within two man-lengths of him sat a pair of eminently stealable girls. Temptation battered at him. One, evidently the older sister, was well muscled and lithe, but plump enough to have curves everywhere. The other was beautiful too, but more slender. They had the black hair and tawny smooth skin of the jaksins. Each wore a short lounging skirt of dainty leather which left few secrets.

Prudence, overwhelmed, hardly put up a fight.

Alyar maneuvered Bru carefully back until he could whisper. He ignored the desperate protests. "Shut up. All you have to do is stay here and wait for me, and when you hear a commotion, screech like a fley. You can do that much, can't you?"

Bru, groaning, finally nodded.

A length from the clearing, Alyar chose a young hair shoot and put the point of his spear in the tender spot at its base. He jabbed with all his weight, then dove for the clearing. The beast's involuntary twitch came as he broke into the open.

The women were scrambling to their feet, with cries of "Beastquake!" and right on schedule Bru cut loose with a fine series of fley screeches. In the confusion nobody noticed that Alyar was a stranger until he scooped up the two girls, one under each arm, and jumped for the fur.

It was hard going, with both of them grabbing at hairs to hold them back, scratching him, and in general being unco-operative. He was panting when he reached Bru.

"Here!" he gasped, considerately tossing him the slender one who'd be easier to carry. "This one's yours."

The plump one knew by now what was happening. Slyly, she went limp until Alyar relaxed; then she twisted suddenly and got her teeth at his left shoulder. He yelled as she took out a respectable divot of flesh, and spun her around so she couldn't reach him again.

There was much screaming behind them, but no pursuit yet. Alyar urged Bru to the base of the nearest eyestalk. "Start climbing!"

"But we'll be trapped up there!"

"No, we won't. Go on!"

They were ten man-lengths up before a few old men and a crowd of women and children appeared at the base of the stalk. Seeing Alyar's spear-hand free part of the time, none acted anxious to follow them.

Now they were high enough to be hurt in a fall, and the girls had prudently stopped struggling. Alyar's twisted her head and glared at him. "My father will feed you to the fleys!"

Alyar grinned. "He'll have to catch us first. What's your name?"

"Go to hell."

He let go of the scale he was clinging to with his right hand, and pinch her in a vulnerable spot. She shrieked.

"If I have to keep pinching you," he said, "we'll probably fall. You'd better tell me your name."

She hesitated, then said icily, "Janeejaksin."

"Hm. You seem to be rich girls. You wouldn't be the Paboss's daughters, would you?"

Janee wouldn't answer, but the other girl did, rather cor-dially. "Yes, and my name's Marisujaksin. Are you going to steal us and make smits of us?"

"They'll never get off this eyestalk," Janee said scornfully.

Alyar motioned Bru higher. The figures around the base grew tiny and the stalk tapered to only half the girth of a man. It swayed a little, and they moved around to what would be the upper side if it bent.

Shouts could be heard now from farther forward; undoubtedly the fighters would arrive soon. Bru looked nervously in that direction. "What are we going to do—bargain with them?"

"No. Listen carefully. You know about people riding a pincer. We're going to get one up here, and when it's close enough, jump onto it and ride it to the ground." Alyar grinned at the protests, put his spear-point between two scales, and jabbed.

In a minute the eyestalk began to bend ponderously downward. Far below they could see the pincer-tentacle starting up to meet it.

"Be lively, now!" Alyar warned.

It took a while for the pincer to arrive. They jumped from two man-lengths, landed on the slanting horny surface, and slid. Alyar, hanging onto Janee with one arm, managed to get the other around a small prong. He threw a glance toward Bru and saw that he'd made out all right too. They waited.

Even though the irritation had stopped, the beast was going through with the scratching after hauling all that weight to such a height. The tip of the pincer sawed deliberately at the place Alyar had jabbed, and then they started down.

The movement was faster than it looked from a distance; still, it was a long way to the ground. Partway down, the beast saw them and the claw halted. They crouched while the stalk bent to bring the immense eye directly over them, but evidently the creature was only wondering what they were up to now, for after a while the tentacle started down again.

Three man-lengths from the ground they jumped, landed, and bounded away out of reach.

Men, shouting, were clinging to long hairs, but nobody was climbing the eyestalk. Perhaps no one wanted to imitate the novel descent. Closer shouts indicated a group coming down through the fur.

"What now?" Bru asked.

It was a reasonable question. Even if they dared go home, they'd have to parallel the whole length of this beast and could hardly avoid interception. Alyar and Bru had discarded their extra clothing, while the girls were almost bare, so warmth would be an absolute necessity when night came.

Alyar looked northward toward the volcano. The Warm Ground was supposed to surround it for some distance; maybe they could reach that before night. There wasn't much time to ponder. Men were already dropping to the ground. He picked up Janee and ran for the nearest cover, which was the Forest. "Come on, we can't stay here!"

Bru didn't have to carry Marisu—she was evidently coming along regardless, even though she wailed a little—so he was able to keep up. "We're not going into the Forest, are we?" he panted.

"Just into the edge to get out of sight. Then we'll decide."

They were still a medium shout ahead when they came to the first colossal uprights; trunks so thick it would take a man many breaths to run around one; towering so high one tended to forget there were any tops. In between were smaller plants, some with flowers that formed a thicket dense as fur.

Alyar paused, thinking of the stories he'd heard abo the Forest. But there was no doubt about how real the danger was behind them, so he held his spear at the ready at plunged into the growth.

Janee opened her mouth to scream, and he hastily muffled it with his hand. "Do you want to attract every Demon in the Forest?"

Her eyes widened and she quit struggling.

He listened to the shouts from outside, then pointed north, "That way."

Bru gaped. "But that's away from home!"

"We can't go home yet. Anyway, the jaksins'll expect us to. They're moving south already. Hear them?"

Inside the Forest, in the deep shade, there was less vegetation so that they were able to move easily. Whenever Janee looked ready to scream, Alyar pretended to see or hear something, and by the time she was wise to that, they were out of earshot.

Their luck didn't last long, though. They heard a sound whirled, and saw a small being on a branch, watching them with malevolent yellow eyes.

The girls whimpered, and Bru moaned, "A Demon!"

It had taken a strange shape, with four limbs and one other appendage that looked like a tentacle. It was covered with short black fur, very thick and fine. Just now it had a set of claws for clinging to the tree.

Before they could run, it opened its mouth and uttered a curse, which sounded like "Meow!"

"Let's get out of here!" Bru whispered.

Alyar knew better. "There's no use running; we're already cursed. The only thing is to try to appease it."

"Maybe we could give it the girls?"

Alyar wavered. He'd become quite attached to Janee though he was a little tired of being bitten and scratched, and he *had* gone to a lot of trouble to get her. "Let's try meat first," he decided.

He got a small piece out of his pouch and extended it on the end of his spear. Heart pounding, he moved closer. The Demon tensed as if to jump at them, then seemed to change its mind. It wrinkled its nose (which Alyar hoped was a sign of favor) and finally stretched out its head and took the meat. It chewed daintily and swallowed.

Alyar let out his breath. Nothing was guaranteed, course, but possibly . . .

The Demon said, "Meow," in a different tone.

Carefully, they edged toward the open. After a few steps Bru began to run. Immediately, there was a loud "MEOW!" and he stopped.

In a moment the Demon came into sight, walking on the ground. Alyar noticed that it had ungrown the claws. As he looked (no doubt reading his thought) it grew them again, stretched out its two front limbs, lengthened its body, and yawned.

They started on, but weren't able to make much time until they found that the Demon wanted to be carried.

At the edge of the Forest, it was disappointing to see how little distance they had covered. The nearest end of the jaksin beast, hunching slowly away now toward the smit beast, was still within three shouts. However, no jaksins were in sight.

Again, Alyar hesitated; troubles seemed to be piling up. Still, he didn't see any choice. "We'll have to go to the Warm Ground," he said.

The girls sobbed a little, and he frowned at them. *"Now what's wrong?"*

"There are terrible outlaws there, and Demons, and—and things."

His patience ran out. "To hell with them! We already have one Demon; do you think it's going to share us with everything on the planet? Come on!"

Janee didn't insist on being carried now; evidently she felt compromised enough to come along. They hurried, stopping only once to finish up their food. They were thirsty, but Hot Water was supposed to come up out of the Warm Ground, and anyway they could wait for the evening rains.

It was dusk, and already beginning to drizzle, when they noticed that the ground under their feet was warm.

This was mostly hardened lava, sloping upward toward the volcano, but with small streams and patches of vegetation.

Before they found a good place to stop for the night, Bru pointed ahead. "Look! That glow!"

They went forward cautiously until they could see what must be a Fire, with people sitting around it. Fascinated, Alyar went closer. Suddenly he heard the girls scream, and simultaneously two pairs of rough hands seized him from behind. He wrenched desperately, throwing himself and the two husky men around, but not getting free. More came shouting, to help pin him down and tie him with ropes. It sounded as if Bru and the girls were being similarly treated.

A man who acted like the leader came running from the Fire. "What have we got here? Scouts?" He began directing squads of spearmen as if he expected an attack. "Two women with them? Funny. All right, you—who're you spying for?"

"What are you talking about?" Alyar demanded, as indignantly as his position allowed. "We're from the smit clan and we're—trying to get home," he finished lamely.

"Clan? From a beast? What are you doing up here, then?"

"We came to keep warm."

"Keep warm? Why didn't you build a Fire?"

"I—we don't believe in Fires."

Laughter arose. "Let him up," the leader said. "He must be telling the truth. Only a fley-eater would be so ignorant."

They took off some of the ropes. Alyar rubbed at various bruises and abrasions, wondering whether he and Bru would be killed or made slaves. The outlaws would surely keep the girls. He wondered whether the Demon were going to give up its property so easily.

As if in answer to the thought, it came strolling into the light, and the leader made a sign nervously. "Damn! A black cat! Is it yours?"

"A black what? It captured us in the Forest."

"It . . . captured you? In the Forest? Then it's a real Demon!"

"Of course! How can you be so ignorant?"

"And you're still alive?"

"It hasn't hurt us yet, but it won't let us get away and it makes us carry it. I think we're uncursed right now. I'm not sure; I sort of lost track."

The man gulped and faced the Demon. "Please forgive us, Demon. We didn't know these people were yours."

The Demon looked at him scornfully and uttered a curse. People moved away, except one young spearman who stood his ground. "It—it sounds just like a cat," he quavered.

The leader knocked him spinning with the sweep of a forearm. "Of course it sounds like a cat! How do you think it would sound when it's in cat form? Do you expect it to speak ingils to us?" He beckoned to several women. "Bring food for the Demon, and offerings of iron and jewels!" He glanced at the four captives, and added, as an afterthought, "Better feed its slaves, too."

Cooked meat was easy to chew, but it tasted odd, and the fruit was completely baffling. Still, they were filling.

The outlaw leader eyed the Demon, which had pre-empted Janee's ample lap. "Where is it taking you?"

Alyar didn't want to admit how little he knew of the nature of things, so he said the most awesome thing he could think of. "To Iron Mountain."

There were gasps. "Oh, what unfortunate people you are!" the leader said. Then eagerly, "When will you go?"

Alyar thought he'd better press his luck. "It wants us to start right away. It only pretends to be asleep like that, to see if we're obedient. Er—I seem to have gotten turned around. Which way is Iron Mountain from here?"

The man pointed with alacrity. "That way! A third of the distance around the volcano. Here, we'll help you get loaded up."

The girls were festooned with necklaces and pendants of rare stones, while Bru and Alyar toted the food and the oddments of iron. The outlaws had hastily gathered a fabulous treasure of the metal—whole spearheads, and even a knife, of it!

Alyar waved and smiled at the outlaws just before they were out of sight, then turned north.

"We'll go upcountry," he said. "They won't look for us there. I'm not sure they won't follow; they probably don't know what this Demon will do any more than we do." He saw some huge rocks not far away, with bushes growing on top. "Let's climb up there."

When they were halfway to the rocks, incredible good fortune struck. The Demon with one hurried "Meow!" scrambled away from Janee and ran back toward the outlaw camp.

"Come on!" Alyar exclaimed. "Maybe we can get out of its circle of influence!"

They climbed the rocks and found they could see the Fire. Presently they knew the Demon had arrived there, for the distant figures scattered. Moments later, faint laments drifted to them.

They spent the rest of the night awake and watchful. "The outlaws will surely be after us now," Bru said, "to get back all this treasure."

"Marisu and I want to be near our clan," said Janee. "Even if—" she blushed—"you make smits out of us, the two beasts would meet once in a while and we could visit."

Alyar looked eastward, where numerous glows marked other outlaw camps. The volcano was a barrier to the north. The outlaws would bar the way to the south, expecting them to head home to the beasts. The only direction left was west, and he found that it pleased him.

"I guess we'll just have to visit Iron Mountain," he said. "Then we'll be such heroes that Pabosses smit and jaksin will have to forgive us."

The girls looked at him with awe while Bru moaned.

When the sun came up they could see the northern end of the Forest, south of which the jaksin beast had been feeding. Past it, surprisingly visible from this altitude, were the two beasts, head-to-head with eyestalks touching.

The Forest ran up close to the steep side of the volcano, leaving only a narrow pass. Beyond that was the river which, turning south, passed the two beasts. Farther up the river, according to legend, was Iron Mountain.

They stayed long enough to see what kind of animals prowled the country and to lay out a course, then climbed down and got started. They walked all day with only a few halts and some minor adventures with strange animals, then found another high place to spend the night. In the darkness they spotted a single Fire west of them. The next morning they detoured around that spot, and entered the narrow pass. Before noon they stood looking down at the river.

The canyon was deeper and wider than Alyar could have imagined, and there was more water at the bottom. The country ahead, though, was so rough that it seemed the easiest way was to climb down and go along the river. It took them half the afternoon to get down.

Not very long after that, Alyar put out his hand. "Wait! I hear voices!"

They were men's voices and seemed to be coming downstream.

He pushed the other three to a hiding place behind some rocks and bushes. When the owners of the voices came into sight around a turn, he gasped. They weren't walking, but riding on the water itself, in something like a big dish.

"Magicians!" Bru whispered.

Two of the men (there were seven) were stroking the water with some kind of wands, flattened at the ends. They acted as if they were fleeing from something, talking in low voices and staring back upstream. Just before they came opposite, it caught up with them.

The first thing Alyar heard was a loud voice, distorted and with an odd accent. He had trouble making out the repeated words. "Halt or I'll shoot. Advance and be recognized. Halt or I'll shoot. Advance—"

The thing came into sight—flying! He gripped Bru's shoulder. "The Iron Fley!"

It was made of the kind of iron that didn't rust, and had only eight legs, not ten. All of them were folded to its sides except one with a larger, oblong foot; that one was extended toward the fugitives.

When they saw it, they jumped out of their dish and sank into the water.

"Halt or I'll shoot," said the Iron Fley again, then hurled its spell. The dish shattered abruptly into small bits and a hissing cloud burst out of the water.

The terrible creature circled over the floating fragments for a few minutes, then flew off upstream. When it was gone the seven magicians appeared, climbing out of the river on the far side.

"Damn it!" said one. "A good boat lost, and not a bit of iron. I *told* you we ought to wait for night!"

"It doesn't make any difference," said another gloomily. "It's always on watch. Nobody's gotten away with any iron for three or four seasons."

"Well," said Alyar, after the magicians had straggled off down the river, "now we've seen it. It certainly put a powerful spell on that floating dish, but it didn't hurt the magicians. Maybe if we're careful it won't bother us."

They followed the twisting canyon and eventually began to hear a roaring noise ahead. It turned out to be the water falling over a cliff, and to go any farther they had to climb out of the canyon again. When they were on top they could see, ahead of them, what was undoubtedly Iron Mountain.

Parts of it were broken or rusted, but most of it was the non-rusting kind. Its shape was a surprise. It didn't look like a mountain, but something made by giants, broken off and a stuck into the ground.

It was wonderful to stand here, beholding the mightiest magic in the entire world. Still, Alyar wasn't satisfied. He felt he must go closer, even—possibly—touch it.

"You'd better stay here. Bru, if anything happens to me, take the girls and run. You can get back to the beasts by going down the river."

Bru was dismayed. "Don't go any closer! You saw what happened to the magicians' dish!"

"They were trying to steal iron." He unloaded the metal he was carrying, smiled at them, and went on.

He'd only covered a hundred man-lengths or so when he heard the distorted voice, coming from over his head. He looked up, then stood rooted as the Iron Fley came spiraling down toward him. He tried to think the purest, most serene thoughts he could, though the fervent wish to be somewhere else kept intruding.

The thing paused a few lengths away. "Advance and be recognized," it said.

He took a faltering hop forward. "Halt or I'll shoot," it said, and he stopped.

"Advance."

He did.

"Halt."

He did.

Finally he was very close to it, and he waited for a spell to hit him.

"Name, rank, and serial number," it demanded. Then, as he was silent, "Speak or I'll shoot."

"I—I'm Alyarsmit! I don't think I'm rank, and I don't know what a serial number is."

"Friend or foe?"

"F-friend. I haven't stolen anything. Just some girls."

The thing made a buzzing sound. "You speak, and you have the requisite number of limbs, and one head. Are you human?"

"Y-yes, I'm human."

"Name?"

"Alyarsmit."

"Smith? Smith?" It buzzed some more. "There was a Colonel John Smith on the roster. Are you his descendant?"

"Yes," Alyar hazarded.

"Mr. Smith, sir, Robojeep twenty-seven four nine reporting. All other jeeps inactivated, sir. No ship's personnel or other passengers accounted for in the last three hundred and seventy-four planetary cycles. Damage to ship unrepairable without human direction. Sporadic raids by savages, possibly degenerate humans, repelled successfully. Will you assume manual control, sir?"

Alyar stuck with "Yes."

"Very well, sir." The Iron Fley descended and walked toward him on six of its legs, then squatted.

He stared at its back. Actually, it didn't have one; it was hollowed out from the top, and in the hollow were—seats! Four of them!

Unable to mistake the meaning, he climbed in and sat down. Nothing happened for a while. Then the creature began to buzz again. "Have you forgotten the controls, sir? The lever on the left is for elevation; the other one for horizontal motion. Would you prefer vocal control?"

"N-no, this is all right."

"Very good, sir." The buzz stopped.

The levers were just in front of him. Gingerly, he reached out and gave the lefthand one a twitch, then yelled and let go of it as they shot upward. They stopped, and he tried again gently. They rose more smoothly.

He experimented with the other and moved forward, backward, and to the sides. He lowered to a height where he was less frightened. "Er—Fley?"

"You spoke, sir?"

"I can go wherever I want?"

"Except into obvious danger, sir. I'm programmed to avoid that."

Alyar flew toward where he'd left his companions. They lay down, lamenting, Janee loudest of all. He eyed her posterior, and Bru's, with some misgivings. The Fley's seats were a little skimpy.

He landed beside them, cleared his throat, and waited until they raised dumfounded faces.

"Get in," he said.

Against feeble protests from the others, he maneuvered the creature (which preferred to be called "Jeep") toward Iron Mountain. When they were close Jeep woke up, buzzed, and a hovered while a great doorway slid open. It carried the four, clinging together, into the hollow blackness within.

Then, quite suddenly—even though the door slid shut behind them—it was light as day inside.

What a cave! Cylindrical, all of fifty man-lengths across, it slanted down until it must reach far below ground. Far down there, where Jeep was taking them, were some level platforms.

As soon as they settled on one, a terrible, huge, clanking monster, also of non-rusting iron, flew toward them. They huddled while it spoke. "Mr. Smith, sir, Roborepairunit seventeen reporting. Ship's power and drive in order. Unable to complete hull repairs, or repair other working and scouting units, without cannibalizing part of living quarters. Do I have Mr. Smith's permission to proceed?"

Alyar gulped several times, and got out "Yes."

"Thank you, sir. The job will require arc cutting and a welding and other high-temperature processes. Will you be here very long?"

"We hope not."

"Very well, sir. I'll begin as soon as you leave."

They sat for a while, wondering what to do. Finally Alyar said, "Jeep?"

"Sir?"

"Would we be permitted to leave?"

"At once, sir."

More buzzing, and the door opened again.

As they flew away, Jeep said, "Sir, Roborepair wants to know whether to repair ship in its present position or move it elsewhere."

Alyar was beginning to feel more confident. "In its present position, I think. For now."

As they turned south, Janee began to sniffle.

"What now?" he demanded.

"I miss my Demon."

Alyar turned to Bro. "Isn't that just like a woman? She wants a Demon again!"

She raised her head and glared at him. "He was cute and soft, and he cuddled against me and made happy sounds. You tamed the Iron Fley, and if you really loved me, you could surely handle one little fluffy Demon!"

Alyar let Jeep stop and hang there while he tried to cope with the effrontery of it. After all he'd been through, stealing her, to have her suggest that he go into more danger just to satisfy her crazy whim!

His hands reached out for the levers again. Shaking his head dazedly, he started northeast to look for the outlaws.

Sometime later, they were headed south again, Janee's Demon asleep in her lap. Jeep was loggy with iron and other treasures extorted from various bands of outlaws. In the two rear seats, Bru and Marisu were holding hands.

He was startled to see two more beasts hunching up from
the south, beyond the smits and jaksins. Four of them together at one time!

When they circled down, they found Pabossmit on his hair,
scowling southward. He cringed when he saw the Iron Fley,
then managed to look both dumfounded and furious when he
recognized Alyar and Bru.

"You young hoodlums! I'm glad that thing caught you!
Look there—those are the grans and the kendies coming,
and Pabossjaksin's so mad he'll join them against us!" His
face softened into the start of a grin as he sized up the two
girls, but then hardened again. "I hope you're proud of yourselves, getting your whole clan killed or made slaves!"

Alyar started toward a clearing. "Come on down, Paboss.
We've got so much magic now, we could laugh at all the
clans in the world." And, to Jeep, "Jeep, can we bring Iron
Mountain over here and fly it around and show these savages they better behave?"

"A bloodless demonstration? Certainly, sir. I'll go aloft at
once and radio."

The four stood in a clearing, with awed smits around them
at a respectful distance. Paboss came pushing through the
hair, as awed as any, but less scared.

"Tamed the Iron Fley!" He began to guffaw. "Stole Pabossjaksin's own two daughters! Haw, haw! Young man,
when I retire . . ." His eyes covered Janee approvingly, then
turned back to Alyar. "You're wounded! What—oh, toothmarks!" He laughed some more. "Didn't I say any girl worth
stealing would put up a fight?"

Alyar happened to be looking toward Bru, who had his
own knot of admirers. Marisu was standing a little behind
him, as a bride should. At Paboss's words, she frowned and
her eyes fixed on Bru's smooth shoulder. Her gaze grew
more intent. She moved slowly forward, her eyes crossing as
they remained on the spot.

Closer . . .

Closer . . .

Bru yelled.

THE FORTUNES OF PEACE

I

THAT SECTOR OF THE GALAXY was Treaty territory—that is, open and unpoliced—so the Terran freighter had every right to be there. Nevertheless, she was a long way from home; and, mankind being just fledged in space, with a relatively weak Space Force, it was no wonder the freighter had run into trouble.

"Taintless" Wend, who was Earthborn but could no longer claim citizenship, sat watching the freighter's image swell on the main view screen of the Kyshan ship aboard which he was either guest or prisoner. He saw no signs of damage, so the freighter must have been taken by subterfuge rather than assault. Junnabl—his present host—was a versatile pirate.

Wend turned to the Kyshan. "Is *this* all you wanted me for? You could navigate her yourself. I know you read English as well as you speak it."

Junnabl grinned. That consisted of curling his upper lip (pasty green like the rest of his skin) and drooping the corners of his mouth, showing several dozen close-packed sharp teeth, while his amber eyes changed not one whit. "Iss true spend effort to learn. Now looks not waste. Have splendid job for you. See, soon."

Wend shrugged. They had him over a barrel. He shouldn't have holed up so close to Kyshan territory.

He heard a shuttle boat coupling to the aft lock, to take them over to the freighter.

Half an hour later, he turned from the captured ship's control console and faced Junnabl. "I won't play stupid. There's nothing about this freighter that wouldn't pass for an ordinary commercial ship, but she's too shipshape, too perfectly tuned up. A TSF crew, and a good one, manned her, I would guess. Where are they now?"

"Iss pleasure hire smart man." Junnabl showed his teeth again. "Are in safe keeping. You guess fast. Iss pleasure hire smart man. You not love TSF. Correct?"

Wend said, "I didn't leave it under the most cordial circumstances. Still, Earth was my birthplace."

The Kyshan laced his longer-than-human fingers before his thick chest. "Am not fool enough to ask big treason. Are sizes of treason, yes? This ship little sneak-play by TSF. Cargo of value somewhere, hidden. I want. When get, crew go free."

Like hell, Wend thought. They're undoubtedly dead. He kept his face impassive and waited.

Junnabl flicked a long palid-green finger at a collar-radio and said for the latter's benefit, in Kyshan, "Bring the Terran skipper's uniform and other things." Then he told Wend, in English, "Were well hidden aboard. Uniform iss now made to fit you. You get idea?"

Wend tried not to scowl. "Sure, I get it. An impersonation. Haven't you ever heard of fingerprints and descriptions?"

Junnabl said placidly, "I hire smart man, expect him fix details. On Norp—you know Norp?—are sealed orders this ship suppose pick up. You get, I get hidden cache, give you back little yacht I find you in, give you bundle money, shake hands, good-bye. Okay?"

Wend couldn't help grinning. He wondered if Junnabl actually expected him to believe that. He said, "I'd have to land on Norp without uniform, first, to look at the setup."

Junnabl laced his long fingers again. "Of course. We go there next."

II

Dressed like some space roustabout, Wend strolled by the TSF office, not too close. It wasn't much—a small concrete building in the local style, on the east side of the spaceport, away from town. He could hear the clack of a typewriter inside. Outside the door a human corporal, wearing a holstered rupter, loitered in the shade of a low, wide spreading tree. Four small aircars were parked to one side of the building. Obviously TSF did little business on Norp, which wasn't surprising. A Terran ship was a rarity here.

What he had to get from the backwater office was a padlocked dispatch case. There was, it seemed, a list of five TSF officers who might call for it. Though the orders Junnabl had found didn't specifically say so. Wend was sure the local C.O. would have photos and fingerprints of all five. The one who'd fallen into Junnabl's hands was a Commander Waldron, which meant nothing to Wend. He didn't think he could risk a direct impersonation, anyway.

Casually, he strolled toward the busy side of the field; turned between two buildings and stopped, pretending to fiddle with the zipper of his jacket. He was careful not to look at the Norpan who went by a little too hastily. So Junnabl had hired people to watch him.

He stepped into the open again and looked for a visiphone booth, choosing one that was exposed on all sides. He didn't want anyone sneaking up and using some listening device. He entered and pulled the door shut.

There was a directory-scanner. He deposited a coin and punched for "Importers"; let the names scroll down across the viewer; stopped the device at "Vassun Garka, Inc., Exotic Foods." If this were the same family . . . He contributed another coin and waited.

A polite Norpan face appeared on the screen. The slit-eyes blinked once. "Apologies, sir. I speak no Terran languages."

Wend answered in Kyshan, which he spoke better than Norpan. "Not needful." He held up a plastic card with one of his aliases on it and an orange triangle in the corner. He waited for the clerk's eyes to widen at the implied credit rating, then said, "Secrecy desired. Is there someone familiar with the star called Hane?"

The face—similar to a Kyshan's but swarthier, the two races having diverged a little—twitched and became impassive. "I have not heard of such a star."

Wend nodded politely. "Perhaps a coincidence of names. I had dealings there once with a Loob Garka, also in the import business."

The clerk said tonelessly, "If you will wait, I will make inquiries, sir." The face vanished.

Minutes passed, then a more mature face appeared on the screen. The eyes glanced at the credit voucher. "I do not know you, sir, nor do I know Loob Garka. But how may I serve you?"

"Perhaps you know me as 'Taintless' Wend."

The face changed just slightly. "Ah."

Wend said, "I am followed. I would discuss mutual profit, but I must evade watchers in a way that would not arouse suspicions."

The teeth showed in a smile. "You flatter me in seeking my arrangements in such a matter. But go, in ten minutes, to the Chief Dispatcher of airtaxis and ask him, loudly enough to be overheard to send you to the Vale of Amethyst Joys. He will, instead, place you with a trustworthy driver who will bring you to the Cradle of Mercies, where I will meet you. It will be arranged that you are not followed."

The Cradle of Mercies, though it undoubtedly catered to the cruder desires as well as the more delicate ones, was relatively quiet and meticulously clean. The lobby was dimly lit, and scented with something like lavender plus sandalwood. Various curtained portals led off it. From one came a buzz of Norpan voices and a fan of light as a provocatively clad female held the curtain aside for a moment to gaze around the lobby.

The attendant who'd instantly approached Wend led him through a different door, along a dim corridor, and into a small, plain, well-lighted room. The Norpan to whom Wend had talked via visiphone sat cross-legged on a thick cushion, across a low table from a similar cushion. The attendant left, closing the door. Wend's host glanced at the bolt on the inside of the door.

Wen—now understanding the courtesy of letting him bolt the door—did so. He appreciated the cushion, too, which meant his host knew enough about him to know he'd be comfortable on it. A strange Terran would be given a chair.

On the low table were two self-warmed bowls holding, respectively, roasted nuts and what looked like an equivalent of barbecued prawns. A generous decanter was neck-full of an amber liquor. Two tumblers of opalescent crystal waited. Wend seated himself and answered his host's slight bow. The Norpan glanced at the decanter, then, as Wend made the palm-up gesture of assent, poured liquor. Not until each had sipped did he speak. "You honor me. I am Vassun Garka, and Loob Garka is my cousin. How may I serve you?"

Wend speared one of the prawns with a small silver skewer. "Mine is the honor. You know, doubtless, that I arrived on a Kyshan corsair."

Vassun turned a palm up. "Yes. Junnabl's."

Wend continued, "Junnabl has conscripted me for a bit of theft. If the booty is what I suspect, I am not adverse to taking some of it. However, I do not want to share it with Junnabl, nor do I care to rely upon his promises.

Vassun looked amused. "You find my own race more reliable?"

Wend grinned. "There are Norpan pirates as deadly as Junnabl. But I feel your own family is more likely to let me live. How is Loob, by the way?"

The Norpan chose a roast nut. "Active, and still unhanged. You mentioned his home base. I hope this project of Junnabl's does not lie in that direction?"

Wend turned a palm down. "Junnabl has mentioned no direction, and does not yet have one. Perhaps I should not have mentioned Hane."

"It does not matter," Vassun said. "The clerk is discreet."

Wend sipped more of the liquor, which was like fortified wine. "Well, here's the project." He told about the secret orders. "What I hope to do is switch dispatch cases. I have a tentative plan that will require certain gadgets I can't buy openly. And I want a small padlock specially made. But mainly, I want help getting free of Junnabl. He has my yacht, but if the booty's what I suspect, I can buy a new yacht."

Vassun looked interested. "And you suspect what?"

"Well, I happen to know that before the Treaty was signed, TSF feared it might be drawn into the fighting somewhere out here. There was a secret cache somewhere, in case supplies were cut off. This freighter Junnabl has captured could not haul much in the way of missiles or other heavy weapons. Nor would food and such be worth recovering. So I think it's fuel. TSF uses a synthetic fissionable similar to the one you use. You know how much *that's* worth per pound. I judge this freighter could stow and lift five hundred tons. I think there'll be that much, or more."

"Ah," Vassun said, reaching for his glass a little quickly. "Yes. And what terms have you in mind?"

"I get one-fourth," Wend said. "You get one-fourth. We load the other half aboard the freighter and send her back to Earth."

Vassun blinked. "I did not know you were such a loyal patriot."

Wend held a palm down. "Earth wouldn't miss the whole cargo too much. But if we took all of it, TSF might feel stung enough to do something. Pass rumors around, if nothing else. If they get half of it back, they'll keep quiet. After all, they won't be anxious to admit trying to recover it."

Vassun considered slowly, turning his tumbler in his long fingers. Finally, "You may be right. But if there are other things at the cache? Munitions?"

Wend told him, "I'm not interested in them, nor is TSF, probably. You can help yourself. Now, here's how I hope to get the secret orders." Wend outlined his plan briefly and described certain gadgets he needed. "If you'll have those ready, I can pick them up when I land again, in uniform, to pull off the switch. Then, as soon as I know what the orders

are, I'll get word to you where you can find us—Junnabl and
me, I mean. I'll devise some way to make myself expend-
able for that long. I can't plan in detail until I see the orders,
which I'll do before I take them to him. Do you follow me?"

Vassun considered briefly. "Yes."

"Fine, then." Wend got up. "I don't want to be a hasty
guest, but Junnabl will be furious that I've dropped out of
sight this long. Will you excuse me?"

"Of course." Vassun stood up and held out his hand, in the
Terran gesture. "One question that has interested me, if you
will permit?"

"Of course."

"Why do you have the nickname you do?"

"'Taintless?' Oh, it goes back to my court-martial. My defense attorney got carried away and used the word. It was so
inapplicable to me, everybody laughed. And it stuck."

Vassun smiled. "Ah. Forgive my curiosity." He waited for
Wend to unbolt the door.

Junnabl did a poor job of hiding his rage. "Wass a very long
look, Terran!"

Wend tried to look injured. "Well, naturally I did more
than stroll by! I made inquiries around town. There's no
Night Duty Officer; just one enlisted guard. I can handle
him, and I've got a plan. I'll need Waldron's dispatch case
and his luggage. You'll have to land me in a shuttleboat and
stay in orbit, giving a false ship's name so I can say I'm
traveling on verbal orders, via available transportation. What
I intend to do is switch dispatch cases."

A slight muddiness suffused Junnabl's face. "Iss not likely
they will be that easy to fool!"

Wend told him, "There's a way to manage it. But you'll
have to be ready to pick me up fast when I walk out of the
place."

III

The Senior Lieutenant on Norp was eager to talk. "Is something up, Commander? We've got . . . we've heard rumors, but they're vague. Will the Treaty blow up?"

Wend (who was calling himself Shea) grinned at him. "No. You'd have to go out of the Lenj sector to find any real fighting, and we're not involved in any way. All I know is I'm supposed to wait here for a ship and further orders." He set Waldron's dispatch case on the corner of the Lieutenant's desk. "Can you lock this up somewhere while I go look for a hotel?"

"Of course, Commander. I'll put it in the safe. If you like, sir, we can phone for hotel reservations."

Wend grinned again. "Thanks, but I'd just as soon look around a little. I've built up quite a thirst. I'll send for my luggage." He moved the two bags closer to the wall, started for the front door, then paused. "Will the Night Duty Officer be able to get me that dispatch case? There's a lot of stuff in it I'm supposed to be studying."

The Lieutenant looked guilty. "We don't have a Duty Officer at night, sir." He glanced at the safe in the rear of the office. "I'll leave the combination with the guard. He's reliable."

Wend nodded. "Thanks. Maybe I'll see you around town tonight."

Norp's orange sun had set when Wend returned to the office, nervous about what lay ahead but glad to have the long afternoon over. The office lights were already on. He wiped his palms on a handkerchief and entered.

The guard was sergeant, Category M.P. That wasn't too good. He stood up. "Yes, sir. Commander Shea?"

Wend nodded. "They didn't tell me it was so hot here. I hope it cools off at night."

"It does, sir, if the breeze is right. Did you find an air-conditioned hotel?"

"Yes, finally." Wend glanced toward the safe. "I left a dispatch case."

"Yes, sir. I'll get it."

Wend followed the man as casually as he could. He had to be close enough to use the small gas-gun Vassun Garka had gotten him. He put a hand in his pocket, ready to draw the weapon. The M.P. knelt and worked at the safe dial. It seemed a long time before he pulled the door open. Wend took one step nearer. He drew the weapon, aimed it and pressed the stud, clearing his throat to camouflage the faint hiss. He must hold his own breath now. He saw the faint mist billow out, dispersing quickly. The M.P. had Waldron's dispatch case out now, was about to swing the safe shut. Wend said abruptly, "Sergeant, my luggage . . ."

The kneeling man turned his head. He started to say something, then looked puzzled. "Your . . ."

"Wend stepped closer. "What's the matter? You look sick!"

The man swayed; put a hand on the floor to steady himself. Belatedly, suspicion flooded his face. He made an awkward move toward his holster; changed his mind and reached to shove at the safe-door. Wend thrust a foot in the way. He had his fist doubled, but the gas was swift. The M.P. toppled, pawed at the floor land lay still. He'd sleep for hours, Vassun had promised, and awake with a temporary amnesia. Wend reached into the safe, seized the dispatch case, tossed Waldron's in, slammed the door and gave the dial a spin, then hurried with the other dispatch case to the desk that held the typewriter.

There was a regulation small padlock on the case. He drew from his hip pocket a pair of cutters—another of Vassun's contributions—and cut the link. He glanced at the door, then opened the case.

He re-read the meat of the orders: "Proceed to given co-ordinates and make sure there is no pursuit before approaching the planet. At specified latitude and longitude, fly a search pattern, using ship's metal-detector to locate the cache. Ap-

proximately ten feet of soil and loose rock must be removed."

He studied the description of the planet. A lifeless, uninvit-
ing one, and not handy to anywhere. He memorized all figures, then found the office's disposal-slot and thrust into it
the orders, the gas-gun, the cut padlock and the cutters.

He looked for TSF stationery without a local address,
found it, added carbon paper and a second sheet, rolled the
whole into the typewriter and sat frowning anxiously. He
had to make decisions fast. Did he want to tell Garka the
true location of the cache? He thought not. The Garkas
weren't cutthroats—not ordinarily—but they were capable
of seizing the loot and pondering the agreement later.

Inspiration came. He glanced at the door and at the inert
man near the safe, then, laboriously, with muttered curses,
began to type.

When he'd finished, the fake orders read, in part, "You
will identify yourself before landing, then present these orders to the garrison Commander."

The co-ordinates he gave were not those of the cache
planet. He hoped—this was one of his risks—that they
wouldn't be familiar to Junnabl. They were the co-ordinates
of the uncatalogued, little known star called Hane.

He addressed the envelope to Garka Imports, put a copy of
the faked orders in it and went to drop it in the mail-slot.
Then he looked hastily around the office to make sure he'd
left no evidence. He hurried to the unconscious guard,
dragged him to the Duty Desk and arranged him on the floor
as if he'd fainted and fallen from his chair. Finally he put the
faked orders in the dispatch case and locked that with the
special two-key padlock Vassun had gotten made for him.

As he stepped from the office with the case under his arm,
an airtaxi swooped down for him.

Junnabl, a flat key gripped between long thumb and forefinger, looked up from the dispatch case with a scowl. "What
iss this?"

Wend glanced at the two-key padlock. "It's a common security device in TSF," he lied. "I suppose the C.O. on Norp has the second key. I had no chance to find out for sure."

Junnable stared at him coldly for a moment, then, in an angry motion, drew a rupter and blasted the padlock. Wend ducked to avoid splattering metal. The Kyshan jerked the case open and reached greedily for the thin envelope inside. He tore that open, unfolded the orders and began to read, silently but with lip-movement, holding the document so Wend couldn't see it. His face muddied. He darted a look at Wend, then went back to the orders.

Wend could tell when the alien reached the end and started through. He could tell when Junnabl began to repeat the space co-ordinates to himself.

Suddenly the pirate stiffened. His eyes went wide, then narrowed. The glance he threw at Wend was half-absent.

God, Wend thought, with a sudden knot in his middle, *He recognizes those co-ordinates!*

After minute Junnabl looked at him again. "I can not pay you off yet."

Wend tried to act surprised and angry. "What do you mean? I've done my part of the job!"

The pirate's teeth showed. "Iss other part of job. And iss something strange. You will come with me. But you will not enter control room during trip." He gestured for a guard.

Wend protested a little, but went with the hard-faced crewman. As he left the patrol room, he heard Junnabl placing a ship-to-planet radio call.

The call was to Garka Imports.

The trip would take a little more than a hundred hours, assuming Junnabl went direct to Hane. All Wend knew was that the freighter was in acceleration and would be ready to Translocate in a few hours.

He could only guess what Junnabl had said to Garka, or what Garka's reaction was to the call. Garka might have let something slip.

Not that Junnabl needed any more alerting. Wend's impulsive use of Hane an ambush point had been a bad misstep. At the best, Junnabl knew the Garkas were involved somehow. Very few people knew where Hane was—the star was rather isolated, with only one livable planet—but obviously Junnabl knew. And he'd be wondering hard how it was that a TSF garrison should exist there. He'd assume there was some deal between TSF and the Garkas.

What made it especially galling was that Vassun wouldn't get the envelope Wend had mailed him until hours after Junnabl's call.

Then, too, there was the chance that someone at the TSF office just might sort through the outgoing mail and wonder what business they had with Garka Imports.

And just in case Wend ran out of things to worry about, there was something peculiar about Hane itself, or the area around it. The time he'd been there, he'd been piloted in by a Loob Garka henchman. Ships, he knew, had on occasion blundered into something fatal near Hane; and the Garkas might just be angry enough to let Junnabl do likewise.

IV

Wend spent most of the trip in his cubicle—the one that had belonged to Commander Waldron. When he did wander about the ship, there was always at least one Kyshan guard with him and others within call. They let him visit most parts of the ship, but made it plain he was to touch nothing. He stayed alert for any chance to overpower a guard or seize a weapon, but these weren't amateurs. The deep-chested, stocky Kysh moved like cats and were as ready as cats, and they knew how much distance to keep between him and themselves. Unless he got an unexpected break, he'd have to play out the hand he'd dealt himself.

The freighter was in Translocation now, flashing through some limbo that only abstruse mathematics could describe. Wend had no way of knowing for sure they were headed for Hane. When he asked Junnabl their destination, it was only to maintain his pose of co-operation. Junnabl told him nothing.

He wondered about Junnabl's flotilla. No doubt it would be somewhere handy if needed.

The hours crawled by, and he began to watch his chronometer. Hane, if that is where they were headed, shouldn't be far now.

Then—at about the right time—he heard the sounds and felt the vibrations that meant they'd popped into normal space again. The ship's artificial gravity shifted and wavered, trying to fit itself to deceleration, and finally succeeded. And now Wend was herded to his cubicle and told to stay there.

He sat on the bunk listening to the sounds of the ship. Work was going on somewhere—repairs or alterations to the machinery.

Presently he felt a jar. Something—a shuttleboat, maybe—had coupled on. Shortly after that, there were complex maneuvers. He could not tell what was going on, but they might be matching orbits with something. Were they in orbit around Hane? If so, where was Loob Garka?

There was another mild jar—the shuttletboat was pushing off, perhaps. Then silence. The gravity, at about one-third G, was steady. He listened. The air-conditioners hummed. And what was that other sound? A generator, to keep the ship's minor machinery running. But the drive was silent.

So they *were* in orbit somewhere, or drifting free.

They? He hadn't heard a sound since the shuttleboat's departure to indicate anyone but himself aboard.

He was on his feet swiftly, senses taut. He tried the door and found it unlooked, saw no guard in the corridor. He ran toward the central well; found only dim standby lights on. He turned on full lighting, hauled himself up the ladder to the control room, flipped switches and studied instruments.

The main computer was dead. So were the drive and, of course, the radio. He wasn't going anywhere, and he wasn't going to call help. But the artificial gravity remained at a third-G, and the view screens were working. He turned on the main one.

The brilliant star that crawled across the screen could be Hane, twenty or thirty million miles away. That it crawled as it did meant the ship had a slow end-over-end tumble. He began increasing magnification, and cranking the view to follow the star.

A dimly lit oblong blob caught his eye. That was another ship within a few miles of him, faintly illuminated by Hane's distant light. He could see she was a derelict, holed in more than one place. Watching her, he suddenly realized that she, and his own ship, were in orbit about something.

He started to look for that, but before he found it he saw other ships—dozens of them—all apparently unmanned, many of them damaged, swinging in parking orbits. The orbits were fantastically quick. His own wasn't much over five minutes. They averaged, he'd guess, four or five hundred miles in radius. "God," he muttered, "what kind of gravity-monster . . ."

It took him half an hour to spot it, and then he saw no disk—just an odd localized distortion of the light from distant stars. Something too small to see had a gravity sufficient to hold these ships in their tight orbits.

Had they gotten caught by accident? Hardly. The orbits were precisely circular, obviously planned. This must be Loob Garka's junk pile, where he hid captured ships—too far from Hane to reflect much light, close enough to be reached in a hurry.

And Junnabl knew about it. Wend saw the Kyshan's audacity now. He'd hidden Wend here where Loob would least suspect, while Junnabl went to negotiate with Loob. At least, that meant Junnabl hadn't mentioned Wend to either Vassun or Loob. Message drones would have undoubtedly flashed between Vassun and Loob long before now.

But what was this monstrous gravity-well? It could only be a chunk of nuclear matter—a "bone" of some dead star, perhaps—of fantastic density. No wonder it didn't reflect Hane's light. Its surface gravity was too high!

So Hane had a companion—a dark, secret, dwarf-monster. Thinking back over bits of gossip he'd heard, stories of what had befallen wandering ships, he could understand. He wondered if, in fact, there weren't a number of tiny black dwarfs around Hane. It would take a multiple system to explain some of the stories.

God help a ship that, approaching normally in the plane of the visible star's planets, blundered too close to one of these things! Tidal forces alone could destroy her.

Well, he was safe here for the moment. He got up to make a quick tour of the ship, to see what they'd left him.

This freighter—*Wargentin* was her name—was, overall, a squat cylinder about as long as she was wide. Amidships, halfway between the flat ends and parallel with them, was the circular Main Deck, nearly ten feet thick, which contained among other things the artificial gravity machinery. Within the ship it didn't behave entirely like natural, mass-induced gravity. It focused in (or, more precisely, "drew from") opposite directions *toward* the main deck, so that it was reversed in the two halves of the ship. The focusing made the pull in the control room, sixty feet forward, virtually as strong as at the deck itself. Farther away—outside the ship—the force reverted, by degrees, to the natural laws, including the inverse-square one, and pulled centripetally toward the ship from all directions.

Forward of the main deck were the living quarters and various other things, arranged radially around the central well. Gravity forward was usually kept at one-third G. Aft, the reverse-direction gravity might be low, just enough to hold loose cargo "down," or might be turned off entirely. Machinery and non-liquid storage were mostly aft.

Wend went down the central well, looking in various compartments. He reached the central hatch and went on through the deck—carefully, because the abrupt change in gravity could mess up reflexes. He found only standby lights beyond, and about a twentieth-G.

Half an hour later he started back to the control room. There was no better weapon aboard than a kitchen knife. Small but necessary parts of the drive were gone. The ship would stay livable for a long time. But she was parked until the drive components were put back.

He checked and found that they'd left all of it. So, then, they had transferred to Junnabl's ships.

It wasn't quite true that he was confined here. The two standard spacesuits were in place and in working condition. If he preferred, he could put one on and go out to die in space.

He paced the control room. "Damn it! With all this machinery . . ." He forced himself to sit down and think.

One thing Junnabl didn't know was the deal he, Wend, had made with the Garkas. Therefore, Junnabl wouldn't expect him to recognize Hane. All of that would change, though, as soon as the Kyshan was convinced the Garkas knew nothing of any TSF base. That would prove that Wend had tampered with the orders, and the whole thing would come clear, and Junnabl would hurry back for him. Probably the Kyshan would Translocate away to throw off pursuit, then sneak back. But that wouldn't take long.

Wend got out a handkerchief and wiped his palms. Risking death for a big prize was one thing, but being tortured for information, by experts, was something else. Junnabl would break him completely, until he was utterly incapable of lies.

He had to communicate with Loob Garka, quickly.

Could he rig a radio of some sort? Sure—to communicate within a million miles or so. But it would take more than a crude spark-gap transmitter to reach Hane. Anyway, transmission that far would take many hours.

Well, he needed a message drone, then. He'd already looked to see if there were any aboard, but now he made another trip, looking everywhere he might be stowed. Junnabl had made sure there weren't any.

He went back to the control room and stood scowling at the view screen. What were his chances of reaching one of the other ships in a spacesuit? About as good as his chances of throwing a pebble left-handed and hitting a bee in flight a hundred feet away. Nevertheless, he tracked the closer ones and calculated as well as he could without the computer. The next ship out passed within two miles, regularly. But with relative speeds like this, a free jump of two hundred yards would be considered risky.

Still, he didn't have much to lose. At worst, he'd die in the suit and frustrate Junnabl. He studied the ship. She was Lenjan; a freighter, but no longer and slimmer than *Wargentin*. She was holed amidships, but looked sound otherwise. Like all the others, including *Wargentin,* she had just enough end-over-end tumble to keep her aligned along her orbit.

The chances of reaching her at all were so infinitesimal that odds against finding message drones aboard her didn't make much difference.

He swiveled the viewer, waited for the next ship down to pass under him and studied her. A Norpan freighter. The pass was farther away, and the relative motion greater, so he rejected that alternative.

If he did make a try for the Lenj ship, he'd have to take along some bars of fuel. That was one thing that wouldn't be left in a long-parked ship, and he'd need power for lights and to warm up the tiny drone and project it, assuming he found a drone. So said aloud, "Hell! I'm thinking as if I really expected to make it out there."

Now that he'd decided to try, though, he couldn't bear pondering any more. He hurried to get one of the suits. By the time he lugged it to an airlock and went aft for three fuel bars in their canisters and attached them to the suit, *Wargentin* had made five or six orbits and was overtaking the Lenj ship again. "Damn! I won't make it this pass."

He'd have to hurry even to get ready for the next one. He sat down and forced himself to think everything through. He must, he realized, turn off *Wargentin's* gravity so it wouldn't fight the suit's feeble drive. And he'd better leave early, so he wouldn't overshoot the outer orbit and not have time to correct.

He started toward the suit—then stiffened with a sudden thought.

Gravity . . .

These parked ships didn't drift together, over any ordinary period of time, because their masses were insignificant. But *Wargentin* had gravity—and he could turn it up, fore and aft! Why couldn't he use it to pull two ships together?

Excited, he looked at his chronometer. Nine hours since Junnabl had left. How soon would he be back? It would take many passes to bring the orbits together. At the present distance, the pull would be only a fraction of a G. Did he have time? Would it work at all? He didn't see why not.

He reached for the controls, cranked the viewer around. A quarter-hour to the next pass. "Relax," he growled. "You've got a long job ahead of you."

He made sandwiches and coffee, gulped them down, then paced the compartment. *Wargentin* gradually gained on the other ship. Finally he sat down, turned up the gravity to a full two G's, and let the pressure shove him into the chair. He stared at the screen, though he knew there'd be no visible response in the first pass. He'd been in tight spots, situations where he more than half expected to die within minutes. None of those times, he thought, were worse than this enforced waiting.

But by the fourth pass, the Lenj ship's image was bigger on the screen. And somehow the time came when he turned off all gravity, suited up and went outside.

V

The Lenj ship seemed to creep slowly toward him. Instinct said, "Now!"

He turned on the suit's drive, felt the boot soles press against his braced feet, saw *Wargentin* drop from beneath him. Straight out, he drove—that was the first thing; get out there in plenty of time. Hane was behind him now, and all he saw was the Lenj ship, against a starfield, seeming to grow and to tilt slowly so the stern pointed at him like a cannon coming to bear. His breath was harsh and rapid in his earphones. Was he going to overshoot? He turned off the drive; stabbed a finger at an auxiliary control to turn him head-on; saw that he wasn't badly out of line. Strange, he thought, how that monstrous gravity he couldn't even feel checked his outward drift like a chain. He was in the ship's orbit, now, following her at equal velocity. Hane swung into view ahead. He aligned himself just below the ship and toward the side where she was holed and touched his drive lightly. A minor correction took him within yards of the jagged wound. He maneuvered to face it and used a back-thrust very gingerly. He didn't want to gash the suit's plastic on some metal thorn.

He got in safely, his suit lights making weird shadows in the wrecked compartment. A hatch, leading inward, gaped open, too bent to be closed. But beyond the next compartment was a sound hatch. Once through that, he was in the ship's core, hauling himself along very slowly because the heavy fuel-canisters attached to his suit must be coaxed, not jerked.

He knew where the converter-room would be and found it. Some of the markings he couldn't decipher, but the two charging ports were unmistakable. He moved to them, got into the right position and turned on his suit's footing drive to push his boot soles against the deck. Anchored, he worked clumsily at the port covers until he got them hinged open. Now he detached a canister from his suit, muttering profane thanks to Earth for adopting standard-size fuel bars, wrestled the canister into position so it hung top-down before him. He unscrewed the top, then gave the canister a sharp upward tug. It slid free, leaving the heavy bar suspended. He maneuvered that into the port and, holding himself down with one hand, shoved hard at the bar. It moved sluggishly (but with mass!) into the tube. Through his gloves, he felt the jolts as it tripped the mechanical starters, bringing standby batteries to life. He stood anxiously by watching a panel until a tiny light came on. He let out his breath in relief. The ship had power now, whatever else she might lack. He put the second bar in its port, leaving the third in a rack. "Didn't need a spare after all." He started for the control room.

He flipped master switches and studied telltale lights. The drive wasn't in working order, of course—they'd have seen to that, after parking the ship here. There was no stored air, so he'd have to stay in his suit. And the main computer wasn't working. That latter was bad; he couldn't compute the distance to Hane. He'd have to guess and send several drones (if there were any!) set for various distances and hope one would space-in fairly close.

He studied the console lights, frowning over the alien symbols. That small bank of lights just might be . . . He looked around, saw several closed doors, clumped over to one and opened it. Empty—a suit storage locker. He tried another. This was the communications cubbyhole. He turned on lights. Yes! Those five small ports would be tubes leading to the drone-launching turret! Shakily, he opened one of the ports—and saw the blunt end of a message drone. He released a catch and drew it out. It was about a foot long and three inches thick, with a bulge at the middle. The drive would be there, at the center of gravity. He peered at setscrews mentally translating the Lenj calibrations into miles. Well . . .. He checked the other four ports; found drones in them. He'd send all five, set for distances ranging from twenty to thirty billion miles. If the planet didn't happen to be on the far side of Hane . . ..

He made the settings, locked all the port-covers and studied the controls again before doing anything. He ought to let the drones warm a while longer, anyway. Now—how did he feed his message in? That phone-jack might be where a microphone plugged in—but where was the mike? Hastily, clumsily, he began to search. None here. He fumbled at his suit; unreeled its extension cord; tried the plug. It didn't fit the alien jack. He clumped out to the main console, found no mikes. He went back and hauled a drone out of its nest. Was there a panel that he could hold against the voice-vibrator of his suit helmet? No. These drones had to be fed their messages electronically. He swore and slammed the thing back into its port. Well, they'd space-in and send out their carrier-waves, and just possibly Loob Garka might hear one of them and make the right guesses. He stood in the doorway of the cubbyhole, waiting for Hane to swing into view on the main screen, then pressed the stud that sent the drones to the turret.

A needle flickered on a dial. He stared at it in dismay—he didn't have to read the alien symbols to know what it meant. A ship had spaced-in somewhat close.

Junnabl.

He waited tensely for the Hane to come into position, dead ahead, then stabbed at the firing-stud. He couldn't feel any jar, of course, as the tiny drones leaped away, but five lights blinked on a panel. Barring malfunction, they were locked on Hane now. They'd keep themselves aligned and Translocate as soon as they had velocity. He hoped their drives were strong enough to overcome the monstrous gravity behind them.

He'd done all he could. He went to the viewer, cranked it to find *Wargentin,* saw Junnabl's flagship nestled alongside her. So the pirate knew by now that Wend was gone, or would, after a hasty search of the ship. And as soon as the next pass near this Lenj ship, the whole thing would be obvious.

Wend could, of course, slip out and try to hide in space, but Junnabl's radar would spot him at once. He might as well wait here. He began thinking what he'd do when they came.

Another two hours had fretted by. His suit air reeked of perspiration. A shuttleboat, with two suited figures riding piggyback, was coming cautiously toward the Lenj ship.

Wend waited, peering out one edge of the jagged hole. Gripped in his right hand was the third fuel-bar—as good a club as he'd been able to find, if unwieldly. The two suits detached themselves from the boat and closed in, separating, cautiously. Wend drew back to one side to avoid a flashlight that searched into the hole. Gripping a handhold with his left hand, he got ready to swing the fuel bar with his right.

Time passed, and the temptation was tremendous to peek out; but he resisted it. Finally the flashlight beam stabbed in at a sharp angle and wobbled around the wrecked compartment. He got the fuel-bar moving very slowly. The flashlight itself poked into the hole, and a moment later a suit blocked out the stars. He strained hard at the bar. With painful slowness, it swung around; threatened to tear itself from his gloved hand, so that he had to pull at it very hard. The flashlight beam caught it. The suited pirate went motionless, then, realizing the significance of the slow-motion swing, tried frantically to dodge. But the heavy bar moved on ponderously, sweeping him back out of the hole, sending him in a head-over-heels tumble. Wend was already moving. He launched himself out after the tumbling figure. The flashlight was spinning away uselessly; so was whatever weapon the pirate had held. Wend reached him, got behind him, waited until the balance was right and gave him a shove that sent the pirate spinning anew and Wend shooting feet-first to one side. A rupter beam slashed across the ship's hull, spilling incandescence in a shower. Wend was already curving up and around the hull, working frantically at his drive controls to keep aligned. Another rupter beam missed him narrowly, then he was beyond the hull. He took quick evasive action, straining the suit's drive to push him outward, careful not to move retrograde to the ship because that would mean being pulled down toward the small dark gravity-monster. He got turned so he could see back. The shuttle boat was in sight, waiting for the two suited men to reach it. Junnabl's ship was headed this way. The suit radio was a clamor of harsh Kyshan oaths. Soon the radar would find him. *Well,* he thought savagely, *I gave it a try. And I'm not going to let them take me alive. Junnabl will never know where that cache is!*

But Junnabl—Wend saw presently—had other problems.

Missiles, ghostly in Hane's distant light, were streaking toward the pirate ship. It fought them off desperately with counter-missiles while it leaped into acceleration, out of orbit and away. More missiles pursued. But Junnabl, Wend could see, would get velocity enough to Translocate before ever being hit.

Smaller missiles came after the shuttleboat. It veered frantically, away from them. Wend gasped, "God! Not retrograde!" But already the boat, orbital speed lost, was spiraling down, its drive vastly overworked trying to fight that gravity. It wouldn't go all the way in, of course. But the tidal forces—

He turned on his suit transmitter, then waited to get his voice under control. "Loob Garka? This is Taintless Wend. Do you hear me?"

It took them minutes to make a transmission on his wavelength. "Wend? This is Loob Garka. I have a fix on you. What in hell are you doing? Trying to hijack one of my ships?"

Wend's chuckle was shaky. "I was just guarding her for you. Evidently one of those message drones was close enough."

Loob said amusedly, "You need not have wasted so many. Don't you think I have listening devices out around Hane? But you're lucky they were Lenj drones. That was the only thing that told me where they'd come from!"

VI

The cache hadn't been hard to find, and no harder to dig up. Wend sat with Loob and with Vassun Garka, who was newly arrived from Norp. Wend asked the latter, "What did Junnabl say when he called you?"

Vassun showed his teeth. "He said he had a contract with TSF to pick up cargo for them. He didn't mention you. I was startled, at first. But when I got your letter, I understood. Now, about this division—"

Loob interrupted, "It was a thing I don't like, your giving him Hane co-ordinates. I do not see that we are obligated to keep the agreement."

Vassun said, "We'll give you your fourth, but considering events I'm inclined to agree with Loob about the rest. Can you tell me any reason, other than you already have, why we should send half back to Terra?"

Wend tried to lie casually. "Well, no. Except that the letter I sent you wasn't the only one I sent."

Vassun considered, looking almost pleased. "Ah. And if you are not free to intercept it within a certain time, someone will open it, yes? But you could be bluffing."

Loob took a healthy swig of the refreshments and grinned. "I like a good bluff. And this Earthman is a valuable acquaintance. Let us keep the agreement."

Wend said, "Fine. And you'll make an additional profit buying my fourth from me at your usual scandalous rates. I won't find it convenient stuff to peddle around myself. I'll have to run, and fix up a new alias, since Junnabl's still alive to talk."

Loob veered at Vassun. "You see?" Then he peered at Wend. "I understand you have lost your yacht. Now I happen to have on hand a fine small ship, a rebuilt military scout. I will sell it to you at a very reasonable price."

A FLASK OF ARCTURAN

Date: April 29, 2017.
From: President.
To: Vice Presidents, Regional Managers.
Subject: Loose Handling of Information

THE CHAIRMAN OF THE BOARD has asked me to call to your attention a disturbing laxity in the handling of proprietary Company information. There has been too much casual discussion of Company plans, expenditures, technical processes and formulas. The Chairman and the rest of the Board were quite disturbed that a competitive distiller was able to learn in advance of publication details of our newest advertising campaign based on the virtues of our splendid new hardwood whiskey bottles. This leak of information will force us to spend additional millions of dollars educating the public to the fact that only our particular wooden container, with its special wood unique interior design, confers the benefits described.

We of course want to maintain and promote interdepartmental co-operation and smooth working relationships, but it is considered desirable that there be less fraternization between personnel of different departments. Naturally this will have to be approach with tact and subtlety.

In particular, Technical personnel must stop casually revealing details of secret processes and materials to Sales personnel. Accounting and Sales must stop discussing selling prices, markups, salaries, commissions, etc., with Production and with Research. And Purchasing must stop revealing potential or actual fluctuations in raw material markets, to Sales and Production. This constant hubbub of gos-

sip creates anxieties and dissatisfactions and is definitely in-
imical to the best interests of Interstellar Distilleries, Inc.

The Chairman and I want you to give this your personal attention and to enlist tactfully the co-operation of your department heads and managers.

Cordially,
Ellingsworth J. Pough, President

Date: May 12, 2017.
From: Hdqtrs. Purchasing.
To: Production Manager, Arcturus V.
Subject: Requisition for Pencils.
No. V-744-6-2129.
No doubt subject requisition become garbled in the sub-
space transmission. As received, it calls for 500,000 lead
pencils, medium soft, cedar, yellow lacquered, with red rub-
ber erasers. How many new pencils did you actually want?

I. Haggel.

Date: May 14, 2017.
From: Production Manager, Arcturus V.
To: Hdqtrs. Purchasing.
Subject: Requisition for pencils.
Half a million was right. However, under separate cover I
am entering an additional requisition for another half million, along with ten dozen pencil sharpeners, you know, the
kind you fasten on the wall. Make sure they're good quality
so they won't wear out. It doesn't matter what color the
sharpeners are, but make sure the pencils are exactly as req-
uisitioned, and that the whole shipment gets here by the date
specified.

Otto Stehdenbed.
Prod. Mgr.

Date: May 17, 2017.
From Hdqtrs. Purchasing.
To: Production Manager, Arcturus V.
Subject: Pencils.

We are still not sure we have the figures right, and if we do, we do not think we can approve the requisition. What possible use could you have for that many pencils and sharpeners?

I. Haggel.

Date: May 19, 2017.
From: Production Manager, Arcturus V.
To: Hdqtrs. Purchasing, Att'n I. Haggel.
Subject: Delayed requisition and obstructionist tactics.

If you can't okay the pencils yourself, get the Old Man to do it, and while you're talking to him inform him that the first month's quota of wooden bottles won't be met because you're diddling around with my requisitions. Also ask him to explain to you why my reason for wanting the pencils is none of your damned business. As for the sharpeners, I want them to sharpen the pencils with.

O. Stehdenbed.

Date: May 20, 2017.
From: Shipping· Dept., Earth.
To: Production Manager, Arcturus V.
Subject: Rush shipment. ON 2017-V-93952.

We are shipping this morning, special express, your order for one million pencils and ten dozen sharpeners. It is costing the Company seventeen thousand dollars extra to get these to you by the date demanded. If you had taken the trouble to enter your order a few days earlier, we could have shipped by regular freight.

E. O. Hippus,
Shipping Clerk.

Date: May 25, 2017.
From: Director of Research
To: Production Manager, Arcturus V.
Subject: Request for Development of New Process. Refer NP D No. V-2016-37.

I have your memorandum inquiring as to progress on subject project.

It has been less than thirteen months since you entered this request. Considerable laboratory time has been expended on this project, and a number of promising leads developed. However, press of other work (you yourself have several other requests in) coupled with personnel shortages and a limited budget, have delayed the project. Would you like us to assign it an "A" priority, or perhaps a "B"?

This project deals with a process for hollowing out wooden blocks, leaving a rather complex inner surface. It is regrettable that you find it necessary to be so uninformative as to the process you are currently using. (We presume that this is something you already have in production.) It would help immeasurably if you could at least inform us as to the finished product involved. We can only conjecture from the incomplete specifications you supplied that it is some kind of a food container. If so, you should so advise us so that we may start getting clearance from the Federal and Interstellar Food and Drug Administrations. We are sure you are well acquainted with this Company's liabilities in regard to edible products.

We find that we have used up all the sample blocks of wood you sent us. Since you specify that no other wood is satisfactory, could you send us another supply?

I. Ben Dopenoff, PH. D
Director of Research

Date: May 28, 2017.
From: Director of Sales.
To: President.
Subject: Wooden Bottles Program.

As you know, E.J., we are ready to hit the market with this thing. TV and Feely-Smelly space is all hired, and everything's ready to go, and it's unthinkable that we should fall on our faces now by not having the product ready on time.

I was asking Otto out on Arcturus when the shipment of bottles is coming in. Attached is a Photostat of his reply, which seems to reflect a negative attitude. I know you'll grasp the seriousness of this at once, and will want to make your own inquiries.

Goodwin Grype.

Date: June 2, 2017.
From: Production Manager, Arcturus V.
To: President.
Subject: Goddam wooden bottles.
Yes boss they'll be there. Otto.

Date: June 3, 2017.
From: Headquarters Accounting.
To: Production Manager, Arcturus V.
Subject: Pencils and Sharpeners.
As you know, such items as office supplies must be accounted under Supervisory Overhead. You have erroneously reported a month's usage of pencils and sharpeners under Production Costs.

We are returning your Monthly Operating Report for May, 2017. Please file a Corrected Report promptly so we can clear your books for May.

D. U. Plicate.

Date: June 6, 2017.
From: Special Field-Representative. (Confidential).
To: President (personal).
Subject: Production Manager, Arcturus V.
E.J.: Otto acting oddly. You may have to replace him. I'll be in with a verbal report day after tomorrow.

Date: June 8, 2017.
From: President.
To: Production Manager, Arcturus V.
Subject: Arcturus operations.
Otto, what's going on? WHAT IN HELL'S A PENCIL-BURGER?

Date: June 8, 2017.

From: Vice President in charge of Efficiency Cost Examination.

To: President.

Subject: Savings, office supplies.

E.J.: I'm rather proud of some savings we've been able to effect lately, and I'm sure you'll appreciate having one particularly substantial item called to your attention.

Some of our divisions have been using considerable numbers of lead pencils. Working with our suppliers, I was able to find a new experimental pencil, just coming into production, which is nearly nine per cent cheaper in wholesale lots. Instead of being made from prime solid cedar, this new pencil has a composition moulded around the lead, made from ground waste wood with a synthetic glue binder. As I understand it, the saving results from the use of the substitution of moulding for the old cutting and shaping processes.

We are always alert for opportunities to reduce costs and thus augment our profits. I think we can be forgiven a little pride when we are as successful as we have been in this case.

I.C. Abuck, Vice President.

Date: June 11, 2017.

From: Ex-Production Arcturus V.

To: President.

Subject: Pencilburgers.

Enclosed is my resignation, which I am completing while I'm still able to write.

First of all, let me inform that your shipment of 250,000 wooden bottles will *not* arrive on schedule. They are all ready to go, but I think when you hear about them you won't want to waste shipping costs. We may as well leave them here.

Secondly, I'll explain about the pencilburgers. It's very simple. The only way to make the damned bottles is the way the original samples were made. (If I'd known how those were made I'd never have come out here.) The dominant race on Arcturus V is a race of intelligent termites, about two inches long. That is, the individuals are two inches long. They produce and trade around the galaxy all sorts of carved wooden goods. They're very artistic, and good scientists too in their way. The wood bottles they make have just the right chemistry, and some damned thing in the pattern of their inner surfaces, to give whiskey the mellowness and special boost we advertise.

As you may or may not know, we've been trying for a year to get Research off its fanny to develop some mechanical way of hollowing out the bottles, but they haven't come up with anything, so when the deadline got close I went ahead and contracted with the termites to have them do the work. We take a block of wood and shape it on the outside, then they eat their way in through the neck and shape it on the inside the way it's supposed to be.

About four months ago I discovered that there's something about an ordinary lead pencil from Earth that makes it a great delicacy here. We grind up a pencil, lead and all, except for the little brass part and the rubber eraser. Some of the termites like it without any rubber. Others like it with the rubber sliced or ground up and sprinkled on, like onion in a hamburger. We serve a pencilburger between two small slabs of ordinary local wood instead of a bun.

They don't give a damn about Terran money if they can get pencilburgers instead.

Now, I was very thorough in my requisitions and specified the exact kind of pencils I needed and all, but some jackass went ahead and shipped some new kind that seems to be made out of sawdust instead of good aromatic cedar. I was out in the hills supervising some lumbering when they came in, and no one found out what was happening until over a hundred thousand pencilburgers had been doled out to the termites.

I tell you, E.J., I wouldn't believe it if I hadn't seen it. There was something about those pencils that made the termites absolutely ribald. The word is too mild. Think of the worst drunk you've ever been on, or seen, and multiply it by ten and imagine it went on for seven or eight days.

The first day wasn't so bad. They did carve all sorts of pornographic pictures and mottos on all the wooden buildings, and put a lot of equipment out of commission. The second day they got into the files and ate up all the records. Ordinarily they don't care much for paper, but they were too drunk to care. The third day they attacked personnel. They weren't vicious; just playful. One of their favorite tricks was to eat their way quietly up through the seat of a wooden chair someone was sitting on, and—

But all that we could have stood. On the fourth day we discovered that they'd gotten into the insides of the bottles.

I don't know what the hell they did, but I can describe the results. If you take good whiskey and put it in one of those bottles, the following changes occur within one day:

1. The alcohol content drops to nil.

2. The color changes to sickening green.

3. The taste becomes awful. I can only describe it as tasting like vinegar in which spoiled salt herring have been soaked.

There were other things that happened, but I haven't time to describe them. Everything considered, we're all happy to come through it alive.

I personally am in hiding from the Termite government, with a price on my head. I am also avoiding my former human employees, who seem to blame me for the whole thing. One bunch even went around looking for a rope, but fortunately the drunken termites had chewed them all up.

I'm starting for the hills as soon as I mail this report. I'm taking two loaves of bread I managed to steal from the commissary, and ten of the original sample bottles that are still filled with the good whiskey. I also have in my knapsack a few thousand of the old cedar pencils, with which I hope, after things have cooled down a little, to propitiate the Termite authorities or a least bribe my way to the spaceport. I thought I might head out to the Lesser Magellanic Cloud, or somewhere.

You can apply my last month's salary against the whiskey.
Good-by and good luck,
Otto Stehdenbed

Date: June 15, 2017.
From: President.
To: Vice Presidents, Regional Managers
Subject: Intercompany communications.

Sometimes the stupidity of some of our employees approaches downright treason. I refer to the disastrous and completely unforgivable breakdown in interdepartmental coordination in the recent matter of handling requisitions for our former plant on Arcturus V.

How can we advance, or even stay in business, if our right hands do not know what our left hands are doing?

Of course we don't want to jeopardize the secrecy of any valuable proprietary Company formulas or processes, nor do we want plans, costs, remunerations, etc., bandied about carelessly. But I want each of you to ...

THE DRUG

AMOS PARRY, a regional manager for Whelan, Inc. (Farm & Ranch Chemicals & Feeds), had come to work a few minutes early and was waiting in the lab when Frank Barnes arrived. He saw that the division's chief chemist was even more nervous than usual, so he invested a few minutes in soothing small talk before saying, "Frank, Sales is beginning to push for that new hormone."

Immediately, Barnes came unsoothed. "Bill Detrick was on the phone about it yesterday, Mr. Parry. I'm sorry I was abrupt with him."

Amos grinned. "If you were, he hasn't had a chance to mention it to me yet. But I think we'd better light a fire under the thing. We'll probably get a blast from Buffalo before long. How many men do you have on it?"

"Well, two helping with routine work, but I've done most of it myself, evenings and weekends. I didn't want anybody to know too much about it. Mr. Parry, I'm worried about it."

"Worried? How do you mean?"

"Well—let me show you the litter we've been testing it on."

The pigs were in pens outside the lab. Amos had seen figures on weight gain and general health (the latter was what promised to be sensational) but hadn't seen the animals for two weeks. He eyed the first bunch. "How old is that boar pig?"

"Not quite four months."

Amos was no expert, but he'd spent many hours on customers' farms and he thought the animal looked more mature than that. So did the shoats in the same pen, though they tended more to fat. All of the group had an odd look, certainly not normal for Yorkshires of their age. He thought of wild hogs. "Is it just the general health factor?" he asked.

"I don't think so, Mr. Parry. You remember I told you this wasn't actually a hormone."

"I know. You wanted to call it that for secrecy, you told me."

"Yes, sir, but I didn't tell you what it really was. Mr. Parry, are you familiar with hypnotics? Mescaline, especially?"

"No, I'm not, Frank."

"Well, it's a drug that causes strong hallucinations. This is a chemical derivative of it."

Amos grinned again. "Pipe dreams for hogs?"

He quit grinning as implications struck him. If this thing didn't pan out, after the money they'd spent and the rumors that had seeped out, there'd be some nasty questions from Buffalo. And if it did, and they began selling it . . .

"What would it do to human beings?" asked Amos.

Barnes avoided his eyes. "That's one of the things I'm worried about," he said. "I want to show you another pig."

This one was isolated in its own pen, and it looked even stranger than its siblings. In the first place, its hair was thicker, and black. There was an oddness in its shape and a vaguely familiar sinuousness in the way it moved that made Amos' skin prickle.

"What's wrong with it?" he asked.

"It's healthy except for the way it looks and acts."

"Same litter and dosage?"

"Yes, sir—all of them got just one dose. The effects seem to be permanent."

They were leaning over the fence and the animal was looking up at them. There was an oddity in its eyes; not intelligence exactly, but something unpiglike. Abruptly, it stood up on its hind legs, putting its forefeet against the fence and raising its head toward them. It squealed as if begging for attention. Amos knew that pigs made affectionate pets. Drawn to it as well as repelled, he reached down and patted it, and the squealing stopped.

It was standing too easily in that position, and suddenly Amos recognized what was familiar about it. He jerked his hand away, feeling a strong desire for soap and water. "How long's it been this way?"

"It's changed fast in the last week."

Amos looked toward the doorway of the lab, just inside of which a large black tomcat sat watching them. "Is the cat out here a lot?"

Barnes' eyes went to the cat, widened, and turned back to the pig. He looked as ill as Amos felt.

When Amos got to his office his sales manager was already waiting. His mind only half present, Amos sized up the stuffed briefcase and the wider-than necessary smile as he responded automatically to the amenities. "Just get back?" he asked.

"Early train. Darned planes grounded again." Detrick looked full of energy, though he'd undoubtedly rushed home, shaved, showered and changed, and hurried to the office with no rest. He sat down, extracted papers from the briefcase, and beamed. "Wrote up the Peach Association."

He'll give me the good news first, Amos thought. "Fine, fine," he said. "The whole year?"

"Yep. Got a check from the Almond Growers, too. All paid up now."

"Good," said Amos, and waited. It came. "Say, I was talking to Frank Barnes about that new hormone he's got and he seemed a little negative about it. When do you think we can have it?"

It was a temptation to answer with false optimisms and duck the issue for a while, but Amos said, "The slowest thing will be State and Federal testing and registration. I'd say not less than a year."

Detrick nodded. "Competition's selling more and more stuff that's not registered."

"Fly-by-night outfits and they're always getting caught."

Detrick smiled. "Every night they fly away with more business."

Amos managed a smile, though the argument was old and weary. "We'll put it up to Buffalo if you want to, Bill. You know I can't okay it myself."

Detrick dropped the subject, not being a man to beat his head against a stone wall if there were ways around it, and for the next hour Amos had to listen to the troubles: competition had cut prices on this, upped active ingredients in that, put such an such a new product on the market (Whelan's factories and warehouses already groan under a crippling diversity of products but Sales didn't feel that was *their* problem) and even the credit policies needed revising. But the worst of all was a fifteen-thousand-dollar claim for damage to pear trees, caused by a bad batch of Whelan's arsenical insecticide.

Amos got rid of Detrick with a few definite concessions, some tentative ones, and some standoffs. He made sure no one was waiting to see him and told his secretary he didn't want to be bothered before lunch.

He had a lunch date with a customer and dreaded it—it meant three or four highballs and overeating and an upset stomach later. Before then, though, he had a few minutes to try to get his mind straighten out. He mixed a glassful of the stuff he was supposed to take about now. The Compleat Executive, he thought; with physician and prescription attached. It didn't seem possible that this same body had once breezed through anything from football to fried potatoes.

Mechanically, his mind on the lab's pigs, he got a small bag of grain out of a desk drawer. He hoped nobody (except his secretary, of course) knew he wasted time feeding pigeons, but it helped his nerves, and he felt he had a right to one or two eccentricities.

They were already waiting. Some of them knew him and didn't shoo off when he opened the window and scattered grain on the ledge outside. A few ate from his hand.

It was a crisp day, but the sun slanting into the window was warm. He leaned there, watching the birds—more were circling in now—and looking out over the industrial part of the city. The rude shapes were softened by haze and there was nothing noisy close by. He could almost imagine it as some country landscape.

He looked at his watch, sighed, pulled his head in and shut the window. The air conditioner's hiss replaced the outside sounds.

Not even imagination could get rid of the city for long.

Going through the outer office, he saw that Alice Grant, his secretary, already had her lunch out on her desk. She was a young thirty, not very tall and just inclined to plumpness. She wore her blonde hair pulled back into a knot that didn't succeed in making her look severe, and her features were well-formed and regular, if plain. Amos noticed a new bruise on one cheek and wondered how long she'd stay with her sot of a husband. There were no children to hold her.

"I'll probably be back late," he said. "Anything for this afternoon?"

"Just Jim at two-thirty and the union agent at three."

The lunch didn't go too badly, lubricated as the customer liked it, and Amos was feeling only hazily uneasy when he got back.

A stormy session with his plant superintendent jarred him into the normal disquiet. Jim Glover was furious at having to take the fifteen-thousand-dollar claim, though it was clearly a factory error. He also fought a stubborn delaying action before giving Amos a well-hedged estimate of fifty thousand to equip for the new drug. He complained that Frank Barnes hadn't given him enough information.

Amos was still trembling from that encounter when the union business agent arrived. The lunch was beginning to lump up and he didn't spar effectively. Not that it made much difference. The union was going to have a raise or else. By the time he'd squirmed through that interview, then dictated a few letters, it was time to go home.

He hoped his wife would be out so he could take some of his prescription and relax, but she met him at the door with a verbal barrage. Their son, nominally a resident of the house, had gotten ticketed with the college crowd for drunken driving and Amos was to get it fixed; the Templetons were coming for the weekend; her brother's boy was graduating and thought he might accept a position with Amos.

She paused and studied him. "I hope this isn't one of your grumpy evenings. The Ashtons are coming for bridge."

His control slipped a little and he expressed himself pungently on Wednesday night bridge, after a nightclub party on Tuesday and a formless affair at somebody's house on Monday.

She stared at him without compassion or comprehension. "Well, they're all business associates of yours. I wonder where you think you'd be without a wife who was willing to entertain."

He'd been getting a lot of that lately; she was squeezing the role of Executive's Wife to the last drop of satisfaction. Well, since he couldn't relax with his indigestion there was only one thing to do. He headed for the bar.

"Now don't get tipsy before dinner," she called after him.

He got through the evening well enough, doused with martinis, and the night that followed was no worse than most.

At nine the next morning, the call he'd been expecting from Buffalo came through. "Hello, Stu," he said to the president of the company.

"Hello, Amos. Still morning out there, eh? How's the family? Good. Say, Amos; couple of things. This big factory charge. Production's screaming."

"It was definitely a bad batch, Stu."

"Well, that's it, then. Question is, how'd it happen?"

"Jim Glover says he needs another control chemist."

"Hope you're not practicing false economy out there."

"We wanted to hire another man, Stu, but Buffalo turned it down."

"You should have brought it to me personally if it was that important. It's going to take a big bite out of your year's profit. Been able to get your margin up any?"

Amos didn't feel up to pointing out that Sales wanted lower prices and the union wanted higher wages, so that the margin would get even worse. He described a couple of minor economies he'd been able to find, then mentioned the contract with the Peach Association.

"Yes, I heard about that," said the president of the company. "Nice piece of business. By the way, how you coming on that animal hormone?"

That was the main reason for the call, of course. Detrick had undoubtedly phoned east and intimated that Amos was dragging his feet on a potential bonanza. "I was going to call you on that, Stu. It'll take a year to test and get registered and—"

"Amos, I hope you're not turning conservative on us."

The message was plain; Amos countered automatically. "You know me better than that, Stu. It's the Legal Department I'm worried about. If they set up a lot of roadblocks, we may need you to run interference."

"You know I'm always right behind you, Amos."

That's true, thought Amos as he hung up. Right behind me. A hell of a place to run interference.

He knew exactly what to expect. If he tried to cut corners, the Legal Department would scream about proper testing and registration. Production would say he was pushing Jim Glover unreasonably, and everyone who could would assume highly moral positions astraddle the fence. A ton of paperwork would go to Buffalo to be distributed among fifty desks and expertly stalled.

Not to mention that this was no ordinary product. He realized for the first time that the Government might not let him produce it, let alone sell it. Even as a minute percentage in feeds. If it was a narcotic, it could be misused.

His buzzer sounded, and he was surprised when Mrs. Grant announced Frank Barnes. It was out of character for Frank not to make a formal appointment first.

One look told Amos what was coming. He listened to Frank's resignation with a fraction of his mind while the rest of it mused upon the purposeful way things were converging.

Barnes stopped talking and Amos said mechanically, "You've been part of the team for a long time, Frank. It's especially awkward to lose you just now." It was banal, but it didn't matter; he wasn't going to change the man's mind anyway. He looked closer. The timidity was gone. So were the eyeglasses. A frightening thought struck him. "You've taken some of that drug."

Barnes grinned and handed a small vial full of powder across the desk, along with a file folder. "Last night," he said. "Between frustration with the job and curiosity about this stuff, I yielded to temptation."

Amos took the vial and folder. "What are these for?"

"So you can destroy them if you want to. I've doctored up the lab records to make the whole thing look like a false alarm. You're holding all that's left of the whole program."

Amos looked for signs of irrationality and saw none. "Do you feel all right?"

"Better than you can imagine. But let me tell you what you're up against. I can at least do that for you, Mr. Parry."

"Thanks. Don't you suppose you could call me Amos now?"

"Sure, Amos. First of all, you were right about that pig trying to imitate the cat. He couldn't do much because he only had a pig's brain to work with." He stopped and grinned, evidently at Amos' expression. "I'll try to explain. What is an animal? Physically, I mean?"

Amos shook his head. "You've got the floor."

"All right. An animal is a colony of cells. Different kinds of cells form organs and do different things for the colony, but each cell has a life of its own, too. When it dies a new one of the same kind takes over. But what regulates the colony? What maintains the pattern?"

Amos waited.

"Part of it's automatic replacement, cell for cell. But beyond that there's a control; and it's the unconscious mind." He paused and studied Amos. "You think I'm theorizing. I'm not. That drug broke down some barriers, and I see all this as you see your own fingers moving."

Amos remembered the mention of hallucinations.

Barnes grinned again. "Let's say it's only one per cent awake and walled off from the conscious mind. What would happen if something removed the wall and woke up the other ninety-nine per cent?"

Remembering the pig, it was impossible not to feel a cold seed of belief. Amos dreaded what was coming next; clearly, it would be a demonstration.

Barnes held out his hand, palm up. In a few seconds a pink spot appeared. It turned red, oozed dismayingly, and became a small pool of blood. Barnes let it stay for a moment, then wiped it off with a handkerchief. There no more bleeding. "That's something I can do fast," he said. "I opened the pores, directed blood to them, then closed them, again. Amos, do you believe in werewolves?"

Amos wanted to jump up and shout, "No! You're insane!" but he could only sit staring.

"I could move that thumb around to the other side of my hand," Barnes said thoughtfully. "I'm still exploring, but I don't think even the bone would take too long. You'll notice I don't need glasses anymore."

The buzzer buzzed. Amos jumped, and from habit answered. "Bill Detrick and that customer are here, Mr. Parry," came Alice Grant's voice.

"I—ask them to wait," he managed.

His mind was a muddle; he needed time. "You—Frank— will you stay for a few days?"

"Sure. I'm in no hurry now. And while you're thinking, let me give you a few hints. No more cripples or disease. No ugly people, unless they choose to be. And no law."

"No—law?"

"How would you police such a world? A man could change his face at will, or his fingerprints. Even his teeth. Probably he could do things I can't imagine yet."

The buzzer went again, with Mrs. Grant's subtle urgency. Amos ignored it, yet he hardly knew when Frank left the room.

He realized the chemist had done him a favor. The selfish thing would have been to keep the secret and the boon all to himself; instead, he'd given Amos the choice.

But what was the choice? Suppressing the drug would cost him his job, There was no doubt about that.

He was standing with his back to the door when he heard it open. He turned and faced Detrick's annoyed frown. "Amos, we can't keep this man waiting. He's—"

All of Amos' frustration and the new burden coalesced into rage. He ran toward Detrick. "You baboon-faced huckster!" he yelled. "Get out! Get out! I'll tell you when you can come in here!" He barely caught his upraised fist in time.

Detrick stood petrified, his face ludicrous. Then he came to life, ducked out, and pulled the door shut behind him.

Amos waited no longer; if he had to decide, he wanted the data first-hand. He spread out the file Barnes had left him and looked through it for dosages. Apparently it wasn't critical, so he poured a little of the powder into a tumbler, added water and threw it down. There was a mild alkaline taste, which he washed out of his mouth with more water. Then he sat down to wait.

A monotone seemed to be rattling off trivia; almost faster than he could grasp it, even though it was in his head and not in his ears: "Paris green/ calcium acetoarsenite/beetle invasion Texan cotton/paint pigment/obsolete/should eliminate/compensation claim/ man probably faking infection/ Detrick likes because we only source/felt like hitting him when we argued about it/correspondence Buffalo last year/they say keep/check how use as poison/ damned wife—"

The last thought shocked his intellect awake. "Hey!" Intellect demanded. "What's going on here?"

"Oh; you've broken through," said Unconscious. "That was fast. Fifteen minutes and twenty-three seconds since you drank it. Probable error, one-third second. I've only been awake a few minutes myself. Minute/sixty per hour/ twenty-four hours day/days getting shorter/September/have

raincoat in car/wife wants new car/raincoat sweats plasti-
cizer/stinks/Hyatt used camphor—"

"Hold up a minute!" cried Intellect.

"You want me to stop scanning?"

"Is that what you're doing? Scanning what?"

"Memory banks, of course. Don't you remember the book
we read three years ago? 'Human brain estimated—' Oh, all
right; I'll slow down. You could follow me better if you'd
let me grow some permanent direct connections."

"Am I stopping you?"

"Well, not you, exactly. I'll show you." Unconscious began directing the growth of certain nerve tendrils in the
brain. Amos could only follow it vaguely.

"Fear!" screamed a soundless voice. "Stop!"

"What was that?" Intellect asked, startled.

"That was Id. He always fights any improvements, and I
can't override him."

"Can *I?*"

"Of course; that's mainly what you're for. Wait till I get
these connections finished and you'll see the whole setup."

"FEAR!" shrieked Id. "STOP! NO CHANGE!"

"SHUT UP!" yelled Intellect. It was strange being inte-
grated; Amos found he was aware on two levels simultaneously. While he responded normally to his external environment, a lightning inner vision saw everything in vastly
greater detail. The blink of an eye, for instance, was an
amazing project. Even as commands flashed out and before
the muscles started to respond, extra blood was rushing into
the area to nourish the working parts. Reports flowed back
like battle assessments: these three muscles were on schedule; this was lagging; that was pulling too hard. An infinitesimal twinge of pain marked some minor accident, and
correction began at once. A censor watched the whole opera-
tion and labeled each incoming report: trivial, do not record;
trivial, do not record; trivial, do not record; worth watching,
record in temporary banks; trivial, do not . . .

He felt now that he could look forward to permanent
health, and so far he didn't seem to be losing his identity or

becoming a moral monster (though certain previously buried urges—toward Alice Grant, for instance—were now rather embarrassingly uncovered). He was not, like Frank Barnes, inclined to slip out of the situation at once. He still felt the responsibility to make the decision.

He carried the vial of powder and the lab records home with him, smuggled them past his wife's garrulity (it didn't bother him now) and hid them. He went out with her cheerfully to visit some people he didn't like, and found himself amused at them instead of annoyed. In general, he felt buoyant, and they stayed quite late.

When they did get home, an urgent message was waiting on the telephone recorder, and it jolted him. He grabbed up the hat and coat he'd just laid down.

"What is it?" his wife demanded.

"I've got to go down to the plant." He hesitated; it was hard to say the words that were charged with personal significance. "The watchman found Frank Barnes dead in the laboratory."

"Who?"

"Frank Barnes! My chief chemist!"

"Oh." She looked at him, obviously concerned only with what effect, if any, it might have on her own circumstances. "Why do you have to get mixed up in it?"

"I'm the boss, damn it!" He left her standing there and ran for the garage.

The police were already at the plant when he arrived. Fred's body lay on the floor of his office, in a corner behind some file cabinets, face up.

"What was it?" Amos asked the man from the coroner's office, dreading the answer he expected.

The answer wasn't the one he expected. "Heart attack."

Amos wondered if they were mistaken. He looked around the office. Things weren't disarrayed in any way; it looked as if Frank had simply lain down and died. "When did you find him?" he asked the watchman.

"A little after one. The door was closed and the lights were out, but I heard the cat yowling in here, so I came in to let it out, and saw the body."

"Any family?" one of the city men asked.

"No," said Amos slowly, "he lived alone. I guess you might as well take him to the ... morgue. When can I call about the autopsy?"

"Try after lunch."

Amos watched them carry Frank away. Then he put out the lights and closed up the laboratory. He told the watchman he'd be around for a while, and went to his office to think.

As nearly as he knew, Frank had taken the drug less than twenty-four hours before he had. Death had come late at night, which meant Frank had been working overtime. Why? And why hadn't he been able to save himself?

"Not logical," his unconscious stated firmly. "He should have felt it coming and made repairs."

"This whole thing's a delusion," said Amos dully, aloud.

"No, it isn't," said a peculiar voice behind him.

He whirled and saw the black tomcat grinning up at him. He gasped, wondering if he were completely insane, but in a flash understanding came. "Frank!"

"Well, don't act so surprised. I can tell that you took some yourself."

"Yes—but how—"

"I thought it would be an easy life and I want to stay around here and watch things for a while. There ought to be fun."

"But *how?*"

"I anesthetized the cat and grew a bridge into his skull. It took five hours to transfer the bulk of my personality. It's odd, but it blended right in with his."

"But—your speech!"

"I've made some changes. I'm omnivorous now, too, not just carnivorous—or will be in a few more hours. I can go into the hills and live on grass, or grow back into a man, or whatever I like."

Amos consulted his own inwardness again. "Is this possible? Can a human mind be compressed into a cat's brain?"

"Sure," said Unconscious, "if you're willing to junk all the excess."

He thought about it. "So you're going to stay around and watch," he said to the cat—no, Frank. "An intriguing idea. My family's taken care of, and nobody'll really miss me."

"Except Alice Grant," said Frank cattily. "I've seen the way you look at her. The cat part of me has, I mean. And she looks back, too, when you aren't watching."

"Well," said Amos. "Hm. Maybe we can do something there too."

His own metamorphosis took a lot longer than five hours; he had a much bigger job of alterations to finish. It was nearly two months before he got back to the plant.

He peered in through the window at Detrick, who'd inherited Amos' old office. Detrick was chewing out a salesman. Amos knew what would be happening now; Detrick's ambitious but unsound expansion would have gotten the division all tangled up. In fact, with his sharp new eyes, Amos could read part of a letter from Buffalo that lay on the desk. It was quite critical of Detrick's margin of profit.

The salesman Detrick had on the carpet was a good man, and Amos wondered if he was to blame for whatever it was about. Maybe Detrick was just preparing to throw him to the wolves. A man could hang on a long time like that, shifting the blame to his subordinates.

The salesman was finally excused; and Detrick sat alone with all the frustration and selfish scheming plain on his face. No, Amos thought, I'm not going to turn this drug loose on the world for a while. Not while there are people like Detrick around.

There were no other pigeons on the window ledge except himself and Alice; the rest had stopped coming when Amos disappeared and the feeding ended. For that matter, they tended to avoid him and Alice, possibly because of the abnormal size, especially around the head, and the other differences.

He noticed that Alice was changing the color of her feet again. Just like a woman, he thought fondly.

"Come on, Pigeon," he said, "let's go somewhere else. This tightwad Detrick isn't going to give us anything to eat."

ALL THAT EARTHLY REMAINS

BREATHING A LITTLE HEAVILY in the Andean air, and still dazed at the urgency with which he had been whisked southward (via jet bomber), Dr. Luis Craig walked across packed earth toward a powerful-looking helicopter which, he had just been told, was to take him on the last leg of his trip. He listened tiredly to the unctuous words of his escort, a Lieutenant Rabar who wore the uniform of this Latin American nation's Air Force and who was to fly the helicopter.

Shouts erupted behind them, at the edge of the field. Something snarled at his left ear. The sound was familiar, though not recently so: the crack of a rifle. He hit the dirt.

Another bullet came searching, but now the shouts got themselves organized into crisp Spanish. Sidearms and at least two automatic weapons blatted. There were no more rifle shots. Cautiously he raised his head to look at the knot of uniformed men where the sniper had been.

Rabar stepped forward, offering a hand. "Are you all right, Doctor?"

Craig ignored the hand and got up without help. "Quite, thank you." He had disliked Rabar from the moment of introduction; and now it was in his mind that Rabar stepped carefully away from him *before* the first bullet came.

As casually as he could, he walked to the aluminum ladder hung upon the helicopter's side and hauled himself up. He stopped in the hatch, dignity forgotten, startled at the disparity of the three men already in the ship.

Directly across the cabin sat a gaunt scarecrow of a man in a black priest's hassock. An oxygen mask dangled on his thin chest, suggesting a bloated crucifix. The long, swarthy face was pockmarked, dour and without animation at the moment, except for fierce black eyes that burned steadily into Craig's own. Craig thought of a condor, perched near some nearly ready meal. He was immediately ashamed of the thought.

Forward of the priest sat a brown Indian. His face mirrored dignified resignation to being carried in this hellish contraption to horrible death, or worse.

Occupying the only seat on the hatch side was a tautly uniformed man who eyed Craig coldly.

The priest spoke. His voice was deep and gently strong, caressing the Spanish syllables like a great soft bell. "We are abject, Doctor. We had tried very hard . . . but there are fanatics."

"Eh?" said Craig. "Oh. Well, I am unhurt, as you can see."

"For which, thanks to the Almighty. Our humblest apologies. You speak Spanish exceptionally well, Doctor."

Wondering if there were a question behind the compliment, Craig said, "My mother was Mexican." He did not think it necessary to add that he'd grown up near the border, and had once spent two years as an exchange Professor of Physics at the Mexican university.

The priest nodded once. "I see. It was thoughtful of your government to choose you. And more than kind of you to come. But, forgive me; the shooting has made me forget my manners. This—" indicating the uniformed man—"is General Noriega." He laid a hand on the shoulder of the Indian. "And this one prefers to answer to the name Dientes."

Craig looked at the brown face with interest. Archeology was one of his hobbies, and in this part of the world . . . 'Dientes' was Spanish for 'teeth,' he mused. Abruptly, under his gaze, the immobile face split into a wide nervous smile revealing the source of the nickname. They were large, even and very white.

"And I," the priest was saying, "am called Father Brulieres. Won't you seat yourself?"

Craig tensed in surprise. The name Brulieres had been very much in the news of late. A priest by that name had led

the movement which put the present government in power—
and was still, reputedly, the man who actually ran it.

Craig realized he was still perched awkwardly halfway
into the cabin. Mumbling something, he squeezed his bulky
mountain gear through the hatch and took the empty seat
beside the priest.

Rabar came in, closing the hatch behind him, and went forward to the pilot's seat. He glanced around at his passengers.

It seemed to Craig that he was more interested in faces
than in the condition of seat belts. Rabar worked at switches
and buttons. Engines coughed, then roared. From overhead
came the rising "whoosh" of the vanes. The craft shivered
and lifted.

They went on oxygen at once, and Craig, under the eyes of
the other passengers, was glad to put the breather over at
least part of his face. Imitating the others he pulled down the
earflaps of his helmet. It seemed to have built-in radio, as he
could hear Rabar advising them to strap in. A moment later,
clearing his throat, he discovered that his breather contained
a mike. He was surprised at such advanced electronics here.

They were quickly closed in by mighty cliffs. Below them,
a river tumbled wildly. Where it could find root-holds, fantastic greenery burgeoned, but it did little to disguise the
menacing rock. The cabin's plastic windows gave all too
clear a view.

Turning from the window beside him, Craig found his
eyes wandering to the insignia pinned to the priest's hassock. Of elegantly wrought gold, it was the same emblem
he'd noticed on buildings, vehicles and other government
property here. It looked like a set of football goalposts with
the uprights moved in close together, leaving the crossbar
extending to the sides.

The priest caught his look and gave him what might be intended for a smile. "You wonder about our emblem? It
represents the Church and State standing—what is the expression in your own language? —'four-square' together."

"Oh." Craig realized that the symbol was simply a cross with two posts instead of one. He felt a little annoyed. His own government had told him enough to make him eager to come on this job, but they'd also warned him emphatically not to discuss politics or religion. He supposed the United States needed friends wherever they could be found, but a dictatorship wasn't his notion of a good alternative to Bolshevism.

He realized that the warning had a point. He didn't know how ruthless these people might be, but the shooting back at the airfield hadn't been any game of marbles. For that matter, the whole country, or what he'd seen of it, had an armed-camp air.

He decided the thing to do was to concentrate on the scientific reason for his visit, and now was as good a time to start as any. He leaned toward Brulieres, then realized that wasn't necessary. "Er—are you at liberty to tell me anything about the explosion?"

Brulieres eyed him for a moment, and again there was the hint of a smile. "We could hardly be secretive with *you,* Doctor. You are the expert. How much were you told?"

"Just that there'd been a nuclear explosion of unknown origin. They said there was something spectacular about it."

"Spectacular? *Si!* Your government was gracious enough to accept our request for technical help without demanding details. Security is very difficult, as you comprehend." Brulieres looked absent for a moment. "The explosion occurred at a spot famous in pre-Christian legends, which is why friend Dientes accompanies us. He is considered *experto.*" The intense eyes turned upon the Indian, with a hint of mischief. "Not that he fails to be a good Christian as well."

The Indian crossed himself nervously.

"The explosion," Brulieres went on, "seems to have uncovered some very ancient tunnels. We wish to explore them, but we felt we needed a nuclear physicist along. Especially since there appears the possibility that the explosion originated from the tunnels."

Craig heard Noriega clear his throat. Brulieres glanced at Noriega. "It has also been suggested," the priest said, "that the uncovering of the tunnels is coincidental, and that the explosion was of foreign origin."

Craig thought that over, and was annoyed. "That does not seem likely," he said, a little stiffly. "Nobody is tossing live warheads around."

Noriega spoke for the first time. His voice was crisp and rather high. "You can perhaps speak for your own nation, Doctor Craig; but others too possess missiles."

Brulieres interposed, "You no doubt know, Doctor that a communist putsch very nearly took over this country. The present government has been compelled to very strict measures against a further attempt. Therefore we are not popular with the communist nations."

Craig waved a hand impatiently. "Yes, I know that, but . . ." He realized he was being careless. "I only wish to approach my investigation with an open mind. You say the tunnels were ancient? Incan, perhaps?"

Brulieres shook his head slowly. "They were hardly capable of anything on this scale. One cannot speak so surely so surely of those who preceded the Incas in this place."

Craig pondered, and felt his pulse move faster. "How much have you learned so far?"

"What can be seen from the air. We will be the first to land, if you decide it is safe."

II

They rose with the canyon, and its upper ramparts began to display patches of snow. Ahead loomed solid whiteness. They strained upward and emerged over a snowfield glaring white in the sun, its jagged peaks casting crisp blue shadows. The copter's own shadow danced along beneath them like a crazy gnat.

They aimed for a cluster of five or six peaks dominating everything else. Dientes, twisting nervously in his seat, mumbled something about *"puesto de los demonios."* They flew between two of the peaks and were in a basin formed by the roughly circular cluster.

Zero ground of the explosion was as obvious as an ugly dark blotch on white cloth. Snow had been melted away from an oblong area on the inner slope of one peak, leaving naked rock. Craig stared at what lay revealed. A plateau was carved out of the mountainside, so flat and so precisely oval that there wasn't an instant's doubt that it was artificial. The uphill wall was vertical, following exactly the curve of the ellipse. The wall was in shadow, but Craig could make out the five black tunnel mouths, all of a shape and evenly spaced.

He let out his breath in a grunt as he remembered that this was a blast area and that they were getting close. Hastily, he unhooded one of the instruments, his fingers awkward with excitement. He watched the dial. No serious radiation yet. Rabar looked at him, and he nodded his head to indicate they could go closer.

The radiation increased a little but was still mild. He pondered. The blast had been very clean, and of a low order, melting the snow without even scarring the rock. Apparently it had occurred not far above the surface and over the center of the plateau. He didn't know of any existing warheads that fit the explosion, nor could he believe that either intent or coincidence had placed the blast so exactly.

The copter was hovering now, the other passengers watching him silently. He met Rabar's eyes, and glanced away, uncomfortable. If the priest's eyes reminded him of a vulture's, then Rabar's made him think of a wolf's. They had an odd yellowish tinge, and were at one time alert and devoid of expression. Craig couldn't know where the man fit into things, but he didn't ring true as a simple pilot.

Craig needed no diagrams drawn for him, so far as his own position went. In the first place, the opposition might assassinate him simply to embarrass the government. On the other hand, if he seemed to stand in the way of Noriega's project of making political capital of the explosion, and if Noriega represented a strong faction in the government, that faction might think it worth while to let something happen to him and blame it on the communists.

But the hottest potato of all would be whatever he learned at the spot of the explosion. He could imagine all sorts of fabulous things. So would others, and some of them would go to considerable lengths to know.

An instrument, dangled at the end of a line, showed no bad radiation, so Craig said they could land.

When he stood on the plateau the tunnel mouths seemed like converging black stares. Nevertheless he itched to explore. Impatiently, he led the unloading and stacking of his equipment.

When that was done the group stood for a minute, evidently all feeling the awe Craig did. Dientes was first to break the silence, muttering something under his breath.

Brulieres fixed the Indian with a look that was not entirely severe. *"Christian* prayers, *hijo,* if you please." He turned to Craig. "What can be learned where we stand?"

"I should be able to determine the type of explosion. I will have to take rock samples, and set up some apparatus."

"How long will that require?"

"Less than an hour, with luck."

Brulieres was thoughtful for a while. "In that case, I believe we shall begin reconnoitering the tunnels while you work. But first, let us hear from our expert in demonology."

Dientes squirmed guiltily in his mountain clothing. "I know only what the old tales say, Padre."

"Tell us, if you please. We will decide later whether you have been guilty of *paganismo.* "

"Si, Padre. This place is the home of the Fire Devils. There is no question of the fact. It is precisely as described when I was a small boy sitting at the feet of *los viejos.* "

"Well, then. What manner of devils were they?"

"Creatures of fire, Padre, such that the eye could not behold without being blinded. Brighter than the sun."

"Did they make war upon your people?"

"Those who approached this place were punished with spears of fire. It is told that in ancient times, they were often seen flying through the sky, trailing long tails of white feathers. Sometimes they visited the villages, demanding strange things and frightening the people."

"Do the stories mention these tunnels?"

"No, Padre. The Fire Devils lived beneath the snow. They were seen to vanish into it."

"Without melting it?"

"They could turn off their fire, perhaps. In any event, Padre, who knows what is possible with demons?"

"I know that you need and will receive many hours of strict Christian instruction. How is it that men returned to tell of these things if the devils pursued them with spears of fire?"

"Some escaped."

"Is it definitely told of individuals who were killed?"

Dientes looked thoughtful, and disappointed. "I do not recall the names of any who were slain."

"Bah. Why have there been no reports in recent years?"

Dientes shrugged. *"Quien sabe?* Perhaps the arrival of the true religion has driven away the devils."

"Perhaps," said Brulieres, the corners of his mouth lifting slightly. He turned toward the tunnels. "I think, General, that I will ask you and the lieutenant to explore a little way into one of the tunnels. Come out at once if you see anything that might be dangerous."

Craig opened his mouth to protest, but held back the words. He did ache to get into the tunnels, but he wasn't a free agent here. He watched as the two uniformed men disappeared into the middle tunnel. Their flashlights were quickly lost as they rounded some turn in the tunnel.

Brulieres said to Dientes, "The doctor and I must take some samples of the rock. Will you be good enough to remain here and guard the helicopter?" He laid his hand on the Indian's shoulder. "I see that you are not comfortable in your helmet. You may remove it if you wish. We will call to you if we need you."

Craig realized Brulieres wanted to talk to him alone. He went with the priest. The Indian squatted, apparently quite comfortable without his oxygen. "He is used to high altitudes," Brulieres remarked. "You or I could hardly remain conscious here. I wished to talk to you, Doctor."

"About what, Padre?" Craig felt a little awkward with the title.

"About certain things in our country of which you do not approve."

Craig hesitated. "I . . . am here on a scientific mission."

"Nevertheless, you have ideas in the field of politics? I hope we can be frank with each other."

"Well . . . I have no intention of being critical. As you know, we—that is, in the United States the Church is separate from the government."

The corners of Brulieres' mouth quirked. "What you mean, perhaps, is that you do not understand how the Church can support a totalitarian government. Oh, do not protest; the facts are obvious. We have been called worse names than 'totalitarian.' You do not think it right that the Church should take up actual arms."

"I—yes. Since you put it into words. We have a different concept of religion."

The priest nodded slowly. *"Si.* Once I visited your land. In a way, I envied the priests there. Here, we have had more to contend with than the christening of fat babies and listening to trifling sins of appetite. We are in the front line of battle."

Craig said stiffly, "Do you mean a spiritual battle, or an ideological one?"

This time Brulieres nearly smiled. "Are you so certain, then, that they are not the same battle?"

Damn it, thought Craig, I know better than to argue with a priest. He did not answer for a minute.

Brulieres said gently, "Please forgive me if I am too direct. You do not believe that Evil is a real force?"

Craig could not meet the penetrating eyes. The old doubt edged into his mind: what if he's right and I am wrong?

What if there *is* a personal God? He pushed the thought away, telling himself as he always did that it was just the exposure he'd suffered before he was old enough to think for himself. He said, "I'm a scientist, Padre."

"But not, unless I misjudge you, an atheist?"

"I call myself an agnostic, if you must classify me. I recognize the possibility of some force behind life and mind. I do not believe in a God who is a man with a beard. Nor do I believe in a Devil with hooves and horns."

Brulieres nodded again "We are not so far apart as you may suppose, Doctor. Myself, I have always though that one who claimed perfect faith without the trace of doubt, was either an idiot or a liar. God surely has his reasons for not removing all doubt. In any case I wish to make my position clear to you. It was not happily that I took up what weapons were at hand. Had I the choice, I would choose quite differently." He eyed Craig directly for a moment. "The battle is very real and very clear to me, Doctor. I have done what I must. I hope you will believe that."

Craig's skeptical mind told him that this was just a play for a good press when Craig got home.

His emotions though, wouldn't go along. They cried out that he was looking upon sincerity.

III

The first tests confirmed what Craig had already presumed; that the explosion had been absolutely clean. What radiation existed had originated from molecules in the rock itself or in the vaporized snow.

There was no way of guessing at the type of blast; he only knew that mass had been transformed virtually one hundred per cent into energy in a very short period of time. No process Craig knew even approached it.

He stared again at the tunnel mouths. He was sure now that something had come out of them, risen about seven hundred feet above the plateau and released the blast. He trembled with eagerness to get inside, danger or no.

He had turned impatiently to Brulieres, when somewhere deep in the tunnels, shouting broke out. Two pistol shots echoed hollowly. There was a clatter of running footsteps. Craig found his right hand fumbling at his hip, and felt foolish. He hadn't carried a sidearm since Korea.

Lieutenant Rabar burst from the tunnel, stumbling in the sunlight, his face contorted. He ran straight across the plateau and threw himself over the edge. Dientes, who had jumped to his feet, was only a step behind him. Craig, eyes fastened on the tunnel, realized vaguely that the two must have landed in deep snow, since there was no sound of their falling.

A glow appeared in the tunnel. Craig fought the panic that seized him; stood his ground and was aware of Brulieres beside him. The glow brightened.

Its source came into sight—a ball of dazzling brilliance, oval and about the size of a man's torso. It emerged into sunlight and Craig saw that it was solid. It looked like incandescent metal, but he somehow felt that it wasn't hot. It seemed to move at will and to hover without support.

It acted alive.

It moved a little way toward Craig and Brulieres, then stopped. A tentative rumble came from it, like the beginning of thunder. Something like a tentacle lifted, clutching an object that resembled a flashlight. A blinding lance of heat shot from the object and struck the rock a few yards in front of the two men. A sound came from the rock like ice pressed upon a hot stove. Smoke puffed upward. The beam lasted only an instant, but it left a long curved scar in the rock.

The thing rumbled again, and flashed so brightly Craig threw an arm over his eyes, and heard his own voice cry out wordlessly. His legs tensed to run, but something about the behavior of the thing held him where he was. It seemed unsure of itself, and not really threatening.

When he looked up again, it was moving laterally and up the face of the wall. He saw the flashlight-like object on the ground where it had evidently been dropped.

The oval thing, no longer glowing, lifted fast toward the mountain top. He saw that it was metal, not rusted or cor- roded but dull with age, and he saw the two ragged holes near the middle of it. He strained his eyes for more detail but it grew tiny in the distance and he saw no joints and no pro- tuberances other than the one tentacle. He lost it in the shad- ows of the mountain's brow, then saw it flash momentarily in the sun as it curved up and over.

After a moment he turned dazedly toward Brulieres. But before he could say anything there was a sun-dimming flash of light from beyond the mountain. The ground danced. Sound, echoing from the other peaks and battering its way through the solid rock of the mountain, beat about them like monstrous punishing wings.

As the vast thunder dwindled away, Craig, squinting, saw a tenuous, rapidly dimming mushroom cloud tower above the peak. He flinched, but knew that this would another clean explosion. Most of the cloud was steam. He was sure they were seeing a re-enactment of the blast which had cleared this plateau.

His mind worked in simple patterns: the thing was de- stroyed; it had dropped its weapon.

He started toward the tunnel mouth, but he had hesitated too long. Brulieres, moving very agilely, was ahead of him.

The priest picked up the weapon and turned toward Craig. Craig, still befuddled, wondered mildly at his own detached state of mind: is he going to kill me; I'd love to get that weapon home to the labs; so that's how he keeps warm. (The latter in reference to the heavy underwear he'd glimpsed be- neath the priest's cassock as the padre bent over).

But Brulieres' voice was mild. "Please forgive me for tak- ing possession of this, Doctor. Later, I hope, you will be able to examine it; but I must think first of my own responsibili- ties." He looked at the thing briefly, started to stow it in some fold of his gown, then hesitated. As if unable to resist the temptation, he aimed it at the rock wall and put his thumb on something.

The incandescence squirted out. The rock cried out and yielded up a curl of smoke.

Brulieres turned the thing off at once and turned back to Craig with an expression half guilty; half delighted, like a child with a forbidden toy. Then he sighed and put the weapon away.

Craig had observed what details he could. The thing was an inch or a little more in diameter, perhaps ten inches long. All except one tip was dull and apparently knurled to give a good grip. The tip looked like quartz or some crystal, translucent except the end, which was darkly transparent when not emitting the beam. The trigger was apparently a spot of different color on the body, over which the thumb could be pressed.

Craig thought of the energy stored in that slender cylinder, the necessary insulation, the efficiency of whatever system was used to direct and control the beam. He felt a chill shiver of awe. Then another thought struck him and he looked wide-eyed at Brulieres. "A flaming sword!"

Brulieres gave him a quick glance, and nodded. "Primitives might describe it so."

Rabar climbed back into sight at the edge of the plateau, looking pale. A moment later Dientes poked his head into view.

"Where is the general?" Brulieres demanded.

"Muerto," said Rabar shakily, "in the tunnel. The creature killed him."

The priest's face twitched. "Who shot at it?"

"The general, Padre. He had the only gun."

Brulieres sighed. "Then that is why he is dead. The creature would not have harmed him."

Craig had the same idea. It had used the weapon more as if in bluff, and had apparently carefully gone beyond the mountain to die. He wondered if the two bullet-holes had killed it.

But how many more of the creatures (or machines) waited in the tunnels?

He looked at Brulieres. "Are we going in?"

"By all means. Unless we are stopped." The priest looked thoughtful. "They may be coming out of hibernation or something like it. Can you tell how old this plateau is?"

"Not without taking samples to a geological laboratory. Perhaps not even then, with accuracy. But I would say, some thousands of years."

Rabar was not happy at reentering the tunnel, but set his jaw and came. Craig stood aside to let the lieutenant go ahead of him. Rabar hesitated, then stepped by. Dientes, crossing himself and muttering, evidently preferred coming along to being left alone outside. He followed Craig.

Brulieres swept his flashlight along the tunnel walls, revealing a turn ahead. They rounded it. After a little way it seemed to Craig that the flashlight dimmed. Then he realized that there was other light in the tunnel; the arched ceiling was aglow. It got brighter and Brulieres turned off his flashlight.

"Evidently," he said, "we are expected. Have you noticed the air?"

Craig had not, but he did now; it was warm and the pressure was higher than outside. "One moment," he said, puzzled. He went back to the mouth of the tunnel. As he stepped outside, he felt a gentle resistance as if some force were pushing him into the tunnel. He re-entered, and felt warmth radiating from the ceiling. He rejoined the others.

The floor of the tunnel sloped up gently for a while, then leveled, then turned downward. The walls were vertical and perfect, with a smooth glazed look. The ceiling curved from wall to wall in a perfect arc. There was room for two men to walk side by side by crowding. Craig walked a little behind Dientes.

Soon he took off his oxygen mask and breathed normally. He would have liked to remove his jacket, but there were too many things in the pockets to spill out.

He had counted one hundred seven paces when the tunnel turned again. It was just beyond the turn that they found Noriega's body.

The tunnel branched here; or at least, a narrower tunnel angled up and off from each side. These tunnels were dark, and, Craig found, cold with low air pressure. The same mild resistance guarded their mouths. The General lay sprawled loosely just inside the right-hand branch, head and torso in shadow. He looked simply and peacefully dead.

"Will you lend me a hand, Lieutenant?" Brulieres said. The two of them dragged Noriega into the light.

Craig could see no burns nor any other kind of wound except an abrasion on one cheek which might have resulted from a fall. He started to ask Rabar exactly what had happened, but checked himself. Better not appear suspicious.

He wondered what had happened to the general's pistol, and began to look around it. But again Brulieres was ahead of him. The priest eighteen or twenty yards farther into the tunnel, picking up something. It was the pistol. It went into the cloak as the heat-weapon had.

Craig was watching Rabar and he thought the man looked disconcerted. Craig thought, how's this for a theory: Rabar killed Noriega, took his pistol and started up the tunnel. Maybe he just wanted to learn for himself what was in the mountain, or maybe he planned to murder the rest of the party and make it look like an accident. He met the glowing creature, panicked, put two bullets into it, then dropped the gun and ran.

Craig wondered if the priest shared his doubts about Rabar; but if he did, he didn't show it. The priest was already starting on.

Craig lost count of his steps, but judged they'd gone over a quarter of a mile when the tunnel took a final right angle turn and opened into a great high-domed chamber.

IV

Immediately all question as to the nature of this place vanished. It could only be a military base.

There's something recognizable about weapons, Craig mused, no matter how unfamiliar. Here were gathered great vehicles of war, bristling with the outsize cousins of the heat-tube Brulieres carried and with a myriad other menacing shapes. Yawning black tunnels led away at angles— probably, Craig thought, to hidden exits. Repair machines, some with their work partly finished, were scattered everywhere, silent and with a long-unused air about them. Nearly all of the aerial dreadnaughts (Craig was sure they were that) showed terrible wounds.

The group stared about the chamber in silent awe.

At one place, beneath a trio of round tunnels that aimed steeply upward, was what Craig took to be the main launching area, with ramps for loading ... what? The litter showed clearly where great ships had rested, and that the departure had been hasty. Craig drew in deep trembling breaths and imagined the vast alien argosies lifting upon their mysterious legs of force.

He could see the avarice in Rabar's eyes, and edged closer to the lieutenant. He wasn't going to let the man overpower Brulieres and take the weapons, nor was he going to let him pick up any that might be lying around. Not that Brulieres was being careless. Craig noticed that he kept his distance from everybody, and did not turn his back for long.

They must have stared at the alien machines for quite a while before the priest's deep voice echoed in the chamber. "Come. Another tunnel beckons."

Craig looked where the priest pointed. He saw a tunnel like the one they'd left, about a quarter of the way around the chamber. It glowed with light. All the rest were dark.

He looked again at Brulieres, and was startled at the man's face. It wore a look of glory. Craig shivered. Why, he thought, the man thinks God arranged this for *him*.

Apparently *someone* was arranging things, unless the tunnels and the lights were completely robotic. Craig, ignoring the edge of panic that cut at him, followed the priest toward the entrance to the lighted tunnel.

It was short, with two bends in it (probably, Craig thought, to contain possible explosions). It opened into a smaller, lower-ceilinged chamber which had evidently been an assembly hall for troops, or possibly a mess hall. Dark openings led off it which might lead to barracks. In the far end, a single tunnel glowed with light.

They entered that tunnel, which was another short one, and found that they were indeed in the living quarters. These, if the analogies applied, had been the officers'. There was a small assembly hall, and upon one wall of that were the pictures.

The lighting was arranged to fall mostly upon that side of the chamber. The rock had been smoothed to take the murals. The first glimpse shook Craig so that he walked mechanically toward that wall, momentarily forgetting his companions.

A part of his mind admired the basic technique. Outlines in low relief had been cut into the rock, details delicately etched in and colors brought up, apparently, by altering the composition of the rock itself. As for the style it was somewhere between realism and impressionism. Craig was no expert, but he thought the hand was defter, the viewpoint more penetrating, than any he'd ever seen. The slight alien air only increased the charm of the work.

Whatever sort of beings the aliens had been, they hadn't been an unfeeling race. Emotion leaped from every line of the murals.

The first few told concisely of the establishment on Earth of this outpost, of the local defeat and abandonment. There were some heroic scenes there, but Craig hurried through them, drawn to the next series of paintings, yet unwilling to turn his eyes to them.

They were Biblical and as stunningly familiar as if he'd lived with them all his life.

Feeling churned at his insides again.

One of the first immortalized Noah, or whoever had been the actual hero of the first version of the Flood story. The painting of the sea and the dark doomsday clouds over it was so real that Craig took a step backward. Mountainous wave masses were battered white by an incredible rain. Heaved aslant, decks tumbling water, dwarfed by the seas, was the wooden ship, A few half-drowned domestic animals stared in terror, lashed to their pens on deck. The bearded man who stood on wide-planted giant's legs, rope-like fingers gripping a tiller that strained to escape, was bedraggled but staunch and muscled to meet the sea. A woman clung to one arm. She had been painted not delicately, but with a strong beauty that spoke in thunder of the artist's piercing compassion.

There was the crossing of the Red Sea, and the painting showed clearly how some force held aside the water. The artist had evidently been fascinated by the still-puddled sea bottom.

There were more, but Craig passed them, drawn like a fish on a line to the painting of the man on the cross. The body, more cruelly punished than the Bible recorded, strained in an agony that communicated itself to Craig's own. The face, twisted with pain, sagging with exhaustion, the tortured soft brown eyes, held no bitterness, no accusation.

The accusation was the painting itself. The bitterness and rage (and remorse?) was the painter's own.

Craig, frightened and miserable, looked at the others. Dientes showed only awe and humility. Rabar was holding himself tautly, but terror showed in his eyes. Brulieres shook with overflowing emotions, his face mirroring worship, glory, worry and doubt. He met Craig's eyes. His voice higher-pitched and cracked with feeling, he said, "Have you noticed—this?"

He was standing before a vertical slab of rough stone which had obviously been used to close up a tunnel. The sealing had been done with melted rock, roughly, leaving a groove around the edge. The job suggested haste. Craig's insides writhed at what might lie behind the slab.

He gripped himself, walked over beside the priest. He could make out only a few of the characters of the inscription burned into the slab. He heard his own voice asking, as if from far away, "Do . . . you read Hebrew?"

Brulieres let out a trembling sigh. "With difficulty." He moved slowly closer to the slab, put his fingers to the inscription like a blind man feeling for Braille. Craig saw that his eyes were full of tears. The thin lips mumbled inaudibly.

After a long time Brulieres quit reading and stood there, unmoving. Then he started to speak. His voice was lifeless now, a low uncaring monotone. "Scholars will translate it better, but here is the gist of it."

TO THE DESCENDANTS OF THOSE WITH WHOSE DESTINY I HAVE BRIEFLY MEDDLED: WHEN YOU READ THIS, YOU WILL HAVE ATTAINED A TECHNOLOGY OF YOUR OWN WHICH WILL BE ABLE TO MAKE USE OF THE DEVICES LEFT HERE. ASIDE FROM THEM I LEAVE YOU MY GOOD WISHES, MY APOLOGIES, AND MY LOVE.

WHEN MY RACE ABANDONED THIS PLACE I HID FROM THEM AND STAYED BEHIND BECAUSE I HAD FALLEN IN LOVE WITH YOUR PLANET AND YOUR RACE. I HAVE TRIED TO HELP YOU. I AM NOT SURE I HAVE DONE WELL.

LOOK UPON MY REMAINS IF YOU WILL.

Craig gripped the priest's arm, heard his own words tumbling out: "It proves nothing, Padre! There can still be a God!" He found that he meant it desperately.

The priest turned, stared at him, then looked faintly amused. "Conviction? *Now?* You are a more fortunate man than I."

"No, Padre! Your work! Religion is deeper than . . ."

Brulieres' eyes flashed with some of their old vitality. "My work? This is the God in whose name I have schemed and, Heaven help me, killed." Slowly, mechanically, Brulieres drew the heat-weapon from his garments. He aimed it at the groove around the slab and thumbed the trigger. The rock skirled, and ran to solidify in waxlike lumps. The smoke was acrid in Craig's nostrils.

When the slab was mostly cut around, some inner seal gave way and air sucked loudly into the crack. With a wrenching sound, the slab tore loose. It tilted under some power of its own, and lowered itself to the floor.

Lights, harshly angled and dramatic, flashed on in the small room beyond. It was bare except for the stone platform on the floor, and what rested upon it.

Mechanically, Craig stepped in and moved aside to make room for the others. Brulieres went to the opposite side of the platform and Dientes crouched beside him. Rabar stood hesitantly in the doorway.

The creature was larger than a man and like nothing earthly; many-limbed, built as if for a higher gravity. There was no apparent decomposition or desiccation. The atmosphere of the chamber had evidently been chosen to preserve.

There was still a pungent, half-unpleasant smell, being rapidly drawn away through ducts in the ceiling. There was a face of a sort, and two closed eyes. The face was recognizably strong. The thing might have been called ugly but Craig found a handsomeness about it too. He recognized the drama with which the body was arranged and lighted, and somehow for this last small vanity he loved the creature even more.

Dientes clutched at the priest's robe. "It is a lie, Padre!" And, as the priest remained silent, Dientes turned desperate eyes to Craig. "Mother of God! Will no one say it is a lie?"

Craig fell emotionally depleted. Inside him were a sick regret and a hollowness where something had died, but cold reason remained. If there is no God, he thought, we're just intelligent animals, and we're free to live by our wits. If there is no God, then there is no Devil either.

He pondered that ... and decided with grim amusement that there was Devil enough.

And, in any event, there were needs and desires, friends and enemies. He stepped swiftly around the alien and took the heat-weapon from the priest's limp fingers. He turned toward Rabar, who was (beyond any worthwhile doubt) an enemy, and who was standing in the doorway with an annoying mockery in his eyes. Of *course* he's happy, Craig thought; he's a Bolshevik agent and an atheist. There'll be damned little religion anywhere, now.

He raised the weapon calmly, every nerve and muscle alert, like an animal ready for action. He watched the triumph fade from Rabar's eyes. As his thumb felt unhesitatingly for the trigger, he watched the growth of fear.

SOMEWHERE IN SPACE

I

"I'll come to thee by moonlight, though hell should bar the way." —Noyes.

AS A MAINTENANCE FOREMAN, Ben Auley was close enough to the higher echelons of Tele Ports, Inc., to sense anxiety. In consequence, he was apprehensive as well as puzzled when he was handed a sealed and unmarked envelope, containing a note directing him to report to the General Manager's office.

The receptionist looked at the note, then at him, and took him in to the boss. Ben accepted the boss's handshake and replied mechanically to the brief amenities.

The boss said, "We have you listed as single and without encumbrances. Is that still true?"

"Why, yes; it is, sir—I suppose."

"No serious lady friends?"

"Er, no. Not really."

The boss looked at him for a few seconds, then said, "We have a job for you that may possibly be dangerous. We don't think so, but it may. It's important. If you take it, there's a lifetime pension for you at full pay, above what you may earn if you don't want to retire now. A long vacation, if you want it, and a better job afterward. How does that strike you?"

Ben tried not to look bewildered. "Why, I don't know, sir. I'd have to—can you tell me more about it?"

"I can't, Ben. Unless you accept. Only that it probably involves a series of routine trips and maybe one that won't be routine." He eyed Ben, and continued, "You were on the crew that set up the Uranus station. We have the impression you're—well, an adventurous sort."

Ben didn't find the description unflattering, but it occurred to him that if this assignment he was being offered was worth so much to the company, it might actually be dangerous. Still, the boss had the reputation of being a man you could trust. And the money and the leisure, if he wanted it . . . He said, a little sooner than he really intended, "I'll take it."

The boss grinned briefly, then said, "Okay, here it is. In the last eleven months we've lost nineteen passengers. I mean it literally, *lost* them. They apparently arrived at their destinations and punched the 'Clear' buttons, and that's the last trace we have of them. What do you think of that?"

Ben sat for a minute, dumbfounded. The system was supposed to be reliable to a stupendous number of decimal places. He knew that a few people had suffered hysteria, and that one man, despite the careful health checks, had died of a heart attack. Those things weren't faults of the equipment. But nineteen people . . .! He said, "I had no idea, sir. I—it's hard to believe I wouldn't have heard something."

"We haven't publicized it. After all, the people have just disappeared. They may be walking around somewhere, perfectly safe."

"But the relatives!"

The boss smiled again, grimly. "There aren't any."

"I beg your pardon, sir?"

"No relatives. Oh, a few of them did list next-of-kins— cousins or something like that—but nothing close. You might say these people are unmissables."

"But haven't there been investigations?"

"Of course. But the government's helped us hush it up. I'd rather not think that's because we'll be paying most of the insurance to the government, if it comes to that. Only two of the missing people have beneficiaries. Besides—" the boss hesitated— "I shouldn't tell you this, and I want you to clam up about the whole thing; but two of the men were government agents, travelling incognito."

Ben was still dazed. "I'm very sorry to hear it, sir. But how do I fit in? After all, we've ported millions of people in eleven months. The chances of my stumbling onto anything are pretty small, if you just have the idea of porting me around."

"Not as small as you think, Ben. You fit the category. Young; bigger, more athletic than average; and no troublesome connections. And they've all been trips beyond Mars."

"Oh!" Ben sat up straighter. The implications were clear enough. "But—I'm not welching, sir—if something—I mean somebody—has been kidnapping passengers, won't they spot me?"

The boss smiled the grim smile again. "They, as you put it, seem to have swallowed the two government men. You'll go under a false set of data too. And your baggage will include some innocent-looking tourist's stuff, cameras and whatnot that will actually be weapons. And tools, in case it's some kind of equipment tampering you can fix."

Nearly two months later, prepared for his twenty-third trip of the assignment, Ben stood, nude and itching a little from the antibiotic spray, and watched the machine before him. The data had already been sent ahead. Now the red lights glowed as his baggage, in the small compartment set aside for it, was probed and catalogued down to its last sub-matter particle for transmission. Ben, though he was a practical engineer rather than a theoretician, knew about as much concerning the process as anyone.

It was not Terran technology. It was one of the miracles discovered on Mars, abandoned there by some race not native to that planet or, so the experts said, to the solar system. Man, with his quick grasp of a new toy, had adopted it and used it without understanding the principles on which it was based.

The red lights went out and the screen showed the message, "Baggage received at destination. Ready for passenger."

He lowered himself into the coffin-like chamber that opened for him and lay relaxed, waiting for the lid to close. It was arranged to slide shut slowly, while the interior lighting grew stronger, to avoid a sudden sense of confinement. Ben didn't need such solicitude by now, but it was standard.

He smelled the first whiff of sandalwood perfume that went along with the gas that would put him to sleep. That was a practical safeguard, not a comfort. The probe was fast enough so that the movement of internal organs didn't interfere significantly, but such a thing as a wink or a sudden jerk of a hand might produce a small "freak", as they were called.

He let the swift drowsiness take him.

II

He awoke without much feeling of elapsed time and waited for the lid to slide open, then raised himself carefully and climbed out of the compartment. The cubicle looked all right, as had all the others. A sign said, "You are on Titan, a moon of Saturn. Please check your baggage before pushing the 'Clear' button."

The screen suddenly showed the message "Passenger and baggage at destination." Simultaneously, the red lights went out and the white ones came on.

Ben frowned. The red lights should have stayed on until he pressed the "Clear". In fact, they should not have gone out, nor should the white ones have come on—it should have been impossible—until he'd opened the baggage compartment and removed the contents.

He opened that compartment. There was no baggage in it.

He crouched, really scared now. The screen went blank, and all the lights went off, even the one behind the small screen that said "Inactive". He pushed the "Information" button (so called because it was less suggestive than "Trouble"). Nothing happened.

He turned toward the door out of the cubicle, and as he moved was suddenly aware that gravity was Earth-normal, or near it. He was on no moon of Saturn.

The door opened and he looked into the frightened face of a girl. His own face went hot as he realized that he wasn't wearing as much as a fig-leaf, and he started a move of his hand so banal that, stubbornly, he did not complete it. He said, with as much composure as he could, "My baggage didn't come through."

She said, as if to herself, "Inglish." She stared at him for a second, then said, "Come! You must hurree."

He said helplessly, "My clothes."

Her eyes looked amused for just an instant, then she frowned. "Hurree!"

He thought he'd better follow her, until he found out where he was and what had happened to him.

They stepped from the cubicle into a large room, featureless except for two doors and a line of ventilator openings around the ceiling. The girl opened one of the doors, and light spilled in, so bright Ben threw a hand before his eyes, "Hurree!" she said again.

Shielding his eyes as much as he could, he followed her out into the blinding day. The door luckily, opened on the shady side of the building. She led him along the shade to another door. "In here!"

It was good to be out of the light again. They were in a room filled with machinery of various kinds, including what Ben judged, from the conduits, to be the air-conditioning. She told him, "I think they will not come in here. You must be very quiet. I will bring you food when I can, and when it is dark I will take you to a better place."

He stared at her, then looked around the room. He supposed he could hide behind some of the machinery, if someone merely looked in the door. He said, feeling very helpless, "If my baggage comes, will you bring it to me?"

"It is not going to come."

"But . . . why? I need something to wear."

She looked impatient. "I will bring you something, if it is that important." She turned to go.

"Wait!" he said, stepping forward and taking her by the arm. "Where am I? Who are you?"

She frowned at his hand on her arm, and he took it away. She said, her eyes hard, "I am a slave, as you will be if they catch you." She turned and went out the door.

He explored the room briefly and found nothing he could use for a weapon, and certain bits of equipment he didn't understand at all. He thought he'd better not be prowling around; there might be detectors of some kind. He found a place near one corner, between two bulging machines, and made himself as comfortable as possible. He felt bewildered, but didn't doubt much that the girl was speaking the truth. He puzzled over the fact that she had spoken awkward English at first, but that it had improved with every word.

It was pretty clear that, somehow, he'd been kidnapped.

He sat trying to reason out how it could be done, conscious of how little he really knew about the teleportation. One thing very much on his mind was that the process couldn't be used to duplicate anything. A human, for instance, lay asleep and apparently unchanged until his new self, wherever it might be, came into being. At that moment the old body vanished, with an implosion of air behind it. Neither would the probing—though it could be easily recorded and reproduced as signals by any of a number of means—generate more than a new individual. Therefore, he was stranded. There was nothing the company could do to get him back. Unless, of course, they found a way to repeal what seemed to be a natural law.

The signals must simply have been intercepted. This machine, the one he'd materialized in, was a counterfeit. The kidnappers, whoever they were, obviously could snatch the signals from whatever unguessable, timeless non-space they traveled in. They were able to do more than that. They were able to edit out the baggage, and send false signals back to the origin. It was not clear why they bothered with that last, unless it was simply to delay discovery of the kidnap for a few minutes.

Nothing in his knowledge of the process suggested any way the transmission could be intercepted. He wondered whether he'd get a chance to look at the receiver and materializer here. It might be entirely different from anything he knew, except for the deceptive familiar front. Of course, without tools he couldn't even get the panels open.

An hour or more passed, then the door opened, letting in the awful light. He stayed where he was until the girl's voice said softly, "Food." By the time he stood up, the door had closed again and she was gone.

The food wrapped in a slick tough kind of paper, was baked loaf of some kind of meat with grain and herbs. There were small sweet fruits and a jug of some juice that tasted like spiced lemonade. She had also brought him a length of cloth, quite thin and soft, about nine feet long and less than a foot wide, with fancy ends as if it were a scarf or head-wrapping. He tried to tear it but could not. He devised a way to wrap it where it was most needed, and felt much less vulnerable. He ate what she'd brought, then folded the paper and thrust it into the jug.

He had little relish for more waiting, but he thought he'd better do as the girl said. At least, he'd stay where he was until dark.

He wished he'd had a chance to talk to her more; to get a better look at her. Confused and embarrassed as he'd been, he hadn't noticed much. Her hair was long and black and her eyes a very deep violet. He thought her features could have belonged to a young American Indian maiden, but as he remembered her skin it had an odd tinged, grayish or even with a hint of blue-green rather than brown. He remembered very even, white teeth. And as she'd opened the door of the large room and stood silhouetted against the terrible light, he'd registered an impression of a tiny waist.

III

After what seemed a long time the door opened again and she called to him softly, "Come."

She giggled when she saw how he'd used the scarf, and he blushed miserably. She took the empty jug from him, then led him outside. The blinding light was gone, replaced by what he took for a soft twilight. They stood against the wall and he stared at an unearthly landscape. There were bushes twenty or thirty yards away, and, beyond them, tall bamboo-like trees or shoots. All the shapes and colors were strange. Even the sparse grass in the sandy soil near him was all wrong.

She said, "When you hear me singing go straight toward those closest bushes and hide. Do not go farther until I come for you." She left and went back inside.

He could hear muffled shouts and laughter, somewhere inside the building. Once in a while, from somewhere beyond the building, there were deep animal snarls that sent chills up his spine. After a while he heard the girl's voice begin a quiet little song. He went, quickly, to the bushes and hid himself, learning the hard way that the bushes had thorns. He was still in the building's long shadow.

A rhythmic thudding began, in time with the song. In a minute both sounds stopped, and a deep voice said something in an odd singsong language, with emphasis where it sounded wrong. The girl answered in the same language. The deep voice said something more, and the thudding and singing resumed. Ben waited, trying to control his nerves.

Eventually there was another silence. Then, after perhaps fifteen minutes more, the girl's voice came from behind him. "Here."

He moved cautiously toward her, and found she had changed from the plain light-colored dress she'd worn before to dark trousers and jacket that covered her almost completely. She had something bulky over her arm.

"This way," she said, starting deeper into the trees. After a few yards she stopped and spread the bulky object over something ahead of her. "Cross over these rugs," she said. "Be careful. There is wire beneath, with a deadly voltage."

He hesitated, dumbly, until she urged him again, then went over the wires strung unobtrusively through the trees. He realized what the thudding sounds had been. She'd been beating rugs, as an excuse for bringing them outside. The deep voice must have been a guard, which meant they mustn't dawdle.

She followed him across and hid the rugs a few feet beyond the fence. "The beasts are penned tonight," she said, "so we can go safely, but do not make too much noise. We are going beyond that hill east of here—*that* way is east— and circle around the station when we are out of sight. I will go with you until the trees end, then you must go on alone. I cannot be away any longer. Tomorrow night, or the next, or the next, when I can, I will come to the place where we part, and flash a light twice. Do not come until you see it. Come. We must hurry."

He followed her along what seemed to be a game trail through the trees, around the lower slope of the hill she'd indicated. Through the thick foliage he caught glimpses of a monstrous moon, which, in its brightness, he'd mistaken for a sunset.

He said, "Can't you tell me anything? What world is this? Why have I been brought here, and by whom?" She said nothing, and he went on, "I know I am not in the—in my own system of sun and planets."

She answered, after a minute, "I do not know where your world is, any more than my own. I was taught English because they have been taking people of your race, who sometimes need the care of someone more like themselves. I was a nurse on my own world. That is why they chose me. They take people to sell them as slaves."

He followed her silently for a while, digesting that. Finally he said again, "Who are they?"

"I know almost nothing about them. Sometimes they talk to me but not much. Sometimes I have talked to—but you will not understand about that for a while."

"I— How many of my people have you seen here?"

"Hundreds."

"Hundreds?"

"Yes. Some of them were different tribes. Nations. Not all spoke English."

He said, "You know other Terran languages too?"

"Spanish and German and French and Russian. They started to teach me another one—Chinese, it was called. But they have not taken any who spoke that language."

"You've learned all those languages? You—so young?"

She turned and smiled at him. "Thank you. Sometimes I do not feel young. My race has good memory for sounds."

"I should say!" They walked for a while, then he said, "I haven't even thanked you."

"Today is one of their celebration days, and I knew they would have a party. I do not serve them. They have other slaves, and they do not find me pleasing. I thought with most of them drunk, and the beasts penned, I might save you."

"You—I mean they—were not expecting me, then?"

"The machine chooses. We do not know until a bell rings. They were all away, making some kind of ceremony, and I was all alone in the building. I did what I could."

"I don't know how to thank you. I hope you haven't put yourself in danger."

"There is always danger, of one kind or another. And what have I to lose?"

"I'm . . . very sorry, and very grateful. Maybe I can help you. It won't be more than a night or two before I see you again, will it?" he asked.

"If Fate wills it."

"Well . . . Where are you taking me?"

"To a place where you can live. I can do no more. I do not understand about the machines, and they watch them closely most of the time. Go carefully, now. We are near the end of the trees."

They stopped where the dense growth gave way to a stretch of desert. Not far south, a mighty butte or dune reared into the sky, but Ben only noticed it vaguely. He'd stopped in his tracks and was staring at the moon.

It was three or four times the apparent diameter of Luna, and brighter. It was still low in the southeast, but fully above the horizon now, and casting long shadows. It was more than three-fourths full. In the middle of it, occupying a large part of its area was a great brooding face. It was broad-chinned and strong, with a skull as bald as an apple; intelligent despite its ruggedness. Something in the expression, the lines of care, tugged at the emotions.

The girl said, a little impatiently, "You will have plenty of time to stare at it. It is the face of a man whose people lived here long ago. You must go now, to the mountain, as fast as you can. If anything approaches you, do not run from it until you are sure it is hostile. If it seems too curious, growl at it." Suddenly she smiled. "Let me hear you growl."

Feeling very foolish, Ben growled.

She said, "I think that will do," and turned to go.

"Wait!" he said, and seized her hand. "I—" He stopped abruptly and stared down at her hand. It had no thumb. He let it drop.

She looked at him almost sullenly for a moment, then said, "In my world it is normal." Then she was gone.

He stood for a moment; half inclined to follow her, then turned and went toward the mountain. As he trudged through the sand, picking up his pace as he remembered he was supposed to hurry, he saw that it was really a mountain, farther away then he'd thought at first, with trees along its crest.

When he'd walked for perhaps twenty minutes he saw something loping toward him from the left. It was big, and it scared him, but he held his pace. As it got nearer he saw that it was like a huge overgrown puppy, with a big, ludicrous, short-muzzled head and enormous feet that were awkward in the sand. It dashed toward him so purposefully that he stopped and turned to face it, knowing he couldn't outrun it in the sand but ready to dodge. It halted a few yards away and cocked its head, staring at him. He said something, nervously. It began to make little dashes toward him that might be playful, or might not, with little grunting sounds that were not doglike. He growled at it as convincingly as he could, and it cowered back.

He went on, keeping an eye on it. It followed, making the grunting sound. Finally, too worried to keep on, he stopped and began talking to it. It edged closer. He held out his hand, talking soft nonsense, and saw that it trembled a little as it approached. He got a glimpse of its teeth and felt better. They were not carnivorous.

Finally it was close enough to sniff his fingers, then it let him stroke it. After that it lost its fear and came close, rubbing against him and grunting happily. He treated it with respect. Friendly or not, it stood on all fours almost as high as his shoulder and its mouth could have taken his whole head in. He found it was not so bulky as it looked, because its fur, thick-looking but not substantial when he touched it, stood out from its body. He guessed that might be a protection from the fierce sun, though with such moonlight he didn't see why anything had to be out in the daytime. Of course, a moon had dark phases too.

It stayed with him for possibly half an hour, then stopped and picked up its ears as if listening. After a second it broke into a gallop and went back the way it had come.

It took him a few minutes more to reach the mountain. He saw that it was really a curved ridge, concave toward him, tapering down at each end into a lunette. Several small streams trickled down to be lost in the sand before they got far. He couldn't see much more since he was looking into the shadow, but the whole slope seemed to be wooded except where rocky crags broke through.

IV

When he reached the base the mountain loomed over him so that he thought it must be close to a thousand feet high; and from farther back it had looked several times as long. The concavity was deeper than he'd thought. The ends curved around him like a giant revetment.

He sat down by one of the streams and dipped up cool water with his hands, realizing for the first time how tired he was. Now his predicament closed in upon him. He had nothing but the scarf wrapped around him. The girl had said he could live here, but he didn't see how he was going to go about it. He'd never really believed fire could be made by rubbing sticks together, or striking stones; and though he knew, vaguely, that it was possible to make traps out of natural materials and catch rabbits and such, he didn't know how. Nor did he have any reason to believe there would be small creatures here to catch, or that they'd be edible if there were. He thought, gloomily, that he'd never realized how dependent he was on other people and on the things of society.

A voice said, "Those are the dullest thoughts I've met for a long time. Excuse me; I don't usually probe; but the way you acted I thought you might really be in trouble."

Ben jumped to his feet and whirled toward the voice. There was nothing in sight. Or he thought there wasn't until a spot of nebulosity appeared in the air above him. "Does this make you more comfortable?" it said.

There was no other way to describe it. The voice, quite Terran and matter of fact—and even peculiarly familiar—simply came from the thing, which might have been a small dense cloud of smoke or colored gas except that it had definite edges that did not diffuse or waver, aside from a slight undulation.

"I just vibrate the air," the thing said. "Isn't that a convenient way to talk? I could plant ideas in your brain, but I think that would disturb you."

Ben was paralyzed with fear, or horror. Finally he managed to say, "What . . .?"

"Don't be such a primitive," the thing said, and chuckled. "I'm not going to eat you. And as for your own survival, that will be very easy. You can make fire if you must, though I can't permit you to kill any of my other guests. But you won't need it. There are plenty of fruits and berries for you to live on, and maybe I will fetch something to lay eggs for you."

The easy manner of the speech calmed Ben little. He said, "Who are you? I—I guess I should say, what are you? Are you just a cloud of gas?"

"Hardly. That is a manifestation I assumed when you were so frightened at hearing me. I can drop it. See?" The thing vanished suddenly, but the voice remained. "I see you like me better visible. How about this?" It reappeared, but luminous this time.

"Energy," Ben said, dumbfounded. "You must be pure energy!"

"Not at all. I can be, but it's boring. I told you this is just a manifestation. I could materialize as a biped if I wanted to, but it would take time and I see no reason to pamper you that much."

"Then . . . what are you?"

"I am the mountain."

Even after he got over his first disbelief, Ben could not adjust emotionally to a mountain's being alive. He thought of it as an immense beast lying there, and when he tried to climb the slope his instincts rebelled and he turned back.

The manifestation disappeared after chiding him once for being timid, and left him alone for a while. He found enough fruit to satisfy him when he was hungry and otherwise sat through the night with his back against a tree.

When weary hours had passed the voice spoke to him again. "The moon will be setting before long. If you want to see the desert you'd better climb up now."

"I . . . No, thanks; I'm comfortable here."

"It's up to you, but you won't be safe down here in the daytime."

Ben thought about that for a few minutes, and his imagination supplied fears enough to get him on his feet. He started toward the slope. The voice said, "Go over to that stream on your left and follow it up. It's the easiest way."

The closest stream on his left was approximately in the middle of the curve, and flowed out the farthest into the sand, maintaining a ribbon of greenery. He found there was a trail of sorts, with what seemed to be wide stone steps in the steepest places. He did not have it to himself. Small creatures kept scuttling before him, all headed upward, and there was one dim shape ahead of him that stopped now and then to stare back. It looked as big as a man but walked mostly on all fours and was furry.

It took him probably an hour to reach the top, where the green plants gave way suddenly to pale things like the ones the girl had led him through. No doubt this was where the sun hit.

The southern slope was more even, or looked so from here and much more gradual that the green side. It was sparsely covered with the light-hued plants. He studied one beside him. It looked like bamboo with wide paper discs flaring from each joint. At the tops, which were in some cases forty or fifty feet up, hung flowers like big corn-tassels but maroon-colored in the moonlight. The stalks and discs were almost white, just tinted with yellow-green. The plants made a dry rustling noise in the faint breeze.

The desert stretched away southward as far as he could see, though he thought there were a few hills on the horizon. To the west it was the same. In the east was a line of hills, wooded with the pale shoots, he thought. A river or perhaps a dry bed ran diagonally from the east to the south, with a few trees of dark green visible in its canyon.

The low hills from which he'd come seemed to be only a projection of the range in the east, as they didn't go far west. Beyond them was a mass that might be mountains, but he couldn't see now.

The moon was touching the horizon in the southwest. It had evidently not gotten very high at any time, which would mean that he was not far from the planet's North Pole. He stood staring at the face on the moon, and now the voice spoke to him. "Are you looking at my ancestor?"

"Your ancestor?"

"Don't be so shocked. Your own race may evolve as I have . . . depending on a number of factors."

Ben felt prickly again. He'd forgotten for a while that he was standing on a live being. He controlled his revulsion as well as he could. "It must have taken millions of years. Many millions."

"No. Not millions; nor hundreds of thousands, even. Think of how you came here. If your own body can be broken down into impulses of energy, then rebuilt as it was, why should it not be rebuilt in a different form?"

Ben shook his head, unable to grasp it.

The voice said, "That's the way it started. Our world was almost too hot for us to survive, after a near collision and change of orbit, so we had to adapt. We used a process similar to the one your own race has inherited, but we changed the chemistry of our bodies. We switched from carbon to silicon because it was more plentiful and we could arrange broader temperature tolerance, and from water to a synthetic fluid. Not many generations after that we perfected our control so that we had immortality, if we wanted it, and could change ourselves still farther. I've been a mountain for many thousands of years now, though I sometimes change size or shape to fit circumstances. But my ancestor's face there reminds me that I was once a biped, which is probably why I take the trouble to talk to you. I sometimes have such whimsies. Though I'm glad to say they do not rule me."

Ben was beginning to lose his horror of the voice, but the elusive familiarity of it bothered him. "Why," he asked impulsively, "do you sound so familiar to me?"

The voice chuckled. "Don't you recognize it? I picked the voice most deeply engraved in your subconscious."

Now it flooded over Ben, and he stood quiet, wondering how he'd failed to recognize it. His father had died when

Ben was eleven. After a while he said, "It's not very comfortable to have my mind read."

"I don't do it often," the voice said. "But since curiosity is my only reason for tolerating guests, I reserve the right."

Ben didn't see what he could do about it. He stared at the moon, which was farther gone now. "Who was he?"

"A man who led my race through a great crisis. It is all in my accumulated memory, with a billion other stories I haven't recalled for a long time. I've pretty much outgrown reminiscence."

"So they put his face on their moon."

"A good idea, don't you think? It's still there, while the last trace of their cities is gone."

Ben napped a little on the top of the mountain, which was level and smooth, until dawn awoke him.

The sun, as he expected, arced low along the southern horizon. He could not look at it directly, nor could he stand it upon his skin. Even early in the morning, the desert and the hills within sight looked dry and sweltering. Only the curved shady side of the mountain showed moisture. He thought the mountain must produce water, or draw it up from some cool depth.

Now he got to know the other guests, as the voice called them. They were mostly quadruped, and furred with the strange hair he'd found on last night's dog-like trail companion. One of the small things, rat-sized and with a prehensile tail let him stroke it and he examined the fur. Each hair grew out from the skin as a stiff quill, then burst into a crown or parasol of very fine wool at the end. The hairs seemed to be mobile, or at least a shrug of the skin moved them in a wave-like motion that might be for ventilation.

Few of the creatures were afraid of him, or of each other, though some of them kept a distance. He saw the large animal that had come up the slope ahead of him, or one like it; a plant-eater and not belligerent. It looked at him with resigned, sad eyes, and he wondered how long it had been separated from its kind.

Later in the morning he saw why everything had come up the slope.

A band of terrible things came scuttling from among the trees in the direction of the slave base. Their heads, bodies, and rasp-like tails were vaguely crocodilian, but instead of crawling they darted swiftly on four pairs of upright legs. Sometimes they reared their necks aloft and held the front pair of legs before them like arms, their taloned paws ugly and grasping. They were flushing out and catching small things that lived in the sand. And later they came to the shade of the mountain and stopped to drink from the largest of the streams.

The voice said, "See how hungrily they look at my guests. They don't belong to this world; the slavers brought them. They'd love to get up here if they dared."

"How do you keep them off?"

"Shrug them off, usually. I can cook up quite an earthquake. If that doesn't stop them I have other ways, of course."

Ben said, "I guess I ought to thank you for your protection."

"You owe me no thanks. I only tolerate you, all of you, as a diversion. Don't get the idea there's any sentiment in it. If you walked out there and got caught by those things or died of sunburn, I wouldn't stir an atom to help."

"Oh," said Ben. "But you could move from this spot then, if you wanted to?"

"What a question! Didn't you see the manifestation over your head last night? Here, look at it again!"

"I saw that," Ben said, "but it wasn't very far from the rest of you. I assumed . . ."

"I'm not flattered by your assumption. I could send a thousand energy-vortices patrolling the planet; I do send out a few to keep in touch. I could split into a thousand parts and fly away as a swarm of meteors. I could visit your own world that way if I wanted to, and pummel it into lifelessness without hurting myself; or I could go by instantaneous translation. I can do almost anything within the laws of nature. With time and raw materials, I could grow into a planet, or a sun."

"I'm sorry if I offended you."

"You can't offend me. Are you accusing me of atavism? I told you I'd outgrown such childish things as egotism."

"Oh. I'm sorry. You sound so . . . Well, human."

"That's because I'm talking to you. Naturally, I only display facets of my intelligence that you can grasp."

"I see. I guess—I've been meaning to ask you if you had a name, but I don't suppose you'd bother with one."

"You might call me Lith, since I am mostly stone now. Of course that's only a concession to you and your own language."

"Thank you," said Ben. It was a comfort to think that a being like this probably wouldn't bother to swat a fly.

V

He had no way of telling time, but the day seemed longer than a Terran one. It was uncomfortably hot, even where he was, and he took advantage of the cool springs. He didn't have much appetite, because the sweet fruit took it away quickly, but he remained vaguely unsatisfied. What he craved was meat. Under the circumstances, he didn't feel like trying to acquire any.

He went as high as he could without leaving the shade, and stared to the north. He could see the roofs of the buildings where he'd arrived, though the rest of the place was hidden by the bamboo-like stuff around it.

Farther north there were high hills, obscured by heat-shimmer but dry-looking, though there were dark spots.

The mountain talked very little to him during that day, but it did tell him that it soaked up the sun's energy, not only upon its surface but by other means, and stored what it didn't use at once. It answered affirmatively his question whether it made water, and said it moved slowly about finding water-bearing compounds.

He waited impatiently for the day to end, and long before twilight was gone he was at the edge of the greenery, staring across the sand toward where the girl had left him.

Hours passed, and the mountain chuckled at him. Then, at last, he saw two quick flashes of light.

He ran as fast as his bare feet would take him. When he was halfway there, she started out to meet him. She held out a package. "Some cooked meat. And I have brought you a knife." She handed him a simple table knife. "Come. It is not good to stand out here."

They went back to the trees, but before they reached them a movement to one side caught Ben's eye. He turned apprehensively, but it was only the overgrown puppy thing, or another like it. It galloped up and rubbed against both of them, and the girl said, "I see you have made one friend."

"Two," he said, "counting you."

She smiled and they hurried on toward cover, the playful beast coming with them. She said, "We will be all right here, I think. How did you get along at the mountain?"

"Well, it's a little hard to get used to. I was comfortable enough, I guess. But this meat is welcome."

"Why don't you eat some of it now?"

"Too many things on my mind. Did they find out you were away last night?"

"No; but it wouldn't have mattered. When the beasts are penned I can wander where I like, except when they tell me not to. I always have to be there during the day. Tonight I left openly, by the gate."

"You mentioned servants. Are there many?"

"Eight others, now."

"Are any of them human? I mean, like me?"

"Neither like you nor like me. They are happy to be slaves as long as they are taken care of; they are little more than animals. Why did you ask?"

"Well, I was wondering if there were enough to help me overpower the slavers. I've got to get hold of some tools and get at that machine."

"Tools? You could do things to the machine?"

"Maybe."

"None of the others from your world knew anything about the machine."

"It was not their trade. Maybe I don't know enough either, but I've got to try."

"I can't see how you can get to the machine. They were all drunk yesterday, but they will not be that way again for a long time. And you cannot fight them. The other servants would not help, even if they knew how to fight."

"How many slavers are there?"

"Ten or twelve, now. They come and go. They have weapons, and the beasts which they control."

"How long have you been here?"

"Almost two of your years."

"And you don't know where your own world is?"

"No. I do not even know if it still exists. There was a war. I was on my way to an outpost when we were captured."

"You were a nurse?"

"Yes, in our fighting forces."

"Then your people are advanced. Scientifically, I mean."

"We had science, but we did not know much about war."

"Was your world defeated?"

"I do not know."

"Won't your—won't the slavers tell you?"

"They do not know, or care. I have been traded and shipped far. I do know I am not in the same part of the galaxy. The stars are not familiar."

Ben could see very few stars now, but that might be due to the moon's brightness. He wondered how far he was from Earth. He said, "At least you and I have the will to escape. What about tools?"

"There are tools. Four men, if you can call them that, are here permanently, and once they worked on the machine. I do not know where the tools are kept."

Ben said, "By the way, I don't even know your name."

"Naleen."

"Naleen? It's a lovely name. Naleen, you've already done more for me than I have any right to ask; but could you find out about the tools?"

"If you wish. But one man, without weapons . . ."

"Couldn't you sneak me back in the way you got me out?"

"They are usually on duty."

"But there must be some way. Some time."

"I do not know when it would be. I can only promise that when it is possible, I will help you. I am not afraid for myself."

"Do they treat you badly?"

"Most of the time they do not. I do my job and they respect me for that. But I hate them. They . . ."

"They what, Naleen?"

"They treat me like an inferior. They even put me below the other servants, who are of a race that looks more like themselves. And they brought me, as you would an—an object."

"Why do you stay there? You could live on the mountain," he asked gently.

"I ran away once and stayed there four days. I knew they would punish me when I went back, but I could not stay longer on the mountain. I was not free there either. And at least I have my work. Some of the people who come through the machine are sick or terrified and they need me. Besides . . ."

What, Naleen?"

"I live in the hope my own people will find me some day. It is a foolish hope, but I stay near the machine because that is where they would come if they traced me. Can you understand that?"

"I can understand it," Ben said. "Look—I hope I can do more than wait. I may be able to fix the machine so it will take me home, or at least communicate and get help. If I can—go home, I mean—will you come with me?"

She was silent for a while, then she said, "I do not know. What would your people say about me? You thought my hands were ugly."

"I didn't!"

"It was in your face."

"I was only surprised. I swear it."

"And my color."

"Your color is close enough to my own. We have people on Earth who are a little different, too."

"Yes, I know. I was taught a little of that."

"Well, then?"

Suddenly she laughed. "You are a silly man, Ben. So far I have only been able to get you a table knife, and already you are going to fight the universe and rescue me."

It was Ben's turn to be silent. After a minute he said, "I guess it *is* silly. But will you help me try?"

"I have already promised that. I think I must go now."

"When will I see you?"

"When I can come. I do not think it will be tomorrow night, or the next. They will be busy, I think."

"I suppose I'll have to stay on the mountain."

"Until you know this world better. Good night, Ben."

"Good night." This time he held her hand deliberately, not letting himself flinch at its strangeness.

He spent the rest of the night pondering weapons. Possibly he could make a bow and some arrows, but he didn't know how to use a bow and he thought it would take a long time to become adept. The same applied to a sling.

He'd been a good pitcher once. If he could find a number of smooth, round stones about the size of a baseball, he'd at least have something. Beyond that, he thought he'd investigate the bamboo-like stuff with the idea of making spears. Not that he'd be able to throw them, but a six-or-eight-foot pointed shaft would be some protection against animals.

There were no smooth, round stones on the mountain, and if there had been he'd have felt squeamish about using them. He remembered the river to the southeast. Possibly he could get to that and find rounded stones. Maybe he could even make a stone axe, if Naleen couldn't steal him something better.

Before the sun was up he hacked down one of the smaller bamboo-like things and took it to a cooler spot to work on it.

The circular discs were hard but too brittle for anything much. The tassels were fairly tough, and might be braided into a rope. The stalks were very much like bamboo, and each section contained a small amount of thick syrup that had a tart-sweet taste. Ben split the stalk, which was about four inches in diameter, into thirds and chose the strongest parts of each. A six-foot length was sturdy enough to stand a hard thrust. When he had three such crude spears finished, despair suddenly washed over him again. They were ludicrous, compared to real weapons.

Frustrated anger replaced the despair, and he called out, "Lith!"

The voice said, "You're quite bloodthirsty, aren't you? I suppose you're going to ask me for weapons to use against your enemies."

"I'll take any weapons you'll give me, gratefully. What I was going to ask was why you tolerate slavers on your planet. You do think of this as your planet, don't you?"

Lith chuckled. "I'm not really jealous about it. I can always go somewhere else and set up housekeeping, you know."

"But haven't you—don't you feel anything against a crime like slave-trading?"

"Feel? Feelings are immature, Ben Auley. And don't your own people indulge in slave-trading?"

"Certainly not!"

"You sell animals as labor-slave. You even eat them."

"They're not intelligent beings."

"And are you, biped?"

"Why! ..." Ben saw that was a dead end. "Intelligence is relative, of course. And there are different kinds. But beyond a certain point, a being isn't a beast any more. He's civilized."

"Your own point of view. Actually, you could argue that these particular slavers treat their property well. The slaves will be fed and tended, and they'll have a certain amount of leisure to themselves. And since your race is bisexual, you'll be pleased to hear that the slaves are taken from both sexes, and allowed to mingle. Do you really think most of them would be better off free?"

"Why, of course! Freedom is worth more than anything!"

"A concept that some would dispute. I will not help you, beyond keeping the sanctuary here. If you want to bring the girl here, I will tolerate both of you."

"She won't stay here," Ben said. "She's—she has unselfish work to do where she is."

"I know about that. But are you sure she won't change her mind now that you're here?"

"You're certainly an old cynic."

"Just rational."

Ben gave up, and tried to nap.

VI

Fairly early in the day he was awakened by a whooshing sound and saw an aircar of some kind rise from the slavers' camp and head southward, carefully detouring around the mountain. He did not climb up to watch; he'd have to face into the sun if he tried. He looked back toward the base, and listened. There was no more activity that he could see. The day dragged.

Naleen did not signal him that night, or the next. The aircars were busy, so he presumed slaves were coming in. He fought against a listless depression and tried to sleep as much as possible during the day so he wouldn't doze off at night.

The third night, not long after sundown, the two quick flashes came. He jumped up, clumsy with excitement, and ran across the desert as he had before.

He reached her and stood gasping for breath. When he could, he said, "I was worried."

She said, "I could not come sooner. Nine captives have been taken since I talked to you, and everything was under guard. They flew them away. Did you see?"

"I saw aircars. Where do they take them?"

"To another base that I have only heard bits of talk about. I think it is a spaceport where ships of other races land to buy slaves."

"Were they human?"

"One of them was Terran. The rest were of a race that has been taken often. Not an advanced race. They are captured somewhere and sent here by machine, and they always come in batches of eight. Five were female, and one was very sick, with a—a miscarriage, I think. They took her with the rest. I think she will die."

"What about the human?"

"A man. Not very brave and not very intelligent, I think. They took him with the others."

He said, "Did you find out where the tools are?"

"No. I have been very careful, because they are already suspicious that something has happened."

"How do you mean?"

"The day they had the celebration—the day you came— the one on duty was supposed to turn the machine off, but he was drunk and did not. There is a record of your arrival—but he swears it is something wrong with the machine and will not admit it was turned on."

"Do they suspect you?"

"I do not think so. They accuse each other of stealing an extra slave, or of bungling some way and trying to hide it. But they are alert, so I did not dare look for the tools."

"I wouldn't want you to put yourself in danger. Is it dangerous for you to be here?"

"It would be dangerous if I stopped wandering around. I have done it for a long time."

"Do you have to go right back?"

"No. I think I can stay for a while."

"There's one thing I want to ask you. That river east of here. Do you know anything about it?"

"I have been there often. It comes from the north and has water in it all the year. I think there is snow in the north that melts. I do not know where it goes to the south."

"Snow? Does it ever rain here? Right here, I mean?"

"A few showers, not more than nine or ten a year. Why do you ask?"

"I was wondering if a person could live here."

"You do not like the mountain?"

"No. It—I would rather be somewhere else."

"It is the only safe place in the day time."

"Well ... The reason I asked about the river was, I thought there might be some rounded stones there. Small ones, to fit in my hand."

"I have seen such stones there. Do you want me to bring you some?"

"Can't I go there myself, at night?"

"It would be dangerous. Why do you want the stones?"

"For weapons. I can throw pretty well."

She was thoughtful for a moment. "I can take you there. If things approach you must be very quiet."

"All right."

They went back among the trees where there were game trails and followed them east. Ben judged it was about two miles to the river.

The river's canyon, not very deep but fairly wide, was a slash of green across this parched world. The stream itself was only a few yards wide now, and as far as Ben could tell there hadn't been much water for a long time. Still, the whole bed was fertile except where sand or rocks collected.

They walked up the stream, collecting the kind of stones Ben wanted. Suddenly Naleen said, "Stand still for a moment."

Something moved among the trees, and the puppy like thing bounded into sight. Naleen said, "Do not touch it."

They let the thing prance around them, nuzzling at them and grunting its disappointment at not being petted. After a minute something heavy could be heard coming through the trees. A hulking shape appeared, and Ben realized it was an adult of the same species. Another came into sight behind it. They did not seem particularly menacing, but their size was enough to make Ben follow Naleen's advice. The young one was dashing back and forth now between its parents and Ben and Naleen.

Naleen began to talk soothingly. The two big things came closer, slowly, like outsize dogs suspiciously approaching a stranger. Naleen said to Ben, "They know me, but you will have to make friends with them."

Ben let the things come close and sniff him. They had a dignified, ponderous way about them. Slowly, he raised a hand for them to sniff.

It didn't take them long to decide he was all right, and they let him scratch them under the chins. After a few minutes one of them grunted and started back toward the trees. The pup nuzzled at Naleen a second longer, then followed.

Ben had a dozen or so stones in the crook of his left arm. He said, "A few more of these will be enough." They went on.

A little way upstream they came to a quiet pool, shaded by a growth of trees. Naleen said, "I swim here sometimes."

The pool did look inviting. Ben put down his stones and dipped a hand in the water. It was not too chilly. He said, "We don't have suits."

In the dim light, she seemed to look at him with amusement. She said, "Terrans have some strange ideas."

She left him and disappeared into the trees. He stood uncertainly, wondering if he'd offended her, but after a few moments she reappeared, nude and lithe and lovely, and stepped calmly into the water. He stood confused for a moment, then slowly unwrapped his own makeshift garment and went into the pool.

A happiness that was almost childish came over him; an exuberation so that he laughed and splashed water until she had to remind him not to make too much noise. A part of his mind regarded his reactions with amazement. It was strange that such a small thing as a swim, with a girl, could banish his depression and make him forget, almost, his predicament. She seemed to be happy too, laughing lightly. But after a while she said soberly. "I had better go back."

The effect on him was crushing, as if it hadn't occurred to him that they couldn't stay here forever. He stood waist-deep and stared at her. She looked at him for a moment, then turned and waded toward the edge. He followed, his pulse beginning to pound, seized suddenly in vague discontents and urges. She turned in the shadow and stood looking at him, her face unreadable. He took a trembling step forward and she came into his arms. Her body was tense and hot against him. She let out a sigh that was almost a sob and buried her face against his shoulder, clinging to him as if she were desperately afraid he'd let her go.

After their lovemaking they lay together for a time, silent, drawing comfort from each other's arms. Then she said again, "I had better go."

She was quiet and serene now, only laughing a little as she helped him make a pouch of one end of his sash to carry the stones in. She held his hand as they started away.

At the top of the bank she paused and said, "There is something I must do." She went to a clump of the bamboo-like stuff and said, "Will you help me get some of these?"

He didn't understand until he'd broken off a few of the shorter stalks for her. Then she pulled loose the red tassels and chose the longest, toughest strands to tie into her hair, gathering it into a long braid. He said, "Let me help you," and she pulled away from him. "No! I must do it myself."

"Why?"

"It is a custom of my people, when a girl—when she has taken a mate."

He noticed that her thumbless hands were quite deft. The two outer fingers simply turned to oppose one another.

On the way back he said, "Will you be able to come out tomorrow night?"

"I can't tell. I think I will. I will come when I can." They walked in silence for a while, then she said, "I was so lonesome, Ben. I can hardly believe that I am lonesome no more."

Ben said, "I won't be lonesome now either. But we can't expect things to go on. They'll discover me sooner or later, or something else will happen."

"Yes. For as long as it lasts, I will be happy."

"Do you think you can find out about the tools very soon?"

"Not until they get over their suspicions and quarrels. I think it will be several days. Do you really know enough about the machines to send us away, even if you get the chance? How will you find your own world?"

Ben walked glumly for a minute. "I don't know. Maybe I can tell when I look at the machine."

They reached the parting point, and Naleen's serenity broke and she cried a little as he held her.

He slept the rest of the night and napped into the morning, feeling a contentment that made him a little guilty.

Some chattering sounds brought him wide awake, and he found the mountain's other occupants all gathered near the top, nervously watching something on the desert.

When his eyes unblurred he gasped with horror. The puppy-like thing was down there, a hundred yards or so from the base of the mountain, surrounded by the vicious things he'd seen before. It was whirling and darting, trying to find a way out, but the scaley things steadily closed the circle. Ben could hear the victim's terrified grunting. The predators were purposefully silent. Ben grabbed several of his stones and two of the spears and hurled himself down the slope.

One of Lith's manifestations formed in front of him and said, "Don't be stupid. You can't help."

"I can try!" he retorted.

"And get yourself killed. Think for a moment. Do you want to toss away everything for a mindless animal you can't save anyway? What about the girl? What about your own people?"

That brought Ben to a halt, but he blurted out, "You can help! It's practically at your base! You could save it! Can't you see it's only a puppy?"

"The predators seem to have decided it's worth eating. I've noticed you eating protein yourself."

Furious, Ben started down the slope again, but it was already too late. The killers closed in with a rush and the helpless thing went under, its grunts rising shrilly for a few seconds.

At least it was over quickly. Ben turned away, unwilling to watch.

Lith said, "Instead of dwelling upon the agony and terror of the victim, why not think of the predators' satisfaction? They too are living creatures."

Ben would not answer. If the predators, unhurried now about their meal, hadn't been keeping eyes turned toward him, he'd have left the mountain right then. In frustrated rage, he climbed back up the slope and threw himself down on his sleeping-spot.

Naleen did not signal him that night, and he spent the following day in sullen depression. He did not speak to Lith, nor Lith to him.

The next night Naleen's flashlight winked at him early, and he raced toward the meeting-place. She was flushed and laughing at his haste.

She sobered when he told her about the puppy-thing. They went silently toward the river. Finally she said, "I have seen many things die that way. Sometimes my masters put things into the pen, and laugh as the beasts tear them to pieces."

He said, "I wanted to help, but the mountain spoke to me and I hesitated. And I thought of you."

"Only of me?"

"Well, no. Of other things too, but mostly of you. It's the truth."

"You could have done nothing."

"The mountain could have ... Why can't I stay at the river instead? It seems peaceful there."

"It is not peaceful in the day time. There are terrible things, and my masters go there sometimes to hunt or fish. At least the mountain will protect you while you are there."

"I doubt that, if anything made a serious effort."

"I have seen things try. The mountain will not help anyone or anything, but it will not tolerate violence on itself. I do not understand it."

"Neither do I; but I don't like it."

They reached the riverbed and started up the stream toward the pool. Suddenly Ben stopped and gasped. The puppy-like thing was bounding toward them, obviously well and happy. He stood dumbfounded as it reached them anti pushed its way between them, grunting its happiness. He looked at Naleen. She was watching him with wide eyes. He said, "I—I guess it must have been a different one. I was sure it was the same one. I thought it might be coming to the mountain to look for me."

She said her eyes gradually calming, "I suppose there might be others, though I have never seen one."

He petted the thing and laughed with a glee that he could not resist. In a little while the thing's parents came and gravely renewed acquaintances; then, as before, left and took their offspring with them.

Naleen giggled as he pulled her into the thicket beside the pool. She said, "I was afraid you would want to swim first. Then I would have known you did not really love me."

VII

When it was time to go she made him get some more of the red tassels so she could renew the love knot.

As they walked away from the river she said, "I think I know where the tools and instruments are."

He seized her shoulders. "Where? Can we get at them?"

She met his eyes for a moment, then looked away. "You are very anxious to leave."

He stared at her. "Of course! Aren't you?"

"I think you may die trying. I am not anxious for that."

"But—the slaves! I've got to get back and warn my own race!"

"I suppose so. The tools will not be easy to get."

He released her shoulders. "We'll be very careful; plan and prepare. And you'll be going with me."

"If we are lucky," she said, and turned to go. Presently she took his hand as they walked.

He spent the next day brooding, too tense to eat more than a little of the new supply of meat she'd brought him. The first thing he'd need was a map of the base. Naleen could surely draw that from memory. He felt irritated that he hadn't thought to ask her to bring paper and something to write with. Then, when he knew the layout, he'd have to know how the guards were handled and how they behaved, and many other things.

It was strange to ponder calmly the prospect of killing even aliens. He wondered if he'd hesitate, when the moment came—if it did. For that matter, he wondered how he'd go about it. Maybe they were scaley, like their beasts, so that a spear or a knife wouldn't penetrate easily. Maybe their skulls were so thick a blow on the head wouldn't hurt.

The essentials were that he get his hands on the tools and the instruments he needed to examine the teleporter, and that he have a chance to examine it without interruption. At least, that was the immediate problem. Considered that way, stealth might be more to the point than violence.

One thing he had to know about was the bell Naleen had mentioned. That would have to be disconnected before he'd dare touch the machine.

He realized he'd wasted several days already. He could just as well have asked Naleen more.

She was late that night, but when they met he found she'd done some thinking of her own. She had a pencil and some paper, and when they reached the river she drew him a map.

The whole area around the base was a narrow-necked inlet of the desert, surrounded by the low hills, thickets of bamboo-like stuff, and the denser, shorter bushes. Across the neck, which was at the west, was a fence with the only gate in it. The electrified wire was strung around the rest of the circumference.

The building Ben had arrived in was L-shaped and the largest of three. The teleporter was in the leg that ran east and west, while the other leg, at the east, extended south. That was why Ben hadn't seen anything but the one wall.

There were separate buildings for the servants and for the slaves when there were any to put up. They were south of the main building. The landing field and the pen for the beasts were more to the west, near the gate.

Naleen's room and dispensary were in the end or the northern leg of the main building, separated from the large room that held the teleporter cubicle by the attendants' quarters. Those latter consisted of a bunk room and a duty-room. The tools and instruments were in a cabinet in the duty-room, where at least one of the four attendants was supposed to be at any time. Each of the four had keys, but Naleen didn't know if there were any others.

The door from the duty-room to the large room was supposed to be kept locked, but seldom was unless high officials arrived for an inspection. There was a bunk in the duty-room, and sometimes the alien on duty would be asleep.

Naleen had a second door to the outside of the building, so that she came and went as she pleased. However, if she wanted out of the area, she had to get the guard to unlock the gate for her.

She said, "They wouldn't let me out tonight."

Ben was puzzled. "You—oh. You came over the fence."

"Yes. That is why I was so late. When they were suspicious at the gate because I've been out so much lately, I thought I would stay in and pretended I didn't care. But I thought you would worry, so later I sneaked out."

"Would they punish you if they found out? You said they did before."

"I don't think they will look in my room."

"Suppose the bell should ring? They'd miss you then."

"The machine does not bring in slaves at night."

"I would rather you didn't take the chance, though. How did they punish you?"

"I would rather not talk about it."

"Was it pretty bad?"

"Yes. It was bad, but I got over it."

Ben felt upset. After a while he said, "I don't think we ought to wait too long. It sounds to me as if you could sneak me into the place all right. Do you think I'd have a chance to hit the guard over the head, or something, and get his keys?"

"It would not be easy. Maybe—"

"Maybe what?"

"Maybe I could put something in his food that would make him sleep. Then if the outside doors were not locked, I could get in and take his keys without going through their bunk room. Then I could come and get you. But of course they might find him asleep and be waiting for us."

"Can't I sneak in earlier and hide?"

"Maybe. They trade duties sometimes, so I would not know ahead of time which one it would be, and I would not know whether I could get a chance to put something in his food. I can get into the kitchens any time. But I do not know."

"I can't stand to wait much longer."

"You must not try to do anything until I have things arranged."

"But you'll do it as soon as you can? Look, I can always sneak away again if things don't work out, can't I?"

"I do not want you taking the risk if things are not ready."

"You got me out all right before. Promise me you'll try it as soon as you can."

"All right. If you will promise me one thing too, Ben."

"What?"

"Do not leave the mountain until I signal you."

"All right. I promise."

He took the sketch with him when they parted, and went up to the top of the mountain where the moonlight was bright enough so he could study it.

It still bothered him that the mountain might be reading his mind, and that he had to accept its hospitality, but he was in no position to be independent. When he'd learned the map as thoroughly as he could, he sat restlessly, unable to sleep. The sun came up, and he stirred himself to eat a little, and later was able to nap for a while.

When the heat of the day awoke him he doused himself in one of the springs to cool off.

With the knife he was able to hack off a piece of his scarf to carry his throwing-stones in. He puttered with his spears, making some better ones, and napped several times during the day.

Night came, and he alternately sat and jumped up to pace around, waiting for Naleen's signal. When the moon was halfway through its course he knew she wasn't coming, but he refused to abandon the watch until dawn and exhaustion compelled it.

The long day began. There was nothing for him to work on that was worthwhile, so he spent hours practicing with the rocks, until he was afraid to use his arm any more. He bundled them up in the length of cloth and unbundled them a dozen times, fretting over the best way to carry them so they wouldn't bounce too much if he ran. He tried ways of carrying the knife. There was no better way than simply thrusting it under the cloth around his waist.

Mostly he sat and worried.

It might be simply that Naleen hadn't been able to come because there was something going on at the base, but his mind insisted on exploring all sorts of other possibilities. Maybe she was in trouble; or maybe her courage had failed and she was just delaying. He did not think she would go back on her promise entirely. He thought she'd at least come for him and explain.

It was miserable waiting. As dusk fell he forced himself to sit in one place and relax his muscles, though he could do nothing about the tumult inside. The moon, at its full phase now, was near midnight in coming. He tried to convince himself she was waiting for it. The idea didn't take very well. She'd come in the dark before.

Despair pressed heavier and heavier upon him until he couldn't stand it. When the moon began to touch the thickets north of him he grabbed up his weapons and started across the sand. After a few steps he stopped, hesitated, and called out, "Lith!" He was so full of sick despair he was ready to drop his pride and beg information, at least, of the mountain. Lith didn't answer, though Ben called several times and added bitter curses. Ben started on.

VIII

When he was among the trees he tried to find the same path by which she'd brought him the first time.

A line straight from the desert to the buildings would have been only a fraction as far, but there might be good reasons why she came this way. He got onto the wrong game trail and had to retrace, then finally felt he was skirting the right hill. Soon he saw lights ahead and cautiously sought out the place on the north side of the enclosure where she'd taken him across the wires.

Without the thick synthetic-fiber blankets, he wasn't sure how he'd make it across. He spent grudged minutes locating the wires and finding a place where large tree-shoots would let him climb. He went over and worked his way to the bushes where he'd hidden the first night.

This wall of the building had no openings except the one door, as he remembered it, and he could see no light around that. Off to his right, beyond the end of the building, light from somewhere fell on the fence shown by the map.

Beyond the building he heard slow footsteps which he thought must be the guard. They seemed to recede, as though they were moving to the east where the other wing of the building was.

Surely the guard must make a circuit around this side once in a while, and this might be the time.

Crouching, Ben slipped to the building and went along to the western end. He looked around it cautiously. He could see two aircars parked not far from the gate, but the gate looked untended and was no doubt locked. He still couldn't see the source of light but it was somewhere south of the building, possibly on the peak of the roof of the other wing. He heard the footsteps halt and move in a different cadence for a few steps, then stop again. He slipped along the end of the wing to the next corner.

The moon wasn't quite high enough to see; the buildings at the south of the enclosure, and the trees, cut off. He peered around the corner and saw that the light was where he'd guessed. The guard stood under it, unwrapping what looked like a candy-bar. He was biped, but squat and non-human, with no ears or nose that Ben could see, and with piggish eyes under jutting shaggy ridges and a grotesquely wide mouth from which a long pointed tongue flicked like a snake's to taste the stuff he was unwrapping.

Ben, with a shudder, moved back where he wouldn't be seen and fumbled for one of his throwing stones. His heart was pounding so hard he had trouble controlling his breath. Could he hit the guard's head, if it came to that? It had been years since he'd practiced seriously with a baseball. Should he throw hard, or ease up a little to make sure of his aim? Or should he wait and try to use the knife, or one of the crude sprears?

Should he hide instead and hope the guard would go around the building?

It occurred to him that Naleen's room must be inside this very wall. The door would be on the south side of the wing, in plain view of the guard. He considered rapping softly, and decided against it.

The guard's footsteps had not resumed.

From the direction of the gate, but in the shadows to the south of it, came a rasping snarl. He glanced that way. He could barely make out the fence of the pen.

A soft moan came from that direction. He stared hard and almost cried out.

They had Naleen there, naked and exposed on a pole in the middle of the pen, sitting on a crossbar and clinging to the pole. In the dark he could not see her clearly, but he could see the awful sunburn and that her head sagged with exhaustion.

He stood half stunned, realizing slowly that this was her punishment, and that it was his fault. Even if they didn't know about him, they must be punishing her for leaving against orders. His eyes blurred with tears and a tight ache took hold of his throat. He took one step toward her, then caught himself. The guard had to be dealt with first.

Sudden scalding rage burned through him and he almost forgot caution. He tried to control himself, stop the violent shaking of his hands.

The guard said something that sounded amused, and the footsteps began again, coming toward Ben's end of the wing. Ben sucked in a deep breath. This wasn't going to be like pitching to a batter. The first throw had to be right on.

The guard came into sight, looking in Naleen's direction and grinning. Ben hesitated for an awful moment, then with a burst of anger at himself, drew back his arm. Emotion suspended for an instance as his whole being concentrated on the throw. He knew he was not going to miss, and that he was throwing hard enough. The guard was closer than pitching distance.

The stone hit behind the temple, two inches or so from where he'd aimed, but that was good enough. The thud was loud. The alien crumpled, completely limp.

Ben dashed to where the stone had bounced, grabbed it on the run, and whirled toward the pen. Naleen heard him coming and raised her head. He could not make out her features in the shadow.

"No!" she whispered in a weak, cracked voice, "No! They'll—"

He wasn't going to climb over the fence blindly—not without getting in a few blows first. The fence was of heavy wire mesh, with openings of about three inches, and at least twelve feet high. At the top were three strands of wire he thought would be electrified, on brackets that slanted in. He hesitated a moment. He could not throw through the mesh with any accuracy.

Several of the beasts scuttled toward him, raising themselves and clinging to the fence until he almost thought they
were going to climb it, but they avoided the wires at the top.
Their snarls and their struggles to get at him were almost
frantic.

Naleen sobbed weakly, "You promised. You Promised. Go
away before they find you."

He didn't answer. He took one of his spears and jabbed viciously at the underside of a beast. It screeched like rusty
metal and hurled itself, back, the shaft buried in its chest.
Ben impaled two more before they got the idea and backed
away. That was all the spears he had anyway.

Now he clambered up the fence, at one of the metal poles,
being careful not to touch the wires at the top. It was awkward clinging there, but he set himself and got his right arm
free. He tugged the bag of stones around where he could get
at them. Naleen pleaded with him again, and made a move
to climb down. He snapped, "Stay there!" and threw a stone
into one of the gaping mouths. The beast made a muffled
sound and rolled, thrashing, trying to dislodge the stone. The
others, came at him again, hurling themselves up the fence.
One snapped at his bare foot, sticking through the mesh. Ben
gasped with pain and jerked his toes free. More of them attacked, so viciously he had to jump away. He landed off-
balance and went sprawling.

He rolled to his feet and threw stones, sometimes hitting
the wire, sometimes getting them through. He stunned at
least two of the beasts, but there were still a dozen untouched.

Sudden light bathed the area. Aliens came spilling from
the large building, shouting and raising weapons. Naleen
screamed. Ben stood where he was, hoping with cold fury
that they wouldn't shoot him down until they got within
range.

They came at him, seven or eight of them, all armed,
shouting to each other. He stood still until they were near
enough, then raised his arm very fast and threw. He got one

of them in the face and shouted with glee as the blood spurted and the alien went down, gagging. Ben threw again, missed, then got another in the shoulder with a third stone.

The aliens had stopped, amazed, but now the weapons blasted. Ben felt a blow in the middle, harder than he'd ever imagined a blow could be. He tried to throw again but his arm wouldn't work, and neither would the rest of his muscles. He didn't know he was falling until he struck the ground.

He lay for a moment, wondering why he felt so little pain. He could feel it, but it was as if he held it at arm's length, examining it. Then his sight began to blur. He heard Naleen screaming and managed to turn his eyes to see her go down under several of the beasts.

Oddly, he didn't feel grief at her death, or at his own; he only hoped both would be quick. Mostly he was concerned with his anger. He thought that maybe if he lay still he could gather enough strength to get hold of one of the aliens when they approached him. But he knew he had no strength left. He concentrated, with what will was left, on his hate. He wished them every horrible death that could be invented; he willed them to suffer. And then it seemed as if he must be dreaming, or delirious, for he thought he heard a roaring, bursting fury fall upon the aliens and the beasts, shattering them so abruptly they barely had time to scream. He imagined the buildings were blowing up too; he even though he felt the concussion on his skin. But something was being pulled out of him irrestibly, so that he couldn't stay to dream any more.

Reluctantly, he let go of whatever it was and let it be pulled away.

IX

When he began to stir again to consciousness it was with vague memories of nightmares. It took a while for him to collect his thoughts. His rage came back first, then the grief.

His eyes focused on what seemed to be a wall. He was in a bed, and there was a hospital smell.

A voice on the other side said, "Ben."

He rolled over and saw the boss. He lay for a minute letting his thoughts clear. Then he said, "I'm alive?"

The boss grinned. "Unless I'm dreaming too. We don't know how you got back, but you did."

"I got back," Ben repeated, trying to find meaning in the words, beyond the simplest one. "I'm—I'm on Earth?"

"Mars," the boss said. "I came out when you showed up. You've been pretty sick, so we didn't want to move you. How do you feel?"

"Dizzy," Ben said. "Just a little. And hungry as hell."

"I'd better call the doctors."

"No—wait." Ben tried to sort things out better. The alien world, even Naleen, were so foggy in his mind he wondered if he'd dreamt the whole thing. Maybe something had gone wrong with the teleporter; over-dosed him so he'd had a long dream. But he didn't think he'd been headed for Mars. He said, "Didn't they report me anywhere?"

The boss looked at him oddly. "I don't want to press you until you feel all right," he said, "but don't you remember anything?"

"I don't know. Where ... Surely the machine must show a record of departure and arrival?"

The boss shook his head. "You didn't come in a teleporter."

Ben stared at him, and the boss said, "You disappeared for three weeks, then showed up right here, in this bed. Caused a hell of a row among the hospital staff. Ben, what happened? Don't you remember?"

"I remember a lot of things; or think I do. It's—no; I can't tell it to you all at once. It's too wild. Maybe I'm just nuts."

"No, Ben. Something *did* happen to you. For one thing, you've been changed. Your blood is different; and so are other things. Where'd you get tattooed?"

"What are you talking about?"

The boss stood up and pulled down the covers. "Look at your belly."

Ben stared down at himself. The face tattooed, or somehow imprinted, on him was upside down to him, but he recognized it. It was the race of the alien moon. He gasped out, "Lith!"

The boss made a gesture of resignation. "You kept saying that name in your sleep, among other things. Let me get the doctors."

The doctors had to admit, finally, that they couldn't find anything wrong with him except the changes in his blood and certain of his organs, and within a few days they let him go, though they'd have preferred to keep him for study.

He persuaded them that the teleporting had somehow made the changes. There was no use trying to tell them the truth.

He'd had time to adjust to things. It was pretty certain that Lith had saved him, or reconstituted him from memory, through what whimsy Ben couldn't guess. Maybe from nothing more than a cold sense of justice. But that didn't explain the tattoo. That must be a prank, and not a very kind one.

He'd told the boss about it, editing it a little, but nobody else. Lovely maidens rescuing him; mountains that talked; those would most likely have gotten him into the booby hatch.

He thought he was pretty well reconciled, and he was expected back at work after whatever vacation he wanted. He didn't think he'd take much. He needed the work to take his mind off things. It wasn't pleasant not to know whether Lith had reconstituted Naleen too. Even if he had, he'd no doubt sent her back to her own world.

There was a faint glimmer of hope in Ben's mind—one that he wouldn't let himself think of too much—that the experiments he was going to undertake with the teleporters might someday lead to the stars. It was a senseless hope, of course, that he'd ever find her even if they did. But he'd try.

They had fresh clothes that the boss had brought him, and at the desk where he checked out of the hospital there was even a wallet with a new set of identification and credit cards, and plenty of cash. He wondered where his old things had wound up. Maybe on the home world of the slavers, unless they'd been destroyed.

He walked out through the reception room, and stopped abruptly, staring at a girl who stood with her back to him. After a moment he started on, feeling depressed again. Apparently he was going to start seeing Naleen in every woman who happened to look the least like her. This one had the figure, the tiny waist, even the long black hair with a dark red ribbon. But Ben's eyes had gone to her hands, and they had perfectly normal fingers and thumbs. And her skin didn't have the same tint. This girl was dark, but with a Terran brunetteness.

As he passed her she turned, and he stopped again.

Her hands and complexion might be changed, but her eyes weren't. He stood in a kind of paralysis and watched the tears of joy come into her eyes. He did manage to lift his arms, and as she came into them he said under his breath, his own voice choked up, "Lith—you old fraud!"

MAD SHIP

I

FROM DECK TEN, where the pines grew, it was hundred feet up to the sunlamps on the steel bottom of Sea Deck. That was not, of course, three times as hard a climb as the five hundred feet between lower decks, because deck-gravity—a full gee at soil-level—tapered off quickly above any deck. Then, too, the rope ladder here only hung to a platform six hundred feet up in a vast old pine beside the circular hatchway called Central Well. By the time one reached that platform, gravity was less than half a gee, treetops and parasitic flowers were burgeoning joyously, and a vigorous young man need hardly pause for breath before starting up the ladder.

Pryingboy Thorp was already near the top of the ladder, preceding, as a Watch Corporal should, the five men of his squad. The lamp-heat—not too much of it directed toward Central Well—was delicious on his skin. He loved this trip—had, in fact, pestered superiors brashly to get assigned permanently to Sea Deck patrol. He loved the colorful, perfumy mass of vegetation, and even more the feel, this far up the ladder, of virtual free-fall.

How thrilling it must have been for his ancestors, in times before the Catastrophe, to don those legendary pressure-suits and go completely outside the sinus—outside the Ship, even!

Just below the edge of Sea Deck, while he was still weightless, he paused to look down at his squad. Kail, Waran, Arden, and Pendergast were spaced along the ladder, with Muller still on the platform as rear guard.

Pry went a rung higher. Carefully, because sudden weight could play tricks with one's co-ordination he reached up, grasped a knoblike thing that had once been an interior eye of the Ship, and pulled himself onto the narrow ledgelike shelf that ran around the inner curve of Sea Deck's central retaining-wall. His renewed weight felt enormous at first. He leaned against the wall until dizziness passed, then climbed a battered steel ladder and sat straddling the fifteen-foot-high wall. The acrysteel was cool between his thighs.

He glanced around at the circular sea. Light glinted off wavelets stirred by influx-air. There was a smell of fish and sea-plants.

From an excrescence on the steel a few feet away came one of the voices of the insane Ship. "This is Captain Gerlik. I feel your electrical capacitance. By your mass, you must be a grown man. I bless you, my son! Though I am deaf and blind where you are, I bless you." Another voice cut in for a few moments, mouthing gibberish, then Gerlik's voice returned. "Though the universe has passed away, I shall maintain . . ." The sound dribbled away into a mutter and stopped, as if the speaker had forgotten Pry. He shivered a little. He knew the voices were only the minds and personalities of long dead people transcribed into the Ship's computers, but they were eerie.

He wondered why the first rebels, ten or twelve generations ago, hadn't smashed this communicator-outlet along with others. Maybe they'd needed to know whether the Ship stayed alive at all.

This space—called Middle Void—was the biggest in Sinus B, unless there might be bigger ones in the dark, uninhabited, unreachable other half. From where he sat, by turning his head he could see the entire enclosing curve of the sinus wall. Sinus B, the tattered old books said, was a long cylinder closed at both ends, hashed across at intervals with decks having their own artificial gravities, and with various ingresses, ducts, fittings and buried machinery. He knew the dimensions by heart. Fifteen thousand feet long; four thousand in diameter; with the hundred-foot-wide holes in each deck that comprised Central Well.

There were no overhead lamps here in Middle Void. The lamps were in a ring around the sinus wall, fifteen hundred feet above the water. They provided light and heat not only for that round ocean, but also for Upsidedown Sea, three thousand feet above his head.

He tilted back his head and stared up. Had that half of the sinus been peopled too, at some time? No record remained, and the round hole in the middle of Upsidedown Sea— surely the continuation of Central Well—was perpetually dark.

It wasn't likely anyone would ever reach there now, because three thousand feet was much too far to build a ladder or to catapult a grappling-hook, even aside from the complications of inverted gravity.

There were sounds below him, and Fathersface Kail climbed the wall. He grinned at Pry and asked, "All right if I dunk?"

"Sure," Pry said, and watched enviously as the other dropped to the shallows and began to splash about. The Ship maintained the water at a comfortable temperature, the better for the fish crop. But as Corporal, Pry must stay alert.

Not that there was ever anything to observe, except some citizen trying to fish illegally, or a too thick growth of seaweed. It was two hundred years since the last Ship's stooge tried to sneak in, and almost as long since the last robot machine appeared. General opinion was that there was no longer anyone alive outside Sinus B, and no 'pairbots still operating. Nevertheless, he must be watchful.

The rest of the squad arrived one by one—Troublechild Waran, Secondboy Arden, Baldbaby Pendergast—who, however he'd been born, was far from bald now—and Jamestwo Muller—the oldest man of the squad, who *was* beginning to be bald. They all joined Kail in the water.

After a while Waran climbed up beside Pry. Waran was the youngest of the squad, barely nineteen. He stared up at Upsidedown Sea. "Why aren't there any fish up there?"

Pry gave him an amused glance. "Maybe there are. They'd have to be pretty big to see at that distance. Did you ever hear of a fish five or six feet long?"

Waran flushed a little and grinned. "No." He was quiet for a minute. "If the gravity ever failed up there, all that water would fall on us, and some would pour down Central Well! Why is the gravity upside-down there, do you suppose?"

Pry, who'd wondered often enough, shrugged. "Maybe that's part of the Ship's madness. Or maybe it was designed that way when the Ship left Earth."

Waran said softly, "Eight hundred years! And now Earth's gone, with the rest of the universe. How long do you suppose the Ship will last? And will it ever war upon us again? It could stop recycling air, or leave the plant nutrients out. It could leave the sunlamps off, or—or poison the water!"

Pry, irritated, got to his feet. He began shedding his backpack and other gear. "Then I suppose we'd all die." He started around the top of the retaining-wall. "I'm going to have a look at the other side." He went carefully—one certainly didn't want to fall down Central Well—but tried to act nonchalant. The sensible thing, of course, would be to drop to the water and swim or wade; but, except for Waran, the squad were all older than Pry and he didn't want to show timidity.

II

The shallows near the opposite curve of the retaining-wall were normal.

Or were they? His stomach tightened suddenly. That shape out there, distorted to view by the surface and the waves— was it a man lying on the bottom?

Drowned men don't stay submerged.

He dove and swam, after shouting for his squad. The thing had arms and legs, certainly, but ... Then he was close enough to see that it was some kind of limp garment—one that would cover a man all over. Skin prickling, he threw a look up toward the black hole in the middle of Upsidedown

Sea; then, arching himself, he dove and seized an arm of the garment. It felt slick, like the few scraps of old plastic that still existed.

His men gathered around, treading water. Waran, eyes wide, asked in an awed voice, "What is it?"

Pry's own voice was shaky. "It's a pressure-suit! It was right here, on the bottom. There's not enough current to have moved it and it wasn't here yesterday; so, an intruder's come into the sinus sometime during the last dark-cycle here!"

Muller said hoarsely, "There aren't any more people outside the sinus! It must have been some kind of robot!

Pry said impatiently, "A robot wouldn't need a pressure-suit. They don't breathe, and they have their own grav-lifts. So there *are* people out there after all!' He began towing the suit toward the retaining wall.

There was no more talk until they pulled themselves from the water. Then Muller asked, more reasonably, "But why would he abandon it? Do you suppose he drowned? Or maybe the suit just fell from up there!"

Pry suppressed annoyance. "How could that happen, with the gravity reversed up there? Do you see any water falling this way?"

Muller grinned. "No. But why would he abandon it?"

"Because," Pry said, "he's trying to pose as—as one of the people! Maybe in the dark, he didn't realize the suit could be seen from the retaining-wall. But he's gone somewhere below. He could he hiding on Deck Ten. Or lower."

Waran asked shakily, "What would he want?"

Pry shook his head slowly. "As a stooge of the Ship, he may have been sent to prepare the way for some sort of invasion; or he might be here just as a spy."

Muller growled, "He won't find spying easy! Are we going to search Deck Ten?"

"No. Not until we get reinforcements." Pry stared upward. "First of all we're going to send word down to Deck One; then I want to get this thing out of sight in case someone or something's watching from—from up there." He looked at Muller. "You probably know more people on the various decks than any of us do. You take the word down. Tell a few people along the way, but no strangers; and don't delay getting down to Deck One. You'll have to climb down through four or five ladders in the dark."

Muller shrugged. "I've done that plenty of times. Shall I say anything else except . . ."

Pry shook his head. "Just what's happened." In case Muller were intercepted by the intruder—who might have unimaginable weapons, hypnotic drugs, anything—it would be better to keep the report vague.

Muller nodded and hurried toward the down-ladder.

"I wonder," Waran said softly, "what he'll look like? If he'll be normal, I mean." He eyed the suit which, with the water drained out of it, was surprisingly light. "One thing—he's big!"

Pry looked again at the suit. "Yes. There were four sizes of pressure-suit, and this must be the biggest. We'll have to be really alert! Kail, you and Waran stay up here on watch. Pendergast, you go down to the tree-platform on Deck Ten as a lookout. Arden, you follow me down. Both of you make sure your knives are loose in the scabbards!"

Pendergast turned, then hesitated. "How are you going to carry the suit? If he's skulking somewhere, watching the ropes, he'll see it!"

Pry told him, "I'm going to bundle it up and stuff it in my backpack. If we all act casual, even if he does see us he may not suspect anything."

The plastic of the suit—brownish-yellow stuff—seemed incredibly thin to ward off the terrors of open space, though those might be exaggerated in the old tales. There were many thickened parts of the suit, including a thick ridge around the waist, where things were imbedded. There were loops for attaching things. The helmet was semi-rigid, with a horizontal window of clear yellow glass. There were instruments sealed into the helmet, and several turns of wire completely around it near the crown. No doubt it had radio and all the other legendary things.

But it made a small enough bundle to get in a backpack. Pry walked around to the ladder, glanced to make sure Arden was following and started down.

There was five hundred feet or more of clear air before he was among lacelike tendrils of vine, and glad even of that tenuous cover. Then he reached the flaring pine tops and paused to let his eyes adjust to dimmer light.

This was a dim fairy-world, with the light from the sunlamps heavily screened by foliage. Birds that would have had to beat their wings hard in full gravity soared easily here, or hovered with casual wing beats. Squirrels made magnificent slow leaps from branch to branch. There was a distinct ecology of small animals at this level—even cats took advantage of the thick foliage and low gravity, eating what they could catch, drinking water that collected in upturned blossoms during the gentle dark-cycle rains.

Pry continued on down. Gravity increased. The pine-trunks became thick and gnarled, the branches fewer and the light dimmer. He joined Pendergast on the platform. "Hear anything?"

"No. Shall I go on down?"

"Yes." Pry waited while the older man climbed down the ladder of pegs driven into the treetrunk. When Pendergast set foot on the ground and signaled up, Pry could see him only dimly by light coming in laterally from Central Well. Pry went down and they strode the short distance to the retaining-wall of this deck. Pry turned to peer into the gloomy forest. "My guess is, he went farther down while it was dark."

He couldn't be sure, but he shrugged and sent Pendergast down the next ladder.

Deck Nine, five hundred feet below Deck Ten, had a thinner layer of soil suitable for wheat. It was in day-cycle now, but wouldn't be for long. Pry, stepping off the ladder, stood with his hip against the retaining-wall—a low one, here—and stared around at the sinus wall. Intervening low hills hid the base of it and the rim of trees along it—willows taking advantage of the peripheral drain-off ditch. There'd have to be a search there when enough guardsmen arrived.

The sunlamps were hot. One quadrant of wheat, to his left, was nearly ripe. Directly before him was a greener quadrant, while to the right was a crop of alfalfa to re-liven the soil. On the far side of Central Well was the newly-plowed sector. He'd scrutinized all four quadrants, of course, as he came down the ladder.

He waited for Arden to join him and Pendergast. "Wait here a minute, the two of you. I'm going to look at those tracks in the ripe sector."

The tracks, two sets of them, led away from the retaining-wall. A little way out, one set zigzagged, while the other more or less pursued. That might mean some girl leading her man friend on a laughing chase; no one lived on the grain decks, but anyone could visit.

At the best, the pair who'd made these tracks had trampled grain unnecessarily.

Pry followed the tracks to a low hummock. Partway up the slope, one set continued straight on over while the other turned back—retracing carefully to avoid trampling more wheat, which was proper. Stepping in the continuing tracks for the same reason, Pry followed them up the hummock.

From the top he could see the body sprawled face up in the wheat beyond. An area of flattened grain indicated she'd fallen, gotten up to stagger a few steps, and fallen again. He shouted for Pendergast and Arden, then ran toward the girl.

She was perhaps in her early twenties, slight, dark-haired. She wore a tunic of green cloth that left her tanned arms and legs bare. Her moccasins were scuffed. Her hands showed signs of moderate work. Pry guessed she might be from Deck Four or Deck Five, where people lived in the fruit-orchards.

She lay limp, her breathing slow, but Pry saw no sign of injury. Carefully he rolled her over and winced at a round stain of blood on her garment, just at the back of the left arm-hole. Pendergast, coming alongside, grunted. Pry reached under the cloth. There was a small hard object half-

imbedded in the flesh. Gently, he pulled it free and looked at
it.

Arden gasped.

The thing was a very slim bullet—hardly more than a half-
inch needle. Pry looked up at the other two men. "This is a
hypodermic bullet! Do you remember the pictures and descriptions of the pistols?"

He gently pressed her garment against the tiny wound to
make sure she wasn't bleeding any more, then got bandage-
cloth and a bit of dry balsam from his belt-pouch, washed
her wound with water from his canteen, rubbed the balsam
against the still-wet skin and plastered on a bit of cloth. Then
he got to his feet and stared toward the rope ladder. It
seemed very likely that the intruder had gone down at least
one deck farther. "You two stand guard at the ladder. I'll try
to revive her."

III

Within half an hour she began to stir, moaned and tried to
gather her arms under her. Pry knelt quickly. "Lie still! I
think you'll feel better in a few minutes."

She stiffened, but obeyed. Her breathing strengthened.
Presently she lifted her head enough to see him. "Oh!" she
said in a surprised, relieved tone. Her brown eyes, though,
showed fright.

"What happened to you?" he asked.

She drew in her breath. "I—I'd just come up to inspect the
wheat. A man was standing a little way from the ladder. I
nodded and he nodded back, and I walked along the retaining-wall to the ripe sector. I must have stopped and looked
back at him too curiously. He—he acted a little odd, and he
was—was pale; not tanned. I thought he might be some
hermit from Deck Ten. Then he ran toward me and I saw
something in his hand, a sort of pistol, like the pictures in the
old books. I ran and tried to dodge, and he followed me. I
felt a sting at the back of my shoulder. I tried to get across a
hummock, hoping he wouldn't follow, and then ... and

then I began to feel weak. I guess I went a little way and fell down."

"You fell twice," Pry told her, and felt foolish. "What did he look like?"

"Just—just pale. He was clean-shaven, and his hair was cut short. He wore ordinary clothes like anyone. Anyone on the orchard decks, I mean."

"Was he big?"

"Yes. An inch or more taller than you, and heavier. I thought it was odd that such a muscular man wouldn't be tanned."

Pry felt a stir of pique. He was considered muscular enough himself. He demanded, "Did you see him go back to the ladder?"

"No. I didn't look back until I was beyond the hummock, then I—Do you think he's still on this deck?"

"No, I don't. I think he went farther down."

Her eyes widened. "Somebody has to give the alarm! Obviously, with that pistol, he's a—a stooge!"

Pry felt that he was scowling at her. "I've already sent a messenger down. Come on, if you can walk now. We'll build a fire near the ladder."

She looked puzzled. "A fire?"

"The upper decks will be dark by now, and before long this one will, too. I don't want to risk starting down in the dark until reinforcements get here." He flushed, realizing she might interpret that as cowardice. "In this backpack I've got the suit he came down in. I can't risk his getting it back. Without it, at least he's trapped in our half of the sinus."

She stared at him for a minute. "Ah! You mean a pressure-suit! Where did you—"

"We found it on Sea Deck." He helped her to her feet, and urged her toward the ladder.

There was, as on all decks, a small pile of firewood near the ladder, since patrols were likely to camp on any deck through the dark-cycle. Pendergast got busy with a firebow and soon had a blaze going.

The girl looked fairly well recovered by now, and Pry questioned her some more. "Didn't you bring a canteen up with you, or anything?

"Yes, a standard kit. I left it near the ladder rather than carry it with me. I guess *he* took it."

Pry stared away for a minute. "Fine," he said sourly. "Anything to help out his disguise. Well, we'll feed you. I don't want to send you down the ladders in your condition in the dark. Where do you live? On one of the orchard decks?

She flushed, a little angry. "Deck Five. I can get down all right!"

"No. There'll be men coming up the ladders anyway, and you'd slow them down. Besides, I need you here, in case some superior of mine comes up and wants to question you. You're the only person, so far as we know, who's seen the intruder."

She shrugged coldly and settled herself against the retaining-wall, not looking at him. He felt a little ashamed of his gruffness.

Deck Nine was ghostly when the sunlamps went out. There was almost no light from Central Well, since decks Five and everything higher were in darkness too. The fire illuminated a short curve of the retaining-wall and a small half-circle of the grainfield. Cool influx air was wafting down from the ducts between the nark sunlamps. He realized that he and his companions would be here when the rain started; but on a grain deck it was a mere drizzle.

He waited impatiently. Reinforcements ought to be here by now! Finally he got up, threw a leg over the retaining-wall and took a firm grip on the few rungs of metal ladder that were an ancient fixture here.

The girl was on her feet staring at him. "Are you going down? I thought—"

He grinned at the concern in her voice. "No. I'm just going to lean out and look down. There'll be torches, if men are coming up." He let his body hang as far out as his arm would stretch.

His skin began to prickle. Something was unfamiliar about Central Well. Then he gasped. There was no light at all—no dim rings of luminosity marking the lowest decks, which should be out of the staggered dark-cycle before now. No light at all! Or—was that a torch?

The tiny point of light winked off, then on, then off again. He read the signal, half-mumbling it over himself. Presently he pulled himself up and back over the wall into the welcome firelight.

All three companions stared at his face. He said slowly, "All the lamps are off, clear down to Deck One. There's a signal fire there directly below Central Well. They say no one knows what the trouble is. They order all guardsmen to stay on post, wherever they are."

There was a shocked silence. Finally Pendergast asked, "What did they say about Muller?"

"Nothing. That may be just caution, but I think—well, I don't think he ever got to them! I think he was intercepted. I think he's lying somewhere unconscious, or—or dead!" He raised his voice because the tightness in his chest made it hard to speak softly. "Do you see the significance of the lamps all being off at once? The Ship's co-operating with its stooge—making things easier for him. Maybe even without the suit he has some way of communicating with it. Or maybe they're working on a prearranged schedule!"

The girl said in a low, slightly unsteady voice, "We can't live without the sunlamps."

Pry looked at her half-blindly.

He had to get that suit down to Deck One, along with word of what was happening. He moved to the wall again. "I'm going down. Now!"

But before he touched the wall he stopped, rigid with a thought. After a moment he laughed hoarsely.

"What's funny?" Pendergast demanded sourly.

Pry said, "I'm an idiot! Here I'm thinking of climbing down several thousand feet of dark ladder, carrying in my backpack a suit that has grav-lifts. Why don't I simply put it on and float down?"

The trio stared at him. Finally the girl said, "You don't know how to operate it!"

"I can learn! A few experiments—"

"But," she said hastily, as if she were worried about him and sought any argument, "suppose he intercepts you? He may have ways of seeing in the dark. Then—then he'll get the suit back!"

He said, "First he'll have to see me, then he'll have to reach me. And *then* he'll have to take it back!" His heart was pounding now. Why hadn't it occurred to him before to put on the suit? He shrugged off the backpack. "What's your name?" he asked the girl. "Maybe, if they've built bonfires on Deck Five by now, I'll stop and tell them you're all right!"

She glared at him. Finally she said, "Marytwo Garth."

He pulled the suit from the pack and let it fall loose. The closure down the front was open. He thrust in one leg, then the other. He pulled the helmet over his head, worked his arms into place and tugged the front together. He felt for the small knob that was the closure-closer and began to pull.

And the suit spoke to him.

IV

After his first frozen moment of startlement, he realized it was only a communicator built into the helmet. The voice sounded human, but it wasn't Captain Gerlik's.

"Hello," it said again, "who are you?"

It still took him a while to find his voice. Then he said guardedly, "I'm a citizen of Sinus B. Who are *you?*"

The voice chuckled. "I know you're a citizen of the sinus. What's become of the man who wore this suit a few hours ago?"

Pry's mind raced. Did the suit have any way of destroying him? Could the owner of the voice tell precisely where the suit was, or see via it? Pry said cautiously, "We have him under control."

"Oh," the voice said. "Well, my name when I was alive was Ben Tomsun. I'm one of the personalities programmed into the Ship. You people evidently believe the whole Ship's insane. Parts of it are. There were schisms at the time of the Catastrophe, and the computers divided into at least four factions, located in different parts of the Ship. Several of the nineteen human personalities programmed were destroyed. Others went insane, in a way peculiar to a half-machine, half-human intelligence. Two who retained joint control of Sinus B warred against each other, and your own ancestors suffered greatly until they quite reasonably rebelled and seized your half of the sinus. Are you listening?"

Pry felt as if his stomach were full of active beetles. "Yes!"

"Good. Captain Gerlik eventually overcame the other mad personality, or absorbed it—even now we aren't sure about some things. There are parts of the ship under our control— mine and several colleagues'. There are live, sane, healthy humans in the forward part or the Ship, which is called Nose Cone and contains Sinus A. With them and what few repair robots and other facilities remain, we—the sane computer-personalities—have gradually been repairing the Ship and getting ready to seize control of all of it, if possible. We had to work very carefully, because Captain Gerlik can still wreck your end of Sinus B. You have been hostages." The voice paused "Maybe this all sounds like gibberish to you. Have you any knowledge of computers, and of the Ship's life environment machinery?"

Pry was irritated, and still not sure he wasn't talking to a clever madman. He said stiffly, "We have a few books left. I've read them."

There was a hint of a chuckle from the voice.

"Fine; fine. From time to time in the past—not within the last few generations—we've been able to send human agents by a circuitous route into Sinus B. Some have been intercepted by robot machines under Gerlik's control. The rest were all killed by your people." The voice took on a worried note. "You haven't killed the present one, have you?"

Pry thought it wise to say, "No."

"Don't, *please!* The safety of your whole people depends on him!" After a moment the voice added, "Or upon *you.* "

Pry wondered if he heard rightly. "Upon . . . *me?*

The voice sighed. "Yes. Since we've had so little success sending envoys to your people, we decided—once we were able to clear a route for another attempt—to try to enlist one of you as an envoy to us. That was the aim of our present agent. Now it seems that you—I wish you'd tell me your name, and what position you occupy in your society—have voluntarily climbed into that suit. It occurs to me that you might be willing and qualified to come visit us and learn certain things for yourself. Then you could return and persuade others. What do you think of that?"

Pry swallowed hard and stared through the yellow window of the helmet at his two men and the girl. Their faces showed that they'd been hearing every word. "I . . . don't know. What is it you—you'd want me to see?"

"Various things. First of all, that there are sane people who retain the knowledge and technology your ancestors had before the Catastrophe. And that they trust me—us. That would be a big thing for your people to know, wouldn't it?"

"Well—yes."

"Then are you willing to try? To come outside Sinus B and visit us in Nose Cone? I won't lie to you—the trip will be dangerous. Gerlik has resources, and he regards us as infidels, and will destroy any messenger between us and you, if he can, as you would step on a poisonous insect. You still have insects in Sinus B, I think."

"We have insects." Pry's mind was kneading. If there were nothing but the danger described—if it had been only a perilous adventure—how eagerly he'd accept! But his whole people were at stake. Anything the voice said might be a lie.

Once the Ship had him in its control outside the sinus, might it not tamper with his mind in some way? Could it not bend him to its own insanity, and send him back as a subtle poison for his own people?

If he only knew! If he could only make a reasonable guess!

"Well?" the voice said gently.

Pry writhed. "I don't know! I couldn't operate this suit anyway!"

That was true enough.

The voice chuckled again. "Why are you wearing it, then? But it's only a matter of a few simple instructions from me, and a few trials by you. Why are you so reluctant? Are you afraid?"

"No! Not the way you mean."

The voice sighed. "Then you think I'm lying."

Pry moaned. He daren't say yes, and to say no wouldn't help him any. He reached with a trembling hand—awkward enough anyway, because of the gauntlet—for the closure-knob, thinking he had to get out of the suit or go mad. But the voice said, "How could we use you to harm your people? Suppose we could brain-wash you—I guess that would be possible, if we had the desire. At worst, you'd go back to your people with false beliefs. *They* wouldn't be brain-washed. Wouldn't they simply disbelieve?" There was a pause. "Here—to show our good faith, I'll turn the lamps on!"

The deck was suddenly bathed in light. Pry, his eyes protected by the yellow glass, saw Pendergast, Arden, and the girl blink.

The voice said, "With the lights on, your people will see you leave and return. What else are you worried about? That we'll infect you with some deadly disease? Think—if we, or Captain Gerlik for that matter, wanted to destroy your people or beat them to their knees, we could do it by tinkering with your environment. Do you see that?"

"Yes. I—that's true!"

The voice sighed: "Here's another point. You say you have our present agent under control. He'll be a hostage for your own return. Does that help?"

Pry was almost sobbing by now. He ought to wait for his superiors to arrive—they'd be coming, now that there was light—and leave the decision to them. But they'd take the suit away from him, and send someone else, even if they did believe the voice. He was too junior in the guard ... Slowly, his hand dropped from the closure knob.

Anyone else who went would run the same risks, and be the same risk.

He drew in his breath sharply. "How do you operate this suit?"

The voice that called itself Ben Tomsun was talking steadily. "Put your left hand on the rows of little bumps on the left breast of the suit. The row across the top controls the grav-lifts. Pressing the first from the left and the first from the right will set up automatic neutralization of any gravity you're in, so that in effect you weigh nothing. Now—"

Pry's heart was thudding. He might be a traitor or he might not; but he was going through with this or die! He neutralized his weight; he pushed very gently with his feet and floated upward, then pressed bumps and floated down. "I've got that! Now how do I—"

The controls weren't complicated, once they'd been explained. In fifteen minutes he was ready to launch himself up Central Well. He waved a jaunty hand at the trio standing by the rope ladder and grinned at them through the helmet window. Pendergast and Arden stood rigid, staring at him with ludicrous expressions that combined awe, disapproval and envy. The girl's face was harder to read. There was a trace of concern, plus, perhaps, admiration.

V

The first bit of difficulty came when he had to turn over halfway through Middle Void, so he'd be dropping feet-first toward Upsidedown Sea. The suit had a built-in resistance to any change of head-and-foot alignment that had to be counter-acted. Once he achieved it, though, he knew he could do it easily next time.

The retaining-wall around the hatchway in that other sea was identical with the one he knew—except that its sensors and communicators were undamaged. He cringed a little when Captain Gerlik's voice assailed him. "Faithless one! Traitor! What devil's-work have you perpetrated among my people? You shall be punished; do not doubt it. You shall burn through all eternity! Yea, though Heaven and Earth perish . . ." The voice faded into mumblings.

The voice of Ben Tomsun whispered in his helmet. "Pay no attention and keep moving slowly. He can't interpret sanely what he sees or hears."

Later, at Ben Tomsun's direction, Pry turned on lights— one that fanned out in all directions from his helmet, another that lanced straight ahead so he could see farther. He dropped through a space that must correspond to the one above Deck Ten. His light-beam made a dim oval on nearly-bare soil. He asked hesitantly, "Is it all right if I—"

Ben Tomsun said quietly, "Take a few minutes to look around. It's best you know how things are."

Pry moved laterally from Central Well and hovered a few feet above the lifeless deck.

There had been trees here—tall ones, but not pines. A few forked trunks thrust upward like supplicating skeletons. Mostly, though, only stumps remained, chopped off a few feet above ground, the axe-marks showing clearly. The wood was darkened and splintered, with strange deposits of some kind that glittered in the light-beam. He said to Ben Tomsun, "There's something here like broken glass."

"Ice," the voice told him.' "I guess you've never seen it before. There've been no sunlamps here for two centuries. Air circulates through, but isn't warmed. Where are you now? Do you see the metal ladder on the retaining-wall?"

"No. I'm on the opposite side."

Tomsun suggested, "Cross over and look at the dead camp."

Pry complied, and found what Tomsun wanted him to see.

There'd been people, all right. He hovered, staring down and puzzling thing out. There was chopped firewood, and the ancient remains of many fires. So that was what had happened to most of the trees.

He realized suddenly that these folk must have kept a vigil here, on the highest deck they could reach, during a long perpetual night. Had they stared up at his own half of the sinus, where there was still sometimes light?

They must have been near starvation at the last; all of the fifty or more corpses were horribly emaciated—mere skin draped over bones.

But they hadn't all died of starvation. Moving slowly, directing his beam about, Pry gradually built up the story. Many had died in a single way—by having their skulls split open with an axe. Blood had long since turned to a solid dark stuff. He found the axe that had done it, and the wielder.

Angry horror formed within him. Had the man been insane? Had he obeyed some raving of Captain Gerlik? Or . . . had he turned to cannibalism?

No, there was no sign of that. The killer had apparently completed his work, then leaned the axe against a stump and lain down nearby.

Then Pry saw the knife in the corpse's chest, with the fingers of the right hand still clenched around the hilt. Finally he saw the bit of paper clutched in the shrunken spidery fingers of the left hand.

So they'd all been dying, and one—with enough vigor left—had gone around finishing them off quickly, then killed himself. They must have consented; there was no sign of struggle.

An awful thing. But at least they hadn't descended to cannibalism. Pry choked on emotion. He ought, he knew, to go down and try to work that scrap of paper free from the dead hand to read the last message. But he couldn't bring himself to it—not now. If things turned out right, he might do it on the way home; or someone else would do it later.

Slowly, in a carefully-controlled voice, he described the scene to Ben Tomsun, who'd never had a complete description before. When he was finished, Ben Tomsun answered as slowly. "It's about as I'd thought. And it would have been so easy to rescue them, if we hadn't been prevented! So

easy!" There was a pause. "Well, you'd better hurry on. You
have to go down five more decks, then out to the sinus wall.
Be very watchful—keep turning your beam in all directions.
If anything moves, get away from it fast!"

Pry nodded, more than to obey that advice.

There was dead soil and lifeless remains of plants on the
next two decks. On the third one down, there seemed to have
been a fire. That was an orchard-deck, and everything was
charred to stumps.

The next deck down had known not only fire, but something worse. One whole side of the deck was buckled upward. Soil had been thrown aside, leaving bare steel. Ice had
formed there. The sinus wall was pleated like a bit of cloth.

It was the next deck down, though, that showed the full
force of the Catastrophe. Where the sinus wall had joined
the deck, jagged talons of acrysteel splayed upward. The sinus wall had bulged far out and ruptured here, leaving scraps
of itself attached to the deck.

It was through that toothed gap that Pry had to go. Beyond
was darkness that swallowed up his beam.

Ben Tomsun said, "Move about and direct your light
through at various angles. If you see anything move, turn off
your lights and retreat!"

Pry did as he was instructed. But there was no hint of
movement outside. Ten minutes later he went through the
hole.

He paused there, awed. He'd understood that Sinus B was
enclosed within another cylinder that was the outer hull of
the Ship, but he'd had no conception of the distance between. His light couldn't probe it. Near him, the light slashed across great columns like steel bars ten feet thick. Then,
seeing ragged holes in one of them, he realized they were
hollow.

Tomsun's voice said very quietly, "You may as well take
time to go out and look at the hull. We won't be ready to
meet you for half an hour anyway."

"All right." Pry manipulated suit-controls. He must have travelled four hundred feet before his light showed a steel wall, badly rumpled and belled outward. In two places, great patches of thick steel plate had been welded on—to close up ruptures, he supposed. One of the columns which, he realized now, were supports fixing Sinus B within the outer hull had been pulled apart by the awful force, and was crudely pieced together with weld-on girders.

So the hull had bulged *outward,* not inward! He'd been thinking of the damage as some blow from outside. Instead, it must have started with terrible heat; there was plenty of other evidence of that. The softened hull must have been swelled outward by the air-pressure within and ruptured in the two spots. The same thing had apparently happened to the sinus wall.

He shivered. How had the Ship kept *any* of its air? Then he realized how small those ruptures were compared to the immense volume of the ship.

Ben Tomsun's voice cut into his musing. "Where are you now? Can you describe anything unique near you?"

Pry nodded.

"Yes. There are two patches, and a steel column that's been mended near the outer hull."

"That's adequate," Ben Tomsun said. "Drift down to the sinus wall a hundred yards from the base of that column, and on the opposite side of it from the patches. By swinging your light from side to side you can see the curve of the sinus wall. Give yourself partial weight so you can walk and come along it toward the fore end of the ship. That's back toward Deck One. I hope you haven't lost your sense of direction."

Pry mulled that over confusedly for a minute. "Oh I'm all right, I guess—only I didn't know Deck One was at the fore of Sinus B! I—we—supposed it was the opposite!"

"No; it's forward. If you stray off-line, I'll correct you. We can sense you on the sinus wall; that's why I want you to walk. But be alert—Captain Gerlik can sense you too! Swing your light constantly and look behind you. Avoid any place that might be an ambush, such as the bases of the trave-columns." The voice paused. "You are in a compartment now that's seven-hundred-fifty feet long, and you're near the aft end of it. When you reach the forward bulkhead, there'll be a hatch to come through. I'll open it long enough for you to slip through. The danger is this: Gerlik has pairbots of various sizes in the aft end of the Ship that are still operative, and he may try to intercept you. We'll know if they roll along the sinus wall; but if any can fly, we have no way of detecting them. You'll see various stalled machines along the way. Don't worry about them unless they move, but detour around them. Some may be able to swing a tool or a tentacle, or even throw things. But any attack is most likely to come from the rear, and there's only your alertness to rely upon if he has flyable machines. Do you understand?"

Pry said, "Yes. But there's one thing—can't he overhear us talking?"

"No, unless you pass near one of the wrecked machines. Some of them may still have working sensors. Now, I'd like to be able to send a strong escort to meet you, but that won't lie possible for two or three hours, if at all; there are skirmishes going on right now in several different parts of the Ship, and we simply don't have weapons enough to spare. Our actual hope is that Captain Gerlik won't consider you important enough to waste resources on. He won't know you're a Sinus-B dweller, we think—he'll think you're the same agent returning. All right?"

Pry turned his head to cast the light-beam about him. It seemed hardly to scratch the oppressive darkness. "All right. Shall I start?"

"You'd better."

VI

Pry swerved around the fractured trave-column and slanted down to the sinus wall. He gave himself half-weight and started along at a fast walk. The suit hardly hindered him at all—and that was a puzzling thing. How did it lift or move him, or vary his weigh in effect without tugging at his arm-pits or crotch? It must generate some sort of field that worked upon everything in it, or within a certain space. What ancient theory he'd seen hadn't explained it.

He carefully skirted another column and paused to swing his light about him. It dimly showed other columns at vari-ous distances. He started on, swinging it ahead of him—and suddenly stopped in a crouch. What was that his beam had slashed across?

He found the object again—assortment of booms, levers, tentacles mounted on a low three wheeled base. He'd never seen a picture of that kind of repair-robot, but it couldn't be anything else. Was it stirring? Heart thumping, left hand resting shakily on his suit's control-bumps, he swung the light across it again, slowly. Finally he decided it was only the shifting light that had made the thing appear to move very slightly.

He detoured a hundred feet around it. But before he'd got-ten much beyond, he found that he wasn't going to be able to avoid the machines by that far—there were too many of them. Some were as big as the first one he saw. Others were the smaller kind he'd seen pictures of. He saw one biped ro-bot—he knew those too, from the old books—but it was prone and inert, and didn't look much like a man. One of its legs was cut off below the knee-joint. The stub had a fused look, as if some kind of heat-beam had burned it.

There were other signs of violence too. Most of the 'pair-bots had tentacles missing, and he saw several of those am-putated flexible steel members, many-jointed like the legs of insects, lying about.

If there'd been any human corpses after those fearful bat-tles, they were gone now.

He wound his way through the relics. Ben Tomsun said he was off line a little, so he moved to his left.

Presently his beam showed the bulkhead—a vertical wall of steel rising into the darkness. He located the hatch and paused to look behind and to both sides.

Before he approached the hatch he talked to Ben Tomsun.
"There's a machine about twenty yards in front of it."

"Yes; it's been there for about seventy years without moving. There's another not far away from it. You'll have to
pass between. Tell me when you're within ten yards of the
hatch. Our detection's not very precise there."

Pry strode slowly toward the gap between the two machines.
The one nearest the hatch was medium-sized, and a special-
ized sort. It had the tri-wheeled base, and in the center of
that was a vertical column that looked as if it were extensi-
ble—some kind of a hoist. There were half a dozen of the
steel tentacles, and a battery of things shaped like drums.
Those looked familiar, from some picture. Yes—they were
searchlights. He could see the shattered glass now, and the
silvery curved reflectors.

He moved a step closer—and the machine suddenly rolled
to intercept him! Simultaneously there was a loud buzzing in
his helmet. Distracted, he turned to run—and was suddenly
bathed in dazzling light from one side! Through the buzzing
in his helmet, which was maddening, he thought he heard a
faint voice shouting. And now other lights converged on
him. He spun, saw vague shapes rolling toward him and
crouched in pure terror for a moment.

But he wasn't a guardsman for nothing! Shame drove
some of the panic from him. He reached hastily for suit-
controls; he pressed bumps that killed his own lights and
sent him shooting straight up. He darted to one side to escape for a moment the savagely searching lights of the machines and swung his head about, trying to build up a mental
picture of what lay about him. He was going to have to flee
in the dark, and he didn't want to slam into some trave-
column! The lights found him again. He zoomed away errat-
ically, trying to get behind a column; but the searchlights
came from too many directions. He dodged again. If only the
maddening buzz in his helmet would stop. He remembered
Ben Tomsun's saying something about the lowest row of
studs. He pressed one. The buzz broke off for an instant and

resumed on a slightly different tone—but louder, if anything! He tried another bump.

Blessed silence! He went limp with relief. Now at least he could think. He zoomed higher, slanting up toward the outer hull, where the lights would have to reach farther. They hadn't found him now for several seconds; all they did was provide light so he could see his way around. But unless Captain Gerlik or whoever else directed the machines was stupid as well as mad, that wouldn't last for long.

He had to find cover. Back into the sinus? No—he suspected very strongly there'd be an ambush waiting. Some other hatch that opened out of this compartment? He couldn't go around looking for one. Nor could he, apparently, talk to Ben Tomsun; the old books had described radio jamming clearly enough so Pry recognized it.

He needed a place to hide for a while until he could think, or until Ben Tomsun and his allies had time to organize help.

That broken column!

While the slashing lights lasted he shot that way, swerving and trying to stay hidden. He had to stop and wait for a searchlight to swing this way before he could see his objective. Then, when the light had passed, he flew slowly, groping ahead with his arms. He felt the girders, brought himself to a hover and tried to squeeze in between two. Not enough room! He moved to the side, found another gap and slipped in through it. He maneuvered until his body was down inside the hollow column, with only his helmet in the clear so he could see.

His panic was gone now. He knew he was in terrible danger, but it wasn't immediate. He watched the machines rolling about. They apparently knew he'd headed aft and that he'd gone far up toward the outer hull, and they were organized in a line of search, their lights probing aloft. Would they recognize this pieced-together trave-column as a possible hidingplace? If so, he'd have to be ready to move fast! Of course, if the column were hollow and uninterrupted for its full length, he could retreat far down. That wasn't inviting, but at least he could get out of sight.

Then he saw one of the medium sized machines rise slowly from the sinus wall. His midriff contracted.

So some of his mechanical pursuers, at least, had grav-lifts in working order.

Should he leave his concealment and try for the hole back into Sinus B? If he could get through that . . . No. He wasn't going to lead these madman's machines back to his people. So long as Captain Gerlik's fatherly attitude lasted, they'd be all right. Pry mustn't let the Ship find out he was one of them!

Four machines were off the steel floor now. Only one maneuvered easily, but the others could fly and bring their searchlights up near the outer hull. He saw the agile one turn itself slowly in midair and continue on until its wheels touched the outer hull. The event brought him a moment of confusion—he'd been thinking of the outer hull as up, and now suddenly, as he watched the machine begin to roll toward him, he realized that the outer hull could be considered down as well.

All right, he thought angrily, to the devil with that! Up or down, it's coming this way. Its light moved toward his hiding-place. He lowered himself hastily out of sight. Other lights were sweeping the outer hull now too, and reflected light spilled in upon him.

Thinking he'd better reconnoiter into the column, at least, while he had the chance, he let himself fall slowly.

His feet touched something yielding.

Hastily he moved aside and peered at the thing. The dim light from above showed a slick surface. The light strengthened for a moment . . .

He shuddered. The thing was a human corpse in a pressure-suit. He hung there staring at it.

VII

This victim, unlike the frozen ones in the dark hall of Sinus B, hadn't escaped decay. The death-face behind the helmet window was ghastly; the flesh rotted away, the teeth exposed.

The grim relic seemed anchored somehow to the inner curve of the column.

The light faded. Pry hovered for a while until he felt it wasn't coming back, then rose to where he could peer out. The machines weren't far away, but the pattern of the search seemed to be aimed even farther after—where the searchlights showed a warped and ruptured bulkhead, not more than two hundred feet from the hole into the sinus. Did they suspect he'd fled into a farther-aft compartment? Maybe. Or maybe they were just faking—Gerlik might cunningly hope to lure him into the open.

Well, he wasn't going to bite yet. He waited. After a while curiosity prompted him to go down and investigate the suited corpse that hung there so oddly.

Feeling about in the dark, he'd presently solved the thing.

The man, obviously, had been dropping down inside the column—hastily, perhaps, to avoid some pursuit—and had gotten snagged. There, on the otherwise smooth steel, a terrible spike thrust upward and inward—a spike created by the impact of something that had crashed against the outside of the column. That murderous dagger had punched through the plastic suit and into the man's spine.

When? At the time of the Catastrophe? Or more recently, in some furtive reconnaissance into this dark no-man's-land?

Pry brooded about it for a while. He himself might meet some such fate before the hour was out!

Then, slowly, an idea began to crystallize in his mind. He was too late to do anything for the dead man—but possibly the dead man could do something for him!

Did the punctured suit still have power? Of course—it was hanging precisely where he'd let go of it after hoisting it off the snag, which meant it was set on automatic hover. The occupant must have accomplished that much before he died.

With queasy shivers along his spine, Pry worked the grisly thing up the column and got it wedged between two girders, aligned so the head aimed aft and a little down. Then he felt carefully of its control bumps, readying himself to push two. But before he did that he tried his own helmet radio again— and got the same loud, distracting buzz.

Well, he couldn't talk to Ben Tomsun yet, then. Should he wait longer, hoping rescue would come? He thought not. Ben Tomsun must assume he was dead by now. And the longer he waited, the more likely the machines or whoever directed them were to decide he was still in this compartment after all, and concentrate here.

If he could get near the hatch and run back and forth for a moment, wouldn't Ben Tomsun be able to feel him? That was a question. What were his alternatives? To try for the sinus and hide there; to look for some other way out of the compartment; to wait where he was. Or maybe to dash out in a brief attack against the machines.

None of those attracted him.

He took a deep breath and pressed the chosen bumps on the corpse's suit. The girders held it for a moment; then it tugged free and slanted aft, fairly well aimed toward the hole in the sinus wall.

Pry waited no longer, He launched himself in the opposite direction slowly, straining his eyes to see by what dim light bounced this way. He swerved around a column, then tilted himself parallel to it so that, by twisting his helmet, he could see aft. The searchlights were still swinging there. He passed another column.

He couldn't see the suited corpse when they located it, but he could tell by the way the lights swung. Now most of them converged on one spot. His pulse quickened with hope, and he turned his head forward again.

But there was very little light reflecting to this end of the compartment now. He had to go by dead reckoning. When he felt he must surely be near the bulkhead, he drifted very slowly.

Finally his outstretched fingers touched a surface. He moved laterally to make sure it was the bulkhead, then let himself down slowly until he felt the sinus wall beneath his feet.

He looked aft. The machines were headed this way again! Sickness formed in his middle. Should he grope along, hoping to find the hatch by feel? Suppose he ran back and forth where he was? Would Ben Tomsun correctly interpret whatever was felt, or assume it was some light machine? If he only knew more about things!

The machines were coming as if they'd already seen through the trick. Then Pry realized Gerlik could feel him here!

In desperation, he turned on all his lights and directed the beam along the base of the bulkhead. *Where was the hatch?*

There! In dismay, he saw that he'd missed it by nearly a hundred yards. He ran as fast as the suit would let him, swerved around a dead machine and cast a hasty look aft. Search-lights speared toward him now. Was Ben Tomsun alert? Would he understand?

A machine rolled feebly to intercept him. He dodged around it. Another was between him and the hatch—and moving as if to block it physically with its own bulk. Search-lights fixed on him precisely, making him feel as conspicuous and vulnerable as an egg on a table.

Something heavy hurtled through the air, missing him only by two feet, and slammed against the bulkhead at hip-height. He sprinted desperately, seeing that the slowly trundling machine would reach the hatch before he did.

A voice—Gerlik's, no doubt projected via the machines—thundered, "Stop, traitor!"

Then abruptly, the hatch slid open and light spilled through! The slow machine didn't pause. But from the open hatch shot another big shape, blocking the light for an instant. It crashed directly into the blockader. Pry felt the jar and heard the rending of metal and saw objects fly. Then he dodged around the locked-together machines and hurled himself through the hatch. It slammed shut behind him.

And then he stood gasping for breath and staring at four men in suits identical to his own. Each had a pistol of some sort—a heavy kind—in his hand. But the hands hung limp as four pairs of eyes stared back at Pry.

Presently he felt himself grinning. It wasn't all one-sided, this wonder he felt! It was the first time they'd ever seen a man from Sinus B!

One of them grinned back and said in ordinary English, "Turn on your radio."

Pry said, "It's being jammed." But he tried it nevertheless. To his surprise the buzzing was faint, and through it came the voice of Ben Tomsun.

"So you got through alive! I hope you'll let your escort bring you to my compartment at once. After all this, I'm anxious to get a look at you!"

There were several of the big compartments to pass through, all of them lighted and all apparently in friendly hands, then an airlock with double doors. After that one of the four men said, "We're in Nose Cone now."

Nose Cone! A phrase from legends. Pry looked around. The compartment was smaller than the ones he'd just passed through, and there were a number of doors in it—overhead as well as in the floor and walls. From somewhere came the muffled hum and throb of machinery. And then there was a twisting corridor that left Pry with the impression they'd entered a gravity at right angles to the one he'd expected; and there were people, who stared at him, and a glimpse of a tree-covered deck through a doorway. Then, finally, divested of his suit, he stood in a small room, alone except for Ben Tomsun.

VIII

Pry realized he must have resisted, at gun level, the knowledge that Ben Tomsun wasn't a living man; for he was dazed now.

The cabinet of shiny metal was rectangular and more or less the size of a man. That helped a little. So did the horizontal row of small holes at about face-height and the mesh-covered opening below them. These could be thought of as eyes, ears, nostrils and mouth. The voice did come from the mesh-covered opening. But aside from that, it was a simple featureless box, probably of acrysteel.

Ben Tomsun must have known how he felt. "Forgive the way I present myself. I'm not really confined to this box. My personality is scattered among various computer banks of the Ship, all scrambled up with other personalities, history, technologies, Euclidean and non-Euclidean geometries, and data such as the germination-time of peach pits. But I and the other recorded brains prefer these cabinets. They give us at least a tenuous simile to the time when we had live bodies."

Pry stared dumbly for a minute. The first words he blurted were, "You don't *sound* insane!"

Ben Tomsun sighed. "I hope I'm not. I can't explain to you exactly how things are with me. There was the original Ship's computer-intelligence, then human personalities were programmed in, for reasons that were probably partly emotional. But some of us changed. I guess that was inevitable. Gradually we took over many of the Ship's functions. Whether the purely mechanic intelligence would have gone insane at the time of the Catastrophe is something we debate and ponder among ourselves. But Captain Gerlik and a few others did lose their sanity. He and one other were in control of most of the Ship; and as I've told you, they warred between them. Gerlik overcame the other personality, or absorbed it. The rest of us hadn't nearly as much power, but by joining together and by careful maneuvering, we were able to clear him out of Nose Cone and some compartments of Main Hull. We infiltrated the environment-maintenance systems for Sinus B, but couldn't take them over. And that leaves your people in serious danger. There's a reason why we have to get you out of there soon. Well, two reasons, actually—the less urgent being the need to take over and finish repairs."

Pry said, "I can understand that. With the universe destroyed, the Ship has to last as long as is physically possible. Even so ..."

Ben Tomsun chuckled. "That's one of the reasons we wanted you up here—to convince you that the universe has *not* been destroyed! We don't know precisely what Captain Gerlik or his rival told your ancestors at the time of the Catastrophe, nor all of what he's told you since. By the way— won't you please tell me your name?"

"Well ... Pryingboy Thorp. I guess I was, uh, a nosy child."

The voice laughed briefly. "Well, Thorp, this is what happened. We were skirting a cloud nebula—a great mass of dust and gas—when we were unexpectedly thrown off course by a small, dark, very dense, invisible body— probably the core of a long-dead star. It whirled us into the cloud, tail first. Tidal forces—I guess you don't know about those—did some damage, but the worst was the frictional heat. Spots of the hull softened and bulged out and ruptured. You've seen the hasty patches. The heat penetrated far enough to soften the wall of Sinus B too, in one spot. It was touch and go whether we'd survive at all. Captain Gerlik, who was under the worst strain for a long period, went insane. While we were in the cloud, the stars were hidden from us. That's all." The voice paused as if the cabinet were scrutinizing Pry. "You don't look as if you believed me."

Ben Tomsun sighed again. "I wish it were possible to put you in a pressure-suit and send you outside to see for yourself, but that would take too much time. *This* will have to do."

A section of the wall behind the cabinet suddenly slid aside. For a moment Pry thought there was a five-foot-square hole; then he saw that it was a dark screen of some kind.

The screen suddenly blossomed with tiny points of light. At one edge was a convoluted mass of light and dark. Ben Tomsun said, "That luminosity at the edge is the cloud we passed through. The points of light are stars. Have you seen pictures of a starfield?"

Hope and doubt fought a cutlass-battle inside Pry. He swallowed hard. "I've seen small pictures."

"Now," the voice said. The screen suddenly lit all over. There was a mottled pattern of greenish blue. It seemed to shrink in upon itself, and became a half-disc. Pry drew in his breath sharply. "That's a picture of Earth! Is Earth still—"

Ben Tomsun said, "We're far out of telescope-range of Sol, but we have no reason to think that anything's happened to Earth. This is *not* a picture of Earth—it's the next planet we're going to colonize. It's earthlike and primitive. Listen carefully, Thorp! We're in wide orbit around this planet right now. All of us, except for a few who remain aboard Main Hull in orbit to do necessary things, such as repairing the hull and trying to cure Captain Gerlik, will be landing in Nose Cone. Your people will have to clear one of the Sinus B exits your ancestors blocked up and come out the near end. Oh, I don't mean within the next few hours; it'll take time to convince them. And a few people have to land in gravcars—you've read about those? —for preliminary explorations. But *you* will have to start persuading your people. The alternative is that we'll try to take over control of the sinus from Captain Gerlik. And that might end in disaster for your people."

The voice was silent for a minute. "This is a lot for you to swallow in a hurry, I know, but I haven't time to show you more directly, or to let you mull it over. One reason I haven't is that the agent who went into the sinus may be in deadly peril. You have to get back in time to forestall any execution. Now, may I have your decision?"

Pry stood there, so full of feelings he could hardly breathe. He was shocked and angry at such a blunt ultimatum. Yet, if it were all true . . .

To have a *whole planet* to live on . . .

The voice said gently, "If you succeed with your own people quickly, you can be part of one of the exploration teams. Is that any inducement?"

Pry squirmed mentally. He finally burst out, "Damn it! If you're eight hundred years old—"

"Six hundred. I never saw Earth."

"Well, if you're that old, you know how I feel! Of course it's an inducement! Any man . . . But I'm no spy! I wouldn't know the first thing about—about—"

"About spreading a sudden truth? Naturally we wouldn't expect you to work alone. That agent who's already there— if you get back in time—"

Pry trembled for it minute more, then took a deep breath. "All right! What choice do I have, anyway? I—I have to believe you or disbelieve you, and . . ." He stared away for a moment. "I lied to you about that agent. I said we had him under control. We didn't. But if he tries to pose as one of us—"

Ben Tomsun said amusedly, "I knew you were lying."

Pry scowled at the cabinet. "Oh. Well . . . Are you going to tell me how to find him?"

"Not exactly."

"Not—why, in God's name?"

"Because it isn't a 'he', and you've undoubtedly already found her. She was going to call herself 'Marytwo Garth.'"

Ben Tomsun said tersely, "We had to make contact. You, or your ancestors, killed every man we sent in. She volunteered. We aren't playing games, Thorp! Will you work with her?"

Pry turned slowly and took a few blind steps. Such a big suit, and such a small girl . . . But it was clever. And she must have stuck that dart into her own shoulder, calmly abandoned herself to unconsciousness and whatever luck had in store. After first stopping Muller, so he couldn't report.

What a woman!

He whirled back to face the cabinet. "I'll help! And—uh—that exploration team I may go on. Might she, uh, be part of it too?"

Ben Tomsun chuckled.

RAMBLE HOUSE's

HARRY STEPHEN KEELER WEBWORK MYSTERIES

(RH) indicates the title is available ONLY in the RAMBLE HOUSE edition

The Ace of Spades Murder
The Affair of the Bottled Deuce (RH)
The Amazing Web
The Barking Clock
Behind That Mask
The Book with the Orange Leaves
The Bottle with the Green Wax Seal
The Box from Japan
The Case of the Canny Killer
The Case of the Crazy Corpse (RH)
The Case of the Flying Hands (RH)
The Case of the Ivory Arrow
The Case of the Jeweled Ragpicker
The Case of the Lavender Gripsack
The Case of the Mysterious Moll
The Case of the 16 Beans
The Case of the Transparent Nude (RH)
The Case of the Transposed Legs
The Case of the Two-Headed Idiot (RH)
The Case of the Two Strange Ladies
The Circus Stealers (RH)
Cleopatra's Tears
A Copy of Beowulf (RH)
The Crimson Cube (RH)
The Face of the Man From Saturn
Find the Clock
The Five Silver Buddhas
The 4th King
The Gallows Waits, My Lord! (RH)
The Green Jade Hand
Finger! Finger!
Hangman's Nights (RH)
I, Chameleon (RH)
I Killed Lincoln at 10:13! (RH)
The Iron Ring
The Man Who Changed His Skin (RH)
The Man with the Crimson Box
The Man with the Magic Eardrums
The Man with the Wooden Spectacles
The Marceau Case
The Matilda Hunter Murder

The Monocled Monster
The Murder of London Lew
The Murdered Mathematician
The Mysterious Card (RH)
The Mysterious Ivory Ball of Wong Shing Li (RH)
The Mystery of the Fiddling Cracksman
The Peacock Fan
The Photo of Lady X (RH)
The Portrait of Jirjohn Cobb
Report on Vanessa Hewstone (RH)
Riddle of the Travelling Skull
Riddle of the Wooden Parrakeet (RH)
The Scarlet Mummy (RH)
The Search for X-Y-Z
The Sharkskin Book
Sing Sing Nights
The Six From Nowhere (RH)
The Skull of the Waltzing Clown
The Spectacles of Mr. Cagliostro
Stand By—London Calling!
The Steeltown Strangler
The Stolen Gravestone (RH)
Strange Journey (RH)
The Strange Will
The Straw Hat Murders (RH)
The Street of 1000 Eyes (RH)
Thieves' Nights
Three Novellos (RH)
The Tiger Snake
The Trap (RH)
Vagabond Nights (Defrauded Yeggman)
Vagabond Nights 2 (10 Hours)
The Vanishing Gold Truck
The Voice of the Seven Sparrows
The Washington Square Enigma
When Thief Meets Thief
The White Circle (RH)
The Wonderful Scheme of Mr. Christopher Thorne
X. Jones—of Scotland Yard
Y. Cheung, Business Detective

Keeler Related Works

A To Izzard: A Harry Stephen Keeler Companion by Fender Tucker — Articles and stories about Harry, by Harry, and in his style. Included is a compleat bibliography.

Wild About Harry: Reviews of Keeler Novels — Edited by Richard Polt & Fender Tucker — 22 reviews of works by Harry Stephen Keeler from *Keeler News*. A perfect introduction to the author.

The Keeler Keyhole Collection: Annotated newsletter rants from Harry Stephen Keeler, edited by Francis M. Nevins. Over 400 pages of incredibly personal Keeleriana.

Fakealoo — Pastiches of the style of Harry Stephen Keeler by selected demented members of the HSK Society. Updated every year with the new winner.

Strands of the Web: Short Stories of Harry Stephen Keeler — 29 stories, just about all that Keeler wrote, are edited and introduced by Fred Cleaver.

RAMBLE HOUSE's Loon Sanctuary

A Clear Path to Cross — Sharon Knowles short mystery stories by Ed Lynskey.

A Corpse Walks in Brooklyn and Other Stories — Volume 5 in the Day Keene in the Detective Pulps series.

A Jimmy Starr Omnibus — Three 40s novels by Jimmy Starr.

A Niche in Time and Other Stories — Classic SF by William F. Temple

A Roland Daniel Double: The Signal and The Return of Wu Fang — Classic thrillers from the 30s.

A Shot Rang Out — Three decades of reviews and articles by today's Anthony Boucher, Jon Breen. An essential book for any mystery lover's library.

A Smell of Smoke — A 1951 English countryside thriller by Miles Burton.

A Snark Selection — Lewis Carroll's *The Hunting of the Snark* with two Snarkian chapters by Harry Stephen Keeler — Illustrated by Gavin L. O'Keefe.

A Young Man's Heart — A forgotten early classic by Cornell Woolrich.

Alexander Laing Novels — *The Motives of Nicholas Holtz* and *Dr. Scarlett*, stories of medical mayhem and intrigue from the 30s.

An Angel in the Street — Modern hardboiled noir by Peter Genovese.

Automaton — Brilliant treatise on robotics: 1928-style! By H. Stafford Hatfield.

Away From the Here and Now — Clare Winger Harris stories, collected by Richard A. Lupoff

Beast or Man? — A 1930 novel of racism and horror by Sean M'Guire. Introduced by John Pelan.

Black Beadle — A 1939 thriller by E.C.R. Lorac.

Black Hogan Strikes Again — Australia's Peter Renwick pens a tale of the 30s outback.

Black River Falls — Suspense from the master, Ed Gorman.

Blondy's Boy Friend — A snappy 1930 story by Philip Wylie, writing as Leatrice Homesley.

Blood in a Snap — The *Finnegan's Wake* of the 21st century, by Jim Weiler.

Blood Moon — The first of the Robert Payne series by Ed Gorman.

Bogart '48 — Hollywood action with Bogie by John Stanley and Kenn Davis

Calling Lou Largo! — Two Lou Largo novels by William Ard.

Cornucopia of Crime — Francis M. Nevins assembled this huge collection of his writings about crime literature and the people who write it. Essential for any serious mystery library.

Corpse Without Flesh — Strange novel of forensics by George Bruce

Crimson Clown Novels — By Johnston McCulley, author of the Zorro novels, *The Crimson Clown* and *The Crimson Clown Again.*

Dago Red — 22 tales of dark suspense by Bill Pronzini.

Dark Sanctuary — Weird Menace story by H. B. Gregory

David Hume Novels — *Corpses Never Argue, Cemetery First Stop, Make Way for the Mourners, Eternity Here I Come.* 1930s British hardboiled fiction with an attitude.

Dead Man Talks Too Much — Hollywood boozer by Weed Dickenson.

Death Leaves No Card — One of the most unusual murdered-in-the-tub mysteries you'll ever read. By Miles Burton.

Death March of the Dancing Dolls and Other Stories — Volume Three in the Day Keene in the Detective Pulps series. Introduced by Bill Crider.

Deep Space and other Stories — A collection of SF gems by Richard A. Lupoff.

Detective Duff Unravels It — Episodic mysteries by Harvey O'Higgins.

Diabolic Candelabra — Classic 30s mystery by E.R. Punshon

Dictator's Way — Another D.S. Bobby Owen mystery from E.R. Punshon

Dime Novels: Ramble House's 10-Cent Books — *Knife in the Dark* by Robert Leslie Bellem, *Hot Lead* and *Song of Death* by Ed Earl Repp, *A Hashish House in New York* by H.H. Kane, and five more.

Doctor Arnoldi — Tiffany Thayer's story of the death of death.

Don Diablo: Book of a Lost Film — Two-volume treatment of a western by Paul Landres, with diagrams. Intro by Francis M. Nevins.

Dope and Swastikas — Two strange novels from 1922 by Edmund Snell

Dope Tales #1 — Two dope-riddled classics; *Dope Runners* by Gerald Grantham and *Death Takes the Joystick* by Phillip Condé.

Dope Tales #2 — Two more narco-classics; *The Invisible Hand* by Rex Dark and *The Smokers of Hashish* by Norman Berrow.

Dope Tales #3 — Two enchanting novels of opium by the master, Sax Rohmer. *Dope* and *The Yellow Claw.*

Double Hot — Two 60s softcore sex novels by Morris Hershman.

Double Sex — Yet two more panting thrillers from Morris Hershman.

Dr. Odin — Douglas Newton's 1933 racial potboiler comes back to life.

Evangelical Cockroach — Jack Woodford writes about writing.

Evidence in Blue — 1938 mystery by E. Charles Vivian.

Fatal Accident — Murder by automobile, a 1936 mystery by Cecil M. Wills.

Fighting Mad — Todd Robbins' 1922 novel about boxing and life

Finger-prints Never Lie — A 1939 classic detective novel by John G. Brandon.

Freaks and Fantasies — Eerie tales by Tod Robbins, collaborator of Tod Browning on the film FREAKS.

Gadsby — A lipogram (a novel without the letter E). Ernest Vincent Wright's last work, published in 1939 right before his death.

Gelett Burgess Novels — *The Master of Mysteries, The White Cat, Two O'Clock Courage, Ladies in Boxes, Find the Woman, The Heart Line, The Picaroons* and *Lady Mechante.* Recently added is A Gelett Burgess Sampler, edited by Alfred Jan. All are introduced by Richard A. Lupoff.

Geronimo — S. M. Barrett's 1905 autobiography of a noble American.

Hake Talbot Novels — *Rim of the Pit, The Hangman's Handyman.* Classic locked room mysteries, with mapback covers by Gavin O'Keefe.

Hands Out of Hell and Other Stories — John H. Knox's eerie hallucinations

Hell is a City — William Ard's masterpiece.

Hollywood Dreams — A novel of Tinsel Town and the Depression by Richard O'Brien.

Hostesses in Hell and Other Stories — Russell Gray's most graphic stories

House of the Restless Dead — Strange and ominous tales by Hugh B. Cave.

I Stole $16,000,000 — A true story by cracksman Herbert E. Wilson.

Inclination to Murder — 1966 thriller by New Zealand's Harriet Hunter.

Invaders from the Dark — Classic werewolf tale from Greye La Spina.

J. Poindexter, Colored — Classic satirical black novel by Irvin S. Cobb.

Jack Mann Novels — Strange murder in the English countryside. *Gees' First Case, Nightmare Farm, Grey Shapes, The Ninth Life, The Glass Too Many, Her Ways Are Death, The Kleinert Case* and *Maker of Shadows.*

Jake Hardy — A lusty western tale from Wesley Tallant.

Jim Harmon Double Novels — *Vixen Hollow/Celluloid Scandal, The Man Who Made Maniacs/Silent Siren, Ape Rape/Wanton Witch, Sex Burns Like Fire/Twist Session, Sudden Lust/Passion Strip, Sin Unlimited/Harlot Master, Twilight Girls/Sex Institution.* Written in the early 60s and never reprinted until now.

Joel Townsley Rogers Novels and Short Stories — By the author of *The Red Right Hand: Once In a Red Moon, Lady With the Dice, The Stopped Clock, Never Leave My Bed.* Also two short story collections: *Night of Horror* and *Killing Time.*

John Carstairs, Space Detective — Arboreal Sci-fi by Frank Belknap Long

Joseph Shallit Novels — *The Case of the Billion Dollar Body, Lady Don't Die on My Doorstep, Kiss the Killer, Yell Bloody Murder, Take Your Last Look.* One of America's best 50's authors and a favorite of author Bill Pronzini.

Keller Memento — 45 short stories of the amazing and weird by Dr. David Keller.

Killer's Caress — Cary Moran's 1936 hardboiled thriller.

Lady of the Yellow Death and Other Stories — More stories by Wyatt Blassingame.

League of the Grateful Dead and Other Stories — Volume One in the Day Keene in the Detective Pulps series.

Library of Death — Ghastly tale by Ronald S. L. Harding, introduced by John Pelan

Malcolm Jameson Novels and Short Stories — *Astonishing! Astounding!, Tarnished Bomb, The Alien Envoy and Other Stories* and *The Chariots of San Fernando and Other Stories.* All introduced and edited by John Pelan or Richard A. Lupoff.

Man Out of Hell and Other Stories — Volume II of the John H. Knox weird pulps collection.

Marblehead: A Novel of H.P. Lovecraft — A long-lost masterpiece from Richard A. Lupoff. This is the "director's cut", the long version that has never been published before.

Mark of the Laughing Death and Other Stories — Shockers from the pulps by Francis James, introduced by John Pelan.

Master of Souls — Mark Hansom's 1937 shocker is introduced by weirdologist John Pelan.

Max Afford Novels — *Owl of Darkness, Death's Mannikins, Blood on His Hands, The Dead Are Blind, The Sheep and the Wolves, Sinners in Paradise* and *Two Locked Room Mysteries and a Ripping Yarn* by one of Australia's finest mystery novelists.

Money Brawl — Two books about the writing business by Jack Woodford and H. Bedford-Jones. Introduced by Richard A. Lupoff.

More Secret Adventures of Sherlock Holmes — Gary Lovisi's second collection of tales about the unknown sides of the great detective.

Muddled Mind: Complete Works of Ed Wood, Jr. — David Hayes and Hayden Davis deconstruct the life and works of the mad, but canny, genius.

Murder among the Nudists — A mystery from 1934 by Peter Hunt, featuring a naked Detective-Inspector going undercover in a nudist colony.

Murder in Black and White — 1931 classic tennis whodunit by Evelyn Elder.

Murder in Shawnee — Two novels of the Alleghenies by John Douglas: *Shawnee Alley Fire* and *Haunts*.

Murder in Silk — A 1937 Yellow Peril novel of the silk trade by Ralph Trevor.

My Deadly Angel — 1955 Cold War drama by John Chelton.

My First Time: The One Experience You Never Forget — Michael Birchwood — 64 true first-person narratives of how they lost it.

Mysterious Martin, the Master of Murder — Two versions of a strange 1912 novel by Tod Robbins about a man who writes books that can kill.

Norman Berrow Novels — *The Bishop's Sword, Ghost House, Don't Go Out After Dark, Claws of the Cougar, The Smokers of Hashish, The Secret Dancer, Don't Jump Mr. Boland!, The Footprints of Satan, Fingers for Ransom, The Three Tiers of Fantasy, The Spaniard's Thumb, The Eleventh Plague, Words Have Wings, One Thrilling Night, The Lady's in Danger, It Howls at Night, The Terror in the Fog, Oil Under the Window, Murder in the Melody, The Singing Room.* This is the complete Norman Berrow library of locked-room mysteries, several of which are masterpieces.

Old Faithful and Other Stories — SF classic tales by Raymond Z. Gallun

Old Times' Sake — Short stories by James Reasoner from Mike Shayne Magazine.

One Dreadful Night — A classic mystery by Ronald S. L. Harding

Pair O' Jacks — A mystery novel and a diatribe about publishing by Jack Woodford

Perfect .38 — Two early Timothy Dane novels by William Ard. More to come.

Prince Pax — Devilish intrigue by George Sylvester Viereck and Philip Eldridge

Prose Bowl — Futuristic satire of a world where hack writing has replaced football as our national obsession, by Bill Pronzini and Barry N. Malzberg.

Red Light — The history of legal prostitution in Shreveport Louisiana by Eric Brock. Includes wonderful photos of the houses and the ladies.

Researching American-Made Toy Soldiers — A 276-page collection of a lifetime of articles by toy soldier expert Richard O'Brien.

Reunion in Hell — Volume One of the John H. Knox series of weird stories from the pulps. Introduced by horror expert John Pelan.

Ripped from the Headlines! — The Jack the Ripper story as told in the newspaper articles in the *New York* and *London Times.*

Rough Cut & New, Improved Murder — Ed Gorman's first two novels.

R.R. Ryan Novels — Freak Museum and The Subjugated Beast, two horror classics.

Ruby of a Thousand Dreams — The villain Wu Fang returns in this Roland Daniel novel.

Ruled By Radio — 1925 futuristic novel by Robert L. Hadfield & Frank E. Farncombe.

Rupert Penny Novels — *Policeman's Holiday, Policeman's Evidence, Lucky Policeman, Policeman in Armour, Sealed Room Murder, Sweet Poison, The Talkative Policeman, She had to Have Gas* and *Cut and Run* (by Martin Tanner.) Rupert Penny is the pseudonym of Australian Charles Thornett, a master of the locked room, impossible crime plot.

Sacred Locomotive Flies — Richard A. Lupoff's psychedelic SF story.

Sam — Early gay novel by Lonnie Coleman.

Sand's Game — Spectacular hard-boiled noir from Ennis Willie, edited by Lynn Myers and Stephen Mertz, with contributions from Max Allan Collins, Bill Crider, Wayne

Dundee, Bill Pronzini, Gary Lovisi and James Reasoner.

Sand's War — More violent fiction from the typewriter of Ennis Willie

Satan's Den Exposed — True crime in Truth or Consequences New Mexico — Award-winning journalism by the *Desert Journal*.

Satans of Saturn — Novellas from the pulps by Otis Adelbert Kline and E. H. Price

Satan's Sin House and Other Stories — Horrific gore by Wayne Rogers

Secrets of a Teenage Superhero — Graphic lit by Jonathan Sweet

Sex Slave — Potboiler of lust in the days of Cleopatra by Dion Leclerq, 1966.

Sideslip — 1968 SF masterpiece by Ted White and Dave Van Arnam.

Slammer Days — Two full-length prison memoirs: *Men into Beasts* (1952) by George Sylvester Viereck and *Home Away From Home* (1962) by Jack Woodford.

Slippery Staircase — 1930s whodunit from E.C.R. Lorac

Sorcerer's Chessmen — John Pelan introduces this 1939 classic by Mark Hansom.

Star Griffin — Michael Kurland's 1987 masterpiece of SF drollery is back.

Stakeout on Millennium Drive — Award-winning Indianapolis Noir by Ian Woollen.

Strands of the Web: Short Stories of Harry Stephen Keeler — Edited and Introduced by Fred Cleaver.

Summer Camp for Corpses and Other Stories — Weird Menace tales from Arthur Leo Zagat; introduced by John Pelan.

Suzy — A collection of comic strips by Richard O'Brien and Bob Vojtko from 1970.

Tales of the Macabre and Ordinary — Modern twisted horror by Chris Mikul, author of the *Bizarrism* series.

Tales of Terror and Torment #1 — John Pelan selects and introduces this sampler of weird menace tales from the pulps.

Tenebrae — Ernest G. Henham's 1898 horror tale brought back.

The Amorous Intrigues & Adventures of Aaron Burr — by Anonymous. Hot historical action about the man who almost became Emperor of Mexico.

The Anthony Boucher Chronicles — edited by Francis M. Nevins. Book reviews by Anthony Boucher written for the *San Francisco Chronicle,* 1942 – 1947. Essential and fascinating reading by the best book reviewer there ever was.

The Barclay Catalogs — Two essential books about toy soldier collecting by Richard O'Brien

The Basil Wells Omnibus — A collection of Wells' stories by Richard A. Lupoff

The Beautiful Dead and Other Stories — Dreadful tales from Donald Dale

The Best of 10-Story Book — edited by Chris Mikul, over 35 stories from the literary magazine Harry Stephen Keeler edited.

The Black Dark Murders — Vintage 50s college murder yarn by Milt Ozaki, writing as Robert O. Saber.

The Book of Time — The classic novel by H.G. Wells is joined by sequels by Wells himself and three stories by Richard A. Lupoff. Illustrated by Gavin L. O'Keefe.

The Case in the Clinic — One of E.C.R. Lorac's finest.

The Strange Case of the Antlered Man — A mystery of superstition by Edwy Searles Brooks.

The Case of the Bearded Bride — #4 in the Day Keene in the Detective Pulps series

The Case of the Little Green Men — Mack Reynolds wrote this love song to sci-fi fans back in 1951 and it's now back in print.

The Case of the Withered Hand — 1936 potboiler by John G. Brandon.

The Charlie Chaplin Murder Mystery — A 2004 tribute by noted film scholar, Wes D. Gehring.

The Chinese Jar Mystery — Murder in the manor by John Stephen Strange, 1934.

The Cloudbuilders and Other Stories — SF tales from Colin Kapp.

The Compleat Calhoon — All of Fender Tucker's works: Includes *Totah Six-Pack, Weed, Women and Song* and *Tales from the Tower,* plus a CD of all of his songs.

The Compleat Ova Hamlet — Parodies of SF authors by Richard A. Lupoff. This is a brand new edition with more stories and more illustrations by Trina Robbins.

The Contested Earth and Other SF Stories — A never-before published space opera and seven short stories by Jim Harmon.

The Crimson Query — A 1929 thriller from Arlton Eadie. A perfect way to get introduced.

The Curse of Cantire — Classic 1939 novel of a family curse by Walter S. Masterman.

The Devil and the C.I.D. — Odd diabolic mystery by E.C.R. Lorac

The Devil Drives — An odd prison and lost treasure novel from 1932 by Virgil Markham.

The Devil of Pei-Ling — Herbert Asbury's 1929 tale of the occult.

The Devil's Mistress — A 1915 Scottish gothic tale by J. W. Brodie-Innes, a member of Aleister Crowley's Golden Dawn.

The Devil's Nightclub and Other Stories — John Pelan introduces some gruesome tales by Nat Schachner.

The Disentanglers — Episodic intrigue at the turn of last century by Andrew Lang

The Dog Poker Code — A spoof of *The Da Vinci Code* by D.B. Smithee.

The Dumpling — Political murder from 1907 by Coulson Kernahan.

The End of It All and Other Stories — Ed Gorman selected his favorite short stories for this huge collection.

The Fangs of Suet Pudding — A 1944 novel of the German invasion by Adams Farr

The Finger of Destiny and Other Stories — Edmund Snell's superb collection of weird stories of Borneo.

The Ghost of Gaston Revere — From 1935, a novel of life and beyond by Mark Hansom, introduced by John Pelan.

The Girl in the Dark — A thriller from Roland Daniel

The Gold Star Line — Seaboard adventure from L.T. Reade and Robert Eustace.

The Golden Dagger — 1951 Scotland Yard yarn by E. R. Punshon.

The Great Orme Terror — Horror stories by Garnett Radcliffe from the pulps

The Hairbreadth Escapes of Major Mendax — Francis Blake Crofton's 1889 boys' book.

The House That Time Forgot and Other Stories — Insane pulpitude by Robert F. Young

The House of the Vampire — 1907 poetic thriller by George S. Viereck.

The Illustrious Corpse — Murder hijinx from Tiffany Thayer

The Incredible Adventures of Rowland Hern — Intriguing 1928 impossible crimes by Nicholas Olde.

The Julius Caesar Murder Case — A classic 1935 re-telling of the assassination by Wallace Irwin that's much more fun than the Shakespeare version.

The Koky Comics — A collection of all of the 1978-1981 Sunday and daily comic strips by Richard O'Brien and Mort Gerberg, in two volumes.

The Lady of the Terraces — 1925 missing race adventure by E. Charles Vivian.

The Lord of Terror — 1925 mystery with master-criminal, Fantômas.

The Melamare Mystery — A classic 1929 Arsene Lupin mystery by Maurice Leblanc

The Man Who Was Secrett — Epic SF stories from John Brunner

The Man Without a Planet — Science fiction tales by Richard Wilson

The N. R. De Mexico Novels — Robert Bragg, the real N.R. de Mexico, presents *Marijuana Girl, Madman on a Drum, Private Chauffeur* in one volume.

The Night Remembers — A 1991 Jack Walsh mystery from Ed Gorman.

The One After Snelling — Kickass modern noir from Richard O'Brien.

The Organ Reader — A huge compilation of just about everything published in the 1971-1972 radical bay-area newspaper, *THE ORGAN*. A coffee table book that points out the shallowness of the coffee table mindset.

The Poker Club — Three in one! Ed Gorman's ground-breaking novel, the short story it was based upon, and the screenplay of the film made from it.

The Private Journal & Diary of John H. Surratt — The memoirs of the man who conspired to assassinate President Lincoln.

The Ramble House Mapbacks — Recently revised book by Gavin L. O'Keefe with color pictures of all the Ramble House books with mapbacks.

The Secret Adventures of Sherlock Holmes — Three Sherlockian pastiches by the Brooklyn author/publisher, Gary Lovisi.

The Shadow on the House — Mark Hansom's 1934 masterpiece of horror is introduced by John Pelan.

The Sign of the Scorpion — A 1935 Edmund Snell tale of oriental evil.

The Singular Problem of the Stygian House-Boat — Two classic tales by John Kendrick Bangs about the denizens of Hades.

The Smiling Corpse — Philip Wylie and Bernard Bergman's odd 1935 novel.

The Spider: Satan's Murder Machines — A thesis about Iron Man

The Stench of Death: An Odoriferous Omnibus by Jack Moskovitz — Two complete novels and two novellas from 60's sleaze author, Jack Moskovitz.

The Story Writer and Other Stories — Classic SF from Richard Wilson

The Strange Case of the Antlered Man — 1935 dementia from Edwy Searles Brooks

The Strange Thirteen — Richard B. Gamon's odd stories about Raj India.

The Technique of the Mystery Story — Carolyn Wells' tips about writing.

The Threat of Nostalgia — A collection of his most obscure stories by Jon Breen

The Time Armada — Fox B. Holden's 1953 SF gem.

The Tongueless Horror and Other Stories — Volume One of the series of short stories from the weird pulps by Wyatt Blassingame.

The Town from Planet Five — From Richard Wilson, two SF classics, *And Then the Town Took Off* and *The Girls from Planet 5*

The Tracer of Lost Persons — From 1906, an episodic novel that became a hit radio series in the 30s. Introduced by Richard A. Lupoff.

The Trail of the Cloven Hoof — Diabolical horror from 1935 by Arlton Eadie. Introduced by John Pelan.

The Triune Man — Mindscrambling science fiction from Richard A. Lupoff.

The Unholy Goddess and Other Stories — Wyatt Blassingame's first DTP compilation

The Universal Holmes — Richard A. Lupoff's 2007 collection of five Holmesian pastiches and a recipe for giant rat stew.

The Werewolf vs the Vampire Woman — Hard to believe ultraviolence by either Arthur M. Scarm or Arthur M. Scram.

The Whistling Ancestors — A 1936 classic of weirdness by Richard E. Goddard and introduced by John Pelan.

The White Owl — A vintage thriller from Edmund Snell

The White Peril in the Far East — Sidney Lewis Gulick's 1905 indictment of the West and assurance that Japan would never attack the U.S.

The Wizard of Berner's Abbey — A 1935 horror gem written by Mark Hansom and introduced by John Pelan.

The Wonderful Wizard of Oz — by L. Frank Baum and illustrated by Gavin L. O'Keefe.

Through the Looking Glass — Lewis Carroll wrote it; Gavin L. O'Keefe illustrated it.

Time Line — Ramble House artist Gavin O'Keefe selects his most evocative art inspired by the twisted literature he reads and designs.

Tiresias — Psychotic modern horror novel by Jonathan M. Sweet.

Tortures and Towers — Two novellas of terror by Dexter Dayle.

Totah Six-Pack — Fender Tucker's six tales about Farmington in one sleek volume.

Tree of Life, Book of Death — Grania Davis' book of her life.

Triple Quest — An arty mystery from the 30s by E.R. Punshon.

Trail of the Spirit Warrior — Roger Haley's saga of life in the Indian Territories.

Two Kinds of Bad — Two 50s novels by William Ard about Danny Fontaine

Two Suns of Morcali and Other Stories — Evelyn E. Smith's SF tour-de-force

Ultra-Boiled — 23 gut-wrenching tales by our Man in Brooklyn, Gary Lovisi.

Up Front From Behind — A 2011 satire of Wall Street by James B. Kobak.

Victims & Villains — Intriguing Sherlockiana from Derham Groves.

Wade Wright Novels — *Echo of Fear, Death At Nostalgia Street, It Leads to Murder* and *Shadows' Edge*, a double book featuring *Shadows Don't Bleed* and *The Sharp Edge*.

Walter S. Masterman Novels — *The Green Toad, The Flying Beast, The Yellow Mistletoe, The Wrong Verdict, The Perjured Alibi, The Border Line, The Bloodhounds Bay, The Curse of Cantire* and *The Baddington Horror*. Masterman wrote horror and mystery, some introduced by John Pelan.

We Are the Dead and Other Stories — Volume Two in the Day Keene in the Detective Pulps series, introduced by Ed Gorman. When done, there may be 11 in the series.

Welsh Rarebit Tales — Charming stories from 1902 by Harle Oren Cummins

West Texas War and Other Western Stories — by Gary Lovisi.

What If? Volume 1, 2 and 3 — Richard A. Lupoff introduces three decades worth of SF short stories that should have won a Hugo, but didn't.

When the Batman Thirsts and Other Stories — Weird tales from Frederick C. Davis.

Whip Dodge: Man Hunter — Wesley Tallant's saga of a bounty hunter of the old West.

Win, Place and Die! — The first new mystery by Milt Ozaki in decades. The ultimate novel of 70s Reno.

Writer 1 and 2 — A magnus opus from Richard A. Lupoff summing up his life as writer.

You'll Die Laughing — Bruce Elliott's 1945 novel of murder at a practical joker's English countryside manor.

RAMBLE HOUSE

Fender Tucker, Prop.   Gavin L. O'Keefe, Graphics
www.ramblehouse.com   fender@ramblehouse.com
228-826-1783   10329 Sheephead Drive, Vancleave MS 39565

www.ingramcontent.com/pod-product-compliance
Lightning Source LLC
Chambersburg PA
CBHW030343020726
47493CB00003B/659